O. HENRY MEMORIAL
AWARD

PRIZE STORIES
of 1927

O. HENRY MEMORIAL AWARD
PRIZE STORIES
of 1927

CHOSEN BY THE SOCIETY OF
ARTS AND SCIENCES

WITH AN INTRODUCTION BY
BLANCHE COLTON WILLIAMS

Author of "A Handbook on Story Writing,"
"Our Short Story Writers," Etc.
Head, Department of English, Hunter College
of the City of New York

GARDEN CITY   NEW YORK
DOUBLEDAY, DORAN & COMPANY, INC.
1928

FIRST EDITION

ACKNOWLEDGMENT

For the Committee the chairman thanks authors, editors, and agents, with whose friendly coöperation this volume is prepared.

BLANCHE COLTON WILLIAMS.

New York City,
    January, 1927.

CONTENTS

INTRODUCTION

THE JUDGES

1. EMMA K. TEMPLE
2. ISABEL WALKER
3. HARRY ANABLE KNIFFIN
4. KATHARINE LACY
5. FRANCES GILCHRIST WOOD
6. DOROTHY SCARBOROUGH
7. BLANCHE COLTON WILLIAMS
8. ROBERT L. RAMSAY
9. MAXIM LIEBER

First Judges

Final Judges { *Chairman*

1, 2, 3, 4, 5, 6, 7 *Readers, First Judges*
5, 6, 7, 8, 9 *Final Judges.*

IN PREPARING this the ninth volume of the series, the O. Henry Memorial Committee selected more than six hundred stories from some twenty-five hundred published in the year October, 1926, to September, 1927, inclusive. Of these six hundred the best according to the votes of at least two judges are listed in the following pages. From the fifty stories ranking highest were chosen, in the usual process of elimination by five final judges, the fifteen included in this volume.

"Child of God," by Roark Bradford, received four votes for first place, and wins by a number of points. To this story, published in *Harper's Magazine*, April, 1927, is awarded the first prize of $500.

Four candidates were considered for second place. One judge preferred "Singing Woman"; another, "Shades of George Sand" (closely followed by "The Little Girl from Town"); another, "Fear"; two others cast votes for "The Killers." To this last named story, which wins by points, is awarded the second prize of $250. "The Killers," by Ernest

Hemingway, was published in *Scribner's Magazine*, March, 1927.

For the special prize awarded the best short short story, the following were nominated by one or more of the judges: "Another Wife," by Sherwood Anderson; "Sandoe's Pocket," by Elsie Singmaster; "Tommy Taylor," by Zona Gale; "The Scarlet Woman," by Louis Bromfield. "The Scarlet Woman" leads and receives therefore the award of $100. The story was published in *McClure's*, January, 1927.

Among the fifteen stories ranking highest, four happen to be about the American Negro. The increasing representation of this race in brief fiction I observed in my introduction to *O. Henry Memorial Award Prize Stories* of 1925. Of that year Du Bose Heyward's "Crown's Bess" and Julia Peterkin's "Maum Lou" were reprinted; John Matheus's "Fog," Frederick Tisdale's "The Guitar," and Elsie Singmaster's "Elfie" were mentioned. The volume for 1926 reprinted Arthur Huff Fauset's "Symphonesque" and Lyle Saxon's "Cane River." The present collection offers, first, "Child of God." "Never," writes Mrs. Wood, "was the spirit of an age and a people more happily caught than here. The old-time darky and his tales may have been lost in a modern deluge of the nigger minstrel type, that 'extinct species of a race that never existed'; but he comes back into his own in 'Child of God' with his characteristic ideas of a perfect heaven." That the idea of heaven advanced is Willie's idea appears to have eluded those who raised a small storm when they read the story in *Harper's*. The visions Mr. Bradford spreads upon the page with sympathy and naïve simplicity are, of course, the visions vouchsafed to Willie in the few seconds after the trap gave way under his feet and before his body was borne out of jail; just so Willie would have constructed those visions. Added to the dream is something else that is greater art. The supernatural, revealing Willie's experiences after death, is joined to the human dream so well as to defy detection. Who knows when life was pronounced extinct? What part of Willie's dream belongs to earth and what to the heaven of his fancy? "There is art, exquisite art, in the joining," as O. Henry once wrote of another story, and tenuous though the fabric may be, the seam is indiscernible. And how completely the delicately woven stuff covers the hard reality of the green-eyed man's collapse! That ugly blue face and frothy saliva potently declare that the hangman was neatly punished by Willie's ghost. "Mr. Bradford is of course the unquestionable find of the year," writes Mr. Ramsay. "His 'Child of God' would perhaps never have been written if Molnar had not shown us in *Liliom* how interesting it may be to see heaven through a glass very darkly; but it is an amazingly successful transcription into terms of Negro psychology." The chairman suggests that it be read side by side with Ambrose Bierce's "An Occurrence at Owl Creek Bridge"—a tale many times reprinted—for testing its indubitable superiority.

"Bulldog," like the prize winner, makes of an alleged criminal a hero. The black giant, of square and protruding jaw, square and receding forehead, was a fighter, one intent upon vengeance, willing to take punishment. The brute strength that served him falsely in his personal fracases served him and the judge truly in the fifteen-mile odyssey to Ossabaw. Mr. Daniels's use of revealing incident and character prepares acceptance for Bulldog's herculean feat, climax to an escape at once logical and stirring. Call to mind all the thrills you have enjoyed—say, from the many chases in *Les Misérables* on—and compare with them the action from "Stan's yo' back!" to the "cry through the stillness of the night"; you will find that it survives in form, in style, in substance. With right logic and humorous turn the author brings Bulldog back to the opening scene and to the sentence of six months on the farm.

"Done Got Over" dramatizes the struggle between superstition harnessed with petty vengeance against enlightenment aided by generosity. Whoever has lived in the cotton belt knows with what excitation of horror, with what sense of the occult and foreboding of the mysteriously awful the old-time Negroes await the funeral sermon over the manifest ungodly. Intimation of a "preaching-to-hell" draws—or not many years ago drew—an audience keyed to highest expectancy, all sympathy lost in shuddering anticipation of the sinner's doom. The idea seldom occurs that the verdict of the preacher is not irremediable. Perhaps "Done Got Over" falters at the moment of climax, perhaps one may wish that Miss Jinny Pickens had spoken. Her simple act, however, was sufficient—one who knows the Pickenses testifies to this point. The local colour witnesses the authors' careful observation; the atmosphere declares their participation in the drama. They must have seen Draper's yard of prince's feather and dog-fennel; must have smelled the fig leaves in Miss Jinny's back yard, the cape jasmines on Tampa's coffin; surely they felt the agony of Tampa's son.

"Monkey Motions," from a seemingly casual recountal of Sam'l, rises to the perfect description of his dancing. That climax becomes a flashlight to illumine the backward way, to outline clearly details unguessed as salient. Pictures of the dance have always tempted the pen, not infrequently to failure; this instance is successful. "What are you weeping about?" asked Tom. If you have followed with the dancer his exposition of the "origins, methods, and significations" of the Charleston, if through it you have followed his race's history, you may still have no more reason than Aunt Lady, but you will be dropping a tear with her. And your reason may be that so poignant a summary of race history in so short space presents the motive.

"The Killers," second prize winner, one of three photographically realistic studies here reprinted, has been the most talked about story of 1927. In its seeming incompleteness is its superb completeness. Max and Al, the killers, do not get their man this particular evening, but they will get him; and the doom that Ole Andreson knows to be upon him when he says, "There isn't anything I can do about it," is more appalling than would be the actual shot from that sawed-off gun. Unknown horrors are greater than known horrors, a truth of which Mr. Hemingway has taken advantage in leaving the reader to construct the climax. If Ole stays in the room, the slayers will find him; if he goes out, they will find him; in either choice, they will inevitably shoot him. Can such things be? carries its answer: Such things are. Without a word of preachment, the story arraigns a world of presumable law and order. Mr. Hemingway's dialogue, lacking specious suspense or excitement, tells the story. Six or seven hundred words in addition relate the bare action and sketch the setting. In transferring this narrative to the dramatic form no changes are necessary except the conversion of non-dialogue into stage directions; the story is economically perfect. It is not really a story, says Mrs. Wood, "not to be insulted as half-caste 'realism'—just a blazing bit of reality to which you are the unwilling witness. Like the black cook, you 'don't like any of it—don't like any of it, at all!' yet you could no more tear yourself away from that peep-hole in the kitchen than you could resist the weaving head of a cobra. Of course, it is stale comparison to liken 'The Killers' to Greek tragedy, but since that is our golden milestone no other comparison serves."

Of all the stories here reprinted, Maxim Lieber thinks "Night Club" "by far the best. It is a very swiftly moving, sharply outlined story, and the author achieves a remarkable effect with the utmost economy of words." In "Night Club" Miss Brush purports to retail the drab evening of Mrs. Brady, maid, and in so doing adds another instance to examples of old truths: Romance is never at hand, but far away; the searcher fails to see that what he seeks is near home; life is stranger than fiction. The parts of the story are greater than its whole, a six-in-one marvel that tells the stories of (1) a wife who denies her marriage tie, for reasons implied, (2) of a dope fiend, (3) of an unfaithful husband, the wife, and the other woman, (4) of a girl who finds a pair of scissors necessary with her escort, (5) of an elopement, (6) of a girl who marries wealth to save her sister's life. Even summary details convey other stories: "she saw a yellow check with the ink hardly dry." Like "The Killers," this story is of the immediate present. Nothing in fiction has described night-club life so deftly, much less described it from the cubbyhole of a maid who saw nothing.

Third of these photographic studies is "The Little Girl from Town," an exquisite picture of childhood embroidered in tiny, colourful stitches. It reminds the chairman of nothing so much as a treasured piece of tapestry, bought years ago in Bath, in which thousands of stitches portray a small girl, her dog, her parrot, and her flowers. Patricia's beauty and helplessness, set off by the hardier country children's assurance, emphasized by her seeming victory, her pitiful failure, in saving the calf—this slight theme the author has embellished with a wealth of detail. As in the grimmer realism of "The Killers," dialogue does most of the work. The minute accuracy of its transcription reads like a stenographic report edited by an artist. In this story, "quiet and penetrating," to quote Mr.

Ramsay, and in "Eminence" (see page xxii), whose chief character is a relative of Patricia's, Miss Suckow has surpassed her former writing. Interesting by way of comparison for similarity of theme is Nels Anderson's "Old Whitey" (see page xxxi).

Elisabeth Cobb Chapman's "With Glory and Honour," which shares with "Night Club" the element of setting, uses the setting for a different purpose. Hal Levering, who has denied his race, learns by a humiliating lesson what every man of every race must learn, that individual fulfilment depends upon race, pride in race, acceptance of racial possibilities. The work of Irvin Cobb's daughter, "With Glory and Honour," itself a happy testimonial to inheritance, reveals individual power that promises well. In suggestion, choice of detail, and rhythm, the story might be the accomplishment of a master.

In "He Man," Marjory Stoneman Douglas not only tells the experiences of six in a fallen plane ending in the death of all but two, not only describes a struggle with the sea that lasted two days and nights; she achieves victory for endurance and fortitude, no less tokens of manhood than sportsmanship and courage. By vivid pictures, by the wind in the wires, by the omnipresence of the menacing sea, the author brings near the plight of those on the craft. Beautiful writing, forceful writing, carries the story; for example, "Stars were quivering in the enormous rondure of the sky that overhead took on a strange metallic blue and cast upon them a faint luminance that was less than light and only a little less than dark." Isn't that worthy to set beside "L'obscure clarté, qui tombe des etoiles," and Milton's light that served to render darkness visible?

The title "Fear," the fear of men who fly, declares companionship with "He Man." "Fear," second on Dr. Scarborough's list, has the distinction of being the one war story chosen from scores that have done their bit to memorialize the tenth decade after America's entry into the conflict. "Fear" may be, as Mr. Ramsay says, sloppily executed; but, as he also states, it is intensely realized. Mr. Bellah's way with planes is the way of one who has fought in them; his analysis of Patterson's fear is the analysis of a warrior who knows the effect of war on men's minds. Paterson weakened twice, but he recouped in the climax of his berserker rage what he had lost through previous faltering. To read "Fear" is to live again the days of '17 and '18. The story establishes the same point "He Man" establishes: faced by demand for courage, fear flees.

"Jukes," the story of a sailor by sailor Bill Adams, is the survival of many cullings from *Adventure*. No other magazine represented in this book has shown so remarkable a gain in quality. The chairman, who read every number, marvelled at its rapid rise and trusts the ascent is more than temporary. Mr. Ramsay also comments that *Adventure* has had an unusually good year. Mr. Adams, who spent eight weeks in writing Jukes, surely had no prime intention of producing an argument for prohibition; he was concerned to show the weakness of Jukes, that weakness by which tottered Jukes's good resolutions, weakness abetted by crimp and board master. "You an' me is dogs," says one of the sailors; and "Jukes, was you ever beat at anything?" draws no answer. Jukes knows that he has never been other than beaten; his repeated impressment will be repeated—until the end. To read "Jukes" is to taste the ocean's bitterest salt. Mr. Adams need not tell us that he has sailed with many a Jukes. "All these nowadays books about the clipper ships and the beauty of the sea rather weary me at times. The beauty and the grandeur were there. But what a horror was there too. Crews carted around like dogs." Mr. Adams, like Mr. Wetjen, relates stories of the sea with breadth of knowledge and accuracy of detail possible only to a seaman.

Of the four remaining stories two are of the folk. Ada Jack Carver's "Singing Woman," second on Mr. Ramsay's list, celebrates a custom of the French mulattoes on Isle Brevelle of the Joyous Coast. A gruesome and pathetic contest this between Henriette and Josephine, their ninety-nine and ninety-eight funerals proclaiming them last survivors of wailing women, rivals to the death. By easy management, the author permits them to emerge with drawn honours in "my friend, you and me ull quit even"; and, by her usual sympathy in characterizing the lowly, provokes for the old brown women admiration tempered with pity. A near relative of these wailing ones is George Allan England's "Johnny Moaner" (see page xxiv), whose calling led him to kill that he might be supplied with a necessary funeral.

In "Four Dreams of Gram Perkins" Ruth Sawyer weaves one of the oddest yarns ever spun from dream stuff, yet as surely of the Maine folk as "Singing Woman" is of the Isle Brevelle natives. In their climactic progress Zeb Perkins's dreams maintain consistently the ruling passion of Gram's life as well as the character of Zeb himself, self-appointed layer of Gram's ghost. Sardonic humour saves these dreams from the horrific as tenderness redeems Ada Jack Carver's song of death.

"Shades of George Sand!" happens to fall into a category all its own. Mr. Lieber, placing it second, comments on its air of savoir faire and mature quality; the chairman appreciates the rebellion of Mathilde against her environment, her escape into a pseudo-paradise and consequent descent into limbo. Only the clever girl, apparently doomed to rusticity, fired by ancestry, and nourished by experiences vicarious as those which fed Mathilde, can guess with what eagerness Mathilde set out for Chicago. The meanness of Flora Campbell's respectable boarding house and the defection of Mathilde's hero may have struck down momentarily the girl's aspirations; but surely the conference with her tutelary shade gave Mathilde courage to follow her star; and if she has not presided over a salon, she has found something better. The mordaunt, yeasty humour of this tale should leaven the collection, in general a serious collection.

"The Scarlet Woman," in length about that of "The Killers," required greater skill in elimination. Whereas "The Killers" belongs to the true short-story genre in brevity of time, close circumscription of place, and sharply defined conflict, "The Scarlet Woman" is a novel which, paradoxically and exceptionally, succeeds as a short short story. In its 3,000 words, the author, by concentrating the essence of Vergie Winters's life, has escaped a mere synopsis. To say it differently, he has revealed by high lights the passive conflict one woman endured with the social order, a conflict the motive of which is love. The obstacles in the way, too great to be surmounted, Mr. Bromfield has disregarded with a featness that recalls Columbus's triumph with the egg.

THE LISTS

Before consulting the appended lists, please note the following abbreviations:

ABBREVIATIONS

Ad.	Adventure
Am.	American Magazine
Am. Merc.	American Mercury
A. A.	Argosy Allstory Magazine
Arch.	Archer
Atl.	Atlantic Monthly
B. M.	Black Mask
B. B.	Blue Book Magazine
Book.	Bookman
C. W.	Catholic World
C.	Century Magazine
C. T.	Chicago Tribune
Clues	Clues Magazine
C. H.	College Humor
Col.	Collier's Weekly
C. G.	Country Gentleman
D.	Delineator
D. S. M.	Detective Stories Magazine
D. S.	Droll Stories
E.	Echo
Elks	Elks Magazine
Ev.	Everybody's Magazine
Fl.	Flynn's Weekly
F.	Forum
G. H.	Good Housekeeping
H. J. Q.	Haldeman Julius Quarterly
H. B.	Harper's Bazar
H.	Harper's Magazine
H. I. and C.	Hearst's International and Cosmopolitan Magazine
L. H. J.	Ladies' Home Journal
L.	Liberty
McCall.	McCall's Magazine
McClure.	McClure's Magazine
Mun.	Munsey's Magazine

Op.	*Opportunity*
P. R.	*Pictorial Review*
Pop.	*Popular*
R. B.	*Red Book Magazine*
S. E. P.	*Saturday Evening Post*
Scr.	*Scribner's Magazine*
S. S.	*Short Stories*
S. S. M.	*Special Salesman Magazine*
Sun.	*Sunset Magazine*
W. T.	*Weird Tales*
W. S.	*Western Story*
W. H. C.	*Woman's Home Companion*
Y.	*Young's Magazine*

LIST I

Stories ranking highest:

Abbot, Keene, Tree of Life (*Atl.*, Dec., 1926).

Adams, Bill, Jukes (*Ad.*, Nov. 23, 1926).

Alexander, Elizabeth, The Purest Passion (*S. E. P.*, Feb. 5).

Alexander, Sandra, Passion (*H.* Apr.).

Aley, Maxwell, Man Child (*G. H.*, July).

Anderson, Frederick Irving, Wise Money (*S. E. P.*, Aug. 6).

Anthony, Joseph, A Hobo He Would Be (*C.*, Oct., 1926).

Bailey, Margaret Emerson, Common Law (*H.*, Apr.).

Banning, Margaret Culkin, Heads or Tails (*S. E. P.*, May 7);
    The Woman Higher Up (*S. E. P.*, May 21).

Beer, Thomas, Piepowder Court (*S. E. P.*, Oct. 16, 1926);
    The Public Life (*S. E. P.*, Nov. 20, 1926); Curly-
    Tailed Wolf (*S. E. P.*, Apr. 16); Cramambuli (*S. E. P.*,
    May 7); Æsthetics (*S. E. P.*, June 11).

Bellah, James Warner, Fear (*S. E. P.*, Nov. 6, 1926); Boppo's
    Bicycle (*Col.*, Feb. 5); Funny Nose (*S. E. P.*, Feb. 5);
    Old Slithercheeks Takes a Bath (*Col.*, Feb. 26);
    Blood (*S. E. P.*, Apr. 2); The Great Tradition (*S. E. P.*,
    May 28); A Gentleman of Blades (*S. E. P.*, June 11);
    M'Givney's Mustache (*S. E. P.*, Aug. 20).

Blake, Clarice, The Mold (*C.*, May).

Bradford, Roark, Child of God (*H.*, Apr.).

Brady, Mariel, From Four Till Seven (*G. H.*, Nov., 1926);
    April's Fools (*G. H.*, Apr.); Snips and Snails (*G. H.*,
    June).

INTRODUCTION

Brecht, Harold W., Vienna Roast (*H.*, Nov., 1926).
Broadhurst, George, The Motive (*S. E. P.*, July 2).
Bromfield, Louis, "Let's Go to Hinkey-Dink's" (*McCall.*, Sept.).
Brush, Katharine, The Other Pendleton (*P. R.*, Oct., 1926); Night Club (*H.*, Sept.).
Burlingame, Roger, Jacinth (*Scr.*, Oct., 1926).
Burt, Katharine Newlin, Jealous Oberon (*C. T.*, May 15).
Burt, Struthers, Freedom (*C. T.*, Nov. 28, 1926); C'Est La Guerre (*S. E. P.*, Feb. 5); Grandpa (*S. E. P.*, Apr. 23); Soda Bicarb (*S. E. P.*, July 2).
Busch, Niven, Jr., The Wife and the Toreador (*Col.*, Aug. 6).
Butler, Ellis Parker, Bruce of the Bar-None (*Sun.*, May).
Byrne, Donn, Rivers of Damascus (*McCall*, Oct., 1926).
Canfield, Dorothy, Here Was Magic (*W. H. C.*, Feb.).
Carver, Ada Jack, The Old One (*H.*, Oct., 1926); Singing Woman (*H.*, May).
Chapman, Elisabeth Cobb, With Glory and Honour (*C.*, June).
Clark, Valma, Candlelight Inn (*Scr.*, Nov., 1926); The Tact of Monsieur Pithou (*Scr.*, May).
Clarke, James Mitchell, Punishment (*Ad.*, Apr. 1).
Cobb, Irvin S., The Wooden Decoy (*H. I. and C.*, Dec., 1926); This Man's World (*H. I. and C.*, May); Louder Than Words (*H. I. and C.*, June); As Brands from the Burning (*H. I. and C.*, July); Faith with Works (*H. I. and C.*, Aug.).
Cohen, Octavus Roy, Idles of the King (*S. E. P.*, Aug. 6); The Porter Missing Men (*S. E. P.*, Aug. 20).
Connell, Richard, The Lady Killer (*S. E. P.*, Nov. 27, 1926); In Society (*S. E. P.*, Mch. 5).
Cram, Mildred, From a Château Kitchen (*D.*, June).
Crowell, Chester T., The Trick (*S. E. P.*, Apr. 2).
Daniels, Roger, Bulldog (*S. E. P.*, Nov. 13, 1926).
Davis, Elmer, The Ruinous Woman (*C.*, May).
Detzer, Karl W., The Superior Woman (*C.*, Jan.).
Dickson, Harris, On the First Sand Bar (*S. E. P.*, Jan. 15); The Sealed Wager (*S. E. P.*, May 21); Foresight (*S. E. P.*, Aug. 27).
Dobie, Charles Caldwell, Slow Poison (*H.*, July).
Douglas, Marjory Stoneman, The Beautiful and Beloved

(*S. E. P.*, Apr. 2); The Third Woman (*C. T.*, May 29); Stepmother (*S. E. P.*, June 4); He Man (*S. E. P.*, July 30).

Dwyer, James Francis, Dreve of Virginia (*R. B.*, Oct., 1926).

Edmonds, Walter D., Who Killed Rutherford? (*Scr.*, Mch.).

Eliot, Ethel Cook, Heaven Knows (*Arch.*, Mch.).

Ellerbe, Alma and Paul, "Done Got Over" (*Col.*, Nov. 27, 1926).

Fairbank, Janet, The Thin Red Line (*W. H. C.*, Jan.).

Farnham, Walter, David (*Ad.*, Nov. 8, 1926).

Ferber, Edna, Blue Blood (*H. I. and C.*, Mch.).

Fisher, Rudolph, Blades of Steel (*Atl.*, Aug.).

Flynn, T. T., Twenty Fathoms Under (*S. S.*, Apr. 25).

Gale, Zona, A Way of Escape (*W. H. C.*, Oct., 1926).

Gilkyson, Phoebe, The Portrait (*H.*, Jan.).

Gilson, Charles, Three Thieves (*Ad.*, Mch. 15).

Gordon, Eugene, Game (*Op.*, Sept.).

Hackett, Francis, The Cinder (*C.*, Nov., 1926).

Hartman, Lee Foster, The Reek of Limes (*P. R.*, Apr.).

Hemingway, Ernest, The Killers (*Scr.*, Mch.); Fifty Grand (*Atl.* July).

Hergesheimer, Joseph, Collector's Blues (*S. E. P.*, Oct. 2, 1926); Trial by Armes (*Scr.*, Mch.); Natchez (*S. E. P.*, May 21); New Orleans (*S. E. P.*, July 23).

Hervey, Harry, The Lover of Madame Guillotine (*McClure*, Jan.).

Heyward, Du Bose, The Half Pint Flask (*Book.*, May).

Hopper, James, When It Happens (*H.*, May).

Hughes, Rupert, They Were Americans Too (*McCall*, Feb.); The River Pageant (*H. I. and C.*, July).

Hume, Cyril, The Count's China Teeth (*C. H.*, Apr. 2).

Jackson, Margaret W., Birds of a Feather (*McCall*, Oct., 1926).

Jaffé, Margaret Davis, Shut In (*C. W.*, Oct., 1926).

Jordan, Elizabeth, The Little Red-Haired Girl (*C. T.*, Oct. 31, 1926).

Kelly, Eleanor Mercein, Monkey Motions (*P. R.*, Oct., 1926); Emiliana (*S. E. P.*, Oct. 2, 1926); Fête-Dieu (*S. E. P.*, Dec. 18, 1926); Charivari (*S. E. P.*, Feb. 12); Interlude (*S. E. P.*, June 25); Nostalgia (*S. E. P.*, Aug. 13).

A Drink of Water (*H.*, Jan.); Sailor! Sailor! (*P. R.*, July); New Deal (*Scr.*, Aug); Sooth (*H.*, Aug.); Speed (*P. R.*, Aug.).

Stone, Elinore Cowan, An Hour Before Dinner (*Col.*, Dec. 18, 1926).

Suckow, Ruth, Eminence (*Am. Merc.*, Mch.); The Little Girl from Town (*H.*, Aug.).

Synon, Mary, Amy Brooks (*G. H.*, Mch.).

Tarkington, Booth, Mr. White (*S. E. P.*, Mch. 12); Hell (*S. E. P.*, July 16).

Tarleton, Fiswoode, Eloquence (*Ad.*, Oct. 8, 1926).

Taylor, Ellen du Pois, Nostalgia (*H.*, Feb.); Shades of George Sand! (*H.*, Mch.).

Torrey, Grace B., One Medium-Sized Dog (*W. H. C.*, Oct., 1926); Bartley, B. A. (*S. E. P.*, Oct. 30, 1926).

Tupper, Tristram, Three Episodes in the Life of Timothy Osborn (*S. E. P.*, Apr. 9).

Welles, Harriet, The Stranger Woman (*Scr.*, Dec., 1926); Her Highness' Hat (*W. H. C.*, Aug.).

Wetjen, Albert Richard, Shingles out of Bandon (*Ad.*, Oct. 8, 1926); The Covenant of the Craddocks (*Ad.*, Feb. 1); The Strange Adventure of Tommy Lawn (*Ad.*, Mch. 15).

Wiley, Hugh, The *Patriot* (*R. B.*, June).

Williams, Ben Ames, Coconuts (*S. E. P.*, Oct. 9, 1926); Opportunity (*S. E. P.*, Jan. 8); Altitude (*S. E. P.*, Jan. 15); A Needful Fitness (*C. T.*, Jan. 23).

Williams, Jesse Lynch, A Man's Castle (*R. B.*, Feb.).

Wister, Owen, The Right Honorable the Strawberries (*H. I. and C.*, Nov., 1926); Lone Fountain (*H. I. and C.*, Apr.).

Wylie, Elinor, King's Pity (*W. H. C.*, Sept.).

LIST II

Stories ranking second:

Adams, Frank R., Love's Pair o' Dice (*L.*, Feb. 26); Oysters in Season (*L.*, Apr. 2).

Addington, Sarah, Mr. Dickens' Little Boy (*D.*, Dec., 1926); Tornado (*D.*, July); Clodhopper (*D.*, Sept.).

Aldrich, Bess Streeter, "He Whom a Dream Hath Possest" (*Am.*, June).

Aley, Maxwell, Mr. Petty's Garden (*W. H. C.*, Apr.).

Anderson, Frederick Irving, Finger Prints (*S. E. P.*, Oct. 23, 1926).

Andrews, G. G., Fire (*C. T.*, Mch. 6).

Avery, Stephen Morehouse, Where Angels Fear to Tread (*Col.*, Sept. 25, 1926); "Circle Wide, We'll Meet above the Clouds" (*McCall*, May).

Bailey, Temple, So This Is Christmas! (*McCall*, Dec., 1926).

Balmer, Edwin, The Round Bullet (*L.*, Jan. 29); Double Exposure (*L.*, Sept. 3).

Banning, Margaret Culkin, Amateur (*H.*, Dec., 1926); Not in Politics (*S. E. P.*, Dec. 25, 1926); The Favorite Daughter (*Col.*, May 28).

Barker, Elsa, The Jade Earring (*R. B.*, Nov., 1926).

Bechdolt, Frederick, For the Girl Back Home (*H. I. and C.*, May).

Bellah, James Warner, Boppo and the Awful Whiffs (*Col.*, Mch. 12); The Silly Major (*Col.*, Apr. 9); The Gods of Yesterday (*S. E. P.*, Apr. 30); Boppo Refuses (*Col.*, June 11).

Benét, Stephen Vincent, The Amateur of Crime (*Am.*, Apr.).

Blochman, L. G., Ways That Are Dark (*Ev.*, Mch.).

Borden, Mary, An Accident on the Quai Voltaire (*F.*, Mch.).

Borland, Hal, The Heifers (*Book.*, Oct., 1926).

Boyd, Thomas, The Fickle Jade (*C. H.*, Dec., 1926); The Fighting Face (*S. S.*, Dec. 25, 1926); Old Timers (*C. G.*, Mch.); Grandfather's Dog (*Scr.*, July).

Brackett, Charles, The Monster's Child (*S. E. P.*, Oct. 23, 1926); As Suggested (*S. E. P.*, Jan. 22).

Brady, Mariel, Georgia Washington (*G. H.*, Feb.).

Brown, Bernice, Marie Celeste (*D.*, Aug.).

Brown, Royal, The Sixth Hat (*L.*, Mch., 19).

Buckley, F. R., Peg Leg Retires (*W. S.*, Apr. 2).

Burt, Katharine Newlin, Heartbreak Homestead (*L.*, Apr. 23).

Burt, Struthers, Masquerade (*C. T.*, Oct. 3, 1926).

Butler, Ellis Parker, I Beg Your Pardon (*W. H. C.*, June); Happy Harry (*Mun.*, June); Mad Marix (*Mun.*, July).

Canfield, Dorothy, A Basque Windfall (*W. H. C.*, Apr.).

Carman, Dorothy Walworth, Every Thursday (*H.*, Jan.).

Fowler, Richard B., Practicality in Practice (*Scr.*, Feb.);
    Elmer's Imperfect Day (*W. H. C.*, Sept.).

Frost, Meigs, O., They's Always Thoroughbreds (*Ev.*, Jan.).

Gale, Zona, A Winter's Tale (*H. I. and C.*, June).

Gelzer, Jay, Man's Size (*G. H.*, Feb.).

Gilbert, Kenneth, Strength of the Hills (*Sun.*, Sept.).

Gould, Bruce, Sky Scrapes (*B. B.*, Oct., 1926).

Hallet, Richard Matthews, Theed Harlow's Cadenza(*S. E. P.*,
    Apr. 2).

Hergesheimer, Joseph, A Further Study of Plants (*S. E. P.*,
    Oct. 16, 1926); Albany (*S. E. P.*, May 7); Washington
    (*S. E. P.*, June 4); Lexington (*S. E. P.*, June 18);
    Charleston (*S. E. P.*, July 9).

Hopper, James, Stilts and a Complex (*R. B.*, Nov., 1926);
    The Derringer (*L.*, May 7).

Hughes, James Perley, The Glass Stalker (*Mun.*, May).

Hughes, Rupert, The Big Boob (*L.*, May 14).

Humphreys, Ray, In All His Glory (*W. S. M.*, Apr. 2).

Huse, Harry G., Red Symbols (*Ad.*, June 11).

Huston, McCready, The Lamp (*Scr.*, Dec., 1926).

Irwin, Wallace, American Beauty (*S. E. P.*, Jan. 8); Thanks
    for the Buggy Ride (*S. E. P.*, Jan. 15).

Irwin, Will, Through a Loophole in the Law (*L.*, Feb. 12).

Jackson, Charles Tenney, Big Timber (*S. S.*, Feb. 25);
    Fingers (*S. S.*, Sept. 25).

James, Will, The Young Cowboy (*Scr.*, Jan.).

Jerard, Elise Jean, The Treat (*Col.*, May 14).

Johnson, Nunnally, A Portrait of the Writer (*S. E. P.*,
    Oct. 16, 1926).

Johnston, Isabel, The Lavender-Flowered Crime (*McCall*,
    Oct., 1926).

Jordan, Elizabeth, John Henry's Inferiority Complex (*C. T.*,
    July 10).

Kahler, Hugh MacNair, The Puppet (*S. E. P.*, Oct. 16);
    Elbrowroom (*S. E. P.*, Aug. 20).

Kelly, Eleanor Mercein, Las Señoritas (*S. E. P.*, Mch. 26);
    Sky Pastures (*S. E. P.*, Apr. 23).

Kerr, Sophie, The Sloane Temper (*Am.*, Mch.); Hush-Me-
    Dear (*L.*, Feb. 19); Mimi-Mary (*Col.*, Nov. 13, 1926);
    They Told Her Everything (*D.*, May).

Mumford, Ethel Watts, The Scales of Justice (*Mun.*, July).
Nason, Leonard H., The General's Aide (*S. E. P.*, Nov. 6, 1926).
Neidig, William J., Rubies of Mogok (*S. E. P.*, Oct. 9, 1926); The Dagga Smokers (*S. E. P.*, Dec. 11, 1926).
Norris, Kathleen, The Irish Song Bird (*H. I. and C.*, Dec., 1926).
Osborne, William Hamilton, A Rum Proposal (*R. B.*, Oct., 1926).
Pangborn, Georgia Wood, The North Wind (*C. T.*, Dec. 19, 1926).
Parker, Maude, Raise or Quit (*S. E. P.*, Mch. 5); Exploration (*S. E. P.*, June 11).
Patterson, Norma, Ships That Pass (*G. H.*, Jan).
Pattullo, George, Eels (*S. E. P.*, Mch. 12).
Pelley, William Dudley, The Prodigal Angel (*L.*, June 18).
Perry, Peter, the State's Witness (*Fl.*, Oct., 23, 1926).
Post, Melville Davisson, The Leading Case (*Am.*, June).
Pulver, Mary Brecht, They Knew What They Wanted (*S. E. P.*, Dec. 4, 1926).
Reese, Lowell Otus, Fool Ridge (*S. E. P.*, Nov. 6, 1926).
Ritchie, Robert Welles, Rapahoe Bob (*C. G.*, Jan.).
Roche, Arthur Somers, Love Was Different Then (*H. I. and C.*, Feb.).
Roe, Vingie E., Smoke in the Gulch (*McCall*, Jan.).
Rose, Will, Splurgin' (*Scr.*, Jan.).
Ross, Mary Lowry, The Real Mrs. Alward (*S. E. P.*, Nov. 20, 1926); Three Husbands in Paris (*S. E. P.*, May 21).
Russell, John, The Bright Reversion (*Col.*, May 14).
Rutledge, Maryse, Skyscrapers (*S. E. P.*, Apr. 16).
Sangster, Margaret E., Mountains (*G. H.*, May); Loveliness (*G. H.*, Aug.).
Savell, Morton, The Wings of a Lark (*S. S.*, Feb. 25); Bird in Hand (*C. T.*, Sept. 18).
Saxby, Charles, The Little Mercy of Men (*Col.*, Feb. 19).
Schisgall, Oscar, Come On, Row! (*D. S. M.*, Oct. 30, 1926); In Kashla's Garden (*W. T.*, May).
Scott, R. T. M., Peter's Tower (*Am.*, Mch).
Scoville, Samuel Jr., The Mouse and the Lion (*Col.*, Oct. 30, 1926).
Seifert, Shirley, Dumb Bunnies (*Col.*, Nov. 27, 1926).

Weiman, Rita, Dinner Is Served (*R. B.*, Dec., 1926); Slow
　　Torture (*L.*, Apr. 16).
Wetjen, Albert Richard, The First Law of Nature (*Col.*,
　　June 11); The Mate Stands by (*Col.*, July 23).
White, Stewart Edward, "Free, Wide, and Handsome" (*Am.*,
　　May).
Wiley, Hugh, The Power of the Press (*S. E. P.*, Oct. 9, 1926).
Williams, Ben Ames, Skins (*S. E. P.*, Oct. 23, 1926); Aside
　　after Lucre (*S. E. P.*, Dec. 4, 1926).
Williams, Valentine, The Thumb of Fat'ma (*C. T.*, Aug. 7).
Williams, Wythe, En Garde (*S. E. P.*, Oct. 30, 1926); Destiny
　　(*S. E. P.*, Nov. 20, 1926).
Wilson, Mary Badger, Dust Behind the Sofa (*S. E. P.*,
　　Dec. 4, 1926).
Worts, George F., The Nimble Snail (*Mun.*, Oct., 1926).

LIST III

Stories ranking third.
Abbott, Eleanor Hallowell, The Steps That Went up into
　　the Sky (*G. H.*, Nov., 1926); Turkey in the Oven
　　(*W. H. C.*, Nov., 1926).
Banning, Margaret Culkin, Rich Man, Poor Man (*S. E. P.*,
　　Oct. 9, 1926); Delicatessen Love (*C. T.*, Apr. 24).
Bari, Valeska, the Goddess of Liberty (*F.*, July).
Barnard, Leslie Gordon, The Guest of Honor (*L. H. J.*, July).
Barretto, Larry, The Phantom Major (*Ad.*, Nov. 23, 1926).
Bellah, James Warner, Boppo Takes a Bird's-Eye View
　　(*Col.*, May 7); Old Waffle Ear (*Col.*, July 2).
Benét, Stephen Vincent, Miss Willie Lou and the Swan
　　(*C. G.*, Nov., 1926).
Benson, Stuart, Ramadin's Daughter (*Col.*, Oct. 9, 1926).
Boyd, Thomas, Dark in a Shell Hole (*S. S.*, Feb. 10); Two
　　Lean and Hungry Looks (*S. S.*, Apr. 10); Shootin'
　　Keno (*C. G.*, June).
Bretherton, Vivien R., Trinket (*McCall*, May).
Caffrey, Andrew A., Aerial Blue (*Ad.*, Nov. 23, 1926).
Clausen, Carl, On the Midnight Tide (*B. B.*, Nov., 1926);
　　Around the Horn (*C. T.*, June 12); The Shining Door
　　(*R. B.*, July); The Father of His Son (*C. T.*, Aug. 21);
　　The Three of Us (*P. R.*, Sept.).

Douglas, Marjory Stoneman, Too Much Class (*S. E. P.*, Oct. 9, 1926).

Edward, Cecil A., The Russian (*Atl.*, June).

Elliott, Stuart E., Whom the Gods Love (*L. H. J.*, June).

Franken, Rose L., The Lady in the Back (*C. T.*, July 31).

Gale, Zona, Heart of Youth (*L. H. J.*, Oct., 1926).

Goodman, Blanche, Nocturne (*Book.*, Feb.).

Hamilton, H. M., Liberty (*A. A.*, Oct. 23, 1926).

Jones, Vara Macbeth, Danny Goes Druid (*C. W.*, Mch.).

Kroll, Harry Harrison, Good to the Last Drop (*Ev.*, Jan.).

Lea, Fannie Heaslip, The Brute (*G. H.*, Oct., 1926).

Lovelace, Delos, Toe of the Stocking (*C. G.*, Dec., 1926).

McMorrow, Thomas, Hinkle against Fayne (*S. E. P.*, Oct. 30, 1926).

Marquis, Don, The High Pitch (*Col.*, May 28).

Mason, Grace Sartwell, Sweet Tooth (*W. H. C.*, May).

Miller, Helen Topping, A Bird Flies Over (*G. H.*, Oct., 1926).

Montague, Margaret Prescott, Hog's Eye and Human (*F.*, Aug.).

Montross, Lois Seyster, The Golden Legend (*L. H. J.*, Apr.).

Moravsky, Maria, The Ode to Pegasus (*W. T.*, Nov., 1926).

Nebel, Frederick L., Grain to Grain (*B. M.*, Nov., 1926).

Parmenter, Christine Whiting, David's Star of Bethlehem (*Am.*, Jan.).

Pelley, William Dudley, Martin's Tree (*Am.*, Apr.).

Perry, Lawrence, Barbed Wire (*Col.*, Oct. 16, 1926).

Portor, Laura Spencer, One Night (*W. H. C.*, May).

Post, Melville Davisson, The Survivor (*Am.*, Oct., 1926).

Pruden, Oliver, Black Salve (*S. S.*, July 10).

Ritchie, Robert Welles, You Take 'Em as They Flies (*S. S.*, Jan. 25).

Sears, Zelda, Out of the Fourth Dimension (*Mun.*, Oct., 1926).

Shore, Viola Brothers, A Handy Manuel (*S. E. P.*, Oct. 2, 1926).

Shore, Viola Brothers and Fort, Garrett, The Prince of Head-waiters (*L.*, Apr. 9).

Singer, Mary, Fathers (*G. H.*, Aug.).

Singmaster, Elsie, Finis (*Book.*, Aug.).

Speare, Dorothy, Sweet but Dumb (*P. R.*, Apr.).

Steele, Harwood, An Affair of Courage (*S. S.*, Mch., 25).

Synon, Mary, A Girl Called Stella (*P. R.*, Nov., 1926).
Taggard, Genevieve, The Shirt (*Book.*, Nov., 1926).
Tilden, Freeman, The Two-Browning Man (*L. H. J.*, May).
Topham, Thomas, In All His Glory (*D. S. M.*, Oct. 16, 1926).
Treleaven, Owen Clarke, Vengeance (*S. S.*, May 25).
Van de Water, Frederic F., Angels and Yellowjackets
    (*L. H. J.*, Oct., 1926); He Sendeth His Rain (*C. G.*,
    Apr.).
Vance, Louis Joseph, Base Metal (*Col.*, Oct. 30, 1926).
Ware, Edmund, The Boy and the Wind (*Am.*, Aug.); So-Long,
    Old Timer (*L. H. J.*, Aug.).
Weadock, Louis, Bottles and Stoppers (*Clues*, Nov., 1926).
White, Ared, The Watch on the Rhine (*Ev.*, Mch.).
White, Nelia Gardner, "Treasures" (*Am.*, Jan.); Helga (*Am.*,
    Aug.).
Whitehead, Henry S., The Left Eye (*W. T.*, June).
Wolff, William Almon, A Lady of Leisure (*L.*, June 18).

LIST IV

Of short short stories the following rank highest:
Anderson, Nels, Old Whitey (*Am. Merc.*, Jan.)
Benson, Stuart, A Soldier (*Col.*, July 2).
Bromfield, Louis, The Scarlet Woman (*McClure*, Jan.).
Child, Richard Washburn, The Man at the Bottom (*Col.*,
    Aug. 13).
Cohen, Octavus Roy, Stamped Out (*Col.*, Oct. 9, 1926);
    Sunset (*Col.*, Oct. 23, 1926).
Crawford, Nelson Antrim, Frock Coats (*H. J. Q.*, January).
Davenport, Walter, All Aboard (*Col.*, Sept. 17).
Davis, Bob, The Hard-Boiled Egg (*Col.*, Aug. 6).
Dell, Floyd, The Blanket (*Col.*, Oct. 16, 1926).
Doyle, Lynn, Smoke (*Mun.*, Dec., 1926).
Edholm, Charlton Lawrence, The Fame of Usskar (*C.*, Oct.,
    1926).
Fagin, N. Bryllion, The Queerness of Kate (*E.*, Feb.).
Farrar, John, Primrose Pavilion (*Col.*, Jan. 15).
Gale, Zona, Another Lady Bountiful (*H. I. and C.*, Feb.); Blue
    Velvet (*P. R.*, June); Tommy Taylor (*R. B.*, June).
Hare, Amory, Three Lumps of Sugar (*H. I. and C.*, May).
Hecht, Ben, The Lifer (*R. B.*, Feb.); Don Juan's Rainy Day
    (*C. H.*, May).

The short story has known better seasons, says a reader who, moved by indigestion and nausea, forswears the magazine tale of to-day as food unfit. The trouble with this reader lies partly in his having the world too much with him, late and soon. He finds no recreation in reading contemporary fictionists, or fiction about the present of which he is integrally a part. He believes he laments the Stockton and Bunner model; rather he laments the day of Stockton and Bunner. This nostalgia for the dear, dead days that are no more demands a superfiction, a glorification of the past. The demand is satisfied best by fictive biography, which has never known a better season. Because the satiated reader has no desire for short stories, he should condemn them all no more than one who has eaten too many clams condemns all clams.

Yet too many stories of to-day are like O. Henry's clam

shells "from which the succulent and vital inhabitants" have forever departed. A critical reader finds himself saying, "This tale was made on order from the editor," or "So-and-so is writing under too great pressure; he is tired." A disturbing fact is the absence of humour, for humour is the unfailing index to superabundance of vitality.

Among hopeful signs may be mentioned, first, a number of new writers appearing in the better as well as the humbler magazines; several are represented in this volume. Second, from what has been called the incoherent left side and the technically correct right side, a new form may be emerging; I suggest tentatively "The Mold," by Clarice Blake (*Century*, May), and "Sooth," by Wilbur Daniel Steele (*Harper's*, August). Third, the war story is slowly developing out of that emotion remembered in tranquillity which, on occasion, is as necessary to prose as to poetry. The period of recollection has produced good results, chiefly in the work of Thomas Beer, Thomas Boyd, Leonard Nason, and James Warner Bellah. Finally, a number of veterans are creating with undiminished vigour: Irvin S. Cobb, tales of the Tennessee River; Harris Dickson, reminiscences of Mississippi River gambling days; Booth Tarkington, adventures in the supernatural.

In the eight years of *O. Henry Memorial Prize Stories*, no reviewer of the annual collection—so far as I have discovered —has ever suggested a better story of a given year than those included between its covers. The fact is either gratifying or amusing; gratifying if the reviewer recognizes the selections as one of the best possible in the premises; amusing if the reviewer damns the whole lot—unless, to be sure, he damns all stories published in the period.

The Committee know what they demand in a story and read hundreds to salvage the comparatively few which best meet the demand. The first desideratum is a narrative constructed about characters in a struggle or complication having a definite outcome expressed or implied. Every story in this book satisfies this first test. In "Child of God" the struggle is Willie's against the social order; the order crushes him, but by his death he wins; The Killers are out for their man and, though they fail this time, ultimately they will not fail; the Scarlet Woman is at odds with society; Jukes agonizes to escape from the sea—he never will escape; "Fear" is nothing less at bottom than the conflict in Paterson's soul; on the surface it offers a display of spectacular conflicts between enemy planes; "Night Club" hints at a half-dozen conflicts (see page 84); "Singing Woman" relates the final stages in a lifelong rivalry; "He Man" instances a struggle with the sea and hunger; I have spoken of the struggle in "Done Got Over" as one between superstition and enlightenment; of that in "Shades of George Sand!" as one between the individual and environment; "With Glory and Honour" implies pretty strongly that Hal Levering conquered himself before he changed his ways; "Monkey Motions" reveals awkwardness and genius working to final expression; "Four Dreams" relates four vain efforts of Gram; Bulldog's fights and his escape lead to his climactic rescue of the judge; "The Little Girl" symbolizes the helplessness of all childhood through the concrete instance of Patricia's failure.

All writers and all critics are agreed upon other well-known desiderata, which neither the author nor the critic needs consciously to enumerate. Familiarity with the laws and limitations of the art is as necessary to judging fiction as insistence upon them is deplorable if such insistence means undervaluing a narrative that may smash all laws and succeed, it may so happen, because of the fact. He who follows an uncharted way may discover, or he may not discover, new lands.

That standards of reviewers differ may be illustrated by the following quotations drawn from reviewers of *O. Henry Memorial Prize Stories*, 1926:

"Miss Williams's introduction is of great interest, as it takes us behind the scenes with the judges . . . but still the collection itself remains disappointing." — Hartford *Courant*, January 23, 1927.

"Miss Williams in her introduction considers each story with critical seriousness, and analyzes, and praises, and compares, till

"The introduction is, it must be said, an unpleasant piece of work . . . in a style whose lack of distinction is in marked contrast to the stories that follow." — New York *Sun*, January 18, 1927.

"It is at least refreshing after the monotones of praise to which introducing editors have almost invariably treated us; and even though one can't help wondering what she would say of a Chekhov or a Maupassant." —The *Saturday Review of Literature*, May 28, 1927.

"If Wilbur Daniel Steele had never written a better story than 'Bubbles' he would never have achieved the fame and popularity which he not unjustly enjoys." — Richmond (Va.) *News Leader*, January 17, 1927.

"To me the story [Bubbles] is not convincing enough to be really successful. Despite deft craftsmanship the story fails to become important, and even its pattern is beautiful artifice rather than art." —The *Saturday Review of Literature*, May 28, 1927.

"Sherwood Anderson wins the second prize with a story called 'Death in the Woods' in which he is at his worst." —Richmond *News Leader*, January 17, 1927.

"'Death in the Woods' has the curious distinction no story of Mr. Anderson's could

one may not always agree with the specific comment ... that fact need not detract from one's approval of this tempered, tentative editorial attitude as constituting a salutary and genuinely respectable criticism." — New York *Herald-Tribune*, January 30, 1927.

"All competent readers will agree with the official judges as to the wisdom of their first choice. 'Bubbles' is a profound, subtle, and highly finished piece of work." —New York *Sun*, January 18, 1927.

"Mr. Steele's really stupendous story, 'Bubbles'— it is difficult not to overdo superlatives in writing of this appalling little masterpiece ... is one of Mr. Steele's supreme achievements." — Hartford *Courant*, January 23, 1927.

"Of the stories in this book, that by Sherwood Anderson [Death in the Woods] is the most important."— New York *World*, January 19, 1927.

"Mr. Anderson's story strikes the authentic Anderson note. He has seldom done lack, but would have hardly made him the reputation he so magnificently deserves."—New York *Post*, February 5, 1927.

The New York *Times* reviewer (January 23, 1927) remarks, "The relegation of Mary Heaton Vorse's story [The Madelaine] to the back of the book makes the reader wonder if these authorities on the short story . . . really know a story when they see it."

anything more powerful within its limits and never anything more characteristic."—New York *Sun*, January 18, 1927.

The order of the stories (see the table of contents for the 1926 collection) is, after the three prize stories, alphabetical by authors.

CHILD OF GOD

By ROARK BRADFORD

From *Harper's*

WHEN Willie told the preacher that morning that "ev'ything is all O.K., Revund," he meant it from the bottom of his heart. The hawking of the rain crow from the limb of the dead cottonwood. sounded like the song of a mocking bird. The monotonous patter of rain on the tin roof lulled him into gentle restfulness. The damp, dirty stench that floated up from the dark closeness of the cells below him was like a sedative. Even the lyelike coffee served to remind him that the jailer was his friend.

"Cap'm Archie tole me I could have ev'ything I wanted fer brekfus," he explained as he caught the minister sniffing and eyeing the scant remains of the meal. "An' I tole him I b'lieve I'd take some po'k chops an' cawfee, ef'n hit wuz all right. An' hyar it is."

"You mean dar hit wuz," admonished the preacher. "Now yo' flesh is fed, Willie, whut 'bout yo' soul?"

Willie beamed a broad, knowing smile. "My soul," he said tolerantly, "is all O.K. An' Revund," he continued jubilantly, "Cap'm Archie say he gonter bring me a ten-cent cigar to go walkin' up de gallows wid in my mouf." The minister's face was a study in expression. "An' I makes me a speech up yonder"—jerking his arm toward the gallows high in the roof of the jail—"an' den——"

"Den which, son?" Preacher Moore was eager to find a point of contact at which he could begin his prepared message of consolation.

"I'se Glory bound!" Willie declared with enthusiasm.

While the condemned man talked and the preacher listened, the Great State of Louisiana prepared to exact its penalty

I

in the form of the life of Willie Malone because "he did feloniously, wilfully, and of his deliberately premeditated malice
aforethought, make an assault on one Thurston Gibbs, and a
certain gun which then and there was loaded with gunpowder
and buckshot and was by him, the said Willie Malone, had and
held in both hands, he, the said Willie Malone, did then
and there feloniously and of malice aforethought shoot off and
discharge at and upon the said Thurston Gibbs thereby,
and by thus striking the said Thurston Gibbs with the buck-
shots inflicting on and in the body one mortal wound of which
said mortal wound the said Thurston Gibbs then and there
instantly died. And so the said Willie Malone did in the manner and form aforesaid, feloniously and of deliberately premeditated malice aforethought, kill and murder the said
Thurston Gibbs in the Parish of Wilton aforesaid, against
the peace and dignity of the Great State of Louisiana."

It all came out at the trial. Hogs had been running in
Willie's cornfield. The hogs belonged to Mr. Gibbs. And when
Willie asked him to keep them home Mr. Gibbs had cursed
him. Willie then bought a shotgun and some buckshot. Everybody agreed upon that much of it. Willie said he aimed to
shoot the hogs and that when he heard something rustling
the long blades he fired, thinking it was a hog. The district
attorney pointed out that it was impossible to get a witness
who could say what was in a man's mind and, therefore,
he'd leave it to the jury as to whether Willie was hog hunting
or man hunting.

The jury was divided upon the point, but all agreed that
no nigger had any right to shoot a white man's hogs, anyway,
much less shoot a white man. So they found him guilty as
charged.

Willie had rather enjoyed his stay in jail. Two or three
times his lawyer came and talked to him in a low voice and
had him make his cross mark on many important-looking
pieces of paper. It all gave him a feeling of importance hitherto
not experienced.

He liked "Cap'm Archie," too—Cap'm Archie was always
making jokes, and didn't make him do any work around the
jail except a little sweeping. And during the long cool spring
evenings, when the stars twinkled in the sky and the fiddling
of the katydids out in the weed patch back of the jail floated

in between the long iron-barred windows, Cap'm Archie would have one of the short-time prisoners drag his chair back to Willie's own private cage and Willie would sing for him.

Willie did like to sing—church songs, mostly. But sometimes when he felt sad and lonesome he'd sing the one that began:

> "Thirty days in jail,
> Baby, don't soun' so long,
> But de las' frien' I got in dis worl',
> Done shuck her laig an' gone."

There were many verses, and to these Willie had added a hundred others. He was good at that. When they locked up that Caldonie for cutting her husband because he stole one of her hens and a chicken brood and gave it to another woman, Willie celebrated the occasion by adding:

> "He might er stole yo' chickens,
> He might er stole yo' cow,
> Hit don't make no diffunce what he stole,
> You's in de jail-house now."

Cap'm Archie had laughed at that one and it made Willie happy.

Not long after that Cap'm Archie sent for him to come to the office. Cap'm Archie looked sad that day, and it made Willie feel sad. So when Cap'm Archie told him the Supreme Court had turned him down and that he would have to hang Willie was much relieved.

"Shuh! Cap'm Archie," Willie consoled, "dat ain' nothin' to go worryin' 'bout. I thought hit mought er been somethin' wrong, de way you had yo' face strung out. Shuh! Ain' dat de same as de jedge done tole me?"

That afternoon Reverend Moore, Negro preacher, was ushered into Willie's cell, and under his exhortations Willie was converted. He had been converted annually ever since he could remember but he always had been too busy to follow it up. This time he had ample leisure in which to contemplate Christianity and draw mental pictures of it. Willie was keenly interested.

The preacher had spared no detail his imagination could

supply as to the glories of heaven, and these Willie supplemented with the colourful pigments of his own imagination. Heaven was a wonderful place. Willie wanted to go there.

"Hyar dey comes, son," the preacher said kindly. "Git up off'n yo' knees."

Cap'm Archie unlocked the cage door with keys that rattled nervously in his hand. Behind the jailer were half a dozen others—the doctor, two brothers of the man he had killed, the editor of the *Wilton Parish Gazette*, and a short, stubby, mean-looking man that Willie disliked instinctively. He had never seen him before, and the pale-green, watery eyes that squinted out at him through shaggy eyelashes made Willie feel bad. "I loves him too," Willie insisted under his breath. "Got ter love him. 'Makes me love ev'ybody—hit's good ernuff fer me'"—Willie recalled the words from the old song. "An' I guess he is somebody. But I be dog ef'n he looks like much, Ole Green Eyes."

"Ready to go, Willie?" It was Cap'm Archie. His voice was kind and filled with sorrow. Willie hated to see Cap'm Archie like that. But when the jailer's teeth clicked together and he said briskly, "Here, slip your hands into these," it did not sound so sad, and Willie obeyed with alacrity.

"I bet you fergits my cigar, Cap'm Archie," Willie countered as his arms were being pinioned behind him.

"Cut out that damned foolishness! Come on here, nigger. I ain't got all day to fool." It was the stubby little man who assumed charge.

"Makes me love ev'ybody," Willie hummed desperately under his breath. "Hit's good ernuff for me."

"Good ernuff fer anybody," seconded the preacher loudly, happy that he had found some place to enter into the ceremony with the dignity of his calling. "Hit's de ole time religion, and hit's good ernuff fer me!"

As the party marched up the narrow steps to the gallows, the Negro prisoners on the lower tier of cells caught up the refrain and the brick walls of the little jail reverberated with:

> "Gimme dat ole time religion,
> Gimme dat ole time religion,
> Gimme dat ole time religion, Lawd,
> Hit's good ernuff fer me.

"Hit will take you home to Glory,
Hit will take you home to Glory,
Hit will take you home to Glory, Lawd,
Hit's good ernuff fer me."

The climb to the gallows took a remarkably short time and Willie noticed that as soon as they arrived there "Ole Green Eyes" rushed to the rope that was lying handy and began making a loop in the end of it.

"Makes me love ev'ybody," Willie insisted.

Everybody seemed nervous. Cap'm Archie couldn't look at him. The editor was talking with big words to the elder of the Gibbses and said something about "dancing on the air." Willie didn't understand it but he knew he wasn't going to dance on anything. Dancing would send him straight to hell. He had the preacher's word for it.

He edged over toward Cap'm Archie.

"When does I make my speech, Cap'm Archie?" he asked.

The jailer did not look up. "In a minute," he replied. "When you are ready to—when they stand you over there." He pointed to the trapdoor with his foot.

"Come over here, nigger." It was "Ole Green Eyes" again. Willie stood on the trapdoor.

"Makes me love ev'ybody," he kept repeating as the knot was being drawn close to his ear. "Makes me love ev'ybody."

When the knot was finished the little stubby man slipped a black hood over Willie's head and stepped back. A jay-bird on a dead limb of the cottonwood broke out in a scathing chatter of malediction at the crow. A dog howled mournfully in the jail yard below. The katydids in the weed patch opened with a wild symphony of fiddling. "Somethin' 'bout to happen," Willie concluded. "I guess I better make my speech."

He threw back his shoulders and raised his chin as though about to address a large congregation.

"Folkses," he began in a clear, strong voice, "I has a few words I wants to say to y'all——"

"Too late now, nigger." It was that stubby little man. And even as the trap gave way under his feet Willie began:

"Makes me love ev'ybody."

Willie did not finish that line, however. He was interrupted in the midst of it by a long blast on a horn. It was a loud, thundering blast and it startled him. He looked into the direction from which it came and there, charging down the road, he saw four prancing horses drawing a snow-white chariot. It was a beautiful sight. He had seen some such rig the time when he went to the circus at Baton Rouge. But this rig was even prettier than the circus carriages. Big white plumes bobbed from the crown-pieces of the bridles, and the horses pranced and danced along, raising a terrible dust.

"Great day!" he exclaimed. "Class sho' is comin' down de road to-day."

In a minute the carriage was in front of him, and with much suddenness it came to a halt, the horses falling back on their haunches to check the momentum.

"Git up hyar, boy, an' le's git goin'," the driver called down. "Us is late, as it is or—else you is early."

Willie scrambled to the seat beside the driver. As the horses raced onward he enjoyed the thrill of the speedy ride, the wind rushing by his ears, the sparkle of the gold and silver harness, the dexterity with which the driver held the horses in the road with one hand and cracked the whip over their heads with the other.

"You drives right well, boy," he observed. "What's yo' name?"

"Jehu," replied the driver.

"Jehu-which?"

"Jest Jehu," replied the driver.

"Who dat boy wid de hawn in his han'?"

"Gab'l."

The monosyllabic replies of his companion irritated Willie. He wanted conversation and he intended to have it.

"How long you been——" he began, but suddenly Gabriel raised his trumpet to his lips and blew a deafening blast which almost lifted Willie from his seat.

"Hol' tight," cautioned Jehu, and the chariot stopped suddenly.

Willie saw an old man in a black slouch hat and cutaway coat, walking very alertly toward the carriage. His face was cleanly shaven except for a moustache and goatee which gave him a distinguished appearance. Willie instinctively knew that this quality-gentleman was going to ride on the plush seats inside, so he leaped down and opened the door of the carriage. The old man halted a few paces from him and cast a surveying glance at the horses.

"That checkrein is too tight on that off-lead horse," he said. "It is a pity that I have to 'tend to these trifles, but damn it all, I can't stand to see fine horseflesh suffer on account of triflin' niggers."

Willie quickly ran and lowered the checkrein and climbed back to his seat.

"You oughter know better'n to check up dat hoss so high," he admonished Jehu with a proprietary air. "Us likes our hosses to have a heap er room."

Jehu did not reply. He held steadily to the reins, and the carriage fairly flew through the misty haze. Willie wanted to ask for the reins himself. He felt he could drive much more to his own satisfaction but, withal, he admitted, Jehu was doing very well. A minute later, however, when the lead horse bolted just as they approached a long bridge, and Jehu prevented a crash by expert manœuvring of the reins, Willie was glad he was not driving.

"Does dat ev'y time at the bridge," Jehu volunteered as the team settled down to a long gallop across the structure. "Lots er times us misses an' de folks in de chariot gits drownded tryin' to cross Jurdan."

"Dat de Jurdan, huh?" asked Willie. "I be dog," and he gripped tightly to the seat.

The chariot rolled off the bridge and up to the front of a white pearly gate where it stopped. Willie dropped confidently to the ground, opened the chariot door, and assisted the distinguished old passenger to alight. St. Peter swung the big gate open.

"Welcome, Colonel," he said. "It gives me great pleasure to greet you personally after having known you indirectly for these many years. She's waiting for you under the crêpe myrtles. Cherub, escort the Colonel to Miss Julia."

Willie thought that was great, and he was thrilled almost to ecstasy when the old gentleman gave him a curt nod in recognition of his service.

As soon as the old man had disappeared behind the cherub, St. Peter dropped his air of formality.

"Well, well," he said, "if it ain't that worthless Willie Malone. Willie, how'd you git here, son?"

That was language Willie could understand and appreciate.

"St. Peter," he replied, "I jes' got on de chariot an' rid up hyar."

"Well," said St. Peter, "I guess you better try on a pair of wings, then. Here, Cherub. Bring out a pair of wings for old Willie Malone."

St. Peter helped the cherub adjust the wings.

"Now you're fixed, son," he announced. "Fly away!"

And Willie flew. He flew among the golden clouds and down long narrow golden streets. He flew over mansions of gold and sparkling rivers. High into the air and close to the ground he flew. He tried a few fancy turns, such as he had seen birds perform among the chinaberry trees. He dived at the surface of the water and grabbed at the golden fish and then climbed again by lusty flaps of his wings, as pelicans do. And he did it perfectly.

"Doggone my hide," he exclaimed, "dis is somethin' like!"

After a few hours the novelty began to wear off. He was high in the air, maybe a mile high, he estimated. So he pointed one wing at an angle and began gliding down, making a huge spiral as he descended. Halfway down, he reversed the cant of his wings and came down the rest of the way, flying backwards.

He landed right in the midst of a group of other angels who were seated around the Great Throne. Upon the throne sat the Great Lord God. Willie recognized him instantly because of the distinction with which he sat upon his throne and by the carefree tilt of his huge, bejewelled crown almost hiding one eye and by the angle at which the ten-cent cigar was cocked. Willie was a little frightened, and dazzled by the regal splendour of it all, but he settled down noiselessly to the ground, and was made to feel perfectly at home, by the informal greeting he received.

"I bet you want to hear some music, don't you, Willie?" asked the Great Lord God and, without waiting for Willie's reply, he continued, "Little David, play on your harp."

"What shall I play, Great Lord God?" asked Little David.

"Play something calm and low, Little David," said the Great Lord God. "Do not alarm my people."

David struck a chord or two on his harp. It was beautiful. The mellow music floated straight to Willie's heart. One or two of the other angels started humming with the music and, almost unconscious of where he was, Willie added his low, rich bass to the chorus:

"When dat big *Titanic* sunk down in de sea,
All de brass bands played 'Nearer My God to Thee.'
Out on de deep blue ocean de people sleep
In a cold wet cradle, three miles deep.
It's yo' las' trip, *Titanic*."

After several verses Willie began to feel a personal sorrow for the passengers of the *Titanic*. The music stopped suddenly, and the Great Lord God commanded, "Little David, play something quick and lively. Let the skies rock with mirth. Let the heavens open wide. Let the stars and the moon shine out. Let my people shout with joy."

And as soon as the command was issued all the angels began dancing and singing as Little David played:

"Two little babies a-layin' in de bed,
One of'm sick an' de yuther mos' dead.
Sont fer de doctor an' de doctor said,
'Give dem babies some shortnin' bread.'
So put on de skillet an' thow way de led,
Cause mammy gonter make a little shortnin' bread."

Several more songs followed and finally Willie began to tire of singing. The party broke up, the angels flying away in groups of twos and threes. Soon no one was left before the throne except Willie.

Willie felt slightly embarrassed there, with no one around except the Great Lord God. He figured he might be intruding or something, or that perhaps he'd better go out and fly some more. But as he was turning over the idea a tall, kindly looking angel, more strikingly handsome than any he had ever seen, strolled up and sat down familiarly by the side of the Great Lord God. At first Willie thought it was Cap'm Archie. There was kindness and understanding in his face, just like Cap'm Archie's face. But it wasn't Cap'm Archie. Cap'm Archie had no scars on his hands and feet as had this angel.

As he puzzled over the matter he faintly remembered a story his old mammy had told him about a man with scars

on his hands and feet, and he recalled the lines of a song that
Cap'm Archie used to make him sing:

> "They nailed His hands and they rivet His feet,
> An' de hammers wuz heard in Jerusalem street."

Some way, Willie could not place him. But he felt much
more at ease for his presence.

"What you thinking about, Willie?" the kindly angel
asked. "You don't seem to be enjoying yourself so much."

Willie did not know exactly what to reply. He rummaged
through his mind hastily. He had been entirely happy for
ever so long, not a thing had gone wrong. Everybody had
been so nice to him. The music had been beautiful and just
the songs he liked to sing. His wings fitted perfectly and St.
Peter had been wonderful. So had Jehu. And Cap'm Archie
—he had given him everything he could think of and a heap
he did not think of. Of course there was the matter of the
cigar. He wanted to go to the gallows with a cigar in his
mouth. But that wasn't Cap'm Archie's fault . . . and, too,
maybe Cap'm Archie had forgotten the cigar. He had so many
things to think about. Willie concluded that if it were the
cigar he would say nothing about it to the kind angel because
he did not want to embarrass Cap'm Archie. He did not really
want to go to the gallows with a cigar, anyway, he decided.

"But I did want ter make dat speech," he concluded.

"What speech is that?" asked the kindly faced angel.

Willie explained in great detail, and the angel and the
Great Lord God listened intently.

"But hit wa'n't Cap'm Archie's fault," he declared.

"Whose fault was it, then?" demanded the Great Lord
God.

"Hit mought er been—onderstan', I ain' s'cusin' nobody,"
Willie faltered, "but hit mought er been Ole Green Eyes.
But I loves ev'ybody—him, too," he added hastily.

"I know the scoundrel," declared the Great Lord God.
"He's been plaguing me for years and years. But this is too
much." The brow of the Great Lord God clouded in anger and
he shouted with a terrible roar, like seven peals of thunder,
"Cherub, bring me a bolt of forked lightning that I may strike
that man from the face of the earth."

The cherub brought the lightning, and the Great Lord God was about to hurl it. But the kind angel touched his arm gently.

"I wouldn't, Father," said the angel. "He might not have understood that the speech was to have been the biggest thing in Willie's life."

The Great Lord God stayed his hand and turned upon the kind angel. "Of course he understood. That's why he didn't let him make it. He's just low-down mean. I've put up with enough of it."

"But," insisted the kind angel, "it will do no good to strike him down with lightning. It would frighten many people. And it would start new arguments over religion and that would lead to controversies and they would lead to hatreds and hatreds lead to——"

"I've heard that speech a million times, Son," said the Great Lord God, "and you needn't go into details. I admit you are right," and he handed the lightning bolt back to the cherub. "But," continued the Great Lord God, "I will not let this thing pass." His brow clouded in anger again. "I am the Great I am," he roared, "and my commands shall be obeyed." The kind angel sat meekly and argued no further.

"Willie Malone," commanded the Great Lord God in a tone of thunder.

"Yassuh, Great Lord God," replied Willie, jumping to his feet.

"You go right back down yonder and make that speech. He's sitting in the jail office right now with Captain Archie. Now go and do my commands."

Willie lost no time in getting to the jail. As he approached, he noticed a half-dozen Negroes—friends of his—standing in the rain about the big steel door entry to the lower cells. But he hurried by them with only a curt "hy-dy, boys." The fact that they ignored him stung a little but he had no time to lose. He went straight to the office entrance.

The green-eyed man was seated at a table fingering five new ten-dollar bills. The coroner was scratching away with a pen on a big official-looking document. The editor and the two Gibbses were talking in low tones. Cap'm Archie was hunched down in his chair at his desk, looking at the floor.

Willie stood a minute respectfully, hoping Cap'm Archie would notice him and inquire what he wanted.

But Cap'm Archie did not look toward him and Willie tried a scheme that had worked many times for him.

"Cap'm, suh," he said, "don' you want dis ole dirty flo' swep' up er somethin'?"

But Cap'm Archie acted as though he did not hear.

Willie cogitated. Maybe he was worrying about forgetting the cigar.

But as the thought came to Willie Cap'm Archie slowly reached to his vest pocket and drew out a single long black cigar and studied it intently.

"You got the mate to that'n, Sheriff?" Ole Green Eyes quit shuffling the new bills and directed his attention toward the cigar.

"Nope," replied Cap'm Archie, "I ain't got the mate to this'n." And he tightened his grip on the cigar until he had broken and crushed it. "And if I did have it," he added, "I'd damn well keep it."

"No hard feelings, Sheriff," offered Green Eyes. "I see you ain't used to it. Cheer up. It's just another nigger less."

A scraping of feet in the jail hall at the side of the office attracted the attention of both Cap'm Archie and Green Eyes. Willie followed their gaze through the barred hall door and saw six Negroes carrying a long black box toward the big jail door. Behind the box marched Preacher Moore, directing and exhorting as he went.

"There he goes now—out of yer jail and out of yer life. It's all over and yer duty's done."

Cap'm Archie squeezed the cigar tightly, crumbling it into tiny bits.

The green-eyed man essayed a cackling laugh. "And so's mine," he continued, picking up the five bills, "so I guess I'll be going."

Willie had been standing by in respectful silence since the white folks had indicated by ignoring him that they were too busy to talk to him. White people are that way, Willie had learned. Sometimes they will talk with you and laugh with you. And sometimes when they are busy they won't pay any attention to you unless you get in their way or something. Then they will curse you. Willie knew how to get along with white folks.

But things were different now. He had business with Mister Green Eyes.

"Wait a minute, Cap'm, suh," he addressed the green-eyed man.

Green Eyes stiffened, blinked his eyes, passed his hand across his forehead, and frowned. He stuck the money into his pocket quickly and grabbed for his hat.

"Wait a minute, Cap'm," Willie pleaded. "I got ter make my speech."

The green-eyed man turned pale and shut his eyes tightly, gritting his teeth and shaking his head as if in an effort to clear his brain.

"Sheriff," he said with a great struggle for calmness in his voice, "I need a drink. I—I—I'm sort of nervous, I reckon."

"There's the doctor," Cap'm Archie replied calmly, nodding toward the coroner.

"But, Cap'm, suh, wait," interjected Willie, "lemme make my speech——"

The green-eyed man yelled and ran to the doctor.

"Get me a drink, Doctor!" he begged. "A drink! For God's sake. I'm all shot to hell, Doctor. Get me a drink, quick."

"What's the matter, man?" demanded the doctor. "What is it?"

"That damned nigger, Doctor. I'm seein' things. So help me. He wants to make a speech, Doctor——"

"Dat's all right, Cap'm," Willie insisted. "Hit ain't no mean speech."

"O-ww-w-w—Doctor," screamed the green-eyed man. "There he is again."

The coroner and Cap'm Archie caught the hangman and led him to a chair.

"Calm down, man," said the doctor. "Your nerves are upset."

"But that nigger, that damned nigger! I see him."

"Well, he isn't going to hurt you, man. He's——"

"Nawsuh, I wa'n't gonter hurt nobody," Willie assured him. "I jes' was gonter say a few words."

The man struggled wildly, and it was only with the added strength of the two Gibbses and the editor that they succeeded in holding him in his chair. He was alternately crying and cursing, trembling weakly and fighting wildly.

"That damned nigger! I see him! I see him!" he kept shouting. "He wants to make a speech!"

"Hold him until I can fix a hypodermic," ordered the doctor.

"I jes' gonter make my speech," Willie pleaded again in an effort to calm the green-eyed man. "I ain' gonter do nothin' but jes' tawk."

But instead of being soothed, the man became more violent and but for the utmost strength of four men, he would have escaped. They held him, though. Held him in the chair while his eyes glared in wild frenzy, his huge neck swelled even bigger, his face turned purple, and his breath came in short rasping gasps. "Git away, damned nigger. I see you. Ow-ww-ww!"

"I jes' on'y got a few words I wanner say," Willie began again. And after one lunge at the sound of Willie's voice the man quieted down, and his eyes stared glassily at nothing, although his neck still bulged. The colour of his face changed to an ugly blue and his mouth dropped open and dripped frothy saliva. And while the green-eyed man sat limp in the chair Willie Malone completed his speech:

"I jes' wanner say I ain't got no hard feelin's agin nobody an' I don' want nobody to has no hard feelin's agin me. An' I wants to meet you all in heaven."

THE KILLERS

By ERNEST HEMINGWAY

From *Scribner's*

THE door of Henry's lunch room opened and two men came in. They sat down at the counter.

"What's yours?" George asked them.

"I don't know," one of the men said. "What do you want to eat, Al?"

"I don't know," said Al. "I don't know what I want to eat."

Outside it was getting dark. The street-light came on outside the window. The two men at the counter read the menu. From the other end of the counter Nick Adams watched them. He had been talking to George when they came in.

"I'll have a roast pork tenderloin with apple sauce and mashed potato," the first man said.

"It isn't ready yet."

"What the hell do you put it on the card for?"

"That's the dinner," George explained. "You can get that at six o'clock."

George looked at the clock on the wall behind the counter.

"It's five o'clock."

"The clock says twenty minutes past five," the second man said.

"It's twenty minutes fast."

"Oh, to hell with the clock," the first man said. "What have you got to eat?"

"I can give you any kind of sandwiches," George said. "You can have ham and eggs, bacon and eggs, liver and bacon, or a steak."

"Give me chicken croquettes with green peas and cream sauce and mashed potatoes."

"That's the dinner."

"Everything we want's the dinner, eh? That's the way you work it."

"I can give you ham and eggs, bacon and eggs, liver——"

"I'll take ham and eggs," the man called Al said. He wore a derby hat and a black overcoat buttoned across the chest. His face was small and white and he had tight lips. He wore a silk muffler and gloves.

"Give me bacon and eggs," said the other man. He was about the same size as Al. Their faces were different, but they were dressed like twins. Both wore overcoats too tight for them. They sat leaning forward, their elbows on the counter.

"Got anything to drink?" Al asked.

"Silver beer, bevo, ginger ale," George said.

"I mean you got anything to drink?"

"Just those I said."

"This is a hot town," said the other. "What do they call it?"

"Summit."

"Ever hear of it?" Al asked his friend.

"No," said the friend.

"What do you do here nights?" Al asked.

"They eat the dinner," his friend said. "They all come here and eat the big dinner."

"That's right," George said.

"So you think that's right?" Al asked George.

"Sure."

"You're a pretty bright boy, aren't you?"

"Sure," said George.

"Well, you're not," said the other little man. "Is he, Al?"

"He's dumb," said Al. He turned to Nick. "What's your name?"

"Adams."

"Another bright boy," Al said. "Ain't he a bright boy, Max?"

"The town's full of bright boys," Max said.

George put the two platters, one of ham and eggs, the other of bacon and eggs, on the counter. He set down two side dishes of fried potatoes and closed the wicket into the kitchen.

"Which is yours?" he asked Al.

"Don't you remember?"

"Ham and eggs."

"Just a bright boy," Max said. He leaned forward and took the ham and eggs. Both men ate with their gloves on. George watched them eat.

"What are *you* looking at?" Max looked at George.

"Nothing."

"The hell you were. You were looking at me."

"Maybe the boy meant it for a joke, Max," Al said.

George laughed.

"*You* don't have to laugh," Max said to him. "*You* don't have to laugh at all, see?"

"All right," said George.

"So he thinks it's all right." Max turned to Al. "He thinks it's all right. That's a good one."

"Oh, he's a thinker," Al said. They went on eating.

"What's the bright boy's name down the counter?" Al asked Max.

"Hey, bright boy," Max said to Nick. "You go around on the other side of the counter with your boy friend."

"What's the idea?" Nick asked.

"There isn't any idea."

"You better go around, bright boy," Al said. Nick went around behind the counter.

"What's the idea?" George asked.

"None of your damn business," Al said. "Who's out in the kitchen?"

"The nigger."

"What do you mean the nigger?"

"The nigger that cooks."

"Tell him to come in."

"What's the idea?"

"Tell him to come in."

"Where do you think you are?"

"We know damn well where we are," the man called Max said. "Do we look silly?"

"You talk silly," Al said to him. "What the hell do you argue with this kid for? Listen," he said to George, "tell the nigger to come out here."

"What are you going to do to him?"

"Nothing. Use your head, bright boy. What would we do to a nigger?"

George opened the slit that opened back into the kitchen. "Sam," he called. "Come in here a minute."

The door to the kitchen opened and the nigger came in. "What was it?" he asked. The two men at the counter took a look at him.

"All right, nigger. You stand right there," Al said.

Sam, the nigger, standing in his apron, looked at the two men sitting at the counter. "Yes, sir," he said. Al got down from his stool.

"I'm going back to the kitchen with the nigger and bright boy," he said. "Go on back to the kitchen, nigger. You go with him, bright boy." The little man walked after Nick and Sam, the cook, back into the kitchen. The door shut after them. The man called Max sat at the counter opposite George. He didn't look at George but looked in the mirror that ran along back of the counter. Henry's had been made over from a saloon into a lunch-counter.

"Well, bright boy," Max said, looking into the mirror, "why don't you say something?"

"What's it all about?"

"Hey, Al," Max called, "bright boy wants to know what it's all about."

"Why don't you tell him?" Al's voice came from the kitchen.

"What do you think it's all about?"

"I don't know."

"What do you think?"

Max looked into the mirror all the time he was talking.

"I wouldn't say."

"Hey, Al, bright boy says he wouldn't say what he thinks it's all about."

"I can hear you, all right," Al said from the kitchen. He had propped open the slit that dishes passed through into the kitchen with a catsup bottle. "Listen, bright boy," he said from the kitchen to George. "Stand a little further along the bar. You move a little to the left, Max." He was like a photographer arranging for a group picture.

"Talk to me, bright boy," Max said. "What do you think's going to happen?"

George did not say anything.

"I'll tell you," Max said. "We're going to kill a Swede. Do you know a big Swede named Ole Andreson?"

"Yes."

"He comes here to eat every night, don't he?"

"Sometimes he comes here."

"He comes here at six o'clock, don't he?"

"If he comes."

"We know all that, bright boy," Max said. "Talk about something else. Ever go to the movies?"

"Once in a while."

"You ought to go to the movies more. The movies are fine for a bright boy like you."

"What are you going to kill Ole Andreson for? What did he ever do to you?"

"He never had a chance to do anything to us. He never even seen us."

"And he's only going to see us once," Al said from the kitchen.

"What are you going to kill him for, then?" George asked.

"We're killing him for a friend. Just to oblige a friend, bright boy."

"Shut up," said Al from the kitchen. "You talk too goddam much."

"Well, I got to keep bright boy amused. Don't I, bright boy?"

"You talk too damn much," Al said. "The nigger and my bright boy are amused by themselves. I got them tied up like a couple of girl friends in the convent."

"I suppose you were in a convent."

"You never know."

"You were in a kosher convent. That's where you were."

George looked up at the clock.

"If anybody comes in you tell them the cook is off, and if they keep after it, you tell them you'll go back and cook yourself. Do you get that, bright boy?"

"All right," George said. "What you going to do with us afterward?"

"That'll depend," Max said. "That's one of those things you never know at the time."

George looked up at the clock. It was a quarter past six.

The door from the street opened. A street-car motorman came in.

"Hello, George," he said. "Can I get supper?"

"Sam's gone out," George said. "He'll be back in about half an hour."

"I'd better go up the street," the motorman said. George looked at the clock. It was twenty minutes past six.

"That was nice, bright boy," Max said. "You're a regular little gentleman."

"He knew I'd blow his head off," Al said from the kitchen.

"No," said Max. "It ain't that. Bright boy is nice. He's a nice boy. I like him."

At six-fifty-five George said: "He's not coming."

Two other people had been in the lunch room. Once George had gone out to the kitchen and made a ham-and-egg sandwich "to go" that a man wanted to take with him. Inside the kitchen he saw Al, his derby hat tipped back, sitting on a stool beside the wicket with the muzzle of a sawed-off shotgun resting on the ledge. Nick and the cook were back to back in the corner, a towel tied in each of their mouths. George had cooked the sandwich, wrapped it up in oiled paper, put it in a bag, brought it in, and the man had paid for it and gone out.

"Bright boy can do everything," Max said. "He can cook and everything. You'd make some girl a nice wife, bright boy."

"Yes?" George said. "Your friend, Ole Andreson, isn't going to come."

"We'll give him ten minutes," Max said.

Max watched the mirror and the clock. The hands of the clock marked seven o'clock, and then five minutes past seven.

"Come on, Al," said Max. "We better go. He's not coming."

"Better give him five minutes," Al said from the kitchen.

In the five minutes a man came in, and George explained that the cook was sick.

"Why the hell don't you get another cook?" the man asked. "Aren't you running a lunch counter?" He went out.

"Come on, Al," Max said.

"What about the two bright boys and the nigger?"

"They're all right."

"You think so?"

"Sure. We're through with it."

"I don't like it," said Al. "It's sloppy. You talk too much."

"Oh, what the hell," said Max. "We got to keep amused, haven't we?"

"You talk too much, all the same," Al said. He came out from the kitchen. The cut-off barrels of the shotgun made a slight bulge under the waist of his too tight-fitting overcoat. He straightened his coat with his gloved hands.

"So long, bright boy," he said to George. "You got a lot of luck."

"That's the truth," Max said. "You ought to play the races, bright boy."

The two of them went out the door. George watched them through the window pass under the arc light and cross the street. In their tight overcoats and derby hats they looked like a vaudeville team. George went back through the swinging door into the kitchen and untied Nick and the cook.

"I don't want any more of that," said Sam, the cook. "I don't want any more of that."

Nick stood up. He had never had a towel in his mouth before.

"Say," he said. "What the hell?" He was trying to swagger it off.

"They were going to kill Ole Andreson," George said. "They were going to shoot him when he came in to eat."

"Ole Andreson?"

"Sure."

The cook felt the corners of his mouth with his thumbs.

"They all gone?" he asked.

"Yeah," said George. "They're gone now."

"I don't like it," said the cook. "I don't like any of it at all."

"Listen," George said to Nick. "You better go see Ole Andreson."

"All right."

"You better not have anything to do with it at all," Sam, the cook, said. "You better stay way out of it."

"Don't go if you don't want to," George said.

"Mixing up in this ain't going to get you anywhere," the cook said. "You stay out of it."

"I'll go see him," Nick said to George. "Where does he live?"

The cook turned away.

"Little boys always know what they want to do," he said.

"He lives up at Hirsch's rooming house," George said to Nick.

"I'll go up there."

Outside the arc light shone through the bare branches of a tree. Nick walked up the street beside the car tracks and turned at the next arc light down a side street. Three houses up the street was Hirsch's rooming house. Nick walked up the two steps and pushed the bell. A woman came to the door.

"Is Ole Andreson here?"

"Do you want to see him?"

"Yes, if he's in."

Nick followed the woman up a flight of stairs and back to the end of a corridor. She knocked on the door.

"Who is it?"

"It's somebody to see you, Mr. Andreson," the woman said.

"It's Nick Adams."

"Come in."

Nick opened the door and went into the room. Ole Andreson was lying on the bed with all his clothes on. He had been a heavy-weight prizefighter and he was too long for the bed. He lay with his head on two pillows. He did not look at Nick.

"What was it?" he asked.

"I was up at Henry's," Nick said, "and two fellows came in and tied up me and the cook, and they said they were going to kill you."

It sounded silly when he said it. Ole Andreson said nothing.

"They put us out in the kitchen," Nick went on. "They were going to shoot you when you came in to supper."

Ole Andreson looked at the wall and did not say anything.

"George thought I better come and tell you about it."

"There isn't anything I can do about it," Ole Andreson said.

"I'll tell you what they were like."

"I don't want to know what they were like," Old Andreson said. He looked at the wall. "Thanks for coming to tell me about it."

"That's all right."

Nick looked at the big man lying on the bed.

"Don't you want me to go and see the police?"

"No," Ole Andreson said. "That wouldn't do any good."

"Isn't there something I could do?"

"No. There ain't anything to do."

"Maybe it was just a bluff."

"No. It ain't just a bluff."

Ole Andreson rolled over toward the wall.

"The only thing is," he said, talking toward the wall, "I just can't make up my mind to go out. I been in here all day."

"Couldn't you get out of town?"

"No," Ole Andreson said. "I'm through with all that running around."

He looked at the wall.

"There ain't anything to do now."

"Couldn't you fix it up some way?"

"No. I got in wrong." He talked in the same flat voice. "There ain't anything to do. After a while I'll make up my mind to go out."

"I better go back and see George," Nick said.

"So long," said Ole Andreson. He did not look toward Nick. "Thanks for coming around."

Nick went out. As he shut the door he saw Ole Andreson, with all his clothes on, lying on the bed looking at the wall.

"He's been in his room all day," the landlady said downstairs. "I guess he don't feel well. I said to him: 'Mr. Andreson, you ought to go out and take a walk on a nice fall day like this,' but he didn't feel like it."

"He doesn't want to go out."

"I'm sorry he don't feel well," the woman said. "He's an awfully nice man. He was in the ring, you know."

"I know it."

"You'd never know it except from the way his face is," the woman said. They stood talking just inside the street door. "He's just as gentle."

"Well, good-night, Mrs. Hirsch," Nick said.

"I'm not Mrs. Hirsch," the woman said. "She owns the place. "I just look after it for her. I'm Mrs. Bell."

"Well, good-night, Mrs. Bell," Nick said.

"Good-night," the woman said.

Nick walked up the dark street to the corner under the arc light, and then along the car tracks to Henry's eating house. George was inside, back of the counter.

"Did you see Ole?"

"Yes," said Nick. "He's in his room and he won't go out."

The cook opened the door from the kitchen when he heard Nick's voice.

"I don't even listen to it," he said, and shut the door.

"Did you tell him about it?" George asked.

"Sure. I told him, but he knows what it's all about."

"What's he going to do?"

"Nothing."

"They'll kill him."

"I guess they will."

"He must have got mixed up in something in Chicago."

"I guess so," said Nick.

"It's a hell of a thing.'"

"It's an awful thing," Nick said.

They did not say anything. George reached down for a towel and wiped the counter.

"I wonder what he did?" Nick said.

"Double-crossed somebody. That's what they kill them for."

"I'm going to get out of this town," Nick said.

"Yes," said George. "That's a good thing to do."

"I can't stand to think about him waiting in the room and knowing he's going to get it. It's too damned awful."

"Well," said George, "you better not think about it."

THE SCARLET WOMAN

By LOUIS BROMFIELD

From *McClure's*

I CAN see her now as she used to come down the steps of her narrow house between the printer's office and the little shop of Rinehart, the German cobbler—little, rickety steps, never in too good repair, especially as she grew older and the cost of everything increased and that mysterious money of hers seemed to go less and less far in the business of meeting the necessities of life. It was a house but one room wide, of wood painted a dun colour; the most ordinary and commonplace of houses which a stranger would not even have noticed —yet until yesterday, when they pulled it down, a house invested with a terrific glamour and importance. It was a house of which no one spoke; a house which the Town, in its passionate desire to forget (which was really only a hypocrisy), raised into such importance that one thought of it when one forgot the monuments which had been raised to the leading citizens of the community: to the bankers, to the merchants, to the politicians who had made it (as people said with a curious and non-committal tone which might have meant anything at all) "what it was to-day." One remembered it even when one forgot the shaft of granite raised in the public square to remind the Town that John Shadwell had been one of its leading citizens.

I can see her now—Vergie Winters—an old woman past eighty, coming painfully down those rickety steps, surrounded always by that wall of solitude which appeared to shut out all the world. Old Vergie Winters, whose dark eyes at eighty carried a look of tranquil, defiant victory. Vergie Winters, of whose house no one spoke; whose door had been stoned by boys who knew nothing of her story but sensed dimly that she was the great pariah of the Town.

Old Vergie Winters went on and on, long after John Shadwell was in his grave, refusing to give way, living there on the main street of the Town as if she were alone in the vast solitude of a desert. Sometimes she spoke to Rinehart, the cobbler, and sometimes to her neighbour on the other side; and of course in the shops they were forced to sell her things, though in one or two places they had even turned her away— and she had gone without a word, never trying to force her way anywhere.

It all began almost a century ago, before the Civil War, when one day in April Vergie Winters, tall and dark, with great, burning dark eyes set in a cool, pale face, opened the door of her father's house to John Shadwell, tall and handsome and blond, the youngest lawyer in the Town. It happened so long ago that it seems now to have no more reality than a legend, especially when one remembers Vergie only as an immensely old woman coming painfully down her narrow, crooked steps. But it happened; it must have happened to have made of Vergie Winters so great a character in all the community. It must have been the rare sort of love which comes like a stroke of lightning.

He would have married Vergie Winters, they said (the old ones who remembered the beginnings of Vergie's story and passed it on to their children and grandchildren) but there was already a girl to whom John Shadwell was betrothed, and in the background a powerful father, and John Shadwell's career—which Vergie Winters, being only the daughter of a Swiss immigrant farmer, could do nothing to aid.

Long afterward, the Town said, "Look at her! You can see what a drag she would have been on him, with her queer, silent ways. A pity, too, for she was a beautiful girl. A pity she was always bad!"

But they never thought, of course, that if things had been different, Vergie Winters might not have been queer and silent; and now, looking back, one can see that they were quite wrong. It was not Vergie Winters who was a drag on his career. It was the other woman, John Shadwell's wife, who turned into a strange, whining, melancholy invalid before they had been married two years. And what could John Shadwell do? Desert her? It was not possible.

And in the way of such invalids she lived for more than forty years, forty dreary years, complaining, hypochondriac, nagging. She outlived even her husband, a great, vigorous, handsome man, who treated her patiently and with gentlemanly respect.

"It was a pity about John Shadwell's wife," people said. "And she was such a lady, too."

And Vergie Winters? She did not break her heart. She did not marry some stupid lout and give up her life to a dull unhappiness. She did not wither away into spinsterhood. She loved John Shadwell, who knows how passionately, how deeply, in the profound depths of that curious, remote soul of hers? She left her parents ("to set herself up in dressmaking and millinery," so she said), and took a narrow wooden house on Main Street, where she put up a card in the window and sold hats to the women of the Town. And before two years had passed it was to this narrow house that John Shadwell came, secretly—it must have been with an amazing secrecy, for no one even suspected the visits for more than three years. She made no effort to be more friendly with people about her than was required by the simple routine of her trade. She lived placidly, with a strange, rich contentment, inside the walls of the narrow little house. One met her sometimes, usually after darkness had fallen, walking with her slow, dignified step along the streets of the Town. But she was alone . . . always alone.

Only once in all those sixty years was she ever known to leave the house overnight, and that was once, three years after John Shadwell was married, when she went away for a few months, "to visit her aunt in Camden." It was not long after she returned that John Shadwell, "whose poor wife could never have any children," adopted a girl baby. His wife, it was said, made no protest so long as the child had a good nurse and did not worry her. She was "so miserable, always ailing. She would give anything in the world for the health some women had."

"You couldn't blame her," said the Town, "for feeling like that. They say she never has a moment's good, wholesome sleep."

John Shadwell went to the Legislature, the youngest man in the state to hold such an office; and when the time for re-election came the fight was bitter, and into it some enemy thrust the name of Vergie Winters. So the story spread, and so the name of Vergie Winters went the way of most small-town milliners. Millinery was a "fast" business and Vergie Winters was a "fast" woman. A committee called upon her and asked her to leave the Town. And John Shadwell did nothing. If he came to her defense, he was ruined at the very beginning of that precious career. So Vergie gave him up, but she did not leave the Town. In the little parlour with the hats in the window she received the committee, and in that calm, aloof way she told them that they could not force her to leave. They could not prove that she had broken any law. She was a free citizen. She even looked at them out of the depths of those dark, candid eyes, and lied.

"John Shadwell," she said, "is nothing to me. If he has come here once or twice, it is only because he is my lawyer."

She must protect John Shadwell.

And so she sent them away baffled, even perhaps a little intimidated . . . a committee of red-faced, self-righteous townsmen who had known, some of them at least, far worse women than Vergie Winters.

But her trade dwindled. Women no longer came to her for hats, unless they were the shady ladies of the streets. And Vergie Winters never turned them away, perhaps because she needed desperately their trade, perhaps because it never occurred to her, in that terrible solitude to which she had dedicated her life, ever to judge them. They came and sometimes they stayed to talk. A few of them were run out of town, but new ones always took their places. They always went to Vergie Winters for their bonnets.

"She is such a lady. She has such a fine air," they said. And, "It's so restful sitting there in her cool parlour."

But their trade did her no good. "It only goes to show," said the Town.

It was really the beginning of her colossal solitude. She did not go away. She did not flee from the threats that sometimes came to her. She was sure of herself. She would not surrender. And she could wait. She effaced herself from the life of John Shadwell. And when the Town began putting two and two together, she was even forced to give up walking through the twilight in the direction of John Shadwell's house, where from the opposite side of the street she could watch with a furtive eye the little girl who played on the lawn about the iron dogs and deer. She never went out except to buy the few things she needed to eat, and for her trade. It was about this time that a shop run by a Presbyterian elder refused to sell her a spool of thread with which to sew the bright roses on the hats of the ladies of the streets. She did not make a scene; she did not even complain. She went quietly from the shop and never again passed through its doors.

But there were always the gay ladies. They came and went; but there were always some in the town, so it must have had some need for them. They could not live without money, yet they always had it, though they toiled not nor spun, to pay Vergie Winters for their hats. Some died; one or two were murdered in saloon brawls, but Vergie Winters never turned them away. They were her only friends. One wonders what secrets, what confidences they brought to Vergie Winters, sitting there in her narrow little house. One wonders what a dark history of the Town's citizens went into the grave when Vergie Winters was carried down those narrow, rickety steps for the last time. But she said nothing. She simply waited.

At last what she hoped—what she must have known— would happen, came to pass. One cold night while Vergie Winters sat sewing on the gay hats a key turned in the lock, and John Shadwell came back to her. He came in the face of scandal, of ruin, because he could not help himself. It had begun in a flash of lightning when Vergie Winters opened the door of her father's house to let him in, and now John Shadwell found that it went on and on and on . . . There was no stifling it.

Who can picture that return? Who can imagine the sudden upleaping in the calm, withdrawn soul of Vergie Winters— who had such faith in this love that she sacrificed all her life to it?

And so for years John Shadwell came, on the occasions when he was not in Washington, to see Vergie Winters in the narrow wooden house. She kept on with her precarious trade, for she would never while he lived accept any money from him. Besides, she could not, for his sake, afford to arouse suspicions. For herself it did not matter; she could not be worse off.

Thus Vergie Winters and John Shadwell passed into middle age, and there came a time when he no longer sought election but instead became a power behind the throne, a man who shaped the careers of other men. He held power in the palm of his hand and no longer depended on votes. He grew careless, and one night he was seen by a Negro stable boy turning his key in the back door of Vergie Winters's house.

After that there were women who crossed the street in order to avoid passing the window with the gay bonnets; and children, hearing their parents whisper as they drove by on a summer evening, came to understand dimly that some evil monster lay hidden behind the neat fringed curtains. Once, while John Shadwell was away in Washington, boys stoned the house and broke all the windows; but Vergie Winters said nothing. In the morning a Slovak glazier, who was new to the Town and had never heard of its Scarlet Woman, came and repaired the damage; and after he had gone she was seen coming down the narrow steps, in that terrible pool of solitude, as if nothing at all had happened. So far as any one knew, she never spoke of the affair to John Shadwell. She wanted to save him, it seemed, even from such petty annoyances.

And then as the years passed she sometimes saw from her window—the only safe spot from which she might peep—the figure of John Shadwell's adopted daughter, grown now into a girl of twenty. A thousand times she must have watched the girl, always in company with John Shadwell's sister, a large, bony spinster, as the pair came out of the shop on the corner and crossed the street in order that a girl so young and innocent might not have to pass the house of Vergie Winters.

Thus she sat in the narrow, dun-coloured house, working at the gay bonnets, on the afternoon that John Shadwell's adopted daughter was married to a son of the Presbyterian elder who refused to sell Vergie Winters a spool of thread. Perhaps on that afternoon she had a visit from one of the ladies of the street, who sat talking to her (she was such a lady) while the girl in her bridal dress walked down the aisle of the brick Presbyterian church—with no mother sitting in the pew on the right because John Shadwell's wife had been too much upset by the preparations for the wedding.

And one is certain that on the same night, when the

festivities were ended, the figure of a middle-aged man followed the shadows of the alley behind Vergie Winters's house, and let himself in with a key he had carried for more than twenty years. And one can hear him telling Vergie Winters who was at the wedding, and that there never was a prettier bride, and what music they played, and what there was at the wedding breakfast; and assuring her, as he touched her hand gently, that the bit of lace she had given him had been used in the bridal dress. He had told them he bought it himself.

Then, slowly, the town came to accept the state of affairs as a permanent scandal. One seldom spoke of it any longer. One simply knew that Vergie Winters and John Shadwell had been living together for years. He was rich, he was important, he was a power in politics; and now that his career no longer mattered, he had grown indifferent and a little defiant. So far as John Shadwell was concerned, he was a leading citizen nearly seventy years old, the grandfather of children by his adopted daughter.

But with Vergie Winters? She still went her solitary way, making her few bonnets, now a little old-fashioned and *démodé* for all her sedulous reading of the fashion papers. (One can see her, slightly grayed, putting on her spectacles and peering closely at the pages.) And still, as she sat behind the lace curtains at her window, she saw the figure of John Shadwell's daughter, remote and upright and a little buxom, crossing the street and going down the opposite side; only instead of being led by John Shadwell's spinster sister she was leading her own children now. And night after night the figure of John Shadwell, no longer an ardent lover but an old man, following the shadows of the alley (less and less furtively as he grew older) to turn the worn key in the lock and sit there all through the evening with Vergie Winters. What did they do? What did they say to each other in those long winter evenings?

And at last, one night, John Shadwell's wife, peevish and fretful in her tight-closed bedroom smelling of medicines, sent for him at midnight to read to her, only to be told that he had not come in. Again at two o'clock, and again at three— still he had not come in. Even when the gray light filtered through the elms on to the iron dogs and deer, he had not come back. They knew then that he would never return; for he lay dead in Vergie Winters's narrow, dun-coloured house, behind the lace curtains and the gay bonnets. He had belonged to her always, and in that silent, powerful way of hers she had known it from the beginning. In the end he came to Vergie Winters to die. . . .

It made great trouble and embarrassment, and they were forced to wait until midnight of the following day before they were able to take John Shadwell's body from the house of Vergie Winters. And when they did take it, it went out of the same door that had opened so many times at the touch of the worn key, and along the shadows of the alley through which he had passed in life so many times. But even then they were not able to keep the affair a secret. The Town came to know it, and so shut out the last glimmer of tolerance for Vergie Winters. It was no longer a half-secret. It was a scandal which cast darkness upon the name of one of the men who had made the Town (as people said with a curious and non-committal tone which might have meant anything at all) "what it was to-day." The crime was Vergie Winters's. But she could not have cared very much. . . . Vergie Winters, sitting there in her terrible solitude behind the lace curtains, while the procession passed her house—first, the band playing "The Dead March from Saul," and then the cabs containing John Shadwell's daughter, her husband, and John Shadwell's grandchildren, and then one by one the cabs carrying the leading citizens.

The next morning she came down the steps as she had always done, in the same clothes, with the same air of abysmal indifference. She had not betrayed him during life, and in death she would give no sign; and she must have known that on that morning every eye she passed was turned upon her with a piercing gaze, "to see how she took it."

For twenty years longer, Vergie Winters lived in the narrow wooden house, growing poorer and poorer with the passing years. She saw the children of John Shadwell's adopted daughter grow into men and women and have children of their own. But the scandal had grown stale now, though the legend persisted, and only a few must have remembered hazily that the old woman who sat behind the curtains was a great-grandmother. Until one morning the howling of the cat roused

Rinehart, the German cobbler, who broke into the house and found Vergie Winters dead. And when they carried her down the rickety steps on her last journey she went alone, without a band to play "The Dead March from Saul," and without a procession of carriages to follow her into that far corner of the cemetery (remote from the fine burial ground of the Shadwells) where they laid her to rest.

Yesterday they pulled down Vergie Winters's house. There is no monument to her memory save the tiny stone at the head of her grave, paid for with the money saved out of what she earned by making bonnets for the gay ladies of the Town. But Vergie Winters is not dead. When one passes the gaping hole where the little house once stood, one thinks of Vergie Winters. When one passes the granite shaft raised to John Shadwell, one thinks of Vergie Winters. When one sees a Shadwell grandchild or a Shadwell great-grandchild, one thinks of Vergie Winters. For now that time has begun a little to soften the Town, the memory of Vergie Winters has been kept fresh and green with a strange aroma of vague, indefinable romance. When the names of those who crossed the street to avoid her narrow house are forgotten, the name of Vergie Winters will live. Why? Who can say? Was it because the Town never knew a woman called upon to show a faith so deep, a sacrifice so great, a devotion so overwhelming?

I can see her still, an old woman of eighty, hobbling painfully down the rickety steps of her house, with that curious, proud look upon her worn old face, and in the sharp old eyes another look which said, "Vergie Winters was right! John Shadwell belonged to her, from the very beginning!"

JUKES

By BILL ADAMS

From *Adventure*

A BOARDING master's boat was alongside by the fore rigging. The boarding master and his crimp were bringing off the crew; helping the drunken sailors over the bulwarks, and shoving or dragging them into the forecastle.

Alf Jukes came over the bulwarks last. He came without assistance. He was drunk, as were all his fellows, but his drunkenness took a turn different from theirs. As he jumped to the deck he saw the ship's mate by the mainmast.

His attitude revengeful and defiant, Alf Jukes strode up to the mate. He stood face to face with him and cursed him.

The mate paid no attention at all to Alf Jukes. He had heard the same thing, had seen the same thing, too many times from such men as Jukes. He looked at Jukes as unconcernedly as if he looked at a coil of rope or a barrel of tallow.

As the mate turned disinterestedly away, Jukes addressed himself to the ship. Scornfully scanning her from boom to taffrail, from deck to mastheads, from yardarm to yardarm, he cursed her. As if exasperated by her silence, as if maddened by her dignity, he raised his voice higher and higher. Like the mate, the ship paid no heed to him. The wind in her rigging whispered of clean things.

Alf Jukes lifted his eyes to the serene and cloudless sky. Craning his neck, seeming to tiptoe a little, hands clenched and arms upraised, he shouted curses. No answer came from the sky.

Jukes ceased his cursing and walked to the forecastle, in which his comrades were now gathered. Having put the last senseless seaman aboard, having collected from the skipper the price prearranged for them, having pocketed a month's advance pay for each one of them, the boarding master with his crimp was already well on the way ashore. The tug was alongside the ship. The ship's mate leaned on the bulwark and talked with the tugboat men.

Presently the skipper appeared and spoke to the mate, who walked forward and called the sailors from the forecastle.

Alf Jukes came last from the forecastle. Like all his comrades, he reeked of cheap and abominable liquor, but, unlike them, he walked erect and steadily, a fierce remonstrance in his step and bearing. They staggered, cursed, or grumbled listlessly. Some were tall, some short; some wide, some narrow; some bearded, others not. They were of many nations. Some wore dungarees, others shoddy cloth; one, a pair of trousers made of ship's canvas; his upper body covered by a threadbare oilskin jacket. Some wore old cloth caps; one, a battered sun-downer; another a dented derby.

Jukes towered above his comrades. His curly brown head and bony feet were bare. His worn dungaree shirt was unbuttoned. His neatly patched dungaree trousers were gathered by a broad brass-buckled belt. His forearms, hands, and throat were rugged. His breast showed white through his unbuttoned shirt. It looked cold, like marble.

Alone of all the crew, Jukes did not look besotted. The stamp of the sea was on him as on them. But the shore had stamped him less. He scowled toward the shore as he followed his comrades from the forecastle.

Impelled almost as much by instinct as by the brief command of the mate, the crew ascended to the forecastle head, took the windlass bars from their rack and set them in their places. As they leaned their weight upon them some grunted like pigs. Some laughed stupidly. Jukes alone was silent.

The ship lifted a little to the tide beneath her. A flag at her peak fluttered. A wisp of smoke passed over her as the tugboat steamed ahead.

The crew stamped slowly round and round the windlass, heaving the anchor in. The cable clanked at the hawse pipe. Tide and cable spoke of clean and windy things.

The reek of liquor grew fainter. The wind came fresher. The mate said—

"Someone sing!"

One of the sailors began to sing a forecastle song, a chantey, a ballad with a wailing chorus. His voice, at first spiteful, sneering, and contemptuous, the voices of the others, also at first spiteful, sneering, and contemptuous, became presently attuned to the sounds of wind and tide and cable. They no longer cursed, or grunted like pigs. The stamp of the shore was falling from them.

The ship passed swiftly from the harbour heads. The tugboat let go her towline. Some of the men went aloft, to loose sail. Talking in low voices, others waited by sheet and halyard; ready to hoist when the mate's order came. Jukes stood apart, detached, solitary, brooding. He looked like a bear lately released from an unclean cage, and still uncertain of its freedom.

The mate called—

"Hoist away, main tops'l!"

The men grasped the halyards and lay back, setting their weight upon them. Straining to raise the heavy sail, they failed. They tried, and failed again.

"You there! Lend a hand here!" called the mate to Jukes.

The men waited while Jukes slowly approached. As he laid hold on the rope he seemed to shake himself. He drew a long deep breath. He reached up, higher and higher. His great chest expanded.

The mate called—

"All together, now!—*Lay back !*"

The tackle rattled noisily through its three-fold blocks. The sail slid, threshing and filling, to its masthead.

"Bully boy!" said the mate.

A sailor repeated—

"Bully boy!"

Jukes remained silent, sombre, brow-beclouded. While sail on sail was spread, the crew all hauling to his leadership, he took no notice of anyone or anything. He paid no heed at all to their admiring comments.

The shore line faded astern. The day passed. The sun sank. Night fell.

The sailors sat in the forecastle.

"'Ow long was you ashore?" asked one.

"Three days. How long was you?" came the reply.

"I come in the same day as you, then. I been three days ashore."

"We was five months at sea," said the other, "three days in port, an' I don't know nothin' about 'em."

The dozen sailors discussed their stays in port. Not one of them had been ashore over five days. Each had accepted a drink from the boarding master's bottle. Between then and now no one of them knew aught of what had taken place.

"We was two hundred days on the passage out," said one. "We was posted missin'. Four days in port, an' back to sea agin!"

They were from half a dozen different ships.

"How long was you ashore?" asked one, turning to Jukes. Jukes seemed not to hear him.

"He don't know," laughed one.

"We don't none of us know much, or we'd not be here," another grumbled.

"After this v'yage I quits the sea," another asserted.

"Me, too," another.

"Yuss!—You will!" chuckled a third.

"I'll do wot I please," retorted the other.

"Same as you always 'ave! Me, too," another said. "Haw, haw, haw!"

Turning to Jukes the last speaker asked—

"Wot will you do w'en she gits in, ol' matey?"

Jukes rose and left the forecastle. For a long time he sat motionless on the bulwark, his head bowed, his great hands upon his knees, his figure dim against the starry sky. When eight bells struck and his comrades started aft to answer to the muster roll he crossed the deck and reëntered the forecastle. His step seemed to falter as he neared the dingy lamp. Looking about him to make sure that he was all alone, he drew from a pocket a small oilskin package; untied and took from it a faded kerchief—an old bandanna. Loosening the knots, he drew from its crumpled folds an envelope. The envelope, drab and dirty like the kerchief that protected it, bore the mark of a distant port, and of a yet more distant date.

A picture but little larger than a postage stamp fell to the table and lay face up. The letter, dog-eared and torn from much handling, was like the picture—commonplace, yet smiling and hopeful. As Jukes looked hungrily at the picture his face grew haggard. His lips moved as he read the old letter over.

Startled by a shout from the quarterdeck, Jukes thrust letter and picture back within the bandanna, folded the oilskin about them, and hurried out to answer to his name.

A month was gone. Barefooted, bare of arm, Jukes walked from the wheel. The sunset glowed in his weathered face. The sails above him shone. Below him shone the sea. He gave the course to the mate and went to join his fellows on the hatch.

"A fine man that, Mister," said the skipper to the mate.

"'Ow would you like to 'ave a little place ashore?" asked one sailor of another on the hatch.

"I ain't goin' to sea no more after this passage," answered the other.

Jukes lighted his pipe and sat among them. The sea was blue-black; the sky blue-black above. Whispering from horizon to horizon the sea crests murmured of clean, free, windy things.

"'Ow would you like to 'ave a little place ashore?" asked the last speaker of Jukes.

Jukes turned and faced the man. His eyes shining and eager, he drew the oilskin package from his pocket. They gathered round him as he opened it. They passed the picture from hand to hand.

"I wisht as I was 'im," muttered one and another.

They looked at him enviously, seated serene and confident among them.

Another month was gone.

A canopy of cloud hung low over the mastheads. It was without break, or rift, uniform from horizon to horizon. It was of that cold gray that presages snow. Because it was uniform it seemed to be without motion. Beneath it the cañon hollows of the sea were black. From horizon to horizon white sea cataracts roared.

Every two hours a sailor peered from the forecastle. Watching his opportunity, leaving those behind him to close the door, he sprang to the deck. Now running a few steps, now desperately clinging to the wire-tight life line, now leaping high into the rigging to escape the raging sea, he battled a slow way to the wheel; whence the helmsman whom he relieved made an equally precarious passage to the forecastle.

It was midday when Alf Jukes opened the forecastle door. Unlike the others, he did not hesitate, or pause to scrutinize the chances of the deck. Though in the past two days no man aboard had slept, there was no sign of weariness about him. As he opened the door he looked with a casual but comprehensive glance to the gale-whipped and snow-laden sky. Then, stepping to the waist-deep smother of the forward deck, he turned and deliberately banged the door behind him. Head unbowed, gaze straightforward, light hands upon the rigid life line, he strode surefooted through the tempest's rage. When an insweeping sea completely submerged him, the mate, who was watching from by the helmsman's side, made for the chart room and bellowed to the skipper. Jukes's head and shoulders reappeared as the skipper leaped out to the poop deck.

The groan of the ship's hull, the creak and outcry of a hundred straining blocks, the clack of chains and parrals, were inaudible. Had the three masts simultaneously splintered and gone over the side, not a sound would have been heard.

The skipper and mate looked amusedly into each other's faces. Alf Jukes's shoulders, his gripping hands, his arms, the every motion of his entirely reckless body, appeared as the limbs and motions of a gambolling schoolboy. By the toss of his chin, by the shake of his head, by the partings and closings of his stubble-surrounded lips, the universe might observe that Jukes, on his way to relieve the wheel, was singing.

Pointing to the helmsman, the skipper yelled an order into the mate's ear. The mate nodded. Waylaying the man, the mate dragged him into the chart room. So ordered by mate and skipper, the exhausted helmsman sought shelter in the chart house instead of attempting to reach the forecastle.

When sailors looked from the forecastle door to see what was become of Jukes, or of the man whom he had gone to relieve, it was to see the mate gesticulating to them to go back; voicelessly ordering them to remain where they were.

Afternoon passed, and no man ventured to the wheel's relief.

Toward dusk the wind fell, its uproar ending abruptly—as if a multitude of yelling maniacs had leaped from a precipice edge to instant extinguishment. The crests of the sea died down. The horizons widened. For a little while gray ocean rolled under gray sky.

Snow fell. The horizons were blotted out.

Skipper and mate descended to the saloon. Jerking the door of the steward's pantry open, the skipper shouted for the steward. A trapdoor in the pantry deck opened slowly, and the steward, who had laid hidden below, arose. His teeth chattered. For a moment he looked dazedly up at the skipper; then, realizing that the storm was over, that the ship still floated, and that it was long since he had served a meal, passed out to the deck and made haste to the cook's galley.

"We'll set sail when the moon rises," said the skipper to the mate.

Skipper, mate, steward, cook, and sailors buried their noses in pannikins of steaming coffee. Ravenously devouring hash made of pork scraps mixed with pulverized sea biscuit, they forgot the fury of the recent storm, forgot that it was snowing —forgot Alf Jukes.

The ship rolled easily. Blocks whined. Sails flapped. A pleasant odour of tobacco smoke arose in cabin, galley, and forecastle.

The clouds lifted. The snow ceased. A wan light illumined deck and rigging.

"Loose them upper tops'ls!" bawled the mate.

Some of the sailors climbed aloft to cast the gaskets off. Others gathered at the halyards, ready to hoist away. Snow, disturbed by the feet of the climbers, fell on the heads and shoulders of those below. Flapping their arms, shaking their fists, the men on deck swore at the climbers, who, envying them the comparative comfort of the deck, replied with gibes and curses.

A man aloft called—

"All ready on the main!"

The mate said—

"Hoist away!"

The men lay back, straining on the stiff swollen rope. The sail refused to move.

"W'ere's Alf?" asked one of the sailors.

"Jukes!" called the mate, "Jukes!"

They looked aloft, seeking Jukes.

" 'Ee ain't aloft," said one.

"He's at the wheel," said the mate, remembering. "One o' you men relieve Jukes."

"I forgot 'im," said one.

"Me, too," another.

Alf Jukes came forward from the wheel. Snow was thick on his sou'wester, and on his shoulders. Snow was frozen on his sleeves and oilskin trousers. His hands, his lips, were blue.

"Lend a hand here, Jukes," said the mate.

Jukes strode to the halyards and reached up. His great chest expanded as he reached higher and higher.

"All together—*now!*" said the mate.

Jukes laid his weight upon the halyards. The sheaves rattled. The yard began to rise.

"Bully boy!" said the mate. A sailor grunted, "Bully boy!"

Their feet tramping soundlessly in the deep snow, the men ran the topsail to its masthead.

"All ready on the fore," called a man from aloft.

"Go eat," said the mate to Jukes, his accents crisp and clear in the stillness.

Preceding the others, Jukes walked to the fore topsail halyards as if he had not heard.

When sail was set there was neither coffee nor hash left. The cook's skilly pots and hash kids were washed, and hung on the taut wire above his stove. Jukes munched sea biscuit, and took a drink of cold water.

"That fellow Jukes is a good man, Mister," said the skipper to the mate.

"Jukey ain't afeard o' naught," said a sailor, "I wish as I was 'im."

Night passed.

A bright sun shone on the ship at anchor. Sails were furled, ropes coiled. From the fore bulwarks, the sailors watched a boat rowed by two men approaching.

Jukes sat alone upon the forecastle head. Gazing shoreward, he saw masts and spars, steeples and roofs. Chimneys smoked. Windows glinted. Beyond the town he saw low hills, with treetops blowing. His eyes were hungry.

Noticing the approaching boat, Jukes rose to his feet. His teeth clenched, a scowl on his face, he paced to and fro. He looked like a bear come too close to the dwellings of men—

suspicious, undetermined, afraid of the world and of himself.

Hands extended, eyes a-twinkle, faces beaming, a sailor's boarding master and his crimp climbed aboard.

"Did ye have a good voyage, boys? W'ere are ye from? You're come to a good port this time!"

The boarding master entered the forecastle. Seating himself, looking amicably up to the expectant and childish faces of the sailors, he drew a bottle from his pocket.

"The best, boys! I'd never offer ye any but the best."

One of them grasped the bottle.

"Don't swaller it all!" cried one of the sailors.

"'Old 'is arm!" another.

"'S'all right, boys. There's plenty more," grinned the boarding master.

The crimp came from the boat, bottles in his pockets.

The forecastle reeked of cheap and abominable liquor. Presently one of the sailors asked—

"W'ere's Jukey?"

The crimp left the forecastle, to seek the missing man.

"The boys wants you," said he, discovering Alf Jukes alone upon the forecastle head. He took a bottle from his pocket and held it out to Jukes.

Uttering a low coughing grunt, Jukes struck savagely at the crimp. The bottle fell, and broke upon the deck. Cursing Jukes, the crimp beat a hasty retreat.

With a half pannikin of unspilled liquor in it, the lower half of the bottle remained upright against the windlass.

Alf Jukes looked down. Nostrils quivering, fingers twitching, he uncertainly approached the broken bottle. He stooped, lifted the bottle, and stretched out a hand; as if to hurl it to the water. He hesitated; drew in his hand, and sniffed. Another moment and he flung the emptied fragment over the forecastle rail.

"Hey, Jukey! Come on down, ol' son!" called one of his comrades, looking up from the forecastle.

Jukes descended and entered the forecastle. His fellows slapped him on the back. The boarding master thrust a bottle in his hand. As Jukes took it, one of his comrades tried to snatch it from him, and a bellow of laughter rose as the sailor went sprawling on the deck.

The bottles passed around.

"No more ships for me," said one.

"Nor me, boys," said another.

Jukes drank silently.

By and by the sailors shouldered their sea bags and followed the boarding master and his crimp from the forecastle. Jukes towering heedless among them, they shoved and elbowed one another aside, making for the boat. Pointing to other ships near by, they cursed them. They cursed the ship they left. They chattered confidingly to the boarding master, who promised them one and all an easy job on the land. As Jukes grasped the stroke oar and set the pace ashore they shouted their approval.

"Ol' Jukey!" they cried, and "Good ol' Jukey!"

They laughed to see the way the boat drove through the water, with Jukes's great muscles surging her along. They jumped ashore and turned their backs forever on the sea. Without a glance behind, they followed Jukes across the street; Jukes at the boarding master's heels, the crimp behind them all.

Hours passed. Besotted sailors lolled on dirty cots about a dirty room. They quarrelled, forgot their quarrels, and embraced each other. They smoked, and spat, and sang. The leering crimp came in, and went, and came, and went again, and called them each by name—quick-fitted names.

"'Ere, old Cork-fender, lap it up now! It's good for sailor's gizzards."

"Gimme yer empty glass 'ere, Queer-fellow!"

"Young Bandy-shanks, you've 'ad enough! You're young. —Another? All right, then. Wot'd yer mommer say?"

"Aw, haw! haw! haw!"

"Drink hearty, Jimmie Bilge! There's plenty more."

Ignoring their quarrels and embraces, taking no part in their noisy songs, Alf Jukes held out his glass for filling and refilling. The crimp winked at him deferentially.

Evening came. Save for loud snores, heavy breathing, and now and then a mumbled, sleepy oath, the room was quiet. Steady-handed still, Jukes stood erect amidst the wreckage of his fellows and emptied his glass.

In the barroom adjoining, the boarding master reached a

black bottle from beneath the bar. Alf Jukes came from the back room as he replaced it. Resolve in his face, he stepped toward the street.

Three brimming glasses stood upon the bar. Lifting one to his own lips, the boarding master pushed another out toward Jukes.

"Here, big boy! Don't run off so soon!" he quickly called.

Jukes stopped and hesitatingly looked toward the bar. The crimp and boarding master raised their glasses.

Jukes took the proffered glass, lifted, and drained it in one long straight swallow; then turned and strode toward the street door again. Midway, he staggered.

The boarding master and the crimp came from behind the bar. They lifted Jukes, carried him to the dusky street, and dumped him in their boat.

"That fills *her* crew," growled the boarding master with a nod to the riding light of a ship at anchor close inshore.

Dawn was breaking. Stars were fading. Mastheads of anchored ships swayed easily against the opening sky. A ship's mate banged upon the forecastle door, rousing his crew. A drowsy sailor lurched off to the galley, fetching the morning coffee.

"How long was you ashore?" asked one sailor of another.

"Wot day is it?" came the reply. The questioner chuckled. Some surly, some indifferent, they sipped their coffee.

The mate looked in.

"Rouse out here, now! Get up and man that windlass!"

They straggled to the deck. But Jukes lay sleeping still, his face to the bulkhead. The mate stepped in and shook him. He wakened slowly.

"Tumble out, here, you!"

Jukes climbed from the bunk and looked about him.

"Come on, now! You're at sea, my man. Get out of here!"

With a long staggering stride, Jukes passed out to the new ship's deck. The wind blew in his hair. The tide sang by.

Jukes turned, wild-eyed, and faced the mate. Men on the forecastle head looked down and laughed to hear him curse. He gazed up at them, vacant eyed. He looked toward the shore, saw his old ship, and shuddered.

"Come on, my man!" the mate said. "You're at sea."

Alf Jukes ascended to the forecastle head.

"Sing, someone!" said the mate, "sing and let's get her away."

A sailor leaning on a windlass bar began to sing a forecastle song, a chantey, a ballad with a wailing chorus. The tugboat's smoke whirled by. The chorus rose and fell. The cable clanked.

"W'y don't ye sing, shipmate?" a sailor asked of Jukes.

Alf Jukes let go his windlass bar. Fists clenched and arms upraised, his curses ringing loud above his comrades' song, he looked upon the shore.

"Come on, my man," the mate said. "You're at sea."

Weeks were gone by. It was black midnight. No star shone. Sails hung invisible. Long swells rolled sluggishly beneath the keel. The ship's bow rose, dipped to deep hollows, and arose again.

Half naked in the hot night, Alf Jukes lay slumbering. The watch below slept soundly all about him. The watch on deck sat talking on the hatch without.

Sails flapped to the long roll of the ship. Chains clinked upon the lower masts. Blocks chattered squeakily. Now and again a heavy rope, a sheet or lazy tack, thud-thudded against the ship's side. The wheel cluck-clucked. The sailors' voices rose and fell, a mumble from the hatch.

Poring above a chart, the skipper sat in his chart room. Presently he rose, looked out to the dark night, listened awhile, and went below.

An hour passed.

High and sudden, the mate's voice rang above the noises of the night, and, answering quick commands, gloom-hidden sailors leaped up and rushed to the braces.

The skipper ran, pajama-clad and shouting, to the deck. The watch on deck were shouting at the ropes. A deep, long, grumbling roar was all about—the growl of rollers bursting on a reef.

A sailor yelled at the forecastle door, wakening the sleepers of the watch below. Blackness was like a wall. The skipper was shouting orders. The mate was shouting; the grumbling rumble coming closer, louder.

The ship quivered. A rending sound rose sharp above the roar, died, and arose again. A topmast splintered and went overboard. Torn canvas snarled. Blocks skirled. The ship slid on, settling beyond the reef.

Last from his bunk came Jukes. Striking a match, he held it high, and by its feeble flare saw the crazed struggle of his comrades all yelling at the door. Fallen men clutched madly at the feet that trampled them. Water lapped into the forecastle. The match went out. The ship lurched heavily.

Jukes stepped from the emptied forecastle into water knee deep. As he slid barefooted to the rigging, the water rose to his waist. He gripped the shrouds and swung himself aloft. The water followed. He climbed, cat-nimble. The water followed close. He heard a last useless order from the skipper. Someone screamed, "The boat!" A shriek ended in a groan close to him. A hand clutched his bare foot. He bent to grasp the hand; but it slipped, and he touched only water.

Save for the growl and long wash of the sea there was no sound.

Alf Jukes was swimming.

Dawn came, and, treading water, Jukes gazed round the sea. He struck out, swam with strong steady strokes, and presently swung himself upon a piece of drifting wreckage.

The horizon was empty, the sky without a cloud. The sea was flat.

The sun rose. It beat on the bare white skin of Alf Jukes.

Jukes took a little oilskin package from his pocket and wedged it in the centre of the raft. He slipped off his dungaree trousers and dipped them in the sea. The dripping dungarees in his hand, he stood stark naked and once more gazed around. The sea was empty. His head by the raft's edge, he lay down and covered himself as well as he could with the wet dungaree. The sun climbed higher.

Now and again Jukes splashed his great hands in the water, wetting his head and upper limbs afresh. Except upon the raft there was no motion anywhere in sky or sea.

By and by Jukes rose. His eyes searched the horizon. It was empty. He dropped the dungarees and dived deep. He swam down and down, seeking the cooler depths. He glimmered white, far under the unrippled blue water. When he rose to the surface again he held to the edge of the raft. The raft gave no shade. He reached for, and covered his head with, the dungarees. The sun was overhead when he drew himself up, and, holding to the edge of the raft, looked all about again.

Suddenly Jukes hurled himself upon the raft. His body, glistening in the sun, he watched a long green shape dart under him.

For the rest of the day Jukes dipped his dungarees in the sea and covered himself as best he could. All day a sharp green fin cruised slowly round. When the sun dipped there were red fiery patches on the marble-white skin of his back, on his thighs and shoulders.

Stars wakened. Long after day was gone Jukes curled himself in the middle of the raft and went to sleep. Thirst wakened him. He dipped the dungarees in the sea and wrapped them round his neck.

Night passed. At dawn the horizon was empty. Fins cruised to and fro on all sides. Snouts broke the still blue water. The sky was cloudless.

When Jukes dipped his dungarees, jaws snapped on them. He wrenched, and a leg of the dungarees remained in his hands. He wrapped it about his neck, and crouched down. The sun climbed higher.

Jukes rocked a little to and fro. Now and again a low coughing grunt escaped him.

Day passed. Night came, starry and still. Snouts nosed around the raft's edge. Fins darted to and fro, rippling the windless water. Jukes slept fitfully, dreamed, wakened, dozed, and dreamed again. Night passed.

At dawn Jules climbed unsteadily to his feet. His lips were black, his skin scarlet. He moaned. His tongue was swollen.

A quarter of a mile from the raft a dense black cloud was slowly crossing the equatorial sky. A sheer wall of water fell from the cloud to the sea. Flying fish leaped at the rain's foot. White birds preyed on them from above, silver-bellied fish from below. The snouts were gone, to join in the preying.

Staring at the rain wall, Jukes listened to the just-audible s-s-s-s of the doldrum squall.

The squall passed by, came within an eighth of a mile of the raft, dipped under the sea rim, and was gone. The sun rode high in a blue cloudless sky. The snouts were back. Fins rippled the water all about. Jukes crouched, with the wet scrap of dungaree about his neck. Day passed. Night came.

Jukes lay prostrate, face downward. Hours passed. Long

after midnight he lifted his head and tried to climb to his knees. A dim green light winked on the sea far off. He toppled over and was still. Wind ruffled his hair and blew cool upon his brow.

Alf Jukes saw houses with smoking chimneys, windows aglint. Saw masts and spars along a waterfront. Heard singing, far away. A wind blew through green treetops.

When Jukes came to himself he lay in a lamplit forecastle. From near by came the voices of sailors. "I seen a boat wi' two dead men in her one time. None ever knowed wot ship they was from."

"If you follers deep water long enough, it'll git ye."

"Aye. 'Ow many *old* sailors 'ave you ever seed?"

Jukes raised his head painfully and listened. From neck to ankles his body was a fiery blister.

"I been eleven blasted year at sea. I got nuthin'."

"You never will 'ave."

"W'oo cares?"

"There don't no one care. You an' me is dogs."

"This here'll be my last v'yage."

"Aye.—That's wot you says.—Wait."

"Wait yerself. I'm done."

"Haw, haw, haw!"

"There's one as had ought to be cured leastways," and a nod toward the forecastle.

Jukes climbed from the bunk and tottered out into the starlight.

"'Ow are ye, matey?"

"Bring 'im some water."

Jukes gulped cold water down.

"'Ere, mate—you 'ad it in yer 'and."

Jukes took the little oilskin package. They led him back and laid him in the bunk again. They smeared more grease on his burned limbs. They gave him more water.

"Look at 'im!—I'm done."

"Me, too."

As Jukes with fumbling fingers untied the package, they gathered round. He nodded his head. His lips moved. A sailor bent above him, listening.

"'E's done. No more o' ships fer 'im."

FEAR

By JAMES WARNER BELLAH

From *Saturday Evening Post*

I T WAS a little spot, that fear, but it had ached in his heart for months—ever since his first solo flight at Upavon Airdrome. It had come suddenly one morning like the clean pink hole of a steel-jacketed bullet—a wound to be ashamed of—a wound to fight against—a wound that never quite healed. Always it was there to throb and to pinch like the first faint gnawing of cancer. It came with him to the theatre and rankled his mind: "Enjoy this—it may be your last play." It crept into his throat at meals, sometimes, and took away the poor savour that was left to the foods of wartime.

The fear of the men who fly. Sometimes he pictured it as an imp—an imp that sat eternally on his top plane and questioned him on the strength of rudder wires, pointed to imaginary flaws in struts, suggested that the petrol was low in the tank, that the engine would die on the next climbing turn.

It was with him now as the tender that was to take him up to his squadron jolted and bounced its way across the *pavé* on the outskirts of Amiens. The squadron was the last place he had to go to. All the months that were gone had led up to this. These were the wars at last. This was the place he would cop it, if he was to cop it at all.

He shrugged. Anyway, he had had his four days in London and his ten days idling at Pilot's Pool before the squadron sent for him. He braced one shoulder against the rattling seat and reached in his tunic pocket for a cigarette. Mechanically he offered one to the driver. The man took it with a grubby finger.

"Thankee, sor-r."

He nodded and lighted both cigarettes with the smudge of his pocket lighter. Anyway, he was not flying up to 44. That

53

was one flight saved. Funny, that fear—how it came and went like the throb of a nerve in an open tooth. Sometimes the spot was large, and filled his whole being; then again it would shrink to a dull ache, just enough to take the edge from the beauty of the sunrise and the sparkle from the wine of the moon.

There had been a time when it had jumped in every fibre of his soul. He had been a cadet officer then, with only twelve solo hours in the air, under the old rough-and-tumble system of learning to fly. Spinning at that time was an unsolved mystery to him, a ghastly mystery that had meant quick death in a welter of blood, flecked with splinters. Fred Mc-Cloud had gone that way, and Johnny Archamboult. For weeks afterward, Johnny's screams had rung in his ears like a stab of pain, until the mere smell of petrol and fabric dope made the fear crawl into his throat and strangle him. Somehow he had kept on with the rest, under the merciless scourge that lashed one on to fly—and the worse fear of seeing cold scorn in the eyes of the men who taught the lore of thin cloud miles.

The tender twisted and dodged along the hard mud ribbon that ran like a badly healed cicatrix across the pock-scarred face of the fields. Gnarled and bleak, they were fields that had held the weight of blood-crazed men—still held them in un-marked graves, where they had fallen the year before under the steel flail. He had heard stories from his older brother about those fields—the laughing brother who had gone away one day and returned months later without his laugh, only to go away again, not to come back. He had seen pictures in the magazines—— But somehow no one had caught their utter bleakness as he saw it now.

The riven boles of two obscene trees crouched and argued about it on the lead-gray horizon, tossing their splintered arms and shrieking, he fancied, like quarrelling old women in the lesser streets of a village. Close to the roadway, there were a torn shoe and a tin hat flattened like a crushed derby. Poor relics that even salvage could see no further use in. Farther off, a splintered caisson pointed three spokes of a shattered wheel to the sky, like a mutilated hand thrown out in agony. He was seeing it for himself now.

No one could smile at the cleanness of his uniform again

and say, "Wait till you get out. When I was in France——"
He was out himself now. In a day or so he would go over the
line with loaded guns. His instructors at the training 'drome—
thin-jawed men with soiled ribbons under their wings—had
done no more, and some of them had done less. The thought
braced him somewhat. They had seemed so different—so
impossible to imitate—those men. Their war had always been
a different one from his; a war peopled with vague, fearless
men like Rhodes-Moorehouse and Albert Ball and Bishop,
the Canadian; men who flew without a thought for themselves.

It occurred to him with a start that theirs was the same
war as his now. Twenty-five miles ahead of him, buried somewhere in rat runs, between Bapaume and Cambrai, it went on
and on, waiting for him to come—waiting to claw and maim
and snuff him out when he did come. It had seemed so far
away from him in England. When he was at ground school he
had seen it as a place where one did glorious things—he was
young, pitifully young—a place that one came back from with
ribbons under one's wings, with nice clean scratches decently
bandaged. And he had been slightly offended at his brother's
attitude—at the things his brother had said of the staff. Then
he had gone to Upavon to learn to fly. He had soloed for the
first time, and the spot of fear had crawled into his own heart.

They were rattling into the broken streets of a tottering
town; a town that leered at them and grimaced through
blackened gaps in its once white walls. There was a
patched-up *estaminet* with a tattered yellow awning that
tried bravely to smile.

"Albert," said the driver.

The new pilot nodded. Some sapper officers were loitering
in the doorways of the café. Their uniforms were faded to a
rusty brown and reënforced with leather at the cuffs and elbows. Their buttons were leather, too, to save polishing, and
their badges were a dull bronze. He looked down at his white
Bedford-cord breeches and the spotless skirts of his fur-col-
lared British warm—privileges of the flying corps that men
envied. Baths, clean clothing, and better food. The P. B. I.'s
idea of heaven. They called flyers lucky for their privileges and
cursed them a little bit for their dry beds and the wines they
had in their messes, miles behind the line.

The new pilot wondered if they knew what it meant to be alone in the stabbing cold with no one to talk to, no one to help you, nothing between you and the ground save a thin, trembling fabric of cloth and wire and twenty thousand feet of emptiness. That was his fear—emptiness—nothingness —solitude. Those men under the awning could die in company. Not so himself—alone, screaming into the cloud voids, with no one to hear, no one to help, staring with glazed eyes and foam-flecked lips at the emptiness into which one hurtled to death miles below. The price one paid for a bath! He remembered seeing Grahame-White fly at Southport before the war. People had called him an intrepid aviator. The new pilot laughed harshly inside his throat and stared out across the bare fields.

The car topped a slight rise and turned sharply to the left. The driver pointed his grubby finger. "They be comin' in from afternoon patrol," he said. "Yonder is airdrome."

There were three flat canvas hangars painted a dull brown, and a straggling line of rusty tin huts facing them from across the narrow landing space—like a deserted mining village, shabby and unkempt. As he watched, he saw the last machine of the afternoon patrol bank at a hundred and fifty feet and side-slip down for its landing. In his heart he could hear the metal scream of wind in the flying wires. A puff of black smoke squirted out in a torn stream as the pilot blipped on his engine for one more second before he came into the wind and landed. By the time the tender rolled up to the dilapidated squadron office, the machine had taxied into the row of hangars and the pilot was out, fumbling for a cigarette with his ungloved hands. A thin acrid smell of petrol and carbonized castor oil still hung in the quiet air between the shabby huts. Snow in large wet flakes commenced to fall slowly, steadily.

The new pilot climbed down from the tender, tossed his shoulder haversack beside his kit bag, and pushed open the door of the squadron office. The adjutant was sitting on his desk top, smoking and talking to someone in a black leather flying coat and helmet—someone with an oil-streaked face and fingers still blue and clumsy from the cold.

"Paterson, sir, G. K., second lieutenant, reporting in from Pilot's Pool for duty with the 44th."

The adjutant raised a careless finger in acknowledgment. "Oh, yes. How do? Bring your log books?"

"Yes, sir."

"Chuck 'em down. D'ye mind?"

Paterson laid them upon the desk top, still standing to attention. The adjutant smiled. "Break off," he said. "We're careless here. This isn't cadet school."

The new pilot smiled and relaxed. "Very good, sir."

"That's better," said the adjutant; "makes me feel more comfortable. Just give me a note of yourself now." He reached for a slip of paper. "G. K. Paterson, Two Lt. Next of kin?" Paterson gave his father's name. "Age?"

"Eighteen and four twelfths."

"Good!" said the adjutant. "You'll find an empty cubicle in B Block—that's the middle line of huts. You're lucky. Roof only leaks in three places. I'll have your duffel trekked over shortly."

The man in the flying coat blew upon his numbed fingers and smiled. "I'm Hoyt," he said. "Skipper of C Flight. I'm going to take you now, before A gets after you." He turned to the adjutant. "That's all right, isn't it, Charlie? Tell 'em I intimidated you." He grinned.

The adjutant shrugged. "Righto!"

"Come on," said Hoyt. "I'm in your hut block. I'll show you your hole."

They went out into the snow flurry. Mechanics were fussing in little knots around the five tiny machines that had just landed, lining them up, refilling them, and trundling them into the brown musty hangars.

"Le Rhône Camels," said Hoyt. "We've just been over around Cambrai taking a look-see."

Inside one of the hangars, as they passed, Paterson saw something that drew a thin, wet gauze across his eyeballs. On a rough bench just beside the open flap sat a man with his eyes closed and his lips drawn tightly into a straight bluish line. His flying coat was rolled up behind his head for a pillow, and his tunic had been unbuttoned and cut away from his left shoulder. The white of his flesh showed weirdly in the gloom, like the belly of a dead fish. Just below the shoulder, the white was crumpled and reddened as if a clawed paw had been drawn across it. One man was holding his other hand, while another probed and cleaned and dabbed with little puffs of snowy cotton that turned quickly to pink and then to a deep brown.

Hoyt shrugged. "Lucky man. That's Mallory. He was Number Four this afternoon. We never saw a thing. Just happened. Funny." And he smiled. "That's why I was so keen to get you. Can't tell how long it will be before Mallory gets around again, and I've got one vacancy in the flight already." He shrugged. "You'll see a lot of that here—get used to it. It doesn't mean a thing as long as you get back alive."

Paterson looked at him sharply. He wanted to ask him how many didn't get back alive. He wanted to know what had caused the other vacancy in the flight. But people didn't ask those things. People merely nodded casually and went on.

"I suppose not," he said. They tramped on across the airdrome.

"Here we are," said Hoyt. He kicked open the hut door and groped down the dark passageway, with Paterson after him. Presently he pushed back another door and yanked at a tattered window curtain.

The new pilot saw a tiny room, with two washstands, a cot, a folding chair, and a cracked mirror. In a corner were his kit bag and haversack. He pulled out his own cot and chair and set them up; meanwhile Hoyt threw himself down on the other cot and let his cigarette smoke dribble straight upward into the gloom of the pine-raftered roof. Presently he spoke.

"This is a queer war," he said; "full of queer things, and the queerest of these is charity." He laughed in the darkness, and the tip of his cigarette became suddenly pink as he drew the smoke into his lungs. "What was your school?"

"Winchester," said Paterson.

"Right," said Hoyt. "Remember your first day? This is it over again. They've fed you up on poobah at your training 'drome and down at the Pool. They always do. It's part of the system. Just take it for what it is worth and forget the rest. If you want to know anything, come to me and I'll tell you as well as I can. I've been here three months. When I came, I came just as you did to-day, pucka green and afraid to the marrow—afraid of uncertainty. You get over that shortly.

"Our job is a funny one, and we're not here for ourselves, and we're not here to be heroes or to get in the newspapers. The V. C.'s are few and far between." He raised himself upon his elbow. "I'm not preaching self-abasement and a greater loyalty to a cause that is right, mind you. I don't know anything about causes or who started the war or why, and I don't care. I'm preaching C Flight and the lives of five men.

"You saw Mallory over at the hangar. It was teamwork that put him there in his own M. O's hands. Not much, perhaps"— the cigarette described a quick arc in the darkness—"just a slight closing in of the formation—a wave of somebody's hand—somebody else dropping back and climbing above him to protect his tail from any stray Huns that might've waylaid him on the way home. That's what I mean. 'Esprit de corps' is a cold, hard phrase. Call it what you like. It's the greatest lesson you learn. Never give up a man." Hoyt laughed. "They call me an old woman. Perhaps I am. Take it or leave it.

"Slick up a bit and come into my hutch while I scrape off the outer layer of silt. Dinner in half a tick and I'm as filthy as a pig." He vaulted up from the cot and punched his cigarette out against the sole of his boot. At the door he paused for a moment.

"Ever have wind up?" he asked casually.

Paterson stiffened against the question and the small spot of fear danced within him. "No," he said firmly. Hoyt shrugged. "Lucky man." And he went out into the passageway.

At dinner he met the rest of the squadron and the other men in C Flight. Mallory, very pale, with his arm slung in a soft pad of bandages, sat beside him. They were coming for him later to take him down to the base hospital. Phelps-Barrington sat on the other side of Mallory, mourning the fact that the wound was not his, that he might get the inevitable leave to follow. Phelps-Barrington took Paterson's hand with a shrug and asked how Marguerite was in Amiens. "What? You didn't meet Marguerite on your way through? 'Struth!" MacClintock sat across the table beside Hoyt—MacClintock, too young to grow a moustache, but with a deep burr that smelled of the heather in the Highlands and huge pink knees under his Seaforth kilts, muscles like the corded roots of an oak. The other man in the flight, Trent, was down with mild flu. He was due back in a week or so from hospital.

There was a wild argument on about the dawn patrol the next morning. Paterson listened to the fragments of talk that flew like sabre cuts across the glasses:

"He's in a red tripe. I don't give a damn for Intelligence. Saw him this morning myself. Same machine Mac and I had that brush with down at Péronne."

"The next time they'll get an idea for us to strafe a road clear to Cologne for them. What are we—street cleaners?"

"So I let go a covey of Coopers and turned for home. They had it spotted for a battery over at 119 Squadron. I saw the pictures. Right pictures, but wrong map squares as usual. That crowd can't tell a battery from a Chinese labour-corps inclosure. I'd rather be a staff officer than a two-seater pilot."

"Steward, a whisky-soda for Mr. MacClintock and myself. Have one, Hoyt? You, Paterson?"

Cruel, thin, casual talk clicking against the teeth in nervous haste; the commercial talk of men bartering their lives against each tick of the clock; men caught like rats in a trap, with no escape but death or a lucky chance like Mallory's. Caught and yet denying the trap—laughing at it until the low roof of the mess shack rumbled with the echo; drowning it in a whisky for the night.

Afterward, Hoyt came down the passage with him to his room—Hoyt, with his face cleaned of the afternoon's oil and his eyes slightly bright with the wine he had taken.

"We're relieved to-morrow on account of casualties," he said. "I'll tick you out early and we'll go joy riding—see what we can teach each other." He smiled. " 'Night."

Paterson undressed slowly and threw back the flap of his sleeping bag. He ran his fingers softly down the muscles of his left arm. Automatically they stopped at the spot Mallory had been hit. He stretched his thumb from the arm to his heart—seven inches. He shrugged. Nice to go that way. Clean and quick. He sat upon the edge of his cot and pulled on his pajama trousers. Oh, well, this was the place—the last place he had to go to. This was the cot he would sleep his last sleep in. If it weren't a lonely job! That chap in the mess who wouldn't be a two-seater pilot for anything. If he could only feel like that. If he could only feel Hoyt's complacency.

Hoyt, with his calm smile and the two little ribbons under his wings. Military Cross and the Legion of Honour, and three months before he had been green—pucka green!

Paterson blew out the light and turned in. Hoyt was a good fellow—damned decent. Outside he could hear Phelps-Barrington's voice muffled by the snow: "Come on, snap into it! Tender for Amiens! Who's coming?" The yell died in the roar from the car's engine.

Paterson lay for a moment thinking; then suddenly he reached for his pocket flash, snapped it, and stared nervously at the empty cot across the room. There was no bedding on it, nor any kit tucked under it; only the chair beside it, and the cracked mirror.

He got up and padded over in his bare feet. Stencilled on one corner of the canvas there was a name—J. G. H. Lyons. There had been no Lyons introduced to him in the mess. Perhaps he was on leave. Perhaps he had flu with Trent and was down at the base. The spot of fear in his heart trembled slightly and he knew suddenly where J. G. H. Lyons was. He was dead! Somewhere out in the snow, miles across the line, J. G. H. Lyons slept in a shattered cockpit.

The door behind him opened softly. It was Hoyt, in pajamas. "Got a cigarette?" he asked casually.

Paterson turned sharply and grinned. "Righto," he said. "There on the table."

Hoyt took one and lighted it. "Can't sleep," he said. "Come in and take Mallory's cot if you want to. I've some new magazines and I can tell you something about our work here until we feel sleepy."

Hoyt was a good fellow—damned decent.

The cold wet mist lay upon the fields like a soft veil drawn across the face of an old woman who had died in the night. Mechanics, with their balaklavas pulled down across their ears, were running about briskly to keep warm—kicking chocks in front of under-carriage wheels, snapping propellers down with mighty leaps and sweeps until the cold engines barked into life and settled to deep concert roaring. Dust and pebbles, scattered by the backwash, swept into the billowing hangars in a thin choking cloud that pattered against the canvas walls. Hoyt's machine trembled and crept out of the line, with Phelps-Barrington after it. Trent, who had come back from the base the day before, taxied out next.

Paterson waved to the mechanics to pull out his own chocks. They yanked mightily on the ropes, and he blipped his motor with his thumb. Behind him and to the left came Yardley, the new man who had come up from Pool to fill Mallory's place. Then MacClintock, sitting high in his cockpit, rushed out with a roar and a swish of gravel. MacClintock was deputy leader.

Hoyt waved his hand in a quick nervous sweep, and the flight started. Through the mist they roared with their engines howling into sharp echo against the hut walls. A moment later tails whipped up and wheels bounced lightly upon the uneven ground. Then Hoyt's nose rose sharply and he zoomed into the air in a broad climbing turn, with the five others after him in tight formation.

Paterson glanced at his altimeter—five hundred feet. He looked ahead and to the left. There was Bapaume in its raggedness, half drowned in the mist. Suddenly Phelps-Barrington's machine burst into rose flame and every strut and wire trembled like molten silver—the sun. He could see the red rim just peeping up ahead of him and he was warmer for the sight of it. Below, under the rim of his cockpit, the ground was still wrapped in its gray shroud.

They were climbing up in close formation. The altimeter gave them four thousand feet now. He glanced to the left. Yardley waved. Yardley was going through the agony of his first patrol over the line—the same agony he had gone through himself the week before. Only Yardley seemed different, somehow—surer of himself—less imaginative. He was older, too. Behind them, MacClintock, the watchdog, was closing in on their tails and climbing above them to be ready to help if the Hun swooped from behind unexpectedly.

There were clouds above—gray blanket clouds that came together in a solid roof, with only a torn hole here and there to show the blue. Bad clouds to be under. Hoyt knew it and kept on climbing. Almost ten thousand feet now. The ground below had cleared slowly and thrown off most of its sullen shroud. Here and there, in depressions, the mist still hung in arabesque ruffles like icing in a confectioner's window or the white smoke of a railway engine.

The line was under them now, running south and east like a jagged dagger cut, in and out, in and out across the land, not stopping for towns, but cleaving straight through their gray smudgy ruins with a cold disregard and a ruthless purpose. The first day he had seen it, it had seemed a dam to him; a breakwater built there to hold something that must not flow past it; a tourniquet of barbed wire twisted and held by half the world that the blood of the other half might not flow. Some day something would break and the whole thing would give way for good or evil. Curiously, now, like Hoyt, he didn't care which. And suddenly he knew how his older brother had felt, on that last leave, and he had called him unsporting in the pride of his youthful heart!

Hoyt was still climbing. Thin wraiths of cloud vapour groped awkwardly for the six tiny Camels, like ghost fingers, trying desperately to stop them and hold them from their work. Paterson glanced again at Yardley. He had been glad when Yardley came. He was still green himself, but Yardley was greener. It helped buck him up to think about it.

The line was behind them now. Hoyt turned south to pass below the anti-aircraft batteries of Cambrai, and presently they crossed the tarnished silver ribbon of the Somme-Scheldt Canal. Mechanically, Paterson reached for his Bowden trigger and pressed it for a burst of ten shots to warm the oil in his Vickers gun against the bite of the cold air. Then he clamped the joy stick between his knees and reached up for the Lewis gun on his top plane.

His throat closed abruptly, with a ghastly dryness, and his knees melted beneath him. The wing fabric beside his gun was ruffling into torn lace and he could see the wood of the camber ribs splintering as he watched! For a moment he was paralyzed, then frantically he whipped around in his seat and swept the air above him. Nothing. There was the torn fabric and the staring rib and nothing else. MacClintock was gone. Yardley was still there, lagging, with the smoke coming in puffs and streaks from his engine. Then Hoyt turned in a wild climb to the left. Phelps-Barrington dipped his nose suddenly and dived with his engine full on, and at once, where there had been only six Camels, the sky was full of gray machines with blunt noses and black crosses.

Blindly he pressed his Bowden trigger and fired into the empty air, blindly he dived after Phelps-Barrington. Somewhere to the left he saw a plume of black smoke with something yellow twisting in the sunlight on its lower end. A blunt nose crossed his propeller—into his stream of bullets. He screamed and banked wildly, still firing. He saw Hoyt above him. He forgot the machine in front and reached for his Lewis to help Hoyt. He tried to wait—something about the outer ring of the rear sight—but his fingers got the better of him and he fired point-blank.

As quickly as it had begun it ended. There was Hoyt circling back, and two other Camels to the left and below him—four of them. They closed in on Hoyt and he wondered where the two others were. He looked for them—probably chasing after the Huns. He could see dots to the southward—too far away to make out the markings. Hoyt had signalled the washout and they were headed back across the line. Funny those two others didn't come. He wondered who they were. Probably Phelps-Barrington and MacClintock, hanging on to the fight until the last. They worked together that way. He had heard them talk in the mess about it. They'd be at it again to-night, and to-night he could join them for the first time. He'd been in a dog fight! Shot and been shot at! The spot of fear shrank to a pin point.

The brown smudge of the airdrome slid over the horizon. He blipped his motor and glided in carefully. No use straining that top wing—no telling what other parts had been hit. No use taking chances.

Hoyt was standing beside his machine with his glove off, staring at his finger nails. Phelps-Barrington was climbing out. Paterson taxied in between them. The man in the fourth machine just sat and stared over the rim of his cockpit. Phelps-Barrington walked slowly across to Hoyt and laid a hand on his shoulder. Hoyt shrugged and stuffed his bare hand into his coat pocket. Paterson sat with his goggles still on and his throat quite dry. The man in the fourth machine vaulted out suddenly, ripped off his helmet and goggles and hurled them to the ground. It was Trent.

He climbed out of his own machine and walked over toward

Hoyt. Phelps-Barrington, who had a wild word for all occasions—Phelps-Barrington, who led the night trips to Amiens—was silent. When Paterson came up he shrugged and scowled ferociously.

"Is it you, Pat?" said Hoyt. "Thought it was Yardley."

"'Struth!" said Phelps-Barrington. "Let's go and have a drink."

Paterson thrilled as the man slipped an arm through his. For one awful moment he had thought——

"Well," Hoyt said, "those things will happen." And he shrugged again.

"I saw dots to the southward," said Paterson. "Maybe they'll be in later."

"No, little Rollo," said Phelps-Barrington. "They won't be in later or ever. I saw it with my own eyes—both in flames. I thought it was you, and until Trent landed, I thought he might be Mac. But I was wrong. Let's shut up and have a drink!"

Then suddenly he knew, and his mind froze with the ghastliness of the thought. If he'd been quicker—if he'd turned and climbed above Yardley when he saw him lagging, with the smoke squirting from his hit motor—he could have saved him. If he had kept his eyes open behind, instead of dreaming, he might have saved MacClintock, too. In a daze, he stumbled after Phelps-Barrington. That's why Trent had hurled his helmet to the ground and walked off. That's why Hoyt had shrugged and said, "Those things will happen." It was his fault—his—Paterson's. He'd bolted and lost his head and fired blindly into the empty air. He hadn't stuck to his man. He had let Yardley drop back alone to be murdered.

"Look here, P-B," he muttered, "I'm not drinking." He wanted to be alone—to think. So quick it had all been.

Phelps-Barrington grabbed his arm and pushed him stumbling into the mess shack. Trent was slumped down at the table with his glass before him, thumbing over a newspaper. He raised his head as they came in. "Two more of the same, steward—double."

They sat down beside him and Phelps-Barrington reached for a section of the paper.

"It says here," said Trent, "that Eva Fay didn't commit

suicide. Died of an overdose of hashish she took at a party in
Maida Vale the night before."

The steward brought the glasses. Trent raised his and
looked at Paterson. "Good work, son."

Paterson stared at him in amazement. Trent sipped his
whisky and went on reading as if he had never stopped. Some
time later, Paterson left them and went down to the flight
office to find Hoyt. The thought of the morning still bothered
him, in spite of Trent's words, and he wanted to clear it up.
Hoyt smiled as he came in. "Washed the taste out in Faler-
nian?" he asked.

"Some. Look here, skipper—this morning—what about it?"

"What about it?"

"My part—I was fast asleep. I saw Yardley lagging, and I
had a moment to cross above him, but I lost my head, I'm
afraid, and went wild."

The smile faded and Hoyt laid down his pencil. "Do you
really think you could have saved him?"

"He was behind me already when I saw him lagging, just
as you climbed and P-B dived."

"Then you couldn't have helped him, because Mac was
done for when I saw him and climbed, and half a tick after I
climbed, P-B saw Yardley burst into flames. There you are."

"But if I'd kept my eyes back, instead of trusting to Mac?"

"Look here," said Hoyt, "no man can keep his eyes on
everything. Something always happens in the place he isn't
looking. Bear that in mind and forget this morning. You've
seen a dog fight from the inside and lived. Take it easy. You're
not here to do everything. You're here to stick to us. You
might have run away. Remember that and be afraid of it.
Remember if you get away by leaving a pal—he may live to
come back. Then you'll have to face him, and engine trouble
is a poor excuse.

"Trouble with you youngsters is that you've been fed up on
poobah. And the myth of the fearless air fighter. Put it out
of your mind. There's no such thing. Some are less afraid
than others. Some are drunker—take your choice. Class dismissed." Hoyt grinned. "Go get cleaned up. We'll jog into
Amiens for tiffin. Tender in half an hour. Tell Trent and P-B."

They spent most of the afternoon at Charlie's Bar with
some of the men from the artillery observation squadron. For

dinner they went to the Du Rhin and the glasses flowed red. Afterward, in another place, there was a fight, as usual, and chairs crashed like match sticks, until whistles sounded outside and the A. P. M.'s car, siren screaming, raced up the street. They poured out into the alleyway and ran, leaving the waiter praying in high, shrieking French.

Trent had a bottle with him. They rode all the way home singing and shouting to high heaven, forgetting that there were two empty chairs in the mess and that there might be more to-morrow.

> "Take the cylinders out of my kidneys,
> Take the scutcheon pins out of my brain,
> Take the cam box from under my backbone
> And assemble the engine again!"

They were good fellows—Billy Hoyt, P-B, Pat, and Ray Trent. Have 'nother li'l' drink.

They roared along like a Juggernaut, with the exhaust splitting the night air. Sometimes they were on the road and sometimes they were off. No one cared so long as they kept hurtling into the darkness.

Phelps-Barrington was fast asleep. Pat woke him up at the airdrome and tumbled him into the hut.

They stumbled over a kit bag in the doorway. P-B straightened up suddenly. "Good-bye, Mac, old lad, sleep tight."

Trent kicked the bag out of the way. "Damned adjutant! Take P-B in with you, Pat. I'm bunking with the skipper. Might have the decency to take Mac's kit over to squadron office and not leave it lying around the passage. 'Night."

Paterson was quite sober. He tumbled P-B into bed and stood for a moment at the open window, staring out across the ground mist that billowed knee high in the faint night breeze. He rested his elbows on the sill and hid his face in his trembling hands. If he could only be like the others—casual—calloused. If he had less imagination—more sand—stamina—something. MacClintock had planned this night himself, at breakfast. Yardley had left a letter addressed and stamped on his window sill.

Paterson's mind jumped miles to the eastward. He saw the two blackened engines lying somewhere in the bleak fields beyond, ploughed into the ground, with their mats of twisted wires coiled around them in a hideous trap.

Their families would get word to-morrow. "Missing," it would read. And then later: "Previously reported missing, now reported killed in action." And to-morrow—perhaps his own family. Why can't it be quick?

There was a noise behind him. Someone fumbling at the door latch—Hoyt. "Had this bit left. Bottoms up! Quick!" He took the glass and drained it. The liquor bit into his veins and burned him. Hoyt set his own glass down on the wash-stand with a sharp click. "Get into bed now, you idiot. Good-night."

Spiked drink. Hoyt was a good fellow—damned decent. Do anything for Hoyt. Never let Hoyt go. Like my brother—before the war. Good old Hoyt. And he sank suddenly into a dreamless fuddle of sleep.

The weeks crawled on slowly. Paterson felt like a man climbing a steep ladder. Each day was a rung behind him. Each new rung showed an infinite number still ahead, waiting for him to go on, luring him with their apparent safety, waiting for him to reach the one rotten rung that would do him in. Some day he would reach it, and it would crack under him, or his fingers would slip and hurtle him into the abyss under his charred engine.

Offensive patrols and escort for the artillery observation squadron filled their time, with sometimes a road strafe to vary the monotony. These he liked best, for some quaint reason—perhaps because there was less space to fall through. Sometimes there would be a battalion on those roads—a battalion to scatter and knock down like tin soldiers on a nursery floor. Quite impersonal. They were never men to Paterson. Like dolls they ran and like dolls they sprawled awkwardly where they fell.

P-B and Trent and Hoyt carried him through somehow. Mallory was back again, but Mallory never counted much with him. P-B and Trent and Hoyt were a bulwark. They meant safety. It was good to wake up at night and hear P-B snoring on the other cot, to know that Hoyt and Trent were asleep in the next cubicle. It was good to see them stamping to keep warm before the patrol took off in the half light of early morning. So different from one another and yet so alike underneath. Hoyt was nearer his kind than the two others. Tall and spindly like his brother, with a straight, thin nose that quivered slightly at the nostril when he was annoyed. Hoyt, who smiled and sanctioned the childish depravity of little P-B, but never quite met it with his own, although always seeming to, on the night trips to Amiens. Trent, glowering and quiet, with a keen hatred for everything political that he learned in the offices of the London and South Western before the war, when the army to him had meant young wastrels swanking the Guards' livery in the boxes of theatres —wastrels who had died on the Charleroi Road three years before.

Suddenly, from one of his mother's letters, he found that he had been in France almost three months. He stiffened with the thought and remembered what Hoyt had told him that day he had come: "I've been here three months. When I came, I came just as you did to-day—pucka green." He knew then that all his hopes were false. He was the same to-day as he had been that first day. He would always be the same. The spot of fear would always be with him. Some day it would swell and choke him and his hands would function without his frozen brain. He should never have tried to fly. He should have gone into the infantry as his brother had. Too much imagination—too little something. In three months he had learned the ropes, that was all; how to fire and when to fire, where the Archie batteries were near Cambrai, how to ride a cloud and crawl into it—nothing more.

The weeks went on, creeping closer and closer to the twenty-first of March—the twenty-first of March—and with them the feeling crept into Paterson's heart—a feeling that something frightful was to happen. Things had been quiet so long and casualties had been few. C Flight hadn't been touched in weeks. He brooded over the thought and slept badly. He went to Amiens with P-B more frequently. If it was to be any of the three, he knew he wouldn't be able to stand it. His bulwark would crumble and break and he would break with it. On the dawn patrols, those few minutes before they climbed into the cockpits and took off were agony: "This will be the day. It must be to-day. We can't go on this way. Our luck will break."

One day when they were escorting 119, four dots dived on them from behind and he knew suddenly what he would do. Stark, logically, the thing stood before him and beckoned through the wires of his centre section. If a shot hit his plane, he would go down. They were far over the lines, taking 110 on a bombing show. He would wabble down slowly, pushing his joy stick from side to side in a slow ellipse as if he were out of control. Then he would land and run his nose into the ground and be taken prisoner. The others would see him and swear that he'd been hit—and he wouldn't do it until his machine had been hit. That for his own conscience's sake and for the years he would have to live afterwards.

But A Flight, behind and far above, saw the dots and scattered them, and the chance was gone.

Then day by day he waited for another. He knew now that he would do it at the first opportunity. He slept better with the thought, and the minutes seemed shorter now while he waited at dawn for his bus to be run out. All the details were worked out in his mind. If any one of the three were close to him, he'd throw up his hands wildly before he started down. They'd see that and report it. Then when he landed he'd pull out the flare quick and burn his machine so that they would think he had crashed and caught fire. It was so easy!

He spent less time with P-B now. Somehow the old freedom was gone. Somehow Hoyt wasn't the same to him either. He was working with three strangers he had never really known—three casual strangers he would leave shortly and never see again.

On the morning of the fourteenth of March the caller turned C Flight out suddenly, without warning, about an hour after P-B and Trent had returned from Amiens. A special signal had come in from wing headquarters. B Flight had the regular morning patrol, but there was to be an additional offensive patrol besides. A Flight had morning escort and the dusk patrol. That meant C for the special. Paterson could hear Hoyt swearing about it next door. P-B, across the room, uttered a mighty curse and rolled over. Paterson got him a bucket of cold water and doused his feverish head in it. Trent and Hoyt were still cursing pettishly in the next cubicle.

Sleep-stupid, the four of them stumbled into the mess for hard-boiled eggs and coffee. Mallory and the new man, Crowe, were already eating, white-faced and unshaven. They slumped down beside them in silence.

In silence, they trooped across the dark airdrome, buttoning their coats and fastening helmet straps against the cold wretchedness of the March wind. The machines were waiting for them in a ghostly line like staring wasps that had eaten the food of the gods and grown to gigantic size.

They climbed in and taxied out mechanically. B Flight had already left on the regular dawn patrol. They blipped their motors and roared away, leaving their echo and the sharp smell of castor oil behind on the empty 'drome.

Hoyt led them south to the crumpled ruins of Péronne and out to the line, climbing high to get the warmth of the sunlight that began to tint the clouds above them. They were going over to Le Cateau and beyond. Intelligence wanted pictures to confirm certain reports of new Hun shell dumps and battery concentration. The photographic planes were to go out and get them under escort as soon as there was enough light. As additional precaution, offensive patrols were to be kept up far over the enemy's lines to insure the success of the pictures. They passed the sullen black stain that was Le Câtelet and turned to the eastward. The ground was already light and the camera busses would be starting.

Hoyt took the roof at eighteen thousand feet and skirted the cloud wisps, watching below for customers. Paterson watched P-B anxiously. He had been roaring drunk an hour before. Groggy and drunk still, probably. He closed in a trifle and climbed above him, but P-B waved him down and wiggled his fingers from the end of his nose.

He looked ahead and down at Trent. Trent had been drunk, too, but he was steady now, sawing wood above and slightly behind Hoyt.

Then, suddenly, beyond Trent and far below, he saw a Hun two-seater alone. The old stunt. Hoyt shifted and pulled up his nose to climb above it and wait. Trent followed him up. Somewhere above that two-seater, and a half mile behind, there would be a flight of Hun scouts skulking under the clouds, waiting to pounce on whoever dived for the two-seater.

Hoyt knew it for a decoy. Paterson knew it. They would climb above the cloud edge, circle back, and catch the Hun scouts as they passed underneath.

Paterson trembled slightly. This was his chance at last. There'd be a long dive and a sure fight from behind, and in the mix-up he'd wabble down and out of the war via Lazaret VI in Cologne. He glanced around to see if Mallory was above him, and suddenly, out of the corner of his eye, he saw P-B shove his nose full down and throw himself into a straight dive for the decoy bus.

He gazed and shouted "No!" into the roar of his engine. P-B, in a nasty temper and half fuddled, didn't smell the trick. There was one awful second, while Crowe closed up into P-B's place and Hoyt banked to wait above, for the Hun scouts to pounce down on the Camel.

P-B fired, pulled up and dived again, far below them. The Hun two-seater banked sharply and came up and over in an Immelmann turn to get away. P-B caught it halfway over and a trickle of smoke swept out from its engine. Then in an instant Hoyt dived, with the rest of C Flight after him.

The next thing Paterson knew there were two Huns on his tail and a stream of tracer bullets pecking at his left wing. He pulled back on his stick and zoomed headlong up under Mallory. So close he was for a second that he could see the wheels turning slowly on Mallory's undercarriage and almost count the spokes glinting in the sunlight where the inside canvas sheathing had been taken off.

Mallory pulled away from him in a quick climbing turn and the Huns passed underneath, banking right and left. Paterson picked the left-hand one, thundered down on him in a short dive, and let go a burst of ten shots into the pilot's back. He saw the pilot's head snap sideways and his gloved hands fly up from the controls. Then Mallory dived over him after the other one. He turned in a wild split-air and followed Mallory.

There were more Huns below him and to the left, with two of the C Flight Camels diving and bucking between them. He raced furiously into a long dive, picked the nearest, and opened fire again in short, hammering bursts. His Hun wabbled and started down awkwardly in long sweeps. He picked another, still farther below, and pushed his stick forward until the rush of air gagged him. Wildly he fired as he ploughed down on it, and the chatter of his guns stabbed through the roar of his engine. He yelled like a madman, shot under the Hun, pulled up sharply, and fired into its gray mud-streaked belly. There was a fan of scarlet flame and a shock that tossed him to one side. He stalled and whipped out into a spin. Far below him he could see the decoy two-seater trailing a long plume of reddish smoke and flopping, wings over, toward the floor.

Then, suddenly, he saw his chance to wabble down and get away. He ruddered out of the spin and ran his stick once through the slow ellipse he had planned. But somehow he had to force himself to do it. There wasn't the relief he had expected. He looked back. Three C-Flight machines were still above him, fighting madly—P-B, Trent, and Hoyt. No—not this time. He pulled his stick back and climbed up. There were five Huns circling the Camels. It was a long shot, but he fired at the nearest and came up under the tail just as one of the Camels hurtled into a nose dive, twisted over, and snapped off both wings. He saw the pilot's arms raised wildly in the cockpit and no more.

Blood streamed into his mouth. He had torn his lips with his teeth in the excitement. The warm salty tang mounted to his brain. His goggles were sweat-fogged. His fingers ached with their pressure on the joy stick, and his arm was numb to the elbow. In a spasm of blind hatred, he fired. Tracers raced across his top plane and struck with little smoke puffs that ripped the fabric into ribbons. His own bullets clawed at the Hun above him and fanged home.

He threw himself up and over in an Immelmann turn and came under the next, still firing. He let go his stick and jerked his Lewis gun down its sliding mount on his top plane. It fired twice and jammed. He yanked madly at the cocking lug, but it stuck halfway. He hurtled down again in another spin. The ground swept around in a quick arc that ended in clouds and more Hun busses. He caught at his thrashing joy stick. Again the ground flashed through his centre section struts in a brown smudge, with the blaze of the sun hanging to one end of it. Then there was a Camel above him and a Camel below him. He closed in on the one below and squinted at the markings. Hoyt. He looked up at the other Camel, but the numerals on the side of its fuselage were hidden with a torn flap of fabric. Together, the three turned westward and started back.

Presently, near the line, the bus above him wabbled and dipped its nose. He stared at it. It went into a long, even glide that grew slowly steeper as he watched. He looked down for Huns. There were none. The glide became a dive, the dive twisted into an aimless spin, like the flopping of a lazy swimmer turning over in shallow water. The spin flattened and the Camel whipped out upside down, stalled, snapped out again, and again spun downward in that ghastly slow way. Over and over, only to whip out, stall and spin again. It was miles below him now. Nothing to do. Fascinated, he watched it as he followed Hoyt's tail. It was a mere dot now, flashing once or twice in the sun as it flopped over and over. Close to the ground now—closer. Then, suddenly, a tiny sheet of pink flame leaped up like the flash of a far beacon. That was all.

Hoyt was side-slipping below him, and he saw his own airdrome under the leading edge of his bottom wing. He followed Hoyt down. They landed together and taxied slowly in toward the hangars. They stopped side by side and climbed out stiff-legged. Paterson looked down and saw that his right flying boot was torn and flayed into shreds across the outer side. There was a jagged fringe on the skirt of his coat where the leather had been ripped into ruffles. Dumbly, he looked back into his cockpit. The floor boards were splintered and the wicker arm of his seat was eaten away. He shrugged and walked over toward Hoyt. There was blood on the rabbit fur of Hoyt's goggles, blood that oozed slowly down and dripped from his chin piece in bright drops.

"Cigarette?"

Paterson gave him one. They walked into the flight office and slumped into chairs. Hoyt ripped off his helmet and dabbed at the scratch on his cheek. "I'm glad you got out, Pat," he said absently.

Then the fear spot broke and spattered into the four corners of Paterson's soul. He sprang up trembling, with his fists beating the air.

"The dirty lice!" he screamed. "They've killed P-B! They've killed Trent! D'y' hear me, Hoyt?—they've killed 'em! They're gone! They'll never come back! They've——"

Hoyt's voice came evenly, calmly, through his screaming.

"Steady, boy! Steady! You can't help it. No one can. Steady, now!"

A mat of white oil-splotched faces stared at them from the open doorway that led into the hangar. The boy turned wildly. "Clear out!" he shrieked. They vanished, open-mouthed. Hoyt drew him down into a chair. "No, Hoyt, no! Can't you see? P-B and you and Trent have meant everything to me. I can't go on. I've fought this thing till I'm crazy." Hoyt reached quickly and slammed the door. "I've fought it night and day!" He threw up his arms hopelessly and covered his face with his shaking hands.

Hoyt put his hand on his trembling shoulders and patted them. "Steady, now! Steady! None of that!" he said awkwardly.

Paterson's head whipped down across his sprawled arms on the desk top and the sobs tore at his throat in great gusts that choked him. "Oh, God!" he sobbed. "What's it all about, Hoyt? What's the use of it?"

"Steady, son! I don't know. Nobody knows. It just happened, as everything happens. It's much too late to talk causes. We're here and we know what we have to do. That's enough for us. It's all we have anyway, so it must be enough." He took his blood-soaked cigarette from his mouth and hurled it into a corner. It landed with a soft spat.

Someone knocked at the door. "Come in." It was the runner from squadron office. He saluted. "Yes?" said Hoyt.

The man glanced at Paterson's face and snapped his eyes quickly back to the captain's.

"Beg pardon, sir," he said. "Squadron's just been signalled through wing. One of the C Flight machines came down near B Battery, the 212th."

"Who was it?" asked Hoyt.

"Lieutenant Mallard, they reported it, sir. That'll be Lieutenant Mallory, sir, won't it?"

"Yes." Hoyt's voice was quite flat. "Thank you."

The man saluted again and shut the door. Hoyt dabbed at his cheek and reached into his desk drawer for another cigarette. Paterson stood up suddenly and grabbed his arm. "Listen, skipper!" Hoyt's eyes met his calmly. "I'm going to tell you something. I'll feel better if I do. I've been a weak sister in this flight. I've planned for days to go down and let myself be taken prisoner—to get out of it all. I've been sick of it—sick of it, d'y' hear, until I couldn't think straight. I wanted to get out alive. I wanted to get away in any way I could. This morning I broke. I let go and started down——"

Hoyt smiled. "Your trouble, Pat, is that you think you're the only person in this jolly old war."

Paterson stared at him. "But I did! I started down, out of it, this morning!"

"How'd you get here?" asked Hoyt.

"But if I hadn't broken for that moment this morning——"

"That's a lie!" snapped Hoyt. "You're talking poobah! I know how those things happen. If P-B hadn't gone down after the two-seater they'd all be here now; and by the same reasoning, if my aunt wore trousers she'd be my uncle. The important thing is that it's you and me now and nothing else matters. We'll have four brand-new men to whip into shape to-morrow, and whatever you think of yourself, you've got to do it. I can't do much, for I'll be ahead, leading. You'll be behind them and you'll have to do it all. They'll be frightened and nervous and green, but the job's to be done. Understand? You've got to goad them on and get them out of trouble and watch them every minute, so that in time they'll be as good as P-B and Trent—so that when their turn comes they can do for other green men what P-B and Trent did for you. Do you see now what this morning has done for you?" He paused for a moment, and then, in a lower tone—"Afraid? Who isn't afraid? But it doesn't do any good to brood over it."

C Flight did no duty the next day, nor the day following. Hoyt went up to the 212th and identified Mallory for burial, while Paterson flew back to the Pool for the replacement pilots and a new Camel for Hoyt.

In Amiens he heard the first whispered rumours of what was going to happen. Intelligence was ranting for information. Everybody had the story and nobody was right. The hospitals were evacuating as fast as possible. Fresh battalions were being hustled up. It wasn't a push. Anyone could tell that with half an eye. Something the Hun was doing. The spring offensive a month earlier this year. G. H. Q. was plugging the gaps frantically, replacing and reinforcing and wondering where the hammer would fall and what it would carry with it. Hence the pictures that had cost the lives of P-B and Trent.

The air itself trembled with uncertainty, and rumours flew fast and thick.

Paterson flew back with the four new pilots and brought the rumours with him. Hoyt had more to barter in exchange. The talk ran riot at dinner.

"It's a Hun push, all right, but where, nobody knows. We'll have word in a day or so, but it'll be wrong whatever it is, mark what I say!"

And then on the evening of the twentieth things started. A signal came for the major just as they sat down to mess. He went out and presently called out the three flight commanders. When they came back, they took their places thoughtfully. Silence trembled in the room like the hush that precedes the first blasting stroke of a great bell in a cathedral tower. The major swept his eyes down the board.

"You will remain at the airdrome to-night, gentlemen, and remain sober. Officers' luggage is to be packed and placed on lorries which Mr. Harbord is providing for that purpose." He paused for a moment. "This is a precautionary move, gentlemen. We are to be ready to retire at a moment's notice. Flight commanders have the map squares of the new airdrome. You can take that up later among yourselves." He leaned back in his chair and beckoned to the mess sergeant. "Take every officer's order, sergeant, and bring me the chit."

The talk broke in a wild flood that roared and crackled down the length of the table. The tin walls trembled with the surge of it and the echoes broke in hot discord among the rough pine rafters. Offensive patrols for all three flights, to start at five minutes to four A. M. Air domination must be maintained. Wing's instructions were to stop everything at all costs. Go out and fight and shut up. Somebody presented the adjutant with the sugar bowl and asked him if he had his umbrella for the trip back. The adjutant had spent eighteen days without soles to his boots in 1914. He and the medical officer stood drinks for the squadron.

About ten o'clock, Hoyt called the five men of C Flight into his hut. "To-morrow, something is going to happen, I'm afraid, and you've got to meet it without much experience. What I want you to understand is simply this: You've got Pat and you've got me. Follow us and do what we do. We won't let you down so far as it is humanly possible. If the flight gets split up in a dog fight, then fight your way out two and two—and go back to the new 'drome two and two. Don't go separately. Further"—he paused—"if anything happens to me"—Paterson looked up at him quickly and something tugged sharply at his heart; Hoyt went on quietly —"take your lead from Mr. Paterson. You'll be Number 5, Darlington. You'll climb up as deputy leader. And if anything happens to Pat, then it's up to you to bring the rest home." He smiled. "There is a bottle of Dewar's in this drawer. Take a snifter now, if you want it, and one in the morning. It's for C Flight only. Oh, yes, one more thing: The fact that we're moving back to a new airdrome seems to indicate that staff thinks nothing can stop the Hun from breaking through. The fact that nothing can stop the Hun seems to indicate that, for the nonce, we are losing our part of the war. If the thought will help you—it's yours without cost."

The caller rapped sharply and threw back the door. Paterson leaped to his feet half asleep and pushed back the window curtains. The clouds were down to about four hundred feet, lowering in a gray mass over the mist on the airdrome. He went into the next cubicle and turned Hoyt out. Hoyt sat up on the cot edge and ran his hand across his forehead.

"Stop the caller," he said. "Let's see what's what before we turn everybody out." They shrugged into their flying coats and groped down the passage to the major's cubicle in the next hut block.

"Let 'em sleep," said the major. "Can't do anything in this muck. Turn out one officer in each flight to watch for the break and to warn the rest. Send Harbord to me if you see him wandering about."

They woke up the skippers of A and B Flights and told them the news. Paterson took the watch for C. He turned up his coat collar and went out. It was cold and miserable in the open, and the chill crept into his bones. The smoke from his cigarette hung low about him in the still air.

Presently to the eastward there came a low roar. He looked at his wrist watch. The hands pointed to six minutes before four o'clock. The ground trembled slightly to the sound of the distant guns and the air stirred in faint gusts that pulled at blue wraiths of his cigarette smoke. The push had started.

His muscles stiffened at the knees as he listened. The first shock of the guns was raw and sharp in the quiet air; then it settled into a lower, full-throated rumble like the heavy notes of an organ growling in an underground basilica. Now it rose again in its greater volume—rose steadily, slowly, as if it were a colossal express train hammering down the switch points at unthinkable speed. Presently it soared to its highest pitch and held the blasting monotony of its tone. The minutes ticked off, but the guns never faltered in their symphony of blood. At 4:35 one pipe of the organ to the southeastward cut out suddenly and almost immediately began again, closer than before. Again it broke, as he listened, and crept nearer still.

He walked down the line of huts, thrashing his arms and blowing on his cold hands. An impersonal thing to him, yet he shivered slightly and stared upward at the low clouds. Men out there to the eastward were in it. The suspense was over for them. And suddenly he found himself annoyed at the delay, annoyed at the fog and clouds above, that kept him on the ground. He wanted to see what was going on—to know. He turned impatiently and went into the mess. The sergeant brought him coffee, and presently Muirhead of A Flight came in with Church of B.

"It's on," Church said absently. "I suppose this fog means hell up the line."

They drank their coffee and smoked in silence. The sound of the guns crept nearer and nearer, and one by one the rest of the squadron drifted in for breakfast.

Hoyt sat down next to Paterson. "I don't like it," he said. "Something is giving way up there." He went to the window and looked out. "Clouds are higher," he said, "and the fog's lifted a bit. What do you think, major?"

They crowded out of the mess doorway and stood in an anxious knot, staring upward. It was well after six o'clock.

"All right"—the major turned around—"get ready to stand by."

C Flight collected in a little knot in front of Hoyt's Camel, smoking and talking nervously. Paterson kept his eyes on Hoyt and stamped his feet to get the circulation up. A strange elation crept into his veins and warmed him. In a moment now—in a moment. Awkward waiting here. Awkward standing around listening to Darlington curse softly and pound his hands together.

Somewhere behind him on the road, a motor bike roared through the mist, and then to the southward a shell crashed not a thousand yards from the 'drome, and the echo of it thumped off across the fields. Darlington jumped and stared at the mushroom of greasy black smoke. A moment more—a moment now. Paterson reached over and tapped Darlington's sleeve. "Keep your guns warm, old boy." Darlington nodded fiercely.

The major climbed into his cockpit and a mechanic leaped to the propeller. The engine coughed once and the propeller snapped back. The mechanic leaped at it again. It spun down and melted into a circle of pale light. Everyone was climbing in. Hoyt flicked his cigarette away sharply and put a leg up into his stirrup.

They were taxi-ing out into the open ground, with the mechanics running after them. Presently they could see the road. Paterson stared at it in amazement. It was brown and crawling with lorries and troops. Something had happened! A Flight, with the major, sang off across the ground and took the air together in a climbing turn. B Flight waited a brief second and followed. Out of the corner of his eye, Paterson could see the mess sergeant climbing up on the lorry seat beside Harbord, the equipment officer. Then Hoyt waved his hand. Mechanics yanked at the chock ropes and waved them off. They blipped their motors and raced out after Hoyt.

At five hundred feet they took the roof in the lacy fringe of the low clouds. Bad, very bad, Paterson thought. He ran his thumb across the glass face of his altimeter and his globe became wet with the beaded moisture. He could hardly see Darlington's tail. Ahead of them the clouds were a trifle higher. Hoyt led them up and turned northward. Murder to cross the line at that height, with the barrage on. Darlington was lagging a bit. Afraid of the clouds. He dived on Darlington's tail and closed him up on Number 3. Darlington glanced back at him and ducked his head.

Hoyt was circling back now in a broad sweep. Over there somewhere was Cambrai. He looked up for an instant just in time to see the underside of a huge plane sweep over him. He ducked at the sight of the black crosses, but the plane was gone before he could whip his Lewis gun into action. Almost immediately one corner of his windshield ripped away and the triplex glass blurred with a quick frosting of a thousand cracks. He cursed into the roar of his motor and kept on.

They were higher now, but the visibility was frightful—like flying in a glass ball that had been streaked with thick dripping soapsuds. Here a glimpse and a rift that closed up as soon as you looked; there a blank wall, tapering into tantalizing shreds that you couldn't quite see beyond. He fidgeted in his cockpit and turned his head from Hoyt, below him, to the gray emptiness behind. Nothing.

Presently Hoyt banked around, and following him, the compass needle on Paterson's instrument board turned through a half circle. They were going back toward the south again and climbing still higher. An even thousand feet now—just under the rising, ragged clouds. He felt a drop of rain strike his cheek where his chin piece ended. It bit his skin like a thorn and stung for seconds afterward. His goggles were fogging. He ran a finger up under them and swept the lenses.

Then, in a breath, it happened. A gray flash swept down out of the clouds in front of the formation. Hoyt zoomed to avoid it. The Hun zoomed and they came together and melted into each other in a welter of torn, rumpled wings and flying splinters. Something black and kicking rose out and disappeared. The cords stood out in Paterson's neck and his throat closed. Somewhere his stomach leaped and kicked inside of him, trying to get out, and he saw coffee dripping from the dials of his instruments.

In a second he had thrown his stick forward and gone down into Hoyt's place. He didn't dare look—he couldn't look. He was screaming curses at the top of his voice and the screams caught in his throat in great sobs. His goggles were hopelessly fogged. He ripped them off. Behind him the four new men closed in tightly, with Darlington above them as deputy leader.

There was blood again on his lips. He pulled back his stick and climbed. There, somewhere in the clouds, were the men who had done it! All right! All right! His eyes stung and wept with the force of the wind, and his cheeks quivered under the lash of the raindrops. With his free hand, fist clenched, he pounded his knee in stunned anguish until his muscles ached. Hoyt! Hoyt! Then he saw what he wanted and dived down furiously at the shape in the mist. Bullets tore at his top plane and raked across the cowling behind him. He closed on the Hun and sent it spinning. There was another—three— five—nothing but Huns. He dived in between them. Fine! He was screaming again, and firing. He forgot he was flying. The joy stick thrashed crazily between his knees and the ground and the clouds were a muddy gray scarf that swept from side to side across his eyes. Guns were the thing. Once, in a quick flash, he saw tiny men running upside down through the ring sight of his Lewis gun—the gun on his top plane— funny.

His wrists ached and his fingers were quite dead against the Bowden trigger. No, not that; that's a Camel—Darlington. He grabbed at his joy stick and pulled it back. Funny how hard it was to pull it. Another Camel swept in beside him, and another, with startling suddenness. It had been a long time now—a long time. Somebody had been afraid once and there had been a man named Hoyt. No, Hoyt was dead. Hoyt had been killed days before. Must have been P-B. P-B was probably in Amiens by now. He'd left in the tender at six o'clock. And always his guns chattered above the roar of his engine.

Abruptly, the cross wires of his centre section raced up to him from a great distance and stopped just before his eyes. He wondered where they had been all this time. He stared past them into the light disk of his propeller, and again the rain lashed into his face and stung him. He caught at the kicking joy stick and held on to it with both hands—but one hand fell away from it and wouldn't come back. With an effort, he pulled back his stick to climb up under the clouds again. Must be up under the clouds. Must wait and get more Huns. Funny things, Huns. Clumsy, stupid gray things you shot at and sent down. Go home soon, rest a bit and get some more. He laughed softly to himself. Joke. Funniest thing in the world.

The centre section wires clouded up before his eyes and started to race away from him. Here! That's bad! Can't fly without centre section wires. He chuckled a bit over that.

Absurd to think of flying without centre section wires! Come back here! You come back!

Just as his eyes closed, he saw a streak of roadway flicker through the struts of his left wing. There were faces on it quite close to him; faces that were white and staring; faces with arms raised above them. Funny. He whipped back his joy stick with a convulsive jerk, and then his head crashed forward and he threw up his arm to keep his teeth from being bashed out against the compass.

It was very dark—dark except for a dancing blue light far away. He moved slightly. Something cool touched his forehead.

"All right," he muttered; "that's all right now. You just follow me." Someone whispered. He opened his eyes and stared into the darkness. "No," he said quite plainly. "I mean it! Hoyt's dead. I saw him go down."

He felt something sharp prick his arm. "You've got the new airdrome pinpointed, haven't you?" he asked.

A soft voice said, "Yes. Sh-h-h!"

"No," he said, "I can't. Darlington's alone now, and I've got to go back. They're green, but they're good boys." He moved his legs to get up. "There's a bottle of Dewar's——"

"No," said the voice beside him.

"Oh, yes," he said quietly. "Really, this is imperative. I know I crashed."

A stealthy languor crept across his chest and flowed down toward his legs. He thought about it for a moment. "I ought to go," he said pettishly. "But I'm so tired."

"Yes," said the voice. "Go to sleep now."

"Right-o," he said. "You call a tender and wake—me—half—an—hour." He was quiet for a moment more and then he chuckled softly. "Tell 'em it's poobah," he said sharply.

"All right," said the voice. "It's poobah."

His breathing became quiet and regular and footsteps tiptoed softly down the ward away from his bed.

NIGHT CLUB

By KATHARINE BRUSH

From *Harper's*

PROMPTLY at quarter of ten P. M. Mrs. Brady descended the steps of the Elevated. She purchased from the newsdealer in the cubbyhole beneath them a next month's magazine and a to-morrow morning's paper and, with these tucked under one plump arm, she walked. She walked two blocks north on Sixth Avenue; turned and went west. But not far west. Westward half a block only, to the place where the gay green awning marked Club Français paints a stripe of shade across the glimmering sidewalk. Under this awning Mrs. Brady halted briefly, to remark to the six-foot doorman that it looked like rain and to await his performance of his professional duty. When the small green door yawned open, she sighed deeply and plodded in.

The foyer was a blackness, an airless velvet blackness like the inside of a jeweller's box. Four drum-shaped lamps of golden silk suspended from the ceiling gave it light (a very little) and formed the jewels: gold signets, those, or cuff-links for a giant. At the far end of the foyer there were black stairs, faintly dusty, rippling upward toward an amber radiance. Mrs. Brady approached and ponderously mounted the stairs, clinging with one fist to the mangy velvet rope that railed their edge.

From the top, Miss Lena Levin observed the ascent. Miss Levin was the checkroom girl. She had dark-at-the-roots blonde hair and slender hips upon which, in moments of leisure, she wore her hands, like buckles of ivory loosely attached. This was a moment of leisure. Miss Levin waited behind her counter. Row upon row of hooks, empty as yet, and seeming to beckon—wee curved fingers of iron—waited behind her.

"Late," said Miss Levin, "again."

"Go wan!" said Mrs. Brady. "It's only ten to ten. *Whew!* Them *stairs!*"

She leaned heavily, sideways, against Miss Levin's counter, and, applying one palm to the region of her heart, appeared at once to listen and to count. "Feel!" she cried then in a pleased voice.

Miss Levin obediently felt.

"Them stairs," continued Mrs. Brady darkly, "with my bad heart, will be the death of me. Whew! Well, dearie? What's the news?"

"You got a paper," Miss Levin languidly reminded her.

"Yeah!" agreed Mrs. Brady with sudden vehemence. "I got a paper!" She slapped it upon the counter. "An' a lot of time I'll get to *read* my paper, won't I now? On a Saturday night!" She moaned. "Other nights is bad enough, dear knows —but *Saturday* nights! How I dread 'em! Every Saturday night I say to my daughter, I say, 'Geraldine, I can't,' I say, 'I can't go through it again, an' that's all there is to it,' I say. 'I'll *quit!*' I say. An' I *will*, too!" added Mrs. Brady firmly, if indefinitely.

Miss Levin, in defense of Saturday nights, mumbled some vague something about tips.

"Tips!" Mrs. Brady hissed it. She almost spat it. Plainly money was nothing, nothing at all, to this lady. "I just wish," said Mrs. Brady, and glared at Miss Levin, "I just wish *you* had to spend one Saturday night, just one, in that dressing room! Bein' pushed an' stepped on and near knocked down by that gang of hussies, an' them orderin' an' bossin' you 'round like you was *black*, an' usin' your things an' then sayin' they're sorry, they got no change, they'll be back. Yah! They *never* come back!"

"There's Mr. Costello," whispered Miss Levin through lips that, like a ventriloquist's, scarcely stirred.

"An' as I was sayin'," Mrs. Brady said at once brightly, "I got to leave you. Ten to ten, time I was on the job."

She smirked at Miss Levin, nodded, and right-about-faced. There, indeed, Mr. Costello was. Mr. Billy Costello, manager, proprietor, monarch of all he surveyed. From the doorway of the big room, where the little tables herded in a ring around the waxen floor, he surveyed Mrs. Brady, and in such a way that Mrs. Brady, momentarily forgetting her bad heart, walked fast, scurried faster, almost ran.

The door of her domain was set politely in an alcove, beyond silken curtains looped up at the sides. Mrs. Brady reached it breathless, shouldered it open, and groped for the electric switch. Lights sprang up, a bright white blaze, intolerable for an instant to the eyes, like sun on snow. Blinking, Mrs. Brady shut the door.

The room was a spotless, white-tiled place, half beauty shop, half dressing room. Along one wall stood washstands, sturdy triplets in a row, with pale-green liquid soap in glass balloons afloat above them. Against the opposite wall there was a couch. A third wall backed an elongated glass-topped dressing table; and over the dressing table and over the washstands long rectangular sheets of mirror reflected lights, doors, glossy tiles, lights multiplied. . . .

Mrs. Brady moved across this glitter like a thick dark cloud in a hurry. At the dressing table she came to a halt, and upon it she laid her newspaper, her magazine, and her purse— a black purse worn gray with much clutching. She divested herself of a rusty black coat and a hat of the mushroom persuasion, and hung both up in a corner cupboard which she opened by means of one of a quite preposterous bunch of keys. From a nook in the cupboard she took down a lace-edged handkerchief with long streamers. She untied the streamers and tied them again around her chunky black alpaca waist. The handkerchief became an apron's baby cousin.

Mrs. Brady relocked the cupboard door, fumbled her key-ring over, and unlocked a capacious drawer of the dressing table. She spread a fresh towel on the plate-glass top, in the geometrical centre, and upon the towel she arranged with care a procession of things fished from the drawer. Things for the hair. Things for the complexion. Things for the eyes, the lashes, the brows, the lips, and the finger nails. Things in boxes and things in jars and things in tubes and tins. Also, an ash tray, matches, pins, a tiny sewing kit, a pair of scissors. Last of all, a hand-printed sign, a nudging sort of sign:

NOTICE!

These articles, placed here for your convenience, are the property of the maid.

And directly beneath the sign, propping it up against the looking-glass, a china saucer, in which Mrs. Brady now slyly laid decoy money: two quarters and two dimes, in four-leaf-clover formation.

Another drawer of the dressing table yielded a bottle of bromo seltzer, a bottle of aromatic spirits of ammonia, a tin of sodium bicarbonate, and a teaspoon. These were lined up on a shelf above the couch.

Mrs. Brady was now ready for anything. And (from the grim, thin pucker of her mouth) expecting it.

Music came to her ears. Rather, the beat of music, muffled, rhythmic, remote. *Umpa-um, umpa-um, umpa-um-umm—* Mr. "Fiddle" Baer and his band, hard at work on the first fox-trot of the night. It was teasing, foot-tapping music; but the large solemn feet of Mrs. Brady were still. She sat on the couch and opened her newspaper; and for some moments she read uninterruptedly, with special attention to the murders, the divorces, the breaches of promise, the funnies.

Then the door swung inward, admitting a blast of Mr. "Fiddle" Baer's best, a whiff of perfume, and a girl.

Mrs. Brady put her paper away.

The girl was *petite* and darkly beautiful; wrapped in fur and mounted on tall jewelled heels. She entered humming the ragtime song the orchestra was playing, and while she stood near the dressing table, stripping off her gloves, she continued to hum it softly to herself:

> "Oh, I know my baby loves me,
> I can tell my baby loves me."

Here the dark little girl got the left glove off, and Mrs. Brady glimpsed a platinum wedding ring.

> "'Cause there ain't no maybe
> In my baby's
> Eyes."

The right glove came off. The dark little girl sat down in one of the chairs that faced the dressing table. She doffed her wrap, casting it carelessly over the chair back. It had a cloth-of-gold lining, and "Paris" was embroidered in curlicues on the label. Mrs. Brady hovered solicitously near.

The dark little girl, still humming, looked over the articles "placed here for your convenience," and picked up 'the scissors. Having cut off a very small hangnail with the air of one performing a perilous major operation, she seized and used the manicure buffer, and after that the eyebrow pencil. Mrs. Brady's mind, hopefully calculating the tip, jumped and jumped again like a taximeter.

"Oh, I know my baby loves me——"

The dark little girl applied powder and lipstick belonging to herself. She examined the result searchingly in the mirror and sat back, satisfied. She cast some silver *Klink! Klink!* into Mrs. Brady's saucer, and half rose. Then, remembering something, she settled down again.

The ensuing thirty seconds were spent by her in pulling off her platinum wedding ring, tying it in a corner of a lace handkerchief, and tucking the handkerchief down the bodice of her tight white velvet gown.

"There!" she said.

She swooped up her wrap and trotted toward the door, jewelled heels merrily twinkling.

"'Cause there ain't no maybe——"

The door fell shut.

Almost instantly it opened again, and another girl came in. A blonde, this. She was pretty in a round-eyed, babyish way; but Mrs. Brady, regarding her, mentally grabbed the spirits of ammonia bottle. For she looked terribly ill. The round eyes were dull, the pretty, silly little face was drawn. The thin hands, picking at the fastenings of a specious beaded bag, trembled and twitched.

Mrs. Brady cleared her throat. "Can I do something for you, miss?"

Evidently the blonde girl had believed herself alone in the dressing room. She started violently and glanced up, panic in her eyes. Panic, and something else. Something very like murderous hate—but for an instant only, so that Mrs. Brady, whose perceptions were never quick, missed it altogether.

"A glass of water?" suggested Mrs. Brady.

"No," said the girl, "no." She had one hand in the beaded

bag now. Mrs. Brady could see it moving, causing the bag to squirm like a live thing, and the fringe to shiver. "Yes!" she cried abruptly. "A glass of water—please—you get it for me."

She dropped on to the couch. Mrs. Brady scurried to the water cooler in the corner, pressed the spigot with a determined thumb. Water trickled out thinly. Mrs. Brady pressed harder, and scowled, and thought, "Something's wrong with this thing. I mustn't forget, next time I see Mr. Costello——"

When again she faced her patient, the patient was sitting erect. She was thrusting her clenched hand back into the beaded bag again.

She took only a sip of the water, but it seemed to help her quite miraculously. Almost at once colour came to her cheeks, life to her eyes. She grew young again—as young as she was. She smiled up at Mrs. Brady.

"Well!" she exclaimed. "What do you know about that!" She shook her honey-coloured head. "I can't imagine what came over me."

"Are you better now?" inquired Mrs. Brady.

"Yes. Oh, yes. I'm better now. You see," said the blonde girl confidentially, "we were at the theatre, my boy friend and I, and it was hot and stuffy—I guess that must have been the trouble." She paused, and the ghost of her recent distress crossed her face. "God! I thought that last act *never* would end!" she said.

While she attended to her hair and complexion, she chattered gaily to Mrs. Brady, chattered on with scarcely a stop for breath, and laughed much. She said, among other things, that she and her "boy friend" had not known one another very long, but that she was "ga-ga" about him. "He is about me, too," she confessed. "He thinks I'm grand."

She fell silent then, and in the looking-glass her eyes were shadowed, haunted. But Mrs. Brady, from where she stood, could not see the looking-glass; and half a minute later the blonde girl laughed and began again. When she went out she seemed to dance out on little winged feet; and Mrs. Brady, sighing, thought it must be nice to be young . . . and happy like that.

The next arrivals were two. A tall, extremely smart young woman in black chiffon entered first, and held the door open for her companion; and the instant the door was shut, she said, as though it had been on the tip of her tongue for hours, "Amy, what under the sun *happened?*"

Amy, who was brown-eyed, brown-bobbed-haired, and patently annoyed about something, crossed to the dressing table and flopped into a chair before she made reply.

"Nothing," she said wearily then.

"That's nonsense!" snorted the other. "Tell me. Was it something she said? She's a tactless ass, of course. Always was."

"No, not anything she said. It was——" Amy bit her lip. "All right! I'll tell you. Before we left your apartment I just happened to notice that Tom had disappeared. So I went to look for him—I wanted to ask him if he'd remembered to tell the maid where we were going—Skippy's subject to croup, you know, and we always leave word. Well, so I went into the kitchen, thinking Tom might be there mixing cocktails— and there he was—and there *she* was!"

The full red mouth of the other young woman pursed itself slightly. Her arched brows lifted. "Well?"

Her matter-of-factness appeared to infuriate Amy. "He was *kissing* her!" she flung out.

"Well?" said the other again. She chuckled softly and patted Amy's shoulder, as if it were the shoulder of a child. "You're surely not going to let *that* spoil your whole evening? Amy *dear!* Kissing may once have been serious and significant —but it isn't nowadays. Nowadays, it's like shaking hands. It means nothing."

But Amy was not consoled. "I hate her!" she cried desperately. "Red-headed *thing!* Calling me 'darling' and 'honey,' and s-sending me handkerchiefs for C-Christmas—and then sneaking off behind closed doors and k-kissing my h-h-hus-band . . ."

At this point Amy quite broke down, but she recovered herself sufficiently to add with venom, "I'd like to slap her!"

"Oh, oh, oh," smiled the tall young woman, "I wouldn't do that!"

Amy wiped her eyes with what might well have been one of the Christmas handkerchiefs, and confronted her friend. "Well, what *would* you do, Claire? If you were I?"

"I'd forget it," said Claire, "and have a good time. I'd

kiss somebody myself. You've no idea how much better you'd feel!"

"I don't do——" Amy began indignantly; but as the door behind her opened and a third young woman—red-headed, earringed, exquisite—lilted in, she changed her tone. "Oh, hello!" she called sweetly, beaming at the newcomer via the mirror. "We were wondering what had become of you!"

The red-headed girl, smiling easily back, dropped her cigarette on the floor and crushed it out with a silver-shod toe. "Tom and I were talking to 'Fiddle' Baer," she explained. "He's going to play 'Clap Yo' Hands' next, because it's my favourite. Lend me a comb, will you, somebody?"

"There's a comb there," said Claire, indicating Mrs. Brady's business comb.

"But imagine using it!" murmured the red-headed girl. "Amy, darling, haven't you one?"

Amy produced a tiny comb from her rhinestone purse. "Don't forget to bring it when you come," she said, and stood up. "I'm going on out, I want to tell Tom something." She went.

The red-headed young woman and the tall black-chiffon one were alone, except for Mrs. Brady. The red-headed one beaded her incredible lashes. The tall one, the one called Claire, sat watching her. Presently she said, "Sylvia, look here." And Sylvia looked. Anybody, addressed in that tone, would have.

"There is one thing," Claire went on quietly, holding the other's eyes, "that I want understood. And that is, '*Hands off!*' Do you hear me?"

"I don't know what you mean."

"You do know what I mean!"

The red-headed girl shrugged her shoulders. "Amy told you she saw us, I suppose."

"Precisely. And," went on Claire, gathering up her possessions and rising, "as I said before, you're to keep away." Her eyes blazed sudden white-hot rage. "Because, as you very well know, he belongs to *me*," she said, and departed, slamming the door.

Between eleven o'clock and one Mrs. Brady was very busy indeed. Never for more than a moment during those two hours was the dressing room empty. Often it was jammed, full to overflowing with curled cropped heads, with ivory arms and shoulders, with silk and lace and chiffon, with legs. The door flapped in and back, in and back. The mirrors caught and held —and lost—a hundred different faces. Powder veiled the dressing table with a thin white dust; cigarette stubs, scarlet at the tips, choked the ash-receiver. Dimes and quarters clattered into Mrs. Brady's saucer—and were transferred to Mrs. Brady's purse. The original seventy cents remained. That much, and no more, would Mrs. Brady gamble on the integrity of womankind.

She earned her money. She threaded needles and took stitches. She powdered the backs of necks. She supplied towels for soapy, dripping hands. She removed a speck from a teary blue eye and pounded the heel on a slipper. She curled the straggling ends of a black bob and a gray bob, pinned a velvet flower on a lithe round waist, mixed three doses of bicarbonate of soda, took charge of a shed pink-satin girdle, collected, on hands and knees, several dozen fake pearls that had wept from a broken string.

She served chorus girls and schoolgirls, gay young matrons and gayer young mistresses, a lady who had divorced four husbands, and a lady who had poisoned one, the secret (more or less) sweetheart of a Most Distinguished Name, and the Brains of a bootleg gang. . . . She saw things. She saw a yellow check, with the ink hardly dry. She saw four tiny bruises, such as fingers might make, on an arm. She saw a girl strike another girl, not playfully. She saw a bundle of letters some man wished he had not written, safe and deep in a brocaded handbag.

About midnight the door flew open and at once was pushed shut, and a gray-eyed, lovely child stood backed against it, her palms flattened on the panels at her sides, the draperies of her white chiffon gown settling lightly to rest around her.

There were already five damsels of varying ages in the dressing room. The latest arrival marked their presence with a flick of her eyes and, standing just where she was, she called peremptorily, "Maid!"

Mrs. Brady, standing just where *she* was, said, "Yes, miss?"

"Please come here," said the girl.

Mrs. Brady, as slowly as she dared, did so.

The girl lowered her voice to a tense half-whisper. "Listen! Is there any way I can get out of here except through this door I came in?"

Mrs. Brady stared at her stupidly.

"Any window?" persisted the girl. "Or anything?"

Here they were interrupted by the exodus of two of the damsels-of-varying ages. Mrs. Brady opened the door for them—and in so doing caught a glimpse of a man who waited in the hall outside, a debonair, old-young man with a girl's furry wrap hung over his arm, and his hat in his hand.

The door clicked. The gray-eyed girl moved out from the wall, against which she had flattened herself—for all the world like one eluding pursuit in a cinema.

"What about that window?" she demanded, pointing.

"That's all the farther it opens," said Mrs. Brady.

"Oh! And it's the only one—isn't it?"

"It is."

"Damn," said the girl. "Then there's *no* way out?"

"No way but the door," said Mrs. Brady testily.

The girl looked at the door. She seemed to look *through* the door, and to despise and to fear what she saw. Then she looked at Mrs. Brady. "Well," she said, "then I s'pose the only thing to do is to stay in here."

She stayed. Minutes ticked by. Jazz crooned distantly, stopped, struck up again. Other girls came and went. Still the gray-eyed girl sat on the couch, with her back to the wall and her shapely legs crossed, smoking cigarettes, one from the stub of another.

After a long while she said, "Maid!"

"Yes, miss?"

"Peek out that door, will you, and see if there's anyone standing there."

Mrs. Brady peeked, and reported that there was. There was a gentleman with a little bit of a black moustache standing there. The same gentleman, in fact, who was standing there "just after you come in."

"Oh, Lord," sighed the gray-eyed girl. "Well . . . I can't stay here all *night*, that's one sure thing."

She slid off the couch, and went listlessly to the dressing

table. There she occupied herself for a minute or two. Suddenly, without a word, she darted out.

Thirty seconds later Mrs. Brady was elated to find two crumpled one-dollar bills lying in her saucer. Her joy, however, died a premature death. For she made an almost simultaneous second discovery. A saddening one. Above all, a puzzling one.

"Now what for," marvelled Mrs. Brady, "did she want to walk off with them *scissors?*"

This at twelve-twenty-five.

At twelve-thirty a quartette of excited young things burst in, babbling madly. All of them had their evening wraps with them; all talked at once. One of them, a Dresden china girl with a heart-shaped face, was the centre of attention. Around her the rest fluttered like monstrous butterflies; to her they addressed their shrill exclamatory cries. "Babe," they called her.

Mrs. Brady heard snatches: "Not in this state unless . . ." "Well, you can in Maryland, Jimmy says." "Oh, there must be some place nearer than . . ." "Isn't this *marvellous?*" "When did it happen, Babe? When did you decide?"

"Just now," the girl with the heart-shaped face sang softly, "when we were dancing."

The babble resumed, "But listen, Babe, what'll your mother and father . . .?" "Oh, never mind, let's hurry." "Shall we be warm enough with just these thin wraps, do you think? Babe, will you be warm enough? Sure?"

Powder flew and little pocket combs marched through bright marcels. Flushed cheeks were painted pinker still.

"My pearls," said Babe, "are *old*. And my dress and my slippers are *new*. Now, let's see—what can I *borrow?*"

A lace handkerchief, a diamond bar pin, a pair of earrings were proffered. She chose the bar pin, and its owner unpinned it proudly, gladly.

"I've got blue garters!" exclaimed another girl.

"Give me one, then," directed Babe. "I'll trade with you. . . .There! That fixes that."

More babbling, "Hurry! Hurry up!" . . . "Listen, are you *sure* we'll be warm enough? Because we can stop at my house, there's nobody home." "Give me that puff, Babe, I'll powder your back." "And just to think a week ago you'd never even met each other!" "Oh, hurry *up*, let's get *started!*" "I'm ready." "So'm I." "Ready, Babe? You look adorable." "Come on, everybody."

They were gone again, and the dressing room seemed twice as still and vacant as before.

A minute of grace, during which Mrs. Brady wiped the spilled powder away with a damp gray rag. Then the door jumped open again. Two evening gowns appeared and made for the dressing table in a bee line. Slim tubular gowns they were, one silver, one palest yellow. Yellow hair went with the silver gown, brown hair with the yellow. The silver-gowned, yellow-haired girl wore orchids on her shoulder, three of them, and a flashing bracelet on each fragile wrist. The other girl looked less prosperous; still, you would rather have looked at her.

Both ignored Mrs. Brady's cosmetic display as utterly as they ignored Mrs. Brady, producing full field equipment of their own.

"Well," said the girl with the orchids, rouging energetically, "how do you like him?"

"Oh-h—all right."

"Meaning, 'Not any,' hmm? I suspected as much!" The girl with the orchids turned in her chair and scanned her companion's profile with disapproval. "See here, Marilee," she drawled, "are you going to be a damn fool *all* your life?"

"He's fat," said Marilee dreamily. "Fat, and—greasy, sort of. I mean, greasy in his mind. Don't you know what I mean?"

"I know *one* thing," declared the girl with orchids. "I know Who He Is! And if I were you, that's all I'd need to know. *Under the circumstances*."

The last three words, stressed meaningly, affected the girl called Marilee curiously. She grew grave. Her lips and lashes drooped. For some seconds she sat frowning a little, breaking a black-sheathed lipstick in two and fitting it together again.

"She's worse," she said finally, low.

"Worse?"

Marilee nodded.

"Well," said the girl with orchids, "there you are. It's the climate. She'll never be anything *but* worse, if she doesn't get away. Out West, or somewhere."

"I know," murmured Marilee.

The other girl opened a tin of eye shadow. "Of course," she said drily, "suit yourself. She's not *my* sister."

Marilee said nothing. Quiet she sat, breaking the lipstick, mending it, breaking it.

"Oh, well," she breathed finally, wearily, and straightened up. She propped her elbows on the plate-glass dressing-table top and leaned toward the mirror, and with the lipstick she began to make her coral-pink mouth very red and gay and reckless and alluring.

Nightly at one o'clock Vane and Moreno dance for the Club Français. They dance a tango, they dance a waltz; then, by way of encore, they do a Black Bottom, and a trick of their own called the Wheel. They dance for twenty, thirty minutes. And while they dance you do not leave your table—for this is what you came to see. Vane and Moreno. The New York thrill. The sole justification for the five-dollar couvert extorted by Billy Costello.

From one until half-past, then, was Mrs. Brady's recess. She had been looking forward to it all the evening long. When it began—when the opening chords of the tango music sounded stirringly from the room outside—Mrs. Brady brightened. With a right good will she sped the parting guests.

Alone, she unlocked her cupboard and took out her magazine—the magazine she had bought three hours before. Heaving a great breath of relief and satisfaction, she plumped herself on the couch and fingered the pages. Immediately she was absorbed, her eyes drinking up printed lines, her lips moving soundlessly.

The magazine was Mrs. Brady's favourite. Its stories were true stories, taken from life (so the editor said); and to Mrs. Brady they were live, vivid threads in the dull, drab pattern of her night.

SINGING WOMAN

By ADA JACK CARVER

From *Harper's*

LITTLE by little the Joyous Coast was changing.
The old rutted dirt road that fringed the Cane had
been abandoned. The highways cut through the swamps and
marshy lands and fields full of corn and refused to follow the
whim of the river. It seemed to old Henriette relentless and
terrible. It even ploughed its way through people's dooryards,
rooting up ancient landmarks: oaks and chinas and gnarled
crêpe myrtles, their branches bowed to the earth with bloom
—trees under which Henriette in her day had been courted
and won.

Isle Brevelle, where the French mulattoes live, is not lonely
and strange as is an island lost in the sea. With the river curving about it, it is like a maid in the arms of a lover who woos
her forever: "*Lie still, Adored One. Are my arms not around
you? Do you not feel the beat of my heart? Behold the gifts I have
brought, the fruit and the flowers I lay at your feet. You are
round and shining like the sun, more beautiful than the day——*"

The young people on Isle Brevelle liked the changing order,
the feeling of unrest and impatience. Now, in the long summer
evenings they could get in cars and go to town, to see the
sights; or take in the coloured picture show up on the hill.
"*Mais non*, we don't speak to them niggers," they assured
old Henriette. "We don't have nothing to do with them
black folks."

But all this saddened Henriette. For generations now her
people had guarded the blood in their veins. Ignored by the
whites, ignoring and scorning the blacks, they had kept themselves to themselves. But now there was change all about them.
Something was in the air. . . . In her black spreading skirts,

with her black kerchief about her head, Henriette sat on the gallery and watched the gravelled road that was straight and white and went on and on, taking the young folks with it. . . . People didn't die, either, like they used to do, properly in their beds, with time to receive the sacrament and be shrived for their sins. They died just any and everywhere, bumped off by trains or the automobiles that ploughed by on the highway. No wonder the buryings were often hurried, unworthy affairs, without bell or book; to say nothing of singing woman!

Henriette and her crony, fat old Josephine Remon, were the only singing women left on Isle Brevelle. Time was when a singing woman was as necessary as a priest, when no one who was anything could be buried without a professional mourner. In those days Henriette and Josephine were looked up to and respected: the place of honour at table, the best seat by the fireside, the most desirable pew in the church. Finally, instead of being sought after, a wailing woman had to offer her services. Nowadays people seemed to have lost the fear, the dignity of death.

It was the same way with midwifery. Young women nowadays engaged trained nurses, or went to town to the hospitals to have their babies. Nowadays people didn't care *how* they died or were born. They just came in and went out of the world, any old way. . . . All this troubled Henriette, and she sat in her corner and mumbled and grumbled to God about it, "Look like nothing ain't right, not what it used to be . . ."

It had been nearly ten years now since Henriette had wailed for a funeral. Josephine had had the last one, when old Madame Rivet died, six years ago. That made ninety-eight for Josephine and ninety-nine for herself. She was one funeral ahead. How proud she was of her record! She, Henriette, had sung for more buryings than any singing woman in the parish. Of course, old Josephine ran her a mighty close second. Henriette kept an account of her own and Josephine's funerals, in a little black memorandum book locked up in her armoire. On one page was her own name, Henriette; and underneath it ninety-nine crosses in neat little rows of five. On the opposite page was Josephine's name, and beneath it ninety-eight crosses, in neat little rows of five. Well, they had served Death long and faithfully, she and Josephine; where Death had gone they had followed. . . . Time was, when, as a special treat, Henriette would take out her funeral book and name the crosses: "This one was Marie Lombard, and this one Celeste, her daughter. Here was Henri, what died the time the cholera come, in 1860."

Now no one ever thought of Henriette's funeral book. Six years, since Madame Rivet died, it had lain in her armoire. Sometimes she wondered sadly if she would ever wail again. For on Isle Brevelle there was but one person left who, when he died, would want a wailing woman. This person was Toni Philbert, the only soul on Isle Brevelle older than Henriette. Toni and Henriette and Josephine had been young folks together. Now it had got to be a sort of game between the two women as to who would get Toni when Toni died. "If I get Toni," Henriette would say, "me, I'll have two more crosses than you. I'll have a hundred." And Josephine, sitting fat in her chair, would chuckle, "*Mais non*, and if I get him, we'll be even, Etta, my friend."

Toni himself, an old, old man, sans teeth, sans everything, was pleased with the fuss they made over him. Sometimes he would joke with them when he met them at church. "Well, well, old uns. I'm here yet. Hee! Hee! I'll outlive both you girls. Just wait—me, I show you!"

The days on Isle Brevelle were long and filled with the drowsy chatter of ducks and fat red hens. Henriette's prayers for those in purgatory took up part of the time. But a person can't pray forever! Nothing to do but sit and think of the past, and of death and dying. Henriette had always, even when a child, known something lovely and secret about death. What it was she could not have told; but her knowledge made her a good wailing woman. She minded the time, long ago, when the husband of Rose, Toni's daughter, died and left Rose a widow. Such a pretty slip of a thing and so white in her sorrow! Henriette had, of course, done her duty to the dead; she had wailed and sung and beat the earth: "*Under a tree by the river I saw them digging a young grave. Stricken one, desired of Heaven, your eyes that will not look at me—what do they see? How long before I can go to you, as I used to go? . . . down by the water where the reeds are singing. . . .*" But after the funeral (Mother forgive her!), she had gone back to comfort Rose, and unsay all she had said. "Look, Rose, honey, don't take on so. A girl as fresh and sweet as you! Look, he is happy. And the world is full of lovers . . ." At Rose's door grew the lily called "widow's tear"—"widow's tear" because the drop of dew in its heart dries so quickly when the broad, warm sun comes out. . . .

Well, who should know more about death than she, Henriette . . . she who had buried three husbands?

Sometimes when the weather was fine, and the sun not too hot or too bright, old Henriette would put on a clean "josie," and take her stick and hobble down to Josephine's house to sit and talk of old times. She would get one of her grand-children to help her down in the ditch, beside the highroad, where she insisted on walking to avoid the automobiles. When there had been rain Henriette got her feet all wet and muddy, down in the ditch that way. When the weather was dry the automobiles, shrieking by, sprayed her from head to foot with a fine white dust. Sometimes she got into nettles, or cockleburs or ants. And once a rattlesnake had glided across her path. Her grandchildren, who loved her, were dis-mayed and indignant. "Ain't you 'shame, Gran'mamma, walking down in the ditch! How come you don't let us take you to Josephine's in the car?" But Henriette was afraid of cars. "It ain't far. I ruther walk."

Josephine was always glad to see her. She would grunt and grumble and fetch out another shuck-bottomed chair. Then Josephine would make coffee. Josephine was rich. She owned her house and a little store that her son-in-law managed; and her married children lived with her, not she with them. She was very, very fat, what with easy living. How the two old women would gossip, the pleasant air stirred with their pal-metto fans. Now in "American," now in French; talk, talk, talk, talk. "Ain't your tongues ever run down?" Josephine's daughters-in-law would ask, laughing but respectful.

What grand living and dying there used to be, back in steam-boat days! It was like recalling a wedding festival or a Mardi Gras to look back to the yellow-fever scare of 1890. A funeral every day, and sometimes two. She and Josephine had had their hands full. . . . Shucks! the land was too healthy now, what with draining the swamps and such. The people were getting too uppity, outwitting death like that. Good thing after all that the automobiles bumped some of them off, else they never would quit the earth. What if some day folks should rise up and simply refuse to die! Well, what would God the Father have to say about that?

Sometimes Henriette and Josephine would crack mild little jokes, slapping at the flies with their untiring fans. "I seen Toni last week, at the church. He's looking feeble." "*Mais non!*" (A cackle.) "He ain't here for long." Sometimes a shrill and sudden chorus of locusts swelled out of Josephine's trees, and was gone. A sure sign of death. And the two old women would cross themselves. "I wonder who it is *this* time!"

But after all, what did it matter? Some young fool or other run down by an automobile. Some boy shot at the dance hall, over some girl. Whoever it was wouldn't want *them*. The only person on Isle Brevelle who would want a singing woman was Toni, old Toni Philbert, who for nearly twenty years had had one foot in the grave. Looked like he meant to hang on to the earth forever and ever, amen. He had always been like that, a lover of life and living. Heylaw! What a lad old Toni used to be! . . . What a way with the girls!

It was on a sultry August day that Toni Philbert had a stroke. Henriette's grandson came in and told her about it. "I hear tell down at the store that Toni is mighty low. He can't last very long, they tell me."

Henriette was excited. So Toni was sick, very low! She gulped down some coffee and got her stick, and set out for Josephine's house, walking down in the ditch. She was so heavy with news she could scarcely breathe. So Toni was on his deathbed. . . . Thoughts of Toni came to her from the long-ago years. . . . The August sun was veiled in a mist from the river. Already the cottonwoods were changing colour, and the goldenrod was in bloom. Henriette crowded close into the dusty bushes as an automobile flashed past above her on the highroad. So Toni was dying! Well, sometimes she might forget how many grandchildren she had; sometimes she forgot her age, or what year it was, this and that. But she would never forget the time that Toni had kissed her, nor the dress she had worn when he did it, long, long ago. Little enough she had thought of death or singing for death in those days, sitting under the trees by the river in a pink-sprigged challis. What a gallant, insolent lad he had been, old Toni! Of course, he had kissed every girl on the island. But hers was a sort of a special kiss, she had always felt. She was a slim, pretty, green-eyed thing, just turned seventeen. . . .Old Henriette groped along, catching against the bushes and the tumbleweeds at her feet. That was in 1852, long 'fore the war. . . . Old Henriette had warts on her cheeks. "Frogs put 'em there," she sometimes croaked to curious children. "Toadfrogs, out in the swamp." But in those days, when Toni had kissed her, her cheeks were yellow and smooth. Toni had led her down to the river to look at herself. "A minute ago, Henriette, your face was a yellow lily. And now—look!—it's a rose!"

Ah, well, poor Toni was dying! Which one would he want to sing for him, herself or old Josephine? Henriette wondered if Josephine had had any "news." . . . She stopped, heavy with fear. Suppose Josephine had been "asked?" She began to hurry a little. . . . Heylaw! Who was that a-coming, a-coming through the weeds? She screwed up her eyes and peered. It was Josephine, hobbling along down in the ditch, so fat she could scarcely wobble.

The two old women began screeching at each other when they were yet a great way off, and waving their palmetto fans. "Toni, he's very sick! They say that this is the end!" They found a nice spot by the roadside, among the weeds and overgrown summer flowers. It took them a minute or two to get settled. How Josephine grunted and took on, trying to sit! How her hips spread all over the place! Well, Henriette was glad she was thin and could get about some. . . . Butter-and-eggs and Jimson weed grew all around them, giving off rank summer odours. A giant cottonwood reached its arms between them and the sun. . . . "Is you heard from Toni yet?" Henriette· asked, all a-tremble. And Josephine said, "No. Is you?"

Just so, when they were young, they had sat and talked of Toni. "Is you heard from Toni yet?" What a boy he had been for love! . . . Love? Death, the enchantress, was after him now. "If *I* get him," Henriette cackled, "I'll have two more than you." And Josephine laughed, sitting fat in the weeds till their purple juice squashed on her clothes. "*Mais non!* And if *I* get him, we'll be even, Etta, my friend."

A week went by, and another; and it began to look as if old Toni didn't mean to die after all. It was just like Toni to keep death waiting, to flirt with death like that. He always was a tease: "*Well, my beauty, my proud one—all in good time. Don't chafe and paw at the bit. . . .*" And not a word had Toni said about getting a wailing woman! That was just like Toni, too, keeping everyone guessing up to the last.

Every night now Henriette got out her funeral book: ninety-nine crosses for herself. A record any singing woman might be proud of! If only she could get one more, to round out her final five! If only she could get Toni. How she would crow over Josephine then: "Me, I got one hundred crosses. One hundred funerals I've sung for . . ."

One night in early September Henriette, sleepless, lay in her bed. Against her window the trees, uneasy with autumn, pushed and drew away, sighing a little. The moon was up, looking drunken and sodden. It was very warm—good funeral weather, Henriette thought; a fine night for death, with cape jessamine still in bloom and baby owls in the trees. Henriette loved hoot owls. She felt they were kin to her, sisters under the skin. They plied the same trade, she and they. She loved owls and bats and all webfooted creatures, things that live in a green underworld. There were sounds on the highway, the chugging of cars; and into her window flashed the light from an automobile; it sought out the Virgin Mary, wheeled through the room, and was gone. Up and down the roads they went, the automobiles full of young folks—clatter-chug, clatter-chug!—past the unnoticed glory of river and moon and swamp. How little they considered death, the boys and girls on the highway!

The sickly moon went out; and there was lightning in the south. That meant the rain was 'way off, hiding in week after next. . . . Henriette arose very stealthily and crept outdoors to sit on the gallery, where it was cooler. Maybe right now old Toni was dying. . . . Once while she was sitting there her grandson came and poked his head out the door. "You better come to bed, gran'mammy. You'll catch cold out there in your nightclothes." But she shook her head and mumbled, "Let me be." She began to sing, very low, "*He will die, my beloved, my friend, when the good round fruit is ripe; when the time of courting is at an end; when the fields are bare, and the sky is black with the low, long cry of the heron . . ."*

Two weeks later old Toni passed away. And Toni's son came to bid Henriette to the funeral: "Papa, he told us to get you. The funeral's to-morrow at ten."

Henriette, who had moped long ago whenever Toni went off to town, could not shed a tear now he was dead. She was so excited she could scarcely speak; she could scarcely put on her clothes. "Come help me fasten my josie!" she called to her children. . . . So he had wanted *her*, after all, poor old Toni. She had her grandson help her down in the ditch. "Granny!" her grandchildren cried, shocked. "It rained cats and dogs last night. For shame, a old lady like you, walking down in the ditches."

But they couldn't do anything with her. She couldn't rest, she said, until she had seen Josephine. "I must go tell Josie," she said. "Poor old Josie——"

When Henriette neared Josephine's house she began to cackle, her voice like a reed. But Josephine, sitting in her chair, cut her short. "I done heard a'ready. You needn't bother to tell me. . . . Well, me, I'm glad for you, Etta."

Old Josephine sat heavily in her chair, sagging over. How fat and sloppy she looked! And Henriette wondered what memories passed behind her lidless old eyes. . . . Presently Josephine got up and went and made some coffee. "One hundred for you," she muttered, "and ninety-eight for me. Well . . ." To-day old Josephine laced the coffee with anisette, peering at Henriette disapprovingly. "You'll need your strength," she said gruffly, deep in her throat. "Getting your feet all wet that-a-way. You ought to be 'shame', at your age."

But Henriette smiled. She knew Josephine was trying to dull her own disappointment; she knew that Josephine was low in her mind. Henriette drank of the hot, fragrant coffee. On either side of Josephine's steps the bunched-up rosettes of the altheas were very pink in the sunshine; and the red yucca shook out its pretty, globular, rain-filled bells. . . . Henriette didn't stay very long. "I got lots to do. I got to be up bright and early," she said.

But in the morning, when Henriette awakened, she found

that something terrible had happened to her voice. It was gone; she could not speak. Her grandchildren crowded about her bed, concerned and anxious—an old woman is frail as glass! "You see what we told you, Gran'mammy! You got no call yesterday, getting het up and excited just because old Toni is dead and they want you to sing for his funeral. And didn't we tell you stay out that ditch? Walking around in water, just like a duck, at your age."

They scolded and fussed and fumed and put warm flannels on her throat. They gave her a toddy. But it did no good. Her throat hurt, and when she opened her mouth she croaked like a frog—she who in her wailing had had as many stops to her voice as a sounding organ. . . . "Poor Gran'mammy," her children said. "Now she can't sing. And Josephine'll have to go and wail for old Toni's funeral." Henriette lay and moaned a little. If she could only cry as children cry, in her disappointment. But the tears wouldn't come. They had all dried up long ago.

At dusk the family returned from the burying. But out of respect for her feelings, as Henriette knew, they forbore to talk of the funeral and of how nice Josephine had sung and "carried on." They merely said, "Josephine was so fat they had to hold her, to keep her from tumbling down in the grave." But when she thought no one was looking Henriette took her funeral book from under her pillow and made a crossmark under Josephine's name. Now they were even. Her old hands shook and one yellow tear rolled out of one eye. "Poor Gran'mamma," her children said, in whispers. "Poor old Granny . . ."

Sleep did not come to Henriette until nearly daybreak. It began to rain about midnight, a steady rain, long and full of the secrets of autumn. And Henriette lay in her bed and thought about death and dying. She thought about her grandchildren, how good they were. Somehow she always felt sorriest for young people when anyone died. Not for little children, or the very old; but the ones in between. The ones between eighteen and forty, say. They took it hardest. How terrible death was to them, how *everlasting!* If only they could know what *she* knew, she and the little children. . . . Of course, she wailed and carried on; that was her business, her calling. But how often, right in the midst of a funeral, even as she stood and gazed in the grave, she had longed to go and whisper to youth's white, impassioned grief, "There, there, *chère* . . . don't sorrow so hard. Me, I know. I tell you, I *know*." But what she knew she could not have said. . . . Henriette stirred in her bed, sought a new place for her pillow. How often she had longed to say to some bereft mother, she who had buried six, "Do not grieve overmuch, little Mammy. He is not here. See! He is dragging a little tin can for a train, across the white courts of Heaven."

Henriette slept, and after a time a bell tolled in her dreaming. It awakened her. A gray light had come into the room, and the rain was gone. Well, and who could be dead? Somebody old and rich was dead, the bell had been tolling so long. The light about her bed grew brighter, and the ceiling shone with rose. She dozed again; but when she again awakened the bell was still tolling. . . . It must be an old person dead.

Suddenly Henriette became aware of a flow, a movement in the house. The windows rattled; a door was opened somewhere and shut. And then there was a swishing of skirts, a running of feet. Her grandchildren! They crowded about her bed, three-deep, tense and excited. The cheeks of the littlest ones glowed, the way they did when there was bad news to be broken; when the sugar was out, or the cat had fallen down in the cistern. "Granny, what you think is happen? Old lady Josephine's gone!" . . . They crowded closer, to see how Henriette "took it." "Poor Josephine, she got sick in the night and she passed away early this morning."

Henriette sat up against her pillow, blinking. She looked like the kind of old woman children make out of their knuckles, with black-headed pins for eyes. And now the older ones, her daughters, stole into the room on their tiptoes. They took her hands. "How you feel, Gran'mammy? Is your throat all right? Well, they've done sent for you, honey. They said Josephine asked for you in the night, to come and sing for her funeral. . . . . Well, *le bon Dieu* is love you, sho', Mammy."

All day her children were busy, getting Henriette ready: her best alpaca cleaned and pressed; her mourning veil laid out, her gloves and her shoes. Shiny and speckless they must be, to follow the honoured dead. "Mammy," her daughters said, "you stay in bed and rest, so your voice will be good to-morrow." They were nice daughters; they were trying to make her feel prideful again. . . . All day long Henriette lay and gazed out at the white gravelled road, stretching away, on past Josephine's house. Looked like she could see Josephine, sitting there on her gallery, the fat running over!

Well, she would miss Josephine, her old crony. Toni and Josie both gone. It would be queer, a sort of joke, wailing for Josephine's funeral. It would be like singing beside her own grave.

The next morning, at the first peep of day, her children came in to help her. "How you feel, Gran'mammy?" They looked at her and shook their heads. She was so thin and so old. With her friends all gone she seemed like something from some other life. . . . "Well, we won't have Mammy much longer," they said. They crowded about her, solicitous.

Old Henriette sat up in bed. "Fetch me my specs," she grumbled.

They brought her specs, her false teeth, her rosary, and her snake-oil. They washed her feet and rubbed them, and helped her to dress. With her mourning veil on she looked like a little black bride. And when she was dressed and ready they brought her the funeral book. "Now, Mammy, look! Mark it down—one hundred funerals. You've sung for more buryings than anyone else in the parish."

But Henriette stared at the funeral book; she seemed mad about something, offended. "Don't meddle so much," she cackled. "You wait till I come home from Josephine's funeral."

She set out in the ditch, holding tight to her little black bag and her glasses. The grandchildren, who were to go on in the car, stood and watched her sorrowfully. Once she turned back and waved. . . . She was so little, so little and thin, so *perverse!* She hobbled along in the ditch. Her funeral shoes felt stiff and heavy, and caught in the Queen Anne's lace; and whenever an automobile thundered by on the highway, Henriette, terrified, put her hands to her ears. . . . Once, half fainting, she stopped and clutched at the branch of a cottonwood tree. And a loneliness passed over her, a loneliness and a heartache. . . . "Josie," she called, hopelessly, "Josie . . . I'm a-coming . . ."

But when she got to the turn of the road where the willows grew, she faltered, distressed and alarmed. She could get no farther down in the ditch. A freshet poured from a hole in the side of the road, and the ditch in front of her was flooded with water. The black water boiled and licked at her feet, treacherous and angry; and Henriette shrank and backed away. For a moment she stood, trembling, uncertain; and she stared at the road above her that stretched away in the sunlight, on past Josephine's house. Then, tottering and dizzy and sick with fright, she pulled herself up the embankment, and with her face turned toward Josephine's house, began to hobble along on the highway.

"Josie—" she whispered, and a numbness, a darkness took hold of her—"Josie . . . I mind as how, after all, my friend, you and me ull quit even . . ."

WITH GLORY AND HONOUR

By ELISABETH COBB CHAPMAN

From *Century*

IN A cross street of the riant fifties stands the Club Levering, an old brownstone building in a brave new coat of tan plaster, with wrought-iron lamps by its doors and an imposing uniformed figure to bow you out politely, or with the force of a strong arm, in nice accordance to the decorum or lack of it that you preserve within the precincts which he guards.

The Club Levering is not a club; it is a cabaret, a dance hall, and a theatre, with a strong attraction for Broadway luminaries. They drop in after the theatre to hear Hal Levering sing his new songs and to watch the swells, strayed from up town East, dance and enjoy themselves. And they love Hal. "He's a great boy," they say. "An artist. Some kid. Listen to that now. Boy, how he can put it over!"

Levering, born Lipwitz, had been driven to this place by a dim dream. There was struggle behind him, years of the unbelievable struggle of the poor man, of the immigrant Jew, against a relentless city. He could remember dimly a night in southern Russia, the pogrom, flames and the sounds of shots in the dark, driving out the Jew. He had been held up by his mother, crying, on the deck of an immigrant ship to see the Promised City blazing tall and splendid in the sunlight. They had all been held up to see it, he and Lena and Roziska and Leo and little Moses, even though Moses was too young to know what it was all about—and the Promised Land, as it materialized, a tenement in the crowded ghetto, too hard on the little Moses, who died in a few months.

Behind Hal were the years as a singing waiter in cheap cabarets, as a "song plugger," small-time vaudeville, and then a revue; and now marvellously he was Hal Levering, star and part owner of the Club Levering, and packing them in at higher prices than any other night club dared charge.

He had done that single-handed. And he had carried the Lipwitz family with him. Lena was now a dancer, a good one; Isaac, a partner in a clothing store. Rosie had married a doctor. Mama kept house for Lena, and if Papa had been alive, Hal would undoubtedly have found something lucrative for him.

Always his dream had driven him. The dream of the artist, inarticulate, clumsy, hunting for the ultimate beauty. He sang jazz now and he wore fine clothes, while around him were the flash of jewels and the white faces of gaudy women and the throb of Bennie Bernstein's music. Everybody paid him homage, bowing, pounding on the table for Hal Levering, the artist, singing "Abie's an Irisher Now," a song whose words were a cry of pain, written by a Jew in contempt of his race. He sang it gorgeously, with exaggerated gestures, flexible hands, and when he did the part where Abie pretends to be the Irish plug-ugly, one saw the cringe of the homeless race that was ingrained in Abie in spite of the defiant throw of an Irish jaw. It was a beautiful bit of mimicking, and even though he was a Jew he did not mind the ugly words at all.

He had one song, "When My Little Baby Boy Says His Prayers to Me," that never failed to make his hearers cry. And there were tears in his own eyes, when he came off, not because of the song—he knew hokum even when he sang it himself—but because he could "get them" with it. Hal Levering, the artist, his triumph ringing in his ears clapped out by enthusiastic hands.

The grinding afternoon before his new summer show went on; he was in his element. About him were excited waiters arranging their tables, decorators at work on the flowers, Bennie Bernstein in his shirt sleeves, sweating over the new songs, Lilian Laine begging help with the duet they were to sing. And then, as Hal went over his new numbers alone, the waiters and the decorators, Lilian and song-wise Bennie himself, stopped to listen to him.

He had worked that day until his face was gray with fatigue, but when at last he went out for his dinner, he walked bravely, with his head up, a conqueror, Hal Levering of the Club Levering, a king on Broadway.

The opening of the summer show had been an enormous success. The entrance was choked with disappointed people who could not get in, and at the door the page boys battled with the crowd clamouring for tables, among which the lucky ones who had reservations battled their way. And Hal moved from table to table to welcome his guests and receive homage. This was his big night, his triumph, the end, he thought with a choke in his throat, of his struggle toward the ultimate beauty.

Constance Corthwaite came to the Club Levering that night. She had never been there before, but Hal Levering recognized her at once. She was as much a celebrity to Broadway as she was to Fifth Avenue. One saw her everywhere, a pirate of a woman with a face moulded firm in lines of complete and terrible ennui, hunting for amusement, scattering her millions with a disdainful hand. She had been Constance Corthwaite for thirty-five years now, for she had never found a man to hold her interest long enough to marry him.

Levering had gone at once to her table, had been introduced, had accepted a glass of excellent champagne, had bragged, had strutted, had told jokes.

"Your place is quite amusing," Constance Corthwaite said. "I hear you sing very well."

Hal Levering laughed. "That's what they say. Have you ever heard me?"

She shook her head.

"Well, the stuff I do here is—well, no artist can put anything over in a restaurant, but I'm opening in a new act, just a side line, you know, at the Palace next week, and that's where I knock 'em right out of their seats. We've tried it out, and it's great. Next week—come and see me." Then in a magnificent burst of cordiality: "Come around during the show and see it from behind. How'd you like that, huh? See, I do a skit, new songs, new patter—it's a wow!"

She had favoured him with a glance from her long eyes. "Thank you."

"What would you like to have me sing for you now?" he asked.

"Try something good—I should like to see how it went here."

He sang "Sweet Siren" and "Pretty Little Mama" for her.

She did not applaud. He was disappointed. He had realized that she wasn't demonstrative, but he had hoped to win her.

Her friends seemed to enjoy themselves, and he took no more trouble with them. He noticed that they laughed, drank, and danced. Later there was an animated discussion; he could see that from the floor as he sang. Constance Corthwaite's friends were arguing with her. They leaned toward her, protesting. The attitudes were unmistakable. Apparently unmoved, she blew smoke from her nostrils and with a wave of her cigarette turned their attention back to him. They watched him, shrewdly, for a few seconds, and then went off into quiet laughter. Laughter at some joke which that long-eyed woman had designed. From the floor, singing, he saw all this, for his early training had made him observant.

As Constance was leaving she beckoned to him. She stood at the door, wrapped in her dark cloak. He went out at her nod, with alacrity. As he went he wondered what she wanted and decided definitely that he did not like her. "Too damned ritzy," and he thought her ugly and badly dressed, too, but after all she was Constance Corthwaite. Probably she had fallen for him. Most of 'em did.

She recognized his approach with the smallest possible nod.

"Thank you for the songs. We enjoyed them. As I can't watch you 'knock 'em off their seats' at the Palace, I suggest that you come down to my place in the country next week-end and knock us off our seats down there."

She was asking him to visit her. So she *had* fallen for him. They all did. He was inundated with female attentions. But a visit to the Corthwaite place! Well, he had arrived! He accepted blandly.

Mommer and Lena helped him pack. They came from their apartment across the hall to his and favoured him with their advice and assistance. It was a lengthy business. Before he got off, the plush splendour of his rooms was strewn with discarded clothing.

"Take your dress suit, Hermie," advised his mother. "Your new suit for those swells is none too good."

"Wear your lavender sport suit for the golfing."

"A bathing suit."

"Your silk socks, Hermie. Hermie, you have forgot your silk socks, Hermie."

"The lavender suit, Hermie."

He got off at last. His big car seemed to eat the miles, exaltation keeping time to the healthy song of his motor. He went swiftly through the mean towns squatting on the island's edge out to the rolling hills of the North Shore. He dreamed dreams. Now a new billing suggested itself. "Hal Levering—Society's Favourite"—or better, "Hal Levering, Society's Favoured Comedian." In his mind's eye he could see an article in *Vanity Fair*—perhaps—"Hal Levering, the erstwhile mammy songster a belated society discovery."

He turned the nose of the car into the Corthwaite gates and at a reduced speed moved up the driveway. In spite of the explicit directions given him by the policeman in Jonestown, he wasn't at all sure that this was the place.

He had passed, on his drive from New York, many great stone gates, so high and so formidable that they gave only a niggard glimpse of blue stone road, perhaps the outline of proud roofs upheld above the trees, and he had expected the Corthwaite driveway to be at least as fine as the finest of these.

But this was just a comfortable country road, distinguished from its kind only by a pair of lowly stone pillars and a squat frame cottage doing duty as a gatekeeper's lodge.

He drove through a small woodland, not pruned or landscaped at all, turned a corner, and found himself facing an expanse of lawn and a rambling frame house, painted a soft faded yellow and adorned with plain white shutters. The Corthwaite house laid claim to no other beauty than that which is inherent in old colonial houses and in ancient Greek vases, the unadorned beauty of line. Hal Levering was disappointed in it. A butler, not in livery, met him at the door. He was an old man and grumpy.

"Mr. Levering?" he asked. Levering had an uncomfortable feeling that his clothes, his car, and his abilities were all being evaluated, but he dismissed the suspicion as absurd, for the old man's eyes had not moved. He was at the moment holding open the door.

"Miss Corthwaite left word that if she had not returned at the time of your arrival you were to make yourself at home and ask me for anything you might require—sir."

Levering entered.

"The Car?" he asked, and one had, as always, a feeling that he was thinking of it with at least a capital "C." "The Car will be all right there?"

"The chauffeur will take it around if you will give me the keys—sir," said the old man.

"Oh!" There was an appreciative pause from Levering. This place was like one of those English places he had heard of—all service—no show.

The old man led him upstairs, and down a long hall to a bedroom, which like the rest of the house gave the impression of luxury, although the chintz was faded and the old furniture austerely simple.

The windows gave one a view of a garden, a box hedge, and, looming friendly in the rear, fruit trees not bowed as yet with the crop, but holding the green fruit as sturdily as a street lamp its light. That was no drawing room of a garden. The fruit trees were welcome to come in if they liked. "I don't call that much," Levering remarked to the air at large. He compared unfavourably the gay simple little flower beds before him to the marble swimming pool and formal terraces of his friend, Isaac Lowenstein, the moving-picture magnate. He carefully dusted his gray tweeds, straightened his tie an infinitesimal fraction, and from his bag searched out a bottle of brilliantine, and, anointing a comb, smoothed his hair.

Downstairs again, Levering found himself in the great room he had first entered, and through which he had passed too quickly for an impression. Now he frankly took its measure. It did not impress him. It was big, to be sure, but the hangings were not velvet, the upholstery was not rich. He decided that the early-American maple was cool looking but plain, and the dim rosy riot of the chintz, comfortable but cheap. He wondered at the house because he was sure that here, if any place in the world, things would be correct, and he had expected to find a glorified Club Levering with more crystal and more plush and more grandeur.

The old butler found him there and offered liquid refreshment, which was accepted gratefully.

"Did Miss Corthwaite say when she'd be home?" asked Levering. It made him lonely to be left to himself. The din of his days had beaten upon his nerves until solitude was a thing abhorred.

"She did not—sir," said the butler. Hal was offended with his welcome. He was doing Constance Corthwaite a favour in coming all the way down here to the country, and she had made no effort to receive him. Left alone, he looked about him for some source of amusement. Tentatively he opened two small cabinets, hoping vainly that they might contain phonograph or radio. He found only riding gloves, golf balls, a pair of garden shears, and some sheet music. The music offered possibilities, and in that room the big piano was the only piece of furniture that looked like any furniture he had ever seen, but the music was queer stuff. He did not know any of it, nor did he want to.

There were magazines piled on the long centre table, and he looked through them hopefully. Here was the bland impudence of the young intellectuals with their opinions supported by the dignity of a Duncan Phyfe table. If Hal Levering had possessed a subtle mind, he would have fathomed Constance Corthwaite at that instance. Eccentricity upheld by Duncan Phyfe.

Half buried in the pile of papers and magazines he found an old book, *The Book of the Corthwaites*, and in idle curiosity he turned the leaves. There were long lists of names in it, explained by short sentences.

In 1732, Colonel Abednego Corthwaite married Eliza Pepperidge. He settled in the city of Boston and became one of its most prominent citizens. His children were Abednego, Elisha, John, Eliza, Aaron, and Piety. Abednego died in infancy. Elisha married Patience |Cabot. Their children were——

"Good-night!" Levering's surprise was jolted out of him. "What does anybody care who those dead ones married?" But Constance Corthwaite and her kind must care, or the book would not be here. He carried it out on to the porch that gave a view of the garden and the apple trees.

When Constance Corthwaite and the rest of her nouse party returned from the golf links, they found Hal Levering reading. . . .

"In 1802 Solomon Corthwaite married Sarah Emerson," and in his eyes a dazed, bored, yet questioning expression.

"How d'ye do?" said Miss Corthwaite. She did not offer to shake hands. "Sorry to be so late. Golf, you know. Did Lake make you comfortable?" With a little wave of a hand she indicated her other guests, who, apparently without seeing him at all, were settling themselves in the low wicker chairs. "Miss Bromley, Mr.—er—Levering." Miss Bromley, whose sunburned face and quite frankly dirty hands gave evidence that she had played a hard game, indeed, acknowledged the introduction by not the faintest flicker of an eye. She was seemingly impervious to introductions. Her bow was not to be considered as directed at him at all. She merely happened to be bowing at that moment. Miss Paine and Mrs. Douglass and an Englishwoman, Lady Greville, to whom he was in turn presented, acknowledged his presence with equal enthusiasm. The men were more cordial, "My cousin, Mr. Herton, Lord Greville, Mr. Paine, Mr. Taylor, Mr. Valentine."

Levering instantly assumed the genial air of the club. That air, half ingratiating, half bold, wholly impudent. From his smiling lips to the bob of the little blue tassels that held up his blue golf stockings, he radiated cordiality.

They stayed out on the porch for a long time, discussing their golf and the long cold drinks. Levering, whose ignorance of the game was abysmal, and whose drink was finished, found himself rather out of this. Sitting as he was in the centre of the group, it seemed as though he were encircled by silence, while beyond there went on a very animated chatter. And as the dusk slid over them he was conscious of being lonelier than he had ever been in his life.

After dinner that night things picked up a bit. They led him to the piano and settled themselves expectantly around the room waiting to be entertained. They were. He sang them new popular songs and old songs that he had written himself, and he "got them" as he always got them at the Club Levering.

He gave them pathos for a finale, "When My Little Baby Boy Lisps His Prayers at Twilight," and as an encore, "Mamma, Sweet Mamma," in his rich tenor, "Please don't hold out on m-e-e."

Miss Bromley and Mr. Taylor were inspired to do an apache

dance. Lady Greville came over to him. "How quaint!" she said in her staccato voice and clipped pronunciation that he found difficult to understand. "Rippin'—teach it me, won't you?" He made room for her on the piano bench. "See—like this—Ma-ma—sweet Mama—" she picked out the treble with clever trained fingers. In a moment she was playing it very well. "You're some kid at the piano yourself, ain't you?" he said enthusiastically, boldly bending his head to look in her eyes. "But you haven't got it quite. Don't play it like grand opera—see. It's got a wow—like this—SWEET MAMA!"

From a corner Constance Corthwaite watched them with amusement. She looked like a cat luxuriously gorging itself with cream. There was on her face exactly that complacent, contented, and cynical expression.

The next morning he came down late. They had kept him at the piano a long time the night before, and besides, not for years had he risen early. He found the house deserted as it had been the afternoon before. Not until the butler told him they were all out riding did he remember dimly that something had been said about riding, that they had suggested he come along.

Out on the porch there were Sunday papers and warm sunshine. Levering settled himself in a comfortable, soft-cushioned wicker chair and picking up a paper turned to the Broadway page, where he found a flattering notice of the Club Levering activities during the past week. Yes, it was a triumph. Such a notice! "Quaintest night club in town." "Levering's songs draw the élite."

Oh! He'd arrived sure enough, and now here he was the guest of honour at the Corthwaites' house . . . kind of a funny way to treat your guest of honour, though, to leave him alone. . . . But then they knew that an artist had to have time to himself. . . . Sure, that was it. Levering dropped his paper and lay back comfortably. He closed his eyes and savoured his triumph. He was the Kid himself, and running with all these swells. . . . Funny kind of a place, though. No dog, no swank . . . kind of shabby. Not a patch on lots of places. . . . And come to think of it, the people ain't such classy dressers. . . . Not much jewellery on the dames. . . . That English duke's

dinner jacket didn't fit so damn good. . . . Slow kind of crowd;
he didn't get 'em at all. . . . Now when he'd sung that nifty
song it didn't go so big. . . that Corthwaite dame had acted
kinda queer, seemed like she'd almost sneered. . . . But, foolishness . . . she liked him fine, and she liked his stuff, too. . . .

He moved petulantly in his chair.

He wished they'd come back . . . this was a bore . . . no
kind of way to spend Sunday. . . .

He picked up another sheet of the paper, but his attention
wandered, and it fluttered from his hand. "What the hell's
the matter with me?"

It was very still out there. Levering had never felt such
stillness. It pressed on his eardrums. He could fairly hear the
silence. There was no way to escape from one's self in such
quiet. He was acutely uncomfortable. This was nothing like
the Lowensteins' place! Why, Sunday morning at this hour
there would be a crowd of good fellows drinking highballs
and singing and telling jokes, and the marble pool would be
full of people, and like as not someone would climb up one of
those Italian statues of old Lowenstein's and stick a bathing
cap on its head. Sure, there'd be things doing all right.

But this stillness that screamed at you, and this funny little
garden, and no footman in livery, and no marble statues—
hell! This wasn't such a place, and yet——

The stillness gives you funny ideas!

Now, old Lowenstein, he can't be all wrong—but Constance Corthwaite's place can't be wrong at all. This place is
right—for her brand of people. And the house—now, the
house must be right, too. It wasn't what he liked himself, but
it was right. It was bound to be right. It wasn't as if she didn't
always get the best. She could have anything in the world,
and she knew what was right—and she had this. And if this
was right, the Club Levering was wrong. He turned a little
cold at the thought. The club was his creation, it was his
dream, it was, in fact, himself, and it was wrong!

He stooped and picked up a sheet of the newspaper and
folded it gently and exactly.

Corthwaite—she knows. She's the kind that don't make
mistakes about houses.

He was not soothed and comforted in the sunlight now.
He was acutely and miserably fighting with doubt and dis-

trust. For if the Club Levering was wrong, then he was wrong. He had missed. He was cheated. He was being shown a land that he could never enter, and desolately, and suddenly now, he thought it was the only land worth entering.

Oh, the terrible, silent scorn of this house, in its rightness, scorn for him and his land and his dream! Hal Levering was a poet. It seemed to him now that the house behind him had drawn together and was straining to get away from him, just as the people in it strained away from him and left him alone and outside. He tried to reassure himself. There were all kinds of people in the world, and this was America, and he was as good as anybody.

"It ain't so; I'm as good as any of 'em. What'd they ask me here for if I ain't? You big clown you, they asked you here to sing your jazz songs, and so's they could get a good laugh outa you. That's what it was for, you big dummy. Didn't you see that Corthwaite girl sneering? Sure you did. But you wouldn't admit it! These people are right, and you're wrong, Hal Levering. You're a Jew. No, that ain't it either. It's because you ain't a Jew—that's it—because you're pretending you ain't. Because you ain't real. That's it. They got their own names and their own people and the things they've always had, but you—you're what they call a dirty Jew. . . .

"That's what it is about them that's different—it ain't just that they got different styles in architecture—but they ain't pretending nothing. They don't have to."

He remembered the smile that had curled Constance Corthwaite's lips the night before. It grew, it spread, the image of curving lips blotted out all the warm world, and he was alone before them, his heart sick with the humiliation of the degraded artist.

Hal Levering rose from his chair, trembling a little, very white, just as the riding party came strolling through the box hedge.

He looked down at them from the steps of the porch. They came toward him like sublime creatures oblivious of his presence and of his pain, ignoring him as they would always ignore him.

They were talking about someone named Coperbesby. He heard Constance Corthwaite's clear voice say:

"He has the most intense sense of race. A fierce and proud

belief in the Jew, and if you don't understand that he is a Jew, that everything he does is racial and unsullied, you can't understand his music at all."

Levering turned and, blundering against the door, went slowly out of the sun, through the big quiet hall and upstairs. His room had been put in order, and he hated to disarrange it, but he had to hurry, hurry so that he could go quickly, and when you pack in a hurry things get mussed up in spite of you.

The first thing his cronies at the club asked him was if he had had a good time at the Corthwaite place.

Bennie Bernstein, the orchestra leader, Mimi Deland, the specialty dancer, and her lean effeminate partner, surrounded him as soon as he appeared that Monday night.

"Did you have a good time?" they asked him.

"Sure, fine, fine."

Mimi Deland looked at him curiously. "Well, you don't look it."

He turned on her furiously. "What do you mean, I don't look it? What do you want me to do? Sing a song about it?"

She shrugged. "No," simply. "But don't chew my ear off."

"Say, don't get the week-end habit," said Bennie jovially. "That bird you had here last night doing your stuff was awful. We wouldn't keep open a week with him around."

"Pretty bad, huh?" pleased.

"Lousy!"

It was time for his first song. As he stepped to the door that led him to the spotlights and the applause, he said over his shoulder, "Don't worry about me getting the week-end habit; I won't."

"Gee," remarked Deland as he slammed the door on them, "I wonder what they did to him. He's back early, too."

He finished his song, and Bennie dipped his violin to his orchestra, and they began the opening bars of "Abie's an Irisher Now."

At the sound of the first notes, Levering stiffened as though he had been stung; then, turning on his heel, he called harshly, "Don't play that song to-night—or ever again." After which he walked stiffly off the floor, refusing his encore, while the music stopped in the middle of a bar, jarred to a silence that held until Bennie shattered it with his music again.

It was several weeks before Constance Corthwaite came again to the Club Levering. She was quite sure, of course, when Hall Levering fled from her house without a word to any of them, that he had somehow realized his position; but that was not what had kept her from the club. She had been away. Now, to-night, she was in town again and a little bored, and as Hal Levering had once amused her she came to his place in the hope that he might again. He was a hired performer; if she had hurt his feelings, well—she was sorry, but she had no intention of staying away as long as he could give her a moment's entertainment.

The club had not been doing well for the last few weeks. Even Bennie Bernstein's saucy music did not hold the crowds. The reason, of course, was that another man was in Hal Levering's place.

Constance Corthwaite listened to one of his colourless offerings, and then called him to her table.

"Where," she asked, "is Hal Levering? Isn't he going to be here to-night?"

"Nope, he's left for good."

"Really, how disappointing! Where has he gone?"

"Say, lady, you'll never believe me when I tell you; it's the funniest thing you ever heard! You know the money he was getting here—fifteen hundred a week and a rake-off, and he part owner at that——"

"Really?"

"Sure. Well, he came in here one day, nobody expecting it at all, and told 'em he was through—just like that. Through. Told 'em he was going back and be a real Jew, going to give his talent to his people. Can you beat it? They thought he had gone crazy, of course. Fifteen hundred a week and a rake-off—and do you know what he's done?" The objectionable young man paused dramatically. "Say, he's studying to be a cantor in a synagogue—can you beat that?—can you?"

It was a year and more before the Club Levering saw its part owner again. A variety of rumours had floated along Broadway—Levering had gone abroad to study, he had taken a position in a synagogue, he was composing highbrow music —but soon the rumours died away, and all that was left of Levering at his old stamping ground was the flashing red and green sign of the club. Business had fallen off; new places had each in turn engaged the fickle attentions of the city's night-lovers, and the Club Levering was patronized by only a few stragglers. And then the management decided to make one more bid for popular favour with a new revue.

Bennie Bernstein laboured at his piano just as he had the afternoon of Levering's greatest triumph a year before, but the other performers were new. No one now tried to fill Hal's shoes; they had to depend on a speeding chorus to cover up a palpable lack. And as Bennie sweated to get the rehearsal into full swing, the service door opened and a familiar voice sang out: "Hel-lo, Bennie, how've you been? Making the grade O. K., huh?" It was Hal Levering.

"My—God—Hal!" and Bennie leaped from his stool and seized Levering by the shoulders. The other performers gathered around, and to Hal again was given the once so sweet chorus of praise.

"Cut it out—cut it out. Let's get to work here. We gotta give 'em something to knock 'em off their chairs!"

Bennie looked at Levering in astonishment. Was he really coming back? It was too good to be true, but here he was, and Bennie ran over to the piano joyfully. His nimble fingers flew up and down the keyboard, and then, triumphantly, he hammered out the first bars of "Abie's an Irisher Now." Levering, who had been chatting with the chef, who had come running from the kitchen, whirled about with a white face.

"Bennie!" His voice stopped the music with the player's hands suspended in the air, such was its savage earnestness. "Never again that number, Bennie. Levering's a Jewisher now. Don't forget that, hey?" Hal patted his friend on the shoulder. "S'all right, Bennie, but there's been some changes made."

The rehearsal went on under Levering's direction, and when he was satisfied with it he turned to the piano and handed Bernstein several sheets of manuscript.

"Here's some new numbers that I'm going to try," he said.

"Hot dog!" Bernie murmured, as he bent his expert gaze on the neatly written sheets. Then an expression of bewilderment spread over his face. What was this stuff Hal was pulling? He glanced sideways at Levering, who was standing at the edge of the platform, his back turned. With a shake of his head, Bennie played a few bars; then Levering joined in, a new softness, a thrilling timbre, in his rich voice. Again the few in the room stopped their chatter and listened with puzzled expressions, which changed into real wonder and reluctant admiration as Hal sang:

> "Set me as a seal upon thine heart,
> As a seal upon thine arm,
> For love is strong as death,
> Jealousy is cruel as the grave.
> Stir not up nor awake my love
> Until he please."

When he had finished, a silence hung over the place. Hal turned to Bennie. "Try the next one," he said quietly.

And again he sang a verse from the Song of Solomon, set to a wailing accompaniment, that died away to a whisper, rose, swelled, and died away again. It was thrilling, strange, but "Can even Hal Levering get away with that stuff in a night club?" wondered Bennie.

One or two jazz numbers followed, and Hal called off rehearsal. The word spread that Levering was back, and that night, when the lights were dimmed and the chorus twinkled through the opening number, the place was crowded beyond seating capacity.

There was no sight of Levering until after Buck and Wing, those whirling cloggers, had done their turn. Then he appeared, and a burst of applause, punctuated by the staccato click of the little wooden hammers on the tables, showed that he still had a loyal following.

Bennie, at the piano, nervously settled himself, waiting for the noise to cease. Then Hal broke into one of his new songs, those songs that are as famous now as "Eli, Eli." The reaction of the crowd was amazing. Some wept, some applauded, others sat silent, wondering. It was so unexpected, so sudden, that before they realized it Hal had bowed quietly and left the room.

Later he sang several jazz songs, but after the applause he did not join his patrons at their tables; he left the room in spite of clamorous shouts of "C'mere, Hal," "Have a lil one with us, Hal?" "Draw up a chair, Hal."

Sitting at one of the tables were Lord and Lady Greville, Nancy Bromley, and John Taylor. If Levering had noticed the presence of these companions of his week-end at Constance Corthwaite's, he gave no sign.

"I told Constance he'd be back at it within a year," remarked Nancy Bromley, when Levering had left the floor and the lights had again been brightened. "A taste of good fortune to a man like that always goes to the head. . . . Cantor! It is to laugh."

The others were silent; then Taylor spoke: "That's not the man we knew, though. Don't you get the difference? Those first songs were superb. The man who wrote that music is a genius."

"Changed, nothing! That's the same old Levering. I'll prove it to you." Nancy called a waiter and told him to ask Mr. Levering if he would speak to Miss Bromley.

"What are you going to do?" asked Greville.

"Never mind; you'll see when he comes," answered Nancy.

In a few moments Levering appeared and walked through the aisles of tables to where the party was sitting. He did not cross the floor in his old swaggering manner, receiving homage as he went; but with dignity he walked and, reaching the table, bowed quietly to the four people.

"Pull up a chair and have a drink," invited Taylor.

"No, thank you, just the same. Is there anything I can do for you?"

"I am having some people down over the week-end of the twenty-third, Mr. Levering," said Nancy. "I should like very much to have you come."

"That is very kind of you, Miss Bromley," replied Levering quietly; "I should be very glad to come on Saturday evening and entertain your guests. My charge for such an affair is one thousand dollars. I presume you will not want me after eleven-thirty. I must be back in town early, for I sing in a concert Sunday afternoon."

Nancy's face was crimson as she answered, "That will be all right, Mr. Levering." Hal bowed and, turning, walked away.

John Taylor looked with amusement at the discomfited

Nancy and then at the proud set of the head of the Jew who was now a Jew, a Prince of Israel, and a verse that he had learned as a child came to him: "For thou hast made him a little lower than the angels, and hast crowned him with glory and honour."

BULLDOG

By ROGER DANIELS

From *Saturday Evening Post*

NEXT case!" Judge Barringer was brisk. Word had come to him that the railbirds were plentiful down in the marshes of the Big Swamp and he was going hunting. It was Monday morning, and the police-court docket was an unusually large one even for Monday morning.

Out of the group of Negroes waiting in the prisoners' pen, a group so large this morning that it overflowed on to the sunny porch beyond, edged a giant Negro in answer to the turnkey's signal. Rather, he could have been said to plough his way through, for the men and women ranged before him separated as does soft loam under the impelling blade of the ploughshare. Once free of the crowd, the man stepped forward with an easy but awkward shuffle until he stood directly in front of the judge's desk. At that moment Judge Barringer was intently scanning the docket slip and figuring how soon he would be able to get away.

The prisoner's massive head might have been chiselled with an ax from a block of black marble, and not too finely chiselled, at that. It had the sheen of black marble, and was square and formidable, that head, viewed from any angle. The jaw was square and protruding, the forehead was square and receding, the nose was broad and flat. Just now the mouth was spread wide across the shining ebony face.

"Mawnin', Jedge," the big Negro said with a sheepish grin. "Heah Ah is!"

Judge Barringer's head jerked up instantly. He was not accustomed to mawkish familiarity from his charges, nor did he fail to administer stinging rebukes, when such were attempted, in the amount of sentence given as well as in verbal reproof to any and all who might presume to take such liberties. But as he took cognizance of the figure that loomed before him, his expression changed. The frown that had furrowed his forehead did not linger. It could not be said that he smiled, but a look of real recognition, kindly and forbearing, came into his eyes. One hardly frowns at an old acquaintance.

"Well, Bulldog," Judge Barringer said, calling the big Negro by the only name he had, "I haven't seen you for the longest time. Where have you been hiding?"

Bulldog grinned, even a broader grin than before, so that his white teeth showed in a semicircle. "Same place wheah Ah usually is, Jedge Barringer, Yo' Honour. Down on the Fahm wiv Cap'n Jim." The Farm was the chain-gang camp.

"It's too bad, Bulldog," the judge said, shaking his head; "you're big enough to keep out of trouble and mind your own business."

"Yas-suh, Jedge Barringer, tha's jes' what Ah was a-doin', mindin' mah business, an' Ah jes' gits me into trouble jes' the same. Seems lak me an' trouble sticks together lak a pair ob dice." He grinned again. The grin became infectious and Judge Barringer took it up. Even the stolid fat Sam Perks, the turnkey, grinned. Then came a general titter, to be brought to a sudden halt by the judge's staccato gavel.

Judge Barringer had suddenly remembered the railbirds and the Big Swamp. He was off for a three-day hunt, and there were several things he must attend to personally before turning over the affairs of court *pro tem.* to the clerk. With still more than half a heavy Monday docket to be heard from, there was no time for amusement this morning.

"Well, where's the witness against Bulldog? Is the Court to be kept waiting? What has he to say for himself and why isn't he here?"

The patrolman who had arrested the big Negro stepped forward.

"The witness is still in the hospital, judge," he said. "Pretty badly done up and they don't know when he will be out. I guess the case will be continued until he can appear."

"Waste of time," Judge Barringer said crisply. "I know Bulldog." He turned abruptly to the big Negro. "Well, what happened this time? Tell us your side of the story."

Bulldog shuffled from one foot to the other. "It was thisaway, Jedge, Yo' Honour. The las' six months what you give me, they ain't up till to-morrow. Cap'n Jim, he startin' the big 'Geechee Canal to-morrow. Come las' Friday, Cap'n Jim, he say, 'Bulldog, yo' bin a mighty good nigger this trip. Ah'm lettin' yo' out a couple ob days ahaid ob time. Mebby you-all be back so's we kin staht wif the new 'Geechee Canal together.' Ah reckon dat Cap'n Jim be right, Jedge, Yo' Honour, cause heah Ah is!"

As Bulldog broke into another of those infectious grins, it was necessary for Judge Barringer to rap for order, although he was forced to cough to hide his own mirth. Any other morning Bulldog might have been highly amusing entertainment, but the railbirds were calling from the Big Swamp.

"So much for that," Judge Barringer said. "Tell us what happened. Why is this man in the hospital?"

"It was thisaway, Jedge, Yo' Honour," Bulldog repeated the formula: "Ah gits me home an' Ah finds that a yaller Washin'ton nigger been shinin' up to my Sally while Ah bin down on de Fahm. Yassuh, Jedge, Yo' Honour, he's shinin' when I gits home. I comes in de front do' an' he goes out de back. All Ah done, Jedge, was jes' flicked dat nigger, 'cause he don' move fas' enough."

"You just flicked him. What with?" Judge Barringer asked, as the term was a new one to him.

"Wif the back ob mah han', Jedge, thisaway." Bulldog made a snapping gesture with one hand; "jes' lak yo'd flick on a fly, Jedge. Dat's all Ah done to dat measly little nigger. He wasn't big enough to hit."

"So you just flicked him like you'd flick off a fly?" Judge Barringer questioned.

"Yas-suh, dat's all, Jedge, Yo' Honour," Bulldog answered.

"And now this man is in the hospital and they don't know when he will be able to appear. It seems to me that the last time you were here you said you had just made a pass at a man and when they got him to the hospital he was cut in ten different places." Judge Barringer leaned back with an air of resignation. "Bulldog, you're hopeless. I'm going to send you back to Captain Jim for another six months. For the general safety of the community at large, you'd better do your flicking on the new Ogeeche Canal."

"Yas-suh, Jedge, Yo' Honour," Bulldog answered.

Such a remark coming from any other prisoner would have

been impertinence and would have been swiftly treated as such. But between old friends there are no impertinences. Bulldog turned away with a grin and ploughed his way through the crowd in the prisoners' pen to the bench in the rear. Two Negroes got up hastily to make room for him.

The business of the court moved along swiftly. The rail-birds were calling to the judge's bench from the Big Swamp. Bulldog, on the prisoners' bench, was thinking of the convict captain. He liked Captain Jim. "Ah guess he knowed Ah'd be back in time all right," he mused to himself. "Well, Cap'n Jim, Ah'm comin'."

Later that afternoon there was a meeting between the two. "Been waitin' all mawnin' for you, Bulldog," was the convict captain's greeting. "Just you run along and get your work clothes and then you can go over and clean up my quarters."

The regular routine of the check-in was usually dispensed with in Bulldog's case, as it was to-day. Once safe in the convict camp, he caused no trouble. He did the work of seven ordinary men and had withal the stolid patience of a work horse. Only when he was at liberty was Bulldog dangerous, like a colt turned out to grass which suddenly remembers that he can kick. Captain Jim had been busy for several minutes with the other prisoners before he realized that Bulldog still stood back of him, shifting uneasily from foot to foot. He recalled that the same thing had happened on one other occasion and grinned inwardly.

He half turned. "Bulldog, you go over and tell old Henry," Cap'n Jim said, "to give you something to eat."

"Yas-suh, Cap'n Jim," Bulldog said with alacrity, his eyes brightening and his lower lip hanging expectantly at the thought of food. "Dat's what Ah was hopin' yo' was goin' to say, Cap'n Jim. Ah ain't eat since las' night." The sheepish grin spread over his face. "Seems lak Ah cain't relish de bacon and grits what dey gives up to dat city jail. Dey don't know how to feed a nigger lak yo' does, Cap'n Jim."

"So that's why you came back so soon, is it?" the convict captain said with a laugh.

"No, suh," Bulldog answered soberly, his brows knit and his lips protruding. "Ah didn' come back fer no perticular reason, Cap'n Jim. Now Ah stops and figgers it out, Ah guess it jus' happen." His face lit up with an idea as he asked with all the wonder of a small boy, "Cap'n Jim, you-all didn' put no sign on me to make me come back?"

"If you don't get out of here quick I'll put a sign on you you won't forget," the captain exploded.

"Yas-suh," Bulldog called back to him over his shoulder, being already half a dozen paces on his way.

Ten minutes later, garbed in his chain-gang work clothes, with a chain dangling from his waist, Bulldog poked his head through the open window of the cook shanty.

"Ev'nin', Uncle Henry," he said in a mellifluous tone to a gray-haired Negro in cap and apron who was ladling the contents of a huge pot set at the back of the big square stove.

Uncle Henry looked up, his face crinkled with smiles that seemed to close his eyes until they were shiny, laughing dots.

"Dat you-all, Bulldog? Sho' nuff I jes' dis minute 'cided you done dis'point Cap'n Jim an' slumped a fresh ham bone an' two pounds ob meat on it into dat soup. But, Bulldog, boy, for you I fishes it out."

"Yas-suh, Uncle Henry, Ah knowed yo' ain't goin' to see Bulldog starve. Mebbe yo' has a handful ob dem yaller sweet yams." Bulldog's mouth fairly dripped.

"Hush up dat fool talk, boy," the old cook chuckled. "Don' it do my heart good to see them what likes they vittles? Bulldog, yo' am de most satisfactoriest meal hound what I know." Uncle Henry doubled with laughter, in which Bulldog, his mouth already crammed full, joined heartily.

Uncle Henry sincerely liked Bulldog. The giant never referred to the fact that Uncle Henry was a lifer. For twenty-seven years he had been a convict-camp cook. It was as a young man that, under the influence of ten-cent white mule, he had lifted a chair against his legally married wife. In Uncle Henry's mind that dreadful event had always remained as an accident. His whole life was being freely given in atonement. When some of the younger convicts taunted him and called him the old murderer, they left a hurt that remained with Uncle Henry for weeks.

Bulldog shuffled toward the door finally with a sigh. "Ef Ah swallows another swallow, Uncle Henry, Ah busts."

"Boy, come again when yo's hungry; yo' makes me proud."
The old cook chortled, looking after him.

As Bulldog turned into the lane to Captain Jim's quarters,
a small whitewashed bungalow, two hounds bayed a ferocious
greeting.

"Yo' Lady Belle, yo' Junie, hush yo' mouf!" Bulldog bayed
back. Then he grinned and tossed the remains of the fresh ham
bone over the chicken-wire inclosure. The hounds left off
their racket instantly and pounced on the bone, while Bulldog
leaned complacently against the inclosure and eyed them
with satisfaction.

"Dem houn' dawgs go after dat bone lak it was a runaway
nigger," he commented with approval. Though every other
Negro on the place looked upon the bloodhounds as a possible
Nemesis, such a thought had never entered Bulldog's massive
head. To him they were companions, and the fact that he was
allowed to feed them was proof conclusive that he was above
the ordinary regulations of the convict camp.

He turned from the hounds presently and made his way to
a small outhouse, where he procured a pail, a whitewash
brush and a scraper. Captain Jim liked things to look spick-
and-span, and the timbers supporting the bungalow porch
had acquired a reddish-brown mud colour from the recent
rains. Bulldog proceeded at the first job that he knew would
catch Captain Jim's eye. He knew on which side his bread
was buttered.

> "Wasn' it sad to see *Titanic* sinkin' down,
> Wasn' it sad to see *Titanic* sinkin' down;
> Husban's an' wives, little chilluns los' dey lives;
> Wasn' it sad to see *Titanic* sinkin' down."

Verse after verse, in the droning singsong of the old spiri-
tuals, kept time to the whitewash brush. The underpinning of
the bungalow was certainly going to catch Captain Jim's eye
when he came up the lane.

Two and a half hours later Bulldog took up his accustomed
place in line on the way to the mess hall. If he had recently
gorged until he couldn't swallow another swallow, that was
not going to interfere with his doing full justice to Uncle
Henry's supper. And later, spread out at full length in the

bunk room over the mess hall, he lay on his back and slept
the sleep of the just. Sleeping on one's back is said to be
conducive to snoring, but Bulldog was a silent sleeper. If
he was primitive in his mode of living, so, too, he was primitive
in his sleeping hours. Dead to the world he was, yet ready to
be instantly awake.

Once upon a time a fellow convict night guard had taken
the liberty to bring his stick across the soles of Bulldog's bare
feet as he lay asleep. It was a common trick, and as the sleepers were chained to their flat bunks, the guard had only to
step back out of harm's way, while the startled sleeper rubbed
open his eyes and bellowed revenge to the accompaniment of
catcalls from the other prisoners. But the unlucky guard who
had attempted the prank at Bulldog's expense carried an eye
that squinted forever after as a warning to all and sundry
that the giant was equally dangerous, asleep or awake. It
must have been that Bulldog had heard the swish of the
descending stick in his sleep, for the smack of it against the
soles of his feet and the whoosh of his hand striking the un-
witting guard had been nearly simultaneous. So Bulldog slept
the sleep of the just.

He was awake with the sun, and lay there for half an hour
studying his toes, even as a small boy of five or six months
studies them. When a man can do that intently for half an
hour, his conscience isn't bothering him. So to breakfast
presently and to take his place at the head of the squad line.
They were starting the new Ogeechee Canal and Bulldog
knew that Captain Jim meant him to set the pace. It was an
accepted fact that a squad line with Bulldog at its head got
about a week and a half of digging done in a week. It was
useless to try to drive labour out of Negro chain gangs, but
to lead it out of them—that was different. It explained why
Captain Jim needed Bulldog. Winter was coming along and
the new drainage canal must be finished before the flood
rains of spring.

The beginning was to be made some three miles away
from camp, and they marched out in formation, five men to a
squad. The chain-gang squad of five meant two ahead, two
behind, and one in the middle. Each prisoner had a leg iron
around his right ankle, to which was attached the four-foot
squad chain. When they were on the march the squad chains

of each squad were linked together in a common ring, so that if a man attempted to bolt on the road he would have to take four of his companions with him. Even if the bolt were successful, it was poor work for five men, chained together, to beat off pursuit in the swamp. When they worked, each man carried his own chain hooked to a snaffle sewed to his tunic.

But the work line was watched over by a convict guard whose duty it was to sit on a palmetto stump all day with a sawed-off shotgun across his knees. Sometimes a prisoner escaped, but not often.

Bulldog, at the head of tne line, had never tried to escape. When his time was up he had always hurried to town in high glee, but with a certain remote feeling that sooner or later he would be coming back to Cap'n Jim. Once back, he was content to work out his time. He liked to work, he gloried in the fact that he could do the work of seven.

"Ah reckon, big boy, dey hangs yo' dis time." Chinkapin, so named because of his size, was the middle prisoner in Bulldog's squad. He had spoken irrelevantly to the landscape, a dreary waste of cypress knees and cabbage palmetto extending half a dozen miles to the row of live oaks that marked the river line. No one in the squad paid any attention.

"Ah reckon, big boy, dey hangs yo' dis time!" Chinkapin repeated.

This time Bulldog half turned his head to speak, but as he did so three turkey buzzards flapped crazily out of the swamp just ahead and absorbed his attention for the moment. By the time the buzzards had settled out of sight again Bulldog had forgotten Chinkapin.

But the little convict was not to be so readily neglected. "Ah reckon, big boy, dey hangs yo' dis time," he intoned once more.

"Hangs who?" Bulldog demanded bluntly. "Chinkapin, yo' half-size nigger, shut yo' mouf befo' Ah sicks dem eye-pickin' buzzards on yo'!"

"Ah ain' kill nobody," Chinkapin answered glibly; "dem flip-flop death angels ain' lookin' fo' me."

"What yo' mean yo' ain' kill nobody? What lie yo' fixin' to tell now?" Bulldog had stopped and was facing his tormentor. "Who hangs who for what? Yo' tells de truf or Ah smacks yo' cross-eyed."

Chinkapin had an active mind. Although he had never seen him, he had heard about the squint-eyed night guard. Bulldog towered above him. In one glance Chinkapin made full appraisal. Bulldog's hand was the size of a ham. There was no going back now, for the big Negro was evidently riled. The three buzzards taking wing had been an omen. Chinkapin should have realized that before he pressed his point.

"Ah ain' lyin', Bulldog," the diminutive one countered quickly. "My gal done tol' me las' night when she brung mah clo's. Ah'm leavin' Sa'day."

"Who cares when yo' leaves, han'ful? Did Ah ax yo' when yo' leaves? Who hangs for what? Yo' answer me dat in de whole truf or I slaps you pas' an' presen' an' back again!"

Chinkapin shivered. The delay had stopped the whole squad line, and back along the line a convict guard was shouting. But Bulldog was intent only on the little Negro before him.

"Does yo' answer me, Chinkapin, or does I knock you loose?" One hand, open palmed, was raised threateningly.

"Dat Washin'ton nigger died," Chinkapin blurted out in shaking fear. "My gal tol' me when she come las' night."

Bulldog's hand dropped to his side. He stood absolutely motionless, looking blankly at the quivering messenger of bad news. For a full minute he stood there, and to Chinkapin it seemed that death itself was standing there.

"Is yo' tellin' de whole truf?" Bulldog demanded.

"So help me!" quavered the terror-stricken Chinkapin.

"If yo' ain'——"

But the sentence was never finished. One of the guards, alarmed at the sudden halt, had fired into the air as a signal to the others. The report of the gun had an electrical effect on Bulldog. If the Washington Negro had died, he would hang. The three turkey buzzards, frightened by the gun, came winging past. Out of the corner of one eye Bulldog saw them.

"Stan's yo' back!" he commanded quickly, at the same time shoving the four other members of the squad into a huddle. That gave him about six feet of chain to work on. Swiftly he bent. The chain was coiled like magic first around one forearm and then the other. There was a grunt, the ring of metal, and the chain had parted. Bulldog dived headlong off the trail into the palmetto scrub just as the first convict guard came running up. He fired both barrels of the sawed-off shotgun point-blank in the general direction of Bulldog's dive. Then he reloaded and fired again, keeping up the process until the other guards arrived. In a circle they closed in on the place. But the turned-back palmetto scrub revealed nothing. Bulldog was gone.

It was Chinkapin who turned an almost pasty gray face toward heaven as he exclaimed, "May de Lawd have mercy on dis pore little nigger's soul, Ah didn' mean no hahm!"

When he dived, Bulldog landed in the lush swamp grass and proceeded through it bellywise like a snake. He made a hundred yards that way before he got to his feet and broke into a run. The palmetto scrub was slightly higher than his head as he pressed forward ankle-deep in the slime. He came to a halt presently to get his second wind, knowing that he was safe for the immediate present. The convict guards couldn't leave the chain gang. They would have to summon Captain Jim and a posse. By that time Bulldog would be well on his way. But where?

Half an hour later, ploughing his way through the swamp grass to the river, he was still pondering the question when his ear caught the far-away bay of a hound.

"Dere's dat posse, sho' nuff," Bulldog grunted, and put on speed. He was nearing the river and higher ground, and the going was easier. The Big Swamp, on both sides of the river, was mostly tidal backwash. There wasn't a habitation for miles ahead, and once he got to the river, Bulldog felt he could swim downstream and lose himself in the swamps on the other side. Unless the crime were a very terrible one, a white man's posse wouldn't break its neck searching the swamps for one chain-gang Negro more or less. Bulldog, for all his uncouthness, had a rough-and-ready knowledge of the customs of the country. But for one day the chase would be hot; the cry of the hounds, giving tongue, assured the big Negro of that. Even now the dogs seemed to have gained on him, and he stopped to listen. They were much nearer than they had been before. Bulldog's worried face changed to reveal a grin.

"Dem houn' dawgs ain' on no leash. Cap'n Jim done loosed 'em!" He chortled aloud as if to convince himself that his ears had not deceived him. He cocked his head on one side and listened intently. "Sho' nuff! Dat's Lady Belle and Junie."

The river line, with its row of live oaks festooned with Spanish moss, was a scant half mile away now, and the going underfoot was solid. Bulldog broke into a steady run. In a few minutes he had reached the first of the live oaks. Back in the glory days of the old South, these magnificent trees had been set out by some long-since-departed rice planter. Now their branches interlaced.

Bulldog swung himself into a tree, got up among the middle branches, ran out a good-sized limb like some giant monkey, paused, and then swung himself into the next tree. The hounds were close now; he could hear them as he climbed. But they were running the trail far ahead of the posse. Through the second tree and into the third swung the ape-like giant. He kept on until he had reached the fifth, from which he dropped swiftly to the ground. He found a stout section of an old branch, tested it with the weight of his hand, and then swung back in a circle to lie in wait beside his trail.

He did not wait long. The hounds went by in full cry, Junie in the lead, Lady Belle at his heels. The bloodhound cares neither for sight nor sound, but follows his nose. Bulldog closed in behind them and grinned broadly as they came to a baffled halt at the foot of the live oak.

"Yo' Lady Belle, yo' Junie, hush dat racket!"

At the sound of his voice the hounds whirled to face him, baying excitedly at this strange turn of affairs.

"Yo' heah me? Hush dat racket!" Brandishing the broken limb, Bulldog stepped toward them. "Ah feeds yo' wiv mah own han's and yo' runs me down jes' lak Ah was a runaway convic' nigger! Junie, Lady Belle, fo' dat Ah frails yo'!"

The broken limb descended in a sidelong swish and Junie was bowled over. A split second later, in the midst of a protracted howl, Lady Belle got the same treatment. Both hounds scrambled to their feet whimpering.

"Hush dat noise! Yo' ain' hurt!" Again the tree branch came swishing down, but this time above their heads. The hounds were cowed. "Tracks me down lak a runaway convic' nigger, will yo'? Now yo' gits!" Bulldog grunted savagely. "Home, Junie! Home, Lady Belle, befo' Ah cuts loose an' frails yo' good!"

With tails down, both hounds turned and fled. Bulldog sent the tree branch soaring through the air after them. It lit at their heels and sent them scurrying faster.

"Why fo' Cap'n Jim let loose dem houn' dawgs? He might knowed Ah'd frail 'em," the big Negro commented philosophically. It was common knowledge that a bloodhound loose on the trail could be beaten back, or frailed, as usage had it. But time for philosophy was short. Bulldog went down to the river at a jog trot, hesitated at its brink and then dived overboard into the deep water that cut into the live-oak bank. He came up with a snort and struck out for the opposite shore.

The tide was strong and carried him well downstream, which was to his advantage in putting distance between himself and his pursuers. It was in searching for a convenient landing place that he spied a boat pulled up in a bayou. That meant someone else was there, and he allowed himself to be swept farther downstream. It also offered him means of getting upstream with much less trouble than through the swamp. He cut into shore presently, and keeping well under the bank, worked his way around to the boat. It was high and dry, and a pair of oars were tucked under the seats.

Just as Bulldog reached for them there was the reddish-brown flash of a copperhead that had been sunning itself. Outraged at being disturbed, the reptile struck. But the giant Negro was quicker and snatched his hand back out of harm's way.

"Jes' fo' dat, little red snake, Ah whuffs yo'," Bulldog grunted.

Sensing danger, the copperhead squirmed for the gunwale of the boat and the safety of the river. Once more the big Negro was quicker. His heel descended and the snake's head was crushed.

"Whuff!" he grunted. "What Ah tell yo'?" Reaching down, he picked up the remains and tossed them on the sun-baked bank. The whole little drama had consumed not more than ten seconds. Bulldog shoved the boat into the river and clambered quietly aboard.

Once in the current, he pulled upstream, using a long, steady, untiring stroke. As a pickaninny, a flat-bottomed river rowboat had been his hobbyhorse. It would be a full hour before the posse would get within sight of the river, he figured, even if it came that far, now that the hounds were no longer giving cry to guide it. Lady Belle and Junie had cut it straight for home.

Ten miles above the place where he had first struck the river, Bulldog pulled the boat into a bayou, beached it well up among a covering screen of scrub palmetto, and then crawled under it and went to sleep.

The frogs were singing the sun to sleep when he awoke hungry. All along he hadn't had any idea at all where he was going, but that was a matter which could easily remain indeterminate. The gnawing at his stomach was serious. He would starve to death in the swamp; so, as a hiding place, the swamp was cast aside.

"Ah got to git me goin'," he mumbled to himself, his lips protruding as they always did when he was perplexed. In an hour it would be dark. He decided to wait. Presently, in the growing dusk, he dragged the boat down to the river, and tucking the oars under the seats as he had found them, he gave it a heave that sent it well out into the stream. He watched while the current caught it up, nosed it around and bore it from sight in the gloom. "Dey don' git me fo' stealin' no boats," he grumbled dispassionately, "but I sho' would relish me some food."

The yellowest of yellow moons, as big as a house, bathed the palmettos with metallic beauty when Bulldog silently and sullenly struck off through the swamp, heading south. He was going down to the sea, but there was no romance in his going. It was the urge of his stomach that led him that way rather than striking inland. The sea coast below the Big Swamp was a series of wind-swept savannas. It was broken by innumerable inlets and fringed with islands. But there were no settlements along this strip for miles and he would be safe from the sight of men. The beaches offered clams, crawfish, and prawn. He had never been a fugitive before. He was lonely for the companionship of his kind. Most of all, he was hungry.

Hour after hour he went on and on through the swamp, another shadow among a million, yet the only one that moved. His gait was rapid, but not hurried, a relentless, ever-forward swinging rhythm of motion. If he took bearings, he took them subconsciously. He made no plan. At the sea he would find something to eat. His mind travelled no farther than that. He even forgot that he was lonely.

A sudden cry through the stillness of the night sent dread loneliness over him like a pall and stirred every fibre of him, so that he quivered where he stood, as frozen as the other million shadows about him. At once the night had a myriad of tiny sounds that mounted and mounted, until, joined with the pulsations of his own body, they seemed to roar in his ears.

But the cry that had startled him had been human. He sensed that, as he stood listening to hear it again, stood like a statue in the moonlight, motionless and breathless. Had the cry come from above or below him, from before or behind him? He couldn't tell, but as he strained his senses he became gradually aware that he was not alone in the swamp. The moon was well overhead now, and though it was half as bright as day in the upper world, every shadow was as black as pitch. Insects droned, the palmetto leaves caught a fitful breeze and rasped dully, unseen things crackled in the undergrowth.

"Whar yo' is?"

Bulldog jumped two yards at the sound of his own voice, not realizing that he had experienced a psychological moment, that the very stress he had put on his senses of perception had caused him to speak out, just as a householder who fancies he has heard someone outside his door will call out, "Who's there?" And while he stood there unable to decide whether to remain or run, that human cry came to him again, this time almost at his feet.

His teeth chattered now from mental if not bodily fear. Sounds do not come from nothing; and yet, strain his eyes as he would, he saw only a cabbage palmetto and its jet-black shadow in the place from whence it seemed to him the cry had come. Still he stared at the shadow. Something was there. As he stared, he saw it take form. Slowly at first it grew round and whitish, then its shape became more definite. Bulldog was hypnotized by it now, glued to the spot where he stood. He tried to ask it what it was, but his lips refused to move. He was cold now—cold and shivering. Then, with a rush, his breath came back to him. The thing had moved and was looking at him and he knew what he saw.

"Bulldog!" the thing gasped.

"Jedge Barringer! Ah thought yo' was a ghos'!"

"Thank God you've come," the judge said weakly. "I've had an accident. I'm shot in the leg. Not bad, but I lost a lot of blood before I got the flow stopped. I guess I've crawled ten miles trying to find the river and my boat. But I'm all right now. Who's with you? Captain Jim?"

Bulldog heard and yet didn't hear. Judge Barringer had been hunting and had shot himself in the leg. He had tried to reach his boat and had failed. The boat in question was the one Bulldog had found and appropriated; the boat he had later set adrift. The judge thought Bulldog had been sent out to look for him by Captain Jim.

"You black hyena, don't stand there like that!" Judge Barringer exploded feebly. "I'm no ghost. Call Captain Jim."

"Jedge, Yo' Honour, dey ain' nobody heah but me," said Bulldog, simply stating a fact.

"You mean to say you came for me alone?" Judge Barringer was suffering from a terrible ordeal and was not thinking very clearly. "But how did you know——"

He stopped. Bulldog had not come for him. No one had come for him. He had slipped off quietly to hunt alone, expecting to go on that night to Bryan Neck. The whole idea of someone coming for him had been a sort of nightmare of hope when his brain had failed to function properly. He might still be suffering from hallucinations.

"Bulldog!" He spoke to make sure this towering Negro before him was real.

"Yas-suh, Jedge, Yo' Honour." Time and circumstances could not alter custom, and Bulldog's answer was a tribute to habit.

"Bulldog, what are you doing here?"

"Jedge, Yo' Honour, it's thisaway," the big Negro began.

"That's enough," the judge cut in with a sigh of relief. "As long as it's you, I don't give a damn what you're doing here. Just give me a hand and help me get to the river. I've got a boat there in a little bayou between two live oaks."

Bulldog bent and helped the judge to a sitting posture. The judge groaned and then swore.

"Dat boat, Jedge Barringer?" Bulldog asked. "Dat was'n de boat wiv de red paint on de oar handles?"

"Yes, that's the one. So you know where it is? That makes

things easier." Judge Barringer was fast being able to think once more.

"De las' time Ah see dat boat, Jedge, Yo' Honour, she was gwine down de middle ob de 'Geechee all by itself," Bulldog explained honestly.

"You mean adrift?"

"Yas-suh, Jedge, Yo' Honour, jes' lak a ol' tree log."

"All right." It was no time to bewail the loss of a boat. "Then you can take me back in your boat, Bulldog."

"Me, Jedge? Ah swum."

Judge Barringer put out a quick hand to Bulldog's leg. The big Negro's clothes were dry. "You swam across? When?" he asked warily.

"Ah reckon it mus' 'a' been a couple hours befo' dinner-time," Bulldog answered. He knew from experience it was useless to try to lie to Judge Barringer. But the thought of dinnertime prompted him to add hopefully, "Yo' ain't got nuthin' to eat on yo', has yo', Jedge, Yo' Honour?"

"Do you mean to tell me you broke away from the chain gang?"

"No, suh!" Bulldog answered hurriedly. "Ah didn' do nuthin' lak dat. It was thisaway, Jedge, Yo' Honour: Dat Washin'ton nigger die an' Ah cain' see no use in cravin' to hang by mah neck."

Judge Barringer was thoroughly aroused now. "Who told you that nigger died?"

"Chinkapin."

"Where?"

"He's on de chain gang."

"I don't believe it!"

"Befo' de Lawd, Ah wouldn' lie to yo', Jedge Barringer, an' yo' knows it!" Bulldog said fervently.

"I mean I don't believe that nigger died," the judge explained.

"If yo' believes it or don' believes it, Jedge, Yo' Honour, dat don' save mah neck."

"Well, we'll see about that when we get back. In the meantime you can have my word for it, that nigger didn't die."

"Yas-suh, Jedge, Yo' Honour. Ah'll take yo' word for it— on'y, we ain' goin' back," said Bulldog emphatically.

"Do you mean to say you aren't going to help me get out

of here—that you'd go away and leave me?" Judge Barringer looked straight up into the face of the big Negro.

"No, suh! Ah ain' goin' away an' leave yo', Jedge Barringer, but also Ah ain' goin' back wiv yo' an' git hung by de neck for no yaller Washin'ton nigger . . . Ain' yo' even got a san'widge, Jedge?"

Judge Barringer was rapidly, in his weakened state, becoming exasperated. "Now, you listen to me, Bulldog, and don't be a fool. I don't want you to hang any more than you want to hang. Chinkapin never told the truth in his life. If he said that nigger died, he meant it as a ioke, and you jumped to con- clusions and——"

"No, suh, Jedge, Ah ain' jump to nuthing. Jes when Chink- apin say dat nigger die three flip-flop death-angel buzzards come flyin' right ovah mah haid. . . . If yo' ain' even got a san'widge, we goes hungry, both of us; but, Jedge, we ain' gwine back fo' to git me hung." Bulldog was adamant on that point.

"If I had a gun, Bulldog, I'd shoot you!" Judge Barringer threatened.

"Yas-suh, Jedge, Yo' Honour," Bulldog agreed solemnly. "But dat wouldn't be gittin' me hung by de neck. Ah saw oncet a lynch nigger an' his neck was stretch out as long as mah arm. No, suh, Jedge Barringer, when Ah dies Ah dies so dey can put me in de coffin beautiful."

"Can't you do something besides talk like a fool?" Judge Barringer felt that his strength was slipping away from him. The hope that had come with Bulldog's arrival was fast disap- pearing. His head sank resignedly to his chest. His brain was beginning to grow muddled again from sheer exhaustion, when he felt that Bulldog had taken him by the shoulder. From a long way off he could hear the big Negro's voice.

"Jedge Barringer, don' yo' go passin' out. Ah'll git you home someways. Gives me yo' arm an' I totes you to Ossa- baw."

Ossabaw? That was an island at the mouth of the river fully fifteen miles distant. Now Judge Barringer, semi- conscious as he was, knew that Bulldog was crazy. If he should be taken to Ossabaw, he would be farther away from help than ever. He would stay rather where he was. It was warm here, and quiet.

But when the black giant reached down and picked him up he made no protest. He was not even aware that he was being carried. Under this new burden, Bulldog found the going heavy in the swamp and made for the higher ground near the river bank. It was the wind coming up from the sea some two hours later that had a reviving effect on Judge Barringer. He opened his eyes to see a shadow a yard away.

"Is that you, Bulldog?" he asked.

"Yas-suh, Jedge, dis is me."

"If you won't do anything, why do you stay here?" Judge Barringer said petulantly in his weakness.

"Shucks, Jedge, we ain' heah no mo'; we's halfway to Ossabaw. Yo' weighs like ce-ment, Jedge. When Ah gits me a li'l' res' we goes on."

"Halfway to Ossabaw?"

"Yas-suh, Jedge."

Judge Barringer lapsed again. It was useless to try to argue with the crazy hyena. If Bulldog had made up his mind to take him to Ossabaw, he would have to go, being unable to resist. He saw a picture of himself as a fellow Crusoe, fugitive from justice with a chain-gang Negro. But if that leg of his lost its soreness, if he ever was able to get around again, he swore that it would be much better for Bulldog to have hanged. A sudden jolt, a feeling that he was floating, and he knew that they were on their way.

When he opened his eyes again they were still on the go. His injured leg—it had been a flesh wound in the calf— was numb and did not pain him now. It occurred to him that he might even be able to walk. But the side-to-side sway, as he was carried along, seemed much easier; and besides, there was little weight to his body now; he felt as light as a feather. Years after, he was to look back at that moment and wonder what ever had put such a crazy notion in his head. He closed his eyes again.

"Jedge Barringer! . . . Jedge Barringer!" Bulldog was calling to him, but it was cold and he did not want to get up.

"Jedge Barringer!"

That was not Bulldog's voice. He roused himself with a great effort and sat up. A bent old Negro was on his knees before him, his face a picture of despair. Suddenly it was wreathed in smiles of thankfulness.

"Jedge Barringer, yo' is alive, thank de Lawd! Ah been callin' yo' fo' de longes' time until Ah jes' 'bout reckon yo' was a corp'."

"Daddy Ike!" Judge Barringer gasped. "Where did you come from? Where's Bulldog?"

"Down on de plantation, Jedge." The old Negro's face looked puzzled. "How come yo' don' know Ah ain' nebber lef' Ossabaw, Jedge?"

And then Judge Barringer remembered. Ossabaw Island was the seat of the old Depford plantation, now only a relic of the past, and Daddy Ike was the oldest Negro in the section. He still lived in the old ramshackle slave quarters and eked out a living by fishing and raising truck. Everyone knew Daddy Ike, and yet Judge Barringer had forgotten until now. This was the reason they had come to Ossabaw. It was dawn. Bulldog had been carrying him all night. He owed his life to the big Negro.

Daddy Ike misread the judge's thoughts. "Bulldog he gone," the old Negro said quickly. "Yo' fergit all 'bout him, Jedge Barringer, while Ah helps yo' to mah boat."

"That crazy nigger's gone? Where?"

"Yas-suh, Jedge, Bulldog's de craziest nigger in de worl'. Why fo' yo' an' me gib two goobers wheah dat fool nigger's gone? Us is gwine to git yo' home, Jedge. How's yo' laig?" Daddy Ike changed the subject.

Judge Barringer smiled. "Daddy Ike, you old rascal, don't lie to me. Bulldog saved my life. Where is he?"

"Jedge Barringer, Ah don' know. De las' time Ah seed him he was sittin' in mah house eatin' hominy grits an' side meat an' yams an' black-eye peas; an' lissen to me, Jedge, if Ah don't git yo' home and git back dat crazy nigger's gwine to eat me into de po'house. But Ah don' know wheah he is now."

"All right," Judge Barringer laughed. "We'll see about that later. Where's your boat, Daddy Ike? If you'll give me a hand I think I can hobble."

"Dat's right, Jedge, lets us go. Heah's de boat. Bulldog he swum across to de island an' like to scairt me senseless, comin' up to mah do' in dem chain-gang clo's. Ah'd 'a' come across to yo' right away, Jedge, but dat crazy Bulldog said Ah got to feed him fust. If we don' get yo' home he'll eat up all mah winter rations!"

With the old Negro's help, Judge Barringer managed to bear his weight on the uninjured leg and hobble down the few feet of bank to the boat. Ossabaw Island lay like a black blob in the early morning mist a quarter of a mile away. But their way lay in the opposite direction, and Daddy Ike, for all his eighty-odd years, lost no time in pushing off. Bulldog had told him to bring back a pair of overalls and a shirt, and he wanted to get back as soon as possible before the ravenous giant ate him "into de po'house." Also he was genuinely alarmed for the escaped convict's sake and wanted him to get away before the law came after him.

"Yo' ain' gwine to say nuthin' 'bout Bulldog, is yo', Jedge?" the old man asked presently. "Dat nigger's crazy, but fo' all he size, he's jes' lak a baby."

"I'll let you know later," Judge Barringer said absently. He was pondering the question of just what was to be done with Bulldog. He knew that the big Negro would not go far. It was only a matter of time before he would be caught in some shanty or other, giving way to his appetite. But Judge Barringer was also convinced in his own mind that the story of the Washington Negro's death had been a hoax—a hoax that had worked too well. And when they landed at one of the first river settlements where the judge could get a conveyance that would take him back to the city, the first thing he did was to get to a telephone and wait while he had his secretary at the other end give him a report from the hospital.

"Discharged yesterday, Judge," the secretary reported. "It would be pretty hard to find him now. After his experience with Bulldog I guess he's left town."

"All right; didn't want him anyway," said the judge. "Tell Dr. Rafe Kirby to go out to the hospital and wait for me. I'll be there in about an hour, bringing an accident case."

Before the secretary could question him further, he hung up the receiver. Judge Barringer hated personal publicity unless it had to do with politics.

He turned to the storekeeper, whose telephone he had used. "Would you mind telling that old nigger out there I want to see him a moment?"

Daddy Ike came in with his hat in his hand. "What dey say, Jedge?" he asked anxiously.

"That Washington nigger was let out of the hospital yesterday and by now he's halfway home."

"Praise de Lawd for dat!" breathed Daddy Ike.

"And tell Bulldog when he finishes eating that he is to come and report to me before he goes back to the chain gang," Judge Barringer said. The least he could do was suspend sentence, but if possible, he wanted to do something more substantial than that.

Thorough examination by Dr. Rafe Kirby showed that the gunshot wound was superficial. The hardship of crawling mile after mile through the swamp had caused most of the judge's suffering. He was promised that he would be around with the aid of a crutch in a day or two.

"But I thought you went after railbirds, Judge," Dr. Kirby said with a grin when the patient's wound had been dressed.

"Rafe, if you-all don't want me to lose my reputation as a gentleman before this young lady nurse, get out of here quick," Judge Barringer bellowed.

It was the following Monday, still hobbling with the aid of a crutch, that Judge Barringer returned to the bench. There had been no word from Bulldog and he did not quite know what to make of it. When the first case was called, a small Negro, whose head was almost completely shrouded in bandages, stood before him, Judge Barringer looked down compassionately.

"Well, what did you run into—a truck?" he asked.

There was a movement in the prisoners' pen. The Monday-morning crowd was being swayed by some unseen force. Then the force came into view in the shuffling, sheepish form of Bulldog.

"Yas-suh, Jedge, Yo' Honour, heah Ah is!"

"Bulldog!"

Judge Barringer was accustomed to almost anything that might happen in his court, but for the moment he was nonplussed. "Didn't Daddy Ike bring you my message?"

"Yas-suh, Jedge, Yo' Honour, it was thisaway——"

"Why didn't you come to me if you got my message?" Judge Barringer interrupted, his dismay turning to reproof.

"Yas-suh, Jedge, Yo' Honour, Ah'm comin' to dat. It was thisaway," Bulldog pleaded apologetically: "If yo' was to take dem rags offen dat little half-size nigger, yo'd see it was Chinkapin hidin' behin' 'em."

"Chinkapin!"

"Yas-suh, Jedge, de same what tol' me dat lie 'bout dat Washin'ton nigger dyin'. Dis heah Chinkapin cause all de trouble, Jedge, Yo' Honour. If it wasn' fo' Chinkapin's lyin', Jedge, Ah wouldn' 'a' bus' loose from de chain gang. If it wasn' fo' dat little han'ful lyin', I wouldn' hab tote' yo' all de way to Ossabaw. Don' blame me fo' totin' yo' to Ossabaw, Jedge; blame Chinkapin; he done it. Dat Chinkapin nigger's to blame fo' ev'y las' bit ob de trouble. So's when Ah'm comin' from Ossabaw Sa'day night, comin' to see you, Jedge, Ah bumps into dat Chinkapin an' Ah jes nachelly squeeze his lyin' haid fo' him and gib him a couple ob shakes and dat's all."

"Why did you wait until Saturday to come?" Judge Barringer asked.

"'Deed, Jedge, Yo' Honour, how come Ah could come befo' Sa'day? Cap'n Jim didn' let Chinkapin loose offen de chain gang until Sa'day," said Bulldog honestly.

Judge Barringer did not smile this morning. The business before him was too personal. The little bandaged Negro had lied to Bulldog. But in breaking away from the chain gang, Bulldog had been the means of saving the judge's life, for he might never have been found in the swamp. It had been his purpose to suspend sentence on the big Negro, to take him under his wing and get him a job. Now that seemed impossible.

"What do you think I ought to do, Bulldog?" he asked the giant gravely.

"Who, me?" Bulldog looked incredulous. "Shucks, Jedge Barringer, Ah' don' know what yo' ought to do, but Ah knows what yo' is gwine to do."

"What's that?"

Bulldog grew suddenly serious. He had heard enough tales of road gangs in the northern counties of the state, where it was cold in winter, where the prisoners were badly treated, and the food was poor.

"Yo' ain' funnin' wiv me, Jedge, Yo' Honour? Yo' ain'

holdin' it agin me for totin' yo' all de way down to Ossabaw? 'Deed, Jedge Barringer"—and here pathos entered Bulldog's voice—" 'deed, if yo' sen' me anywheres besides to de Fahm, yo'll bus' Cap'n Jim's heart."

Judge Barringer sighed a sigh of relief. "All right, Bulldog, you win. Six months on the Fahm. And you, Chinkapin," he said, turning to the little Negro—"you go with him."

"Yas-suh, Jedge, Yo' Honour," Bulldog grinned. As long as he could be under the gentle tutelage of Captain Jim and Uncle Henry, the cook, he was happy.

"An' yo' kin trus' me, Jedge Barringer," he said solemnly. "Ah won' bus' loose no mo'."

HE MAN

By MARJORY STONEMAN DOUGLAS

From *Saturday Evening Post*

SMALL cold shivers of fright began rippling up and down
Ronny's spine the moment his father stopped the car at
the wharf on the bay front, and Gloria Cargill and Mrs.
Kinney screamed with delight at the waiting parallel planes
of the flying boat. In spite of the warm brilliance of the
Florida morning at ten o'clock, in spite of the salt tang of the
wind that snapped flags on mastheads and ruffled the blue
water between the slips, in spite of the hilarious breakfast
party they had all shared in celebration of Ronny's birthday
trip to Bimini, his feet chilled and his hands went clammy
and the bacon and boiled pompano sat uneasily within him.
Yet the terror that from childhood had ridden him, the fear
of high places, of falling horribly through thin air, and therefore, of all flying, was no greater in him at this moment than
his fear of letting his father know that he was afraid.

He sat mute in the corner of the back seat, his slender
hands gripping at his boyish bony knees. The lucky fact that
no one ever noticed him much anyway gave him a chance to
pull himself together. As his father dashed around to help
out Gloria, and burly Colonel Kinney reached back a hand
for his smart chubby wife, Ronny looked at himself deliberately in the little mirror over the wheel. His tan hid the pallor that he felt. His mild gray eyes steadied as he watched
them, so that they would not betray him. That he did not
show his panic more plainly gave him courage to get out of
the car, carrying Gloria's green-leather vanity case and her
flimsy green-silk coat.

None of the four looked at him as he came up, the tall
awkward boy so acutely aware always that he could never
be the figure of a man that his father was. Ronny looked at

149

him now, shyly, with the spark of his adoration in his eye.

Andrew Burgess always dominated any group. His graying dark hair was bared, flying its shaggy crest of lock above the others. His bronzed handsome face was alert and eager, with only a few folds about the eyes to betray his years. Ronny thought again, as he had since a small boy, with that same little throb of almost hopeless devotion, that his father was the finest man he had ever seen in his life. To Ronny, who at school had followed breathlessly in the newspapers his father's polo exploits, his tennis triumphs, the purses and the ribbons that his racing stable won, Andrew Burgess was also the most brilliant sportsman in the world. His father never in his life refused a high dive or knew the weak sickness of great heights. Never in a thousand years would he have given up practice with the school polo team, as Ronny had, after being in hospital two months with a broken rib, because ever after that when he thought of playing polo the thunder of those following hoofs came sickeningly back to him, the trampling pain, the darkness, the oblivion. His father's ribs had been broken, and his collar bone and his leg, and he had played more dashing polo than ever, after that. But Ronny couldn't. He just couldn't, that was all, no matter how deep within him burned the bitter knowledge that he was a coward.

Sometimes Ronny thought that if his father ever discovered the depths of his son's weakness he would disown him. It was only that as a motherless sickly child Ronny had been given over to the care of the best of nurses, as a mild little boy to the most expensive of schools, that had saved him until now, he was certain, from being found out. This winter in Miami was the first time Ronny had ever been with his father for so many months. It was as if Andrew had suddenly discovered that he was about to be twenty and had decided to make a man of him. As a result Ronny had had desperately to try to live up to what was expected of him by a man who retained all his enthusiasm for sports, even if he were too old now for the more strenuous of them. Ronny had to give up entirely his rather studious, leisurely life. He had no time now for reading, or for the Spanish translations he had been so interested in doing with a young instructor at his college. And he gave up his beloved photography, which for years at school and summer camp and college had absorbed him.

There was time for nothing now, and certainly no excess energy for anything but sports.

He struggled with them, with what valiance he could muster. He worked hard at a golf lesson every day, to improve his indifferent game, while his father and Colonel Kinney tramped their speedy eighteen holes every morning. He worked at tennis lessons for which he had no feeling whatsoever, because it had been one of the things his father had done best. And he spent hours every afternoon with his father and the Kinneys at polo games or at the races, where he bet and lost often, so that his father would not think him a piker, struggling wildly to conceal even from himself how supremely he was bored. It seemed to Ronny that nothing but luck and Gloria Cargill had kept his father from finding him out.

It had been all luck at first. His father happened never to have seen Ronny swinging rather wildly with a brassie, or practising an overhand with his usual awkwardness. Ronny took care always to be swimming among the breakers when everyone else was diving from the tower by the pool. He rather liked swimming, anyway, if he could be left alone at it. He grew brown from work with a medicine ball every morning on the sand, put on a little weight, and tried to remain inconspicuous. His father, incapable of imagining that any real man could be uninterested in the sports he loved, was only vaguely disappointed with him as yet.

If at times he looked a little puzzled at the quiet boy who took no prizes, broke no records at anything, would not play polo, was not handsome and dominant and magnetic, he had not thought about it long enough to be resentful. The boy was young yet. After all, he'd had too much schooling, too many women nurses as a small boy. It was a good thing he'd remembered to take him out of college. There would be still time for his polo.

"Stick with me, old boy!" he would shout to Ronny in one of his lavish moments, when a horse of his had won or he had taken a close game from Colonel Kinney. "I'll make a he man of you yet. Next year, when you're toughened up a bit, we'll look around for a couple of good polo ponies for you and you can get in on the practice games up at Aiken."

Those were the moments that Ronny, writhing inwardly,

hated most. It made the time when his father must find him out seem very near. It was to the putting off of that moment, which would have been the end of everything for Ronny, that Gloria Cargill had assisted.

Ronny did not really like Gloria Cargill. He did not really like big wheezy Colonel Kinney, whose talk was like his father's—all sports and poker and bootleggers—but somehow not the same—a thousand times more monotonous. He did not really like Mrs. Kinney, who was fat and flat faced, who wore the most expensive clothes in the most startling colours and played bridge like an inspired card sharp. He never knew what to say to any of them, and they had a way of screaming with laughter at some embarrassed speech of his and then staring at him curiously, with cold eyes, touched slightly with contempt. They always made him feel that they knew perfectly what a coward he was, if his father did not. But even they were easier to endure than Gloria, for all that she took his father's attention from him.

His father said that Gloria Cargill was the most marvellous woman in New York, and all his world of rich men and expensive women and racing and cards and sport and supper clubs seemed to agree with him. She was the youthful widow of a tire king, and she spent her money like a spoiled empress. She was almost as tall as Andrew, with a lithe figure that was swaying and sleek either in a bathing suit or in one of her fabulous evening dresses. Her hair was wild red gold around the bold beauty of her face. Her brown-velvet eyes had little gold lights in them that burned when they looked at men, and the wet brightness of her mouth showed scarlet down the whole length of a hotel corridor or across a dance floor.

For Ronny the worst of it was that she had discovered that he was painfully shy of handsome women and therefore delighted in tormenting him. She could turn the whole force of her fascination on him, like a headlight, in which he squirmed and blinked miserably, to her laughing delight. She adored running a glittering hand suddenly down his coat sleeve, drowning him in her gusts of perfume, clinging with a burlesque of devotion to his arm and flashing her heady glance into his dazzled eyes. Once or twice Andrew had seen him blanch and jerk his hand back involuntarily and he had been furious, because an assured gallantry to women was to Andrew the fundamental of red-blooded masculinity. He lashed out savagely to the boy, if in a low voice, in one of those sudden rages which reddened his face uncontrollably. The whole thing fixed Ronny in his miserable sense of inferiority.

But if he secretly disliked Gloria, he was grateful to her for taking his father's attention. It seemed that everyone was watching to see if she would marry Andrew. Their world agreed it would be an excellent match, with plenty of money on both sides. Sometimes Ronny had moments of bitter jealousy of her, of this woman like a brass band and an express train, who thought she was good enough for his splendid father. But chiefly he was humbly glad to be effaced. And if she did marry him, perhaps his father would not mind so much finding out, as he must sometime, how much his son was unlike and unworthy of him.

Ronny thought all that over in a flash now, joining them in the full sun upon the wharf. He was trying to keep himself from staring at that flying thing. Gloria caught his somewhat rigid glance and smiled at him brilliantly. He had never seen her beauty so bright and polished and complete. She was all in a green so bright it made your eyes redden to look at it —green shoes and small green hat with a diamond and emerald pin pulled tight down over her blazing gold eyes. There was a flash of emerald light on her finger and a cuff of glittering bracelets on her wrist. And yet she dominated all that flash and glare with the sheer assault of her eyes, her lips, her poise, her conscious charm. Beside her, fattish Mrs. Kinney in her egg-yellow chiffon was almost inconspicuous. Not that Mrs. Kinney cared. Her voice was as loud as Gloria's, if not louder. Her laughter had edges. Ronny saw men around the wharves lingering and staring at the bright group, chauffeurs staring from parked cars and mechanics from the plane shed. The women especially seemed to be carelessly aware of the attention they were attracting. When Gloria glanced about her with quick casual glances, it was as if she trailed her laughter like an insolent plume across all the staring faces, fascinating them and knowing that she fascinated them, although they did not exist. That sort of thing always made Ronny's feet and hands seem enormous and uncomfortable. Now he tried to imitate his father's lordly buoyance, knowing exactly how far he failed.

For one moment he caught the aloof calculation in the eye of the aviator fussing about the plane which was to take them up. Instantly Ronny's fear leaped and tore at him again. A line of perspiration was cold on his upper lip. He was afraid. He could not go up in that thing, to those terrible heights of thin air. He could not. He would not. He would tell his father that he wasn't well. He did feel slightly nauseated already, and dizzy, as if he were looking down from a high building. Little tremors crawled beneath his skin. Nothing in the world could make him go up in that thing, even his father's furious contempt.

Somebody gave him a soft leather helmet, and he buckled it under his chin with clammy fumbling fingers. Colonel Kinney was putting one on over his shiny bald spot. His father never wore anything on his head in Florida, and Gloria and Mrs. Kinney said their hats were quite tight enough. Then they were walking down the slippery plank and getting into the plane.

It was a three-seater. Mrs. Kinney and the colonel took the third seat and Gloria and his father the second. The women got in alertly, their high heels clicking on the deck, their sleek knees flashing among their skirts. His father motioned Ronny to sit next to the aviator, because it was his birthday treat. Ronny got in.

It was like sitting on a leather cushion in a high-sided tin bathtub, behind the smudged dimness of the short windshield. There were things—rods and handles—dangerous-looking things, between Ronny's feet, which he would not have touched for worlds, and behind, overhead, the loom and shadow of the great wings.

Gloria's jewelled hand patted his shoulder. "So nice of you, darling, to have this marvellous birthday!" she was crying, in that gay scream which made his very eardrums cringe. Suddenly the roar of the engine exploded in a thuttering numbness of sound that clamped mufflers on their hearing. Ronny felt his skin chill and crawl. They were off.

At the same time he had a flash of panicky decision that he must not clench his hands where this aviator could see them. There was something careless and matter-of-fact and young about him, which Ronny suddenly wished that he could emulate. So that, while the plane taxied out on the smooth bay water, rocking a little as it curved and thundered between the high black sides of oil tankers, past white bows of yachts, in an increasing blur of speed, he was equally concerned in watching his hands, fixed in a pose of relaxation, on his knees. He was bracing himself for what he knew must come, the first sickening leap upward. It did not come. There was only a slight adjustment in the angle of the seat. The water at a distance looked lower than it had been. And he suddenly realized that they were up, although he could feel no sensation in himself but a quickening of his heartbeats.

All around the plane the sapphire level of the bay was deepening and lowering. The plane ground ceaselessly, climbing with a great, roaring steadiness the orderly staircase of the wind. There was reality in it, and stolidity. Ronny felt a strange sense of lifting upward into a freedom from earthly things, a consciousness of wide salt wind and tremendous reaches of sunny air. He had forgotten about relaxing his hands now, and his heart was pounding, but in him climbed, as the plane climbed, an amazement and a new delight. He was hardly afraid at all. It was astonishing. It was delicious.

As the plane wheeled, lifted its nose, climbed, wheeled, and lifted in enormous roaring circles, the earth wheeled slowly beyond the side. The checkered green, the crowded glistening roof tops of Miami, stretching west to a mist of Everglades and sky, wheeled also. The blue bay floor wheeled, which was at this height bright turquoise, streaked with lime green, which whitened lightly on each side of the lean elbow of the causeway, where cars slid like beetles. Beyond Ronny's right bathtub rim circled the straight lines of trees and streets that were Miami Beach; the apron patches of green that were golf links; the small squares that were hotel roofs, house roofs, patches and rectangles of colour flattened on the ground. Then, as they climbed higher and the plane lurched a little, heading into the vast sea wind, there before them, dim through the windshield, reaching out tremendously to right hand and to left, lay the ocean, a vast lavender miracle, wrinkling a little and reaching out. reaching out so enormously to the stretched horizon that it seemed to rise to meet it, to melt into it, and mingle in, the distance all one smoking, imperceptible blue.

High and far above it, yet somehow not remote, because there was nothing with which to measure the distance between, the plane snored straight eastward now upon the crystal level of its pathway, rocking a little upon its invisible cradling of air, strangely real, strangely prosaic, a thing of wood and metal, weighty, hard to the touch, solid to rest upon, commonplace in a world gone wonderful with high magic, all blue air and bluer unbelievable sea.

Beside Ronny, the aviator's sunburned profile was calm. His hands moved only occasionally now on the controls. His manner was easy and assured. From time to time he glanced about him, out at the sea below his left shoulder; once across Ronny at the sky; and once, with a long narrowed glance, at something behind and overhead, at a wire or strut or something, which for some imperceptible reason had caught his attention. Ronny followed his glance with a little prickling thrill, but found himself nodding and grinning at Mrs. Kinney in the back seat, beyond his father's shoulder, and at Gloria's brilliant, enthusiastic face. His father and Colonel Kinney grinned at him briefly, eyes narrowed and faces still, with the manner of men enjoying themselves sedately. Ronny felt a sudden glow of friendship for all of them. Against the vastness of the background, underlaid still with the thought of his fear, they were familiar and dear and reassuring. He was overwhelmed with thankfulness that he had not shown them how much he had been afraid. The thuttering roar of the engines which shut about them so completely was not so noticeable. Ronny felt a sudden impulse to lean over and tell his father now all about how afraid of things he was. It seemed as if an ordinary tone could have carried and that in this moment of exultation his father would understand and forgive everything. As if Ronny did not know well enough, at the same moment, that the difference between his father and himself was more impenetrable than the roar.

The plane had been moving steadily upon its level above the vast wrinkled ultramarine of ocean for some thirty minutes now. Far behind, the mainland had melted into the mist, that at the horizon blurred from sea colour into sky colour, like the bloom on a grape. Before them the islands were equally obscured. Occasionally the plane lifted or joggled slightly, as the wings bucked the booming trade wind, but on the whole it was stable, lulling into oblivion remembered fears. Ronny was growing happier and happier in knowing himself relaxed, even sleepy, under the numbing drone.

He could let his glance fall down over the side for a minute or two, with no feeling in the pit of his stomach. He grew bolder, making himself stick his head out almost into the wind to stare down. But suddenly then, like a dropped weight, he was hit by a dreadful image of himself leaping to his feet and pitching over there, head first, and hurtling down the vast empty drop. The suddenness of it caught him in the stomach and the throat so that his spine crept. He withdrew his glance hurriedly to the comfortable commonplace within—dials and indicators, floor boards, the aviator's strong freckled hands, and his own feet. They helped to steady him physically, but horror still mounted within him, not so much at the outside world, perilous as it had become again for him, but at the suddenly revealed depths of strangeness in himself. Perhaps it was not only that he was utterly unlike his father but that he was different from all normal men. Perhaps within his very brain crawled the maggots of unbalance. At that moment he felt it was even possible for him to go mad and scream, and leap screaming over there. Ugh! Yet, of course, it was not so. It was only his imagination. But a he man would never have been troubled by fancies as sick as that.

It was at that moment that Ronny, fighting to calm the tumult in him by staring fixedly at the aviator's hands, saw the right one jerk as the whole plane lurched sideways. He saw the aviator throw a glance over his shoulder even while his hands and feet made curt gestures with the controls. The plane righted, but tossed violently before lurching again. Ronny, throwing a look back and up, saw a broken thing hanging and banging at one wing—a great blue hole and long rags of canvas. The vast circle of the sea below them was tipping up and circling like the surface of water in a tilted cup. The man beside him, working tensely, shot a look at him, a queer, tight-lipped grin, and the plane slid downward slowly, circling and nosing, with occasional moments of level. The engine roared as usual, and the air seemed calm.

The conviction that something was wrong, that something was awfully wrong, came to Ronny with a surprising slowness. The very worst things happened to him only in his imagination. When it was a matter of outward affairs which older men had always controlled so much better than he, it was hard to believe them capable of accident. The dark floor of the sea was rushing toward them in dizzy circles. And yet there was no horror in this for him, as there had been in the thought of plunging alone. Something had gone wrong, that was all, and the aviator had told him in that one glance that he was going to make a landing. Ronny had much more confidence in him than he would ever have in himself. They would probably land all right.

It was like sliding down an enormous shoot-the-chute, even to the water at the bottom. The ocean was there, rushing up to the pitch of the plane's nose, a ridged, blurry surface of deep blue. They were going to land all right. Ronny was certain. He was growing a little pleased with himself. There was even a breath of relief at the more familiar level after all that breathless height.

The engine subsided into a low growl. The wind screamed in the wires as if for the first time, and below grew the long rustling rumour of the waves. He could see whitecaps flashing now over brilliant sapphire hollows. Why, these waves were high, he thought confusedly, leaning back against the steepness. The faint scream of a woman behind him came only a second before the shock and bounce of landing, with the crash and drench of flying cold water. When their bouncing slide lost momentum, they were immediately bucked about, tossed and dropped and flung on the strong new element as if in a light, top-heavy dory. The hiss and surge of waves were around them, dark blue water hurling itself northwestward, blue blacks in the hollows and laced with snowy streaks of foam.

Ronny turned at once to look back and grin at his father, still exhilarated with himself and with his sudden sense of adventure. It was like looking at people whom he had not seen for years, who were changed, yet completely familiar. His father met his glance with a face like bronzed rock, in which the eyes were a little fixed. He and they all were engaged in the almost violent business of keeping their balance in the lurching dip and rise of the plane, topheavy as it was and beaten by the wind, upon the strong waves which rose before them, jagged and frowning, which heaved them up with an unremitting power and passed behind them for others hurrying and trampling on.

Gloria Cargill was clinging with one hand to his father's arm, and with the other was straightening her bright green hat. Mrs. Kinney's plucked eyebrows were lifted over the roundness of her eyes in an almost ridiculous expression of amazed protest, and Colonel Kinney, holding her tightly, was crimson to his heavy dewlaps, and swearing visibly. Ronny was happy that he had not yet revealed himself to these courageous people.

The aviator jerked off his helmet and became immediately individual and human. His blue eyes were anxious in a bony, sun-reddened face. His bleached hair bristled on his head, and his eyelashes were bleached. Ronny remembered suddenly that his name was Bill. He looked more disturbed than any of them.

"Well, folks," he said, "I sure am sorry. That strut busted like a match stick. Somebody will get murdered for this, if I have to do it myself. Hope the ladies are all right. There's nothing to worry about, of course. Perhaps I can patch it." He crawled backward between them and on to the back of the fuselage.

"Want any help?" Andrew Burgess called, with his eyes warm and lively again. "Rotten luck. I've been ready for a bottle of beer for the last fifteen minutes. Hope this won't make us too late for lunch."

Ronny, looking up at Bill as he climbed over the seat and seeing the curious slant look he cast down at his father's nonchalance, knew as suddenly as if he had spoken that the matter was to be graver than that. He clung to the edge of his seat as the plane swung down in a smashing burst of spray that flew over them and stung their faces, considering the thing soberly. The violence of those Gulf Stream waves was still almost unbelievable. They had looked down so long upon the seeming flatness of this water. Ronny's clothes were getting wet and he shifted about on his seat to avoid the stinging spray that came inboard.

His father and Gloria Cargill were singing "Where do we go from here?" and "When do we eat?" with voices that seemed a little too boisterous. He knew that Gloria was showing what a good sport she could be, for his father's admiration, who watched her powder her nose and rouge, and do over her lips with the scarlet lipstick. Gloria was lovely, glancing sidewise into her tiny mirror, sidewise up at him. Mrs. Kinney was not singing. Her plump cheeks had gone a little sallow under the rouge, and her bright yellow hat and bright yellow dress looked startling on her. She sat hunched up very close to her husband, with her eyes fixed upon the lifting wave tops. Colonel Kinney patted her hand regularly and watched Bill.

As the plane lifted to a racing wave Ronny could look out over the sea to some distance to more racing blue wave tops with flashes of white boiling at their crests, under the dazzling beat of the sun. The horizon that had shrunk to this, from the vast sweep of the air, was jagged and uneasy with waves, and the sky beyond it was a remote unnoticed blue. It was the sea that had suddenly taken the menace that the air had had; the sea, looming and tossing around the incongruous smallness of the plane, an awkward alien, unfitted for this heavier element. It seemed to Ronny that they sat a little lower among these waves than they had at first.

The aviator, Bill, was slashing at a tangle of stiff canvas and wires and broken sticks under the lower wing. Ronny saw him slip and the tangle drop into the water, where it hung and splashed, held by a single wire. The plane veered suddenly at the crest of a wave and Ronny saw it plunge, stern down, on the wreckage. With a scream from Mrs. Kinney, a broken strut crashed through a thin floor board and in the jagged rip sea water bubbled smoothly, wetting their feet and ankles and legs.

"Hey, look here!" Ronny's father called suddenly. "We're getting wet! Here, Bill; come here and fix this! Put your feet up, Gloria. It's all right, Mrs. Kinney. We'll be all right presently."

Ronny had been certain his father would take charge of things. He was splendid. His voice was loud and confident and reassuring. Only Ronny could not make himself believe that nothing was the matter. Things looked bad to him. Bill's face told him the same thing, slipping and splashing back along the wet fuselage, like a whale back, low in the water.

The water was rapidly filling the cockpit. There wasn't

any use being too cheerful, Ronny was thinking, climbing up to sit crouched uncomfortably on the back of the seat. His father and Gloria did it, laughing. But Mrs. Kinney had to be helped up and then held, perched precariously, her round dismayed eyes still fixed on the coming water. Colonel Kinney held her, with his ruddy face turning a curious congested purple. Ronny saw suddenly that the Kinneys were afraid, and he was sorry for them. It was dreadful to be afraid.

The plane had sunk with the weight of water in the cockpit, but now it seemed not to be sinking any more.

Bill scrambled wetly up beside Ronny and spoke to the others, "This isn't so good, folks, but it isn't so bad. The old bus is knocked out, but it can't sink any more and we're not so far from Bimini now. We may even drift quite near, the way the stream runs. Somebody's sure to pick us up almost any minute, because we're in the direct line of boats from Miami to Bimini and they'll report by and by that we haven't arrived. All we've got to do now is hang on."

His glance met Ronny's on the last words, and Ronny saw that in spite of his cheerful, matter-of-fact voice, his eyes were wide and unwinking. Ronny's own eyes were like that. As they stared at each other for a long moment, Ronny felt a sudden warmth of understanding and comradeship leap between them. After all, Bill was not so very much older than he was, for all the weathered maturity of his face. That glance linked them, by their youth, by their common ability to look at the situation, without too much fear or too much optimism. These others must be protected at all costs.

"Are you with me?" said Bill's glance to Ronny, and Ronny's answered instantly, "You betcha life."

Bill withdrew his gaze abruptly to unlace his shoes and take them off. Ronny did the same, glad to feel his toes free in the water. He watched one shoe float a minute and then go over the side in a slap of water from a running wave. Bill was plucking up the wet cushions from the seats below the water.

"They'll float," he said briefly. "You hang on to this one, Mrs. Kinney. And listen here. The backs of these seats are going to get awfully uncomfortable in about a minute. It would be easier if we all got down on the fuselage, even if it is partly in the water. Then the ladies can hang on to these cushions, too. That's right, isn't it, sir?"

He appealed to Andrew Burgess, and Ronny saw his father brighten visibly, as if glad of something to do. "Perhaps you could show them, sir," Bill further suggested, and Andrew turned and slid back gingerly over the wet surface, lowering himself with one hand on a strut down on the incline, so that he rested with his legs in the water, but his body supported.

"It is better," he said promptly. "Come along, Gloria. Help Mrs. Kinney, Colonel. Here, grab my hand. You won't get any wetter than you are now. It's not half bad."

Ronny and Bill and the colonel, splashing in the water, held Mrs. Kinney and lowered her, quite mute now, down to Andrew Burgess. Gloria went next, laughing. Her green silk dress clung wetly to her lithe figure, and she moved with much more assurance than the other woman, and seemed somehow more suited to the watery and difficult background. Her face was not so tense either, but somehow the bright spots of rouge on each cheek, the darkened eyelashes, the scarlet curve of mouth seemed to stand away from her face a little, as if the flesh were shrinking. After Colonel Kinney had followed them with ponderous caution and a very tight grip of Ronny's shoulder, the four hung there in a row, their eyes looking upward at Bill and Ronny clinging above them, and at the jagged wave crests racing down upon them, with the same look. It was a mute look, guarded, expectant, a little humble. Their lifted eyes made something in Ronny ache with pity for them. They looked so helpless, hanging there, in the smashing dangerous water. They were looking at Bill and him as if the two had suddenly taken on an unguessed power and significance. Ronny tried to think of something else to do for them to still the tightness in his throat.

"Let's cut some of that wire, Bill," he said. "Maybe we can put it around them, so that they wouldn't have to hang on so tightly. Got a knife? I have."

They worked, balancing, slipping, plunging about on top of the fuselage, over which the highest waves sent a skim of water, twisting and cutting and clinging to the wing frames as they could. When four lengths of the wire had been hacked off, Bill slid down to the Kinneys, Ronny to his father and Gloria. There was enough to twist around the body of each, but it was hard to bend it around a strut so that it would stay fastened against the roll and jerk of the plane.

Half the time Ronny was completely in the water, working with one hand, sprawling, while his father helped. When a higher wave reared above them, hissing, they had to stop working and hang on tightly, their heads and shoulders barely above the smother, their bodies banging against the wood.

Once Ronny lost the last piece of wire overboard and had to dive for it, clutching it luckily in the boiling depth below. But the swimming was actually a refreshment to him. To be able to move his cramped limbs freely and surely in this sea removed much of its menace. It was an element with which he was familiar. He came to the surface with a sputtering rush and an overhand that carried him easily back, with a grin for his father's anxious eyes. Ronny had even time to realize that he had never seen his father look at him like that. As Ronny put the wire about him Andrew's right hand lingered on his shoulder and he said, "Nice work, old chap."

Ronny was warm with gratitude for that. His father was being splendid. His colour was good. His voice was assured. He joked occasionally with Gloria or Mrs. Kinney, putting out a hand to help when he could. That was what it meant to have been a good sport all his life, Ronny thought. He simply did not know what fear meant.

Gloria's hair looked funny, wet and plastered about her forehead like that. She had lost her hat somehow, but she was game all right. She was singing a lot of old songs, making them all sing things like "On the Banks of the Wabash" and "Waiting for the Robert E. Lee." Even Mrs. Kinney smiled with stiff lips when there was anything to smile about.

There was not much to do after Bill and Ronny got the wires fixed. They all hung there, the four with the wires, Ronny and Bill wherever they could catch hold of something, half supported by the wallowing fuselage, bumping and hanging in the flounder of water, watching to duck a taller wave crest, and talking now and then, little bursts of talk that ran from one to another of the soaking figures. Their words lagged or renewed like a slow pendulum of vitality.

Presently Bill, who did a good deal of scrambling about, shinned up so that he could hang from the upper wing frame and peer, long and earnestly, out over the wave tops. Mutely everyone watched him. Ronny, standing on the fuselage above them, noticed that the whites of their eyes shone a little.

Bill had been looking steadily at the same place for several seconds. He drew himself up higher, shading his eyes.

"You're looking at something!" Gloria called suddenly.

Bill did not answer. The faces were tense and a similar light seemed to be upon them all—a light of pallor and suspense. They knew that Bill was looking at something. Ronny leaped up beside him.

At first he could see nothing but scalloped blue wave tops and the leap and flash of foam. Then, more to the right, he caught a steady flash that was a wave, but a wave breaking before a boat's bow. When he looked intently he could see, now and then, the gray pointed mass of the bow itself, appearing and disappearing. It was hard to tell how far away it was, or whether it was moving in their direction. Bill waited, motionless, and so did Ronny.

His father called suddenly below them, "For God's sake, boys, if you see something, tell us! And do something about it, can't you? Wave something! Shout!"

Mrs. Kinney shrieked suddenly, strained and off key, "Oh, make them hurry! Make them hurry! We can't stand this any longer!" And the other three all cried things, words and shouts mingled indistinguishably, a babel of sound at the water's edge, incapable of carrying, in that wind, more than a boat's length. Bill and Ronny waved their arms, waved Bill's coat, waved torn strips of canvas, and shouted as if a tension had given way.

Presently the breaking white from the boat's bow and the occasional glimpse of bow itself were gone. There were only the jagged lift of the wave tops and the foaming white of crests.

When Ronny really believed that the boat had gone, that he could not see it any more, that it had really failed to see them, or had ignored them, he stopped waving and let himself drop down to the fuselage. Bill dropped beside him and they stood looking down at the faces below them, the wet faces with the incredulous eyes raised to theirs. Ronny cleared his throat before he shook his head and said, "It went."

"You mean it went?" His father's voice was suddenly harsh and there were reddish veins under the salt water on his forehead. "You didn't wave hard enough! You didn't try to shout! The hounds—to leave us—the dirty dogs! I'll have them arrested for it. I'll make them suffer for it, the dirty skunks, the lou——"

Gloria stopped him with a hand on his shoulder. Mrs. Kinney had gasped once or twice and her eyes had rolled in her plump white face, but Colonel Kinney had both arms around her.

"Hush, Momma, hush," he said. "Never mind. That means we'll see others. The next one will come nearer."

There was then nothing to do but keep on waiting and keep on hanging on. There was no way of knowing what time it was, except that the blazing sun had moved slightly westward down from the zenith. The waves rolled as high, but it almost seemed as if the six had adjusted to their rolling, so that they did it automatically, knowing how high the highest would come. But the ferocity of the sun was an increasing agony. Ronny felt the sting of it under his wet shirt, along his tanned shoulders, and knew how much the others must feel it on the tenderer skin of their faces and shoulders. Colonel Kinney's bald spot glowed an angry crimson. He had lost his helmet long since. And Ronny tore a big piece from his wet shirt and made Colonel Kinney tie it over his head like a hood.

All Gloria's make-up had washed off and her cheeks were red with sunburn and her nose already blistered. Mrs. Kinney's pale face was bright rose colour, and both women's lips were swollen and blistered from the salt water and the sun. Ronny tore other pieces from his shirt to tie over their faces, and the sun was instantly angry on the bared places on his neck and back.

It was a relief to dive into the water after a dropped cushion or to swim around a bit, after their various positions on the fuselage, and yet Bill was right when he warned him, in a low voice, not to tire himself. Ronny contented himself by hanging over the cockpit edge with one hand and letting his body float on the lift and drop of the waves. The sense of high adventure was burning steadily in him; the sense that here at last he was encountering an experience which he could remember all his life.

The waves that came racing at them from the southeast, with their curious impersonal violence, surprised him with their endlessness. It was amazing that there could be so many of them, hurrying and shoving forward, in their leaping up and down. As the blazing sun crept slowly down the long afternoon slope, so that it shone redly in their smarting eyelids, the light changed upon the waves, whitening their leaping tops, intensifying the dark sapphire of their hollows, shadowed in the trough with glossy black. It might have been a gloriously exhilarating sea to sail a boat over. But sunk almost to the chin as they were here, there was little gaiety in it. Deep blue could be bleak, Ronny was learning slowly, and flashes of white sinister, just as the plane that had been so powerful and assured, taking off from water only that morning, floated here so incongruously; alien wreckage that just was able to support itself and their clutched and uncomfortable lives.

The silences were longer between the choppy snatches of talk. Gloria did no more singing. Ronny remembered, as if she had been some other woman, how she had looked that morning, waiting on the pier. That gay brilliant figure had practically no point of resemblance to this sodden one with the drenched, salt-matted hair, the pale swollen lips, the brilliant green silk only dank clinging fabric on the arms and shoulders, the nose and eyelids reddened. Her consciousness of charm, too, had gone—that powerful vibration.

Ronny looked at her now only with pity and concern for the pale woman, silent, with closed eyes and miserably clutching hands where the great emerald still flashed incongruously in the wet. Mrs. Kinney managed somehow to look more like herself, with her plump short figure in the soaked yellow silk clutched by her husband's arm, with a piece of Ronny's shirt tied over her head and forehead. There was in all the faces, it seemed to him, a growing look of withdrawal, of remoteness, as if each one were drifting away from their relations with others to the silent place where ultimately human life exists alone. When one spoke, it was with a forced utterance. A smile took more strength than it had and was more automatic. All their attention was centring, more and more, on the sheer act of endurance.

The sun, just above the western horizon, burned and flared upon their faces, under their blinking eyelids, and the blue waves changed slowly to a cold green against a vast rose-coloured afterglow that held no loveliness for them. In half an hour it would be night, and there was no boat.

Ronny was thinking lingeringly of juicy beefsteak and baked potatoes and a steaming cup of coffee, or fried onions, or even just an orange. Anything to relieve this withering, abominable taste of salt in the mouth. It seemed to him he must have swallowed quarts of salt water already, and his tongue and the lining of his mouth were blistered with it. The feeling of too much salt water swallowed was cold and uneasy also in his stomach.

Bill came floundering beside him. "Look here, buddy, le's you and me try to turn this bus around, so the plane'll be away from the wind. Maybe she'll ride better that way for the night."

Suddenly Ronny saw the night—the night. "Sure," he said to Bill, grateful for activity. But something about his heart was cold.

It was harder to swim than it had been. There was no longer refreshment in the swash of water over his body. The wind skimmed stinging hatfuls of spray over a wave top into their faces. When they reached the rudder they clung to it and breathed a trifle hard, planning their concerted effort. Presently they let go and began pushing, thrashing tremendously with their legs, breathing or gasping when they could. The huge thing was unwieldy and hard to start and, once started, the wind often caught and forced it back on top of them. Ronny's legs began to feel the strain of it and there was a pain in his labouring lungs. Floundering and struggling side by side there, Ronny found that he and Bill were staring grimly into each other's eyes, as if the very abstract intentness of the look, in such moments as their faces were clear of water, was some sort of permanence. And at the moment when they got the thing half about and the wind took it from the new angle, whirling it as they wanted it to go, Ronny caught a twisted grin on Bill's face, a grin and gasp of triumph that reached to him as a glorious thing. It was tremendous. It was unconquerable, he felt, grinning back as best he could as they both hung and panted on the turned plane. He felt warm all over, as if with a great achievement.

By the time they were ranged beside the others again, along the fuselage, the anxious pale faces turned to them, the bodies floundering and awash, the colour had gone from the watery world. There was only a brief green streak of twilight where the sun had gone. To the east the waves were black against the tremendous looming purple of the night. Stars were quivering in the enormous rondure of the sky that overhead took on a strange metallic blue and cast upon them a faint luminance that was less than light and only a little less than dark. By it they could see their own dark shapes, the black parallels of the wings. On the black water the white crests flashed and lengthened and disappeared, ghostly in the dark. The waves snarled now as they leaped toward them. The hissing spray stung like thrown pebbles as it struck their blistered, puffy faces. There was a little relief in the darkness, for the sun no longer burned into their eyeballs, but in its place the phantoms of the black lonely water started about them and the blood went thin.

"I suppose now"—Mrs. Kinney's voice came suddenly and a little shrill, from the shadow she had become—"now that it's dark, nobody can see to pick us up, even if a boat did come?"

No one spoke. It was what everyone had been thinking, Ronny was sure. But it had not been spoken before in so many words.

Then Bill said simply, "It's not likely, Mrs. Kinney. But in the morning it will be different. They'll have heard from Bimini, and the boats will be out sure. We've been drifting a bit or they would have found us sooner."

No one spoke again. They set themselves somehow to endure the night.

Through the noise of the wind humming and shrieking in the wires and of the waves hissing and slapping against the wood, Ronny could hear few sounds which would indicate that human life was here, clinging perilously to what was almost wreckage. His arm ached dully and continuously as he held it tight over the edge of the cockpit, and his bumped and floating body smarted in places where the skin had been rubbed off. Yet he was growing queerly drowsy. His eyelids drooped and a hazy swimming took the place of thought within his head. He must even have dozed once or twice, for a sharp pain in his elbow roused him or a slap of choking water in the face, and he recognized miserably again, what, for a second of blur, he had forgotten—the lost floundering in the dark, the misery in him and in the figures about him.

Once or twice he heard Colonel Kinney speaking gently to his wife and her sharp whimper, as if she, too, had wakened abruptly from a wretched doze, perhaps one in which she had dreamed of warmth and safety and being dry, to the reality of the roaring and sinister dark. Once he heard Gloria swearing to herself, as if unable to stand it any longer, and then stopping abruptly, knowing that it did no good.

The stars were gold and silver overhead in the vast dark vault, and it seemed to Ronny that their tangled and glittering patterns were dragged slowly across up there, like a remote panorama for how many human eyes below them, raised in agony and mute endurance. Only decoration, after all. He must have dozed again, hanging by the other elbow, cheek almost in the water, for presently he started out of oblivion with a hand on his shoulder.

It was Bill, his voice low and humble.

"Look here, buddy," he said slowly and with difficulty, "we'll have to look out. They've begun to slip off. Mrs. Cargill's wire keeps coming unfastened and your father went down once. Coming up with him I hit my head a bit. Would you stick around and watch them while I catch my breath?"

"Hurt bad, Bill?" Ronny whispered anxiously. "Here, hang on to this edge. Hook your elbow over. Take your time, old man. I'll be on the job."

He swam slowly down the side, catching here and there at a foot. "Don't mind. It's me," he said hastily. He counted the dark heads and shoulders out of the ghostly foam. One, Colonel Kinney; two, Mrs. Kinney; three, Gloria; four, his fa—— that head disappeared even as he looked. Instantly he dived, groping downward in the strangling, rushing depths. There was only water in his frantic reaching fingers. Then he felt hair, a shoulder, caught at a thrashing arm. They came to the surface together, staring into each other's shadowy faces, gasping.

"Dad," Ronny whispered in agony, "did the wire come off? You must have let go. For heaven's sake, be careful. You can't tell when——"

For a moment longer the bulk of Andrew Burgess hung and shook a little in the dimness. "Thanks—old boy," he said then. "Guess I wasn't holding on tight enough. Yet hanging on—hanging on's—not much worth while."

"Hush, Dad. Don't." Ronny whispered. "They'll hear you. Think how we'll talk about this when we get back. Just think of the experience of it."

His father said nothing. Ronny hung and watched the stars and tried not to think of those boiling black depths he had encountered, or of the queer tone in his father's voice, or of hot, yellow scrambled eggs. The wind played three distinct wailing notes among the wires, high when the plane was tossed higher on a crest, low and humming in the hollows. The jerk and ache along his arms helped to keep him alert now. He hoped that Bill would be all right. Then Mrs. Kinney cried out, either in a doze or waking from it, and Ronny ached with pity for her, because she sounded like a frightened child trying hard to be good. Ronny could hear the patient fatherly drone of Colonel Kinney's voice, trying to console her. His own father changed his position restlessly, and then Gloria, in one of those restless moments which passed among them all like a long shudder. The night crawled on.

There was no way of knowing what time it was and yet it might not be more than ten o'clock, Ronny thought. People ashore were just leaving hotels to go out for the evening, or dressing gaily for a dance. How strange it was—they here; those other people over there, hundreds of them, thousands of them, laughing and well fed and happy, walking around on pavements under bright lights. He could see them vividly, hear the murmur of their voices, the scuffing of their feet on sidewalks; and yet they could not think of the six here, even imagine them, or their helpless plight in the black devouring ocean, unless there were headlines in a morning paper. How queer things were.

And the stars far overhead moved slightly and slowly on their steady courses, and the black water lifted and lashed and fell, lifted and fell, lifted and fell, and the wind hummed its three notes interminably. Ronny's head swam a little with a creeping weariness. His body was clammy inside and out, and it was extraordinary how his arms could ache.

Then Gloria's wire went loose and she slipped down with a choked gasp and her head went under, and Ronny dived for her—dived with desperation, so that he crashed full into her down there in the strong surge, and came up with her weight caught in his arms. She coughed and tried to swim a little and spluttered and tried to conceal from him that she was crying in sheer wet misery. Then he could not find her piece of wire. It must have gone down, too. He put one arm around her and held her tightly while she recovered herself. Their wet bodies close together warmed each other feebly, and he was grateful for it. Her shivering stopped slowly and she put out a hand to a strut and held on, so that he was relieved of her weight. He took off what was left of his shirt and tied it around her and around the strut but warned her hoarsely not to trust it too much, torn and sodden as it was.

Then he dozed a little, locking his grip and jerking it tight again before it quite relaxed. It seemed to him that a second of real sleep, half a second of sleep, would be an oblivion so delicious that it would make up for everything. It was always just ahead—just ahead—and then salt water smacked in his face and he was wide awake again and his father's head had disappeared, and he had to dive twice before he brought him safely back again and held him while he recovered from the longer immersion.

A fear that was not like any fear he had known yet clutched coldly at his heart. Was it really a possibility—could it be possible!—that he might lose someone down there? Was death really so near to any one of them in this casual adventure?

The stars slid a little; the waters hissed; the wind screamed. Time was an interminable agony, welding impossible moment to impossible moment that crawled, crawled, crawled. Gloria slipped in again, and then his father, and then Colonel Kinney, losing his wire, and Ronny dived again and again. He had lost track of the number of times. He was not even sure which one it was he hauled heavily to the surface, clinging to him and coughing weakly. Now his right leg was getting cramped. The pain shot up the stiffened muscle, needlelike and searing. Suppose it caught him down there next, when he most needed all the strength he had? He was ashamed to rouse Bill, but he had to, and he heard his own voice, husky and humble, as Bill's had been.

Bill roused instantly and took charge. Ronny hooked his arm over the cockpit edge, and the doze that moved upon him was delightful. Yet it seemed only a moment when Bill was calling him again, exhausted, and the stars were altered and it was hours later.

As Ronny moved out to be among the others, and Bill hung gasping, he counted them carefully, to make sure they were all there. His hands lingered on a shoulder, and he saw that it was his father. After a moment his father's voice came to him wearily. "Still—hanging—on," he said. "Don't go doing —too much now. We—depend on—you and Bill—a lot."

The night went like that, passing so slowly, with such a minute succession of incidents, of wretchedness, that it seemed impossible that it could ever end or change above a half-drowned world.

So that when Ronny, floundering on a wave top, with one arm holding up Gloria, happened to see in the east a streak of pale colour, he stared at it for a long time with puzzled, bloodshot eyes, wondering dully what it could be. The glow widened, the sky and sea around it turned pale gray. A streak of burning gold swelled into that. And Ronny cried out suddenly, in his surprise, "Look; it's morning!"

The tender light fell on faces sodden and strained almost beyond recognition. But even as the light grew white and radiant over the crested wave tops and the strange emerald of the waters, animation came into the faces and they were once more his father and Gloria and Mrs. Kinney and the colonel and Bill.

As if light were the supreme necessity, the supreme miracle, they sought it. It was hope; it was food; it was safety; it was life. A faint burst of animation, exclamation, broken words, feeble, husky laughter passed among them like a renewed pledge. They were once more capable of watching the sea to the west, where any moment now a boat might come. Yet no boat came. The flash of spray was only the edge of a higher wave. The drone was only the wind in the wires. Bill, lifting himself up with greater difficulty now, peered out above them over an empty sea.

Presently the reassuring warmth of the sun had changed to the agonizing glare of yesterday. Their faces were a raw crimson against which the wave edges were knife cuts. Their salt-crusted lips were swollen and cracked. Their eyes were bloodshot and inflamed. Ronny and Bill managed to find rags enough about them to make masks to tie over the faces of the four. Ronny and Bill dared not mask themselves. They had to be on the alert now, both of them. For now that the flash of hope was over and the sun glared nearer and nearer to noon, the others slipped down more easily into the blue depths. It was easier to find them there now, that was all.

It must have been afternoon when Colonel Kinney, slipping down almost without a splash, eluded Ronny's grasp. Beneath the surface the big body was only a whirling shadow which Ronny caught lightly once and lost. When Ronny's lungs seemed bursting he shot to the surface empty-handed, with despairing eyes for Bill's anxious look. One full breath and he was down again, fighting down amidst the strong heave and swirl of the waters, and Bill was with him. Twice they clutched each other fiercely. There was no other shape.

Gasping dreadfully the two hung together on the fuselage, staring into each other's eyes. There was nothing to be said. Ronny was thankful for the mask over Mrs. Kinney's eyes. She need not know yet. She was like a dead thing, hanging there, half held by the wire about her, with one hand locked about a strut. She clung as if by no volition of her own, but only the gripping tenacity of the life within her, straining to go on. The sun beat down upon them. The wind screamed steadily in the wires. The eternal water roared and hissed. No one had said anything for hours and hours.

It was late afternoon. "Ron," whispered his father feebly through his mask, "where's the colonel?"

"Gone," said Ronny after a moment. "I—lost him."

His father tore off his mask suddenly. Beneath it the contorted swollen features were almost unrecognizable. "He's lucky," his father rasped. "Why not? Why not?"

"Hush, Dad," Ronny said patiently, "they'll hear you. There'll be a boat before long. There must be."

Andrew Burgess said nothing more. Ronny stared at the haggard, bitter face where the stiff gray hairs bristled about the chin. It smote through his numbed brain suddenly that his father—his splendid father—was an old, old man.

The sunset flared hideously down upon them. Another night came slowly from the west. And Gloria, tearing off her mask, leaned back abruptly in the rag that held her, and tore free. Her lips strained back from her gaunt face in a queer tense smile and she threw both hands over her head and went down suddenly, before Ronny could guess what she had intended. And below there was only the swirl and the silvery bubbles of his own and Bill's frantic search.

When they came back again it was almost night, and Ronny was shaken by a paroxysm of grief which he had not even strength enough to express in sobs. He remembered vaguely how beautiful she had been on that morning, ages ago, when he was a boy, before the flight began.

In that night his father disappeared. It was a night such as Ronny had never dreamed possible. He and Bill were left alone in all the lost world, hanging mute and feeble on each side of the faintly warm figure of Mrs. Kinney. Her wire still held. With the mask off, under the stars, her face was not so ravaged as the others. From time to time she moaned a little and they took turns in chafing gently her clammy hands and feet. She was something infinitely precious that they had left to care for, in the whirling chaos in their minds, in the roaring black about them and the high black over them, punctuated with the glittering smear of stars.

When the sun at last broke up the permanence of that night they blinked their salt-incrusted eyes at each other unbelievably, to see the sun, to see that they were still there—three nameless, shapeless beings, under the incredible light.

Ronny turned his head presently to see a boat come surging toward them with a great fan of spray at the bow—a boat with men in it, with young, dry, smooth faces looking anxiously at them, and waving. Ronny watched it come with no emotion whatsoever. He had always known that it would come. But now that hardly mattered.

When hands clutched and hauled him up, he fought them until he saw they had clutched also Bill and Mrs. Kinney. He felt himself in a dry boat, with something to drink burning in his throat. But he felt nothing. There was nothing to feel. Until they told him, gently, that Mrs. Kinney had been dead for very many hours. Then he cried with terrible retching sobs, vaguely ashamed that Bill should see him so.

"DONE GOT OVER"

By ALMA AND PAUL ELLERBE

From *Collier's*

WOODIE SIMMONS walked past the house three times before he found courage to open the gate. He was trying to decide what he was going to say. His mind switched; no sooner had he chosen sentences than he forgot them and thought of others. He went up the walk at last because he was afraid that if he delayed longer he wouldn't be able to think of any at all.

There were four-o'clocks on either side of the walk, their blossoms furled into tight little yellow and red fists, and beyond them prince's feather, nasturtiums, a chinaberry tree, and a syringa bush all mixed in with tomatoes (the kind that bear small fruit, like red marbles), collards, mint, jimson weeds and white and yellow dog fennel. The Rev. Zachariah Draper spent but little time on things like gardening. But his congregation kept his house in good repair. It was the best in the Negro section of Lower Habersham.

Woodie knocked. There was the sound of a tilted chair let down to the floor, and then of a heavy foot, and Draper came into the doorless hallway that ran through the middle of the house with the slinging slouch that had always made Woodie think of an enormous, sore-footed cat. He had been afraid of the preacher all his life.

"Good-morning," he said, as simply as he could, but he knew his voice had a stilted sound.

Draper straightened and fumbled with his collar, which was unbuttoned. He buttoned it and made a pompous bow. "Howdy, suh? What can Ah do fer yer?"

The boy had the miserable consciousness that he had been mistaken for a white man. He was tall for his seventeen years, with a coffee-and-cream coloured skin; the light shone from behind him; he and Draper had not met for five years, and he wore the kind of clothes that in that place only white men wore: a gray tweed suit, tan Oxford shoes and blue socks, a clean white collar, a blue cravat and a sailor straw hat. He was intensely conscious of them, but they were all he had.

"It—it's jest Woodie Simmons, Brudder Zach," he stammered, dropping desperately into the vernacular in an attempt at conciliation. "Don't yer know me?"

Draper came nearer, and the morning sun shone on his boldly modelled, lustful face until it gleamed like oiled black marble. His huge body seemed to exude health and strength, along with a rank, unpleasant odour of its own and the smell of snuff. He wore enormous carpet slippers on his bare feet, blue overalls, a dirty white stiff shirt without a cravat, and the greenish black frock coat which was his inevitable badge of office. He tilted back his head, his lips curled away from his snuff-chinked teeth and bluish gums, something lightened in his live black eyes and he broke into a great whoop of laughter.

The volume and unexpectedness of it startled the boy. He shrank back as if he had been pushed. His anger rose, but fear and grief made him weak.

"Li'l' Woodie Simmons!" Draper roared. "Li'l' pickaninny Woodie, dressed up lak' *dat!*" He drew an immense blue handkerchief with white polka dots on it from the tails of his coat and wiped his eyes and blew his nose, watching Woodie the while with a malignant shrewdness beneath his feigned amusement. He enjoyed the boy's discomfort and wanted to prolong it. "Tell me, son, do de Yankee white man what's payin' fer yer at dat school up North throw in dem clo'es?"

"He—he pays all my expenses. All the boys dress thisaway. And—and everybody else in the town."

"Do tell! Ah thought mebbe dey'd done made yer er perfesser or somethin'. And now yer's done gradyerwaited yerse'f, is yer gwine take de colonel's place down ter de bank, or be de chief er *po*lice, or what?"

Woodie's eyes filled with tears. He trembled like a colt in a thunderstorm—he was leggy and sensitive and slender like a colt. "Brother Zack," he said timidly, "my father—died—last night."

A swift change went over the preacher. His easy, bantering

air disappeared. He bent forward an intent grave face. Always and innately dramatic, he listened in every line.

"There's nobody but—but you to preach—at his funeral. Will you—will you please do it?"

Draper gazed at the boy for a long moment. "Tampa Simmons daid!" he said slowly. He pursed his lips and narrowed his eyes, nodding his head to emphasize the words. "Tampa Simmons *daid!*"

He still seemed to be listening, but now to something inside himself. His unseeing eyes were turned inward. A change went over his face and illumined his eye. He regarded Woodie with stern dignity. The boy knew the issue had been settled, but not how.

"Yer paw was er backslider an' er Philly-stine. He turned his back on 'ligion. He fought me up an' he fought me down, ever since de day Ah first come ter de Ole Ship er Zion, fifteen years ago. Ah wrastled wid um in de presence uv de Lawd, an' he scandalized mah name."

It was the deep, sure barytone that had won him half his battles. He could turn it on like an organ stop whenever he needed it. It had a strangely moving quality. Woodie felt it in the flesh of his back.

"But de Sperret says ter me: 'Bury um from de Ole Ship an' preach ter his funeral.' Ah feel de Sperret movin' in mah heart, an' dat what it say: 'Bury um from de Ole Ship an' preach ter his funeral.' Yer can tell yer maw Ah'll do it."

Woodie told her two hours later, after he had bought food in the town, made arrangements for the funeral to be held the next morning at nine o'clock—the hour set by Draper— notified their friends, and jogged the three miles back home on the old white mule that had gone down the furrows ahead of his father ever since he could remember.

"Praise de name er Jesus!" she said gently in her soft voice. "Glory be ter Gawd! Ah never thought he'd do it!"

She turned her face to the whitewashed wall where she lay on her bed and began to cry quietly to herself, from relief. Before Woodie could leave the room she had gone to sleep, for the first time in forty-eight hours.

She was a soft, plump little woman, almost the same colour as her son, full of kindness and forgivingness. She had had no part in the feud between her husband and the preacher. She had always gone to church at the Old Ship of Zion. When Draper became a part of it she had accepted him without question. He preached only hate and fear: hate of the unconverted, of the liberal-minded, of white people, and fear of, almost equally, God and the devil, but she didn't see that. She was perplexed and frightened when her husband denounced him as unchristian and withdrew his family from the church. That had been fifteen years ago, when Woodie was a baby.

Other people had followed Tampa Simmons—who was a good deal of a leader in his own right—but not for long. There was fascination in the very boards of the Old Ship and a dread fascination in Draper. His gift of torrential oratory was unlike anything the Piney Woods had known. His congregation whispered that he "had a hand," and shivered with dreadful pleasure, seeing his power as half from Satan and half from God, and wholly interesting. Their meagre lives would have been barren of entertainment, their genuine religious fervour denied an outlet, without Draper and the Old Ship. Everyone had drifted back but the Simmonses.

Woodie's mother had remained away solely from loyalty to his father. As Woodie lingered, looking down at her, he realized with a pang that at any time during the fifteen years she would have returned to the Old Ship, if she could, as a carrier pigeon to its home. She had never really understood how his father felt, nor why. Woodie had understood, even five years ago—when he was too young to talk about it. He could have talked about it now, and now it was too late.

He went into the other room. Pieces of dark cloth had been tacked up at the windows to keep out the light. Two old women were bent together beside the fireless hearth. He had always called them Aunt Caroline and Aunt Miranda, but they were not related to him. He could barely see them in the half dark, but the mound of his father's body beneath a sheet on the bed stood out clearly. Nothing could have lain so still which had not once had life in it. The room smelled of medicine and snuff and food, and somehow faintly of death. The old women were talking in whispers and dipping snuff.

There was another woman in the lean-to kitchen, beside the stove, where he had never seen anyone but his mother.

She was cooking dinner: collards, turnip greens with pork, and crackling bread. The strong odours made him a little queasy. The woman was stout and black and shone with perspiration. She had big, loose breasts and cheeks and lips and shrewd, tolerant eyes. She wore the garbled remains of white women's clothes: shoes broken at the bulges, a black silk skirt that had split on the creases, and a newly blackened waist still damp with pokeberry dye. Her face looked strange to Woodie without its usual half smile. Her name was Maria Knox, and her husband was a truck gardener. He had known her all his life, but when they spoke to each other their words were stiff and unnatural. He had played with her children almost every day until he went away, but now it seemed that it wasn't he who had known them.

He was feeling more clearly and deeply than he had ever felt; the impressions made upon him were going to last until he was an old man, but because he kept seeing himself as if he were someone else, he thought he wasn't much affected, and was disappointed in himself. He couldn't help seeing the house as if it were a stage-set for a play about inferior people, and the people in the house as if they had been actors, and that seemed to him cruel and unworthy.

He went on out of doors and sat on a stump near the house, where his father used to smoke his pipe in the evening. It came to him there that *he* was the head of the family now. Somehow he had to take the place of the strong, resourceful man who was dead. He felt slight and ignorant—incompetent. The flash and fragrance of the spring day seemed inappropriate and unnatural. He held up his hand to shield his eyes. The fresh yellow-jasmine-scented air was strange in his nostrils.

He stared off across the clearing. That, too, seemed like a scene in a play, and yet no other spot of ground was so familiar. The climbing sun lit as if they had been candles the red trumpet flowers that hung on a twisted pine. There had always been a trumpet vine on that tree. . . .

Something moved near the base of the tree. He looked more closely and saw that it was a woman. She was waving her hand—beckoning. He got up and walked across the clearing.

As he came nearer he recognized a spry, birdlike creature

who played the melodeon in the Old Ship. He remembered that she used to give him tea cakes.

"Why, howdy, sis? Charity?" He held out his hand.

She took it and peered at him with nearsighted eyes from a kindly face as wrinkled as a nanny-oak ball.

"Howdy, Woodie? Yer sho' has growed lak' er weed! De spittin' image uv yer maw! Ah called yer over hyeh ter keep from disturbin' her. Ah—Ah got somethin' ter tell yer."

Her eyes blinked rapidly; she put her head first on one side and then on the other with quick little jerks and her fingers worked nervously together.

"Dat low-down nigger, dat Zach Draper"—she looked around uneasily—"when he preach ter yer paw's funeral ter-morrer, he gwine—gwine"—her voice shook—"*he gwine sen' his soul ter hell!*"

Woodie stared in blank amazement. "He's go'n'er do *what?*"

"*He gwine sen' yer paw's soul ter hell!*"

"But—but how can he? What's *he* got to do with it? Don't everybody know Pappy was a good man? Do you think anybody will believe him?"

"*Ev'ybody* b'lieve um! Ain't he de preacher? An' ain't yer paw laid his 'ligion down? Fer fifteen years he ain't gone ter church nowhar!"

"There warn't anywheres else to go but the Old Ship."

"That ain't gwine make no diff'rence ter most folks. Dey'll say Brudder Zach's got de right ter decide 'bout dat. He's er powerful man when it comes ter de 'splainments uv de Sper-ret!"

Woodie had the feel of things crumbling down inside of him. "I'll—stop him somehow!" he said in a choked voice; but he felt frightened and confused. He looked into the troubled eyes of the little organist. "What can I do, sis—Charity?" he faltered.

"Ah dunno, chile! Ah dunno! Ah's knowed yer paw all mah life, and, preacher or no preacher, Zach Draper ain't fitten ter tote swill fer um!"

"Can't you—can't you change him somehow? Can't you talk him out of it?"

"Ah's done tried ter! Ah's talked ter um till he won't listen ter me no mo'."

Woodie shook with sudden anger. "Did you tell him he's ornery—lowdown—mean?"

"Gawd A'mighty, boy, Ah dassent! Ah'm skeered uv um! Ev'ybody's skeered uv um!" She lowered her voice almost to a whisper: "Dey do say he's got er han'!"

Woodie shivered. You got a "hand" from a conjure doctor, and it gave you supernatural power over your enemies. He had thought, off at school, that he had come to regard such things as nonsense, but down here a deep live current of terror ran through the people, and he found himself tingling to it as he used to do.

Woodie stood for a long time beneath the swaying trumpet flowers, thinking. There was one person who could stop Draper if she would. Miss Jinny Pickens could stop any coloured man or woman in that county from doing anything. His grandfather and grandmother had belonged to her, and he had seen his father and mother turn to her in every emergency. He went to her now as naturally as they would have done.

But first he told the three women what Charity had said, and made them promise to help him keep it from his mother.

From the other side of the gentle tree-smothered valley that stretched before it the house lifted itself with its old air of remote nobility, but when he had walked up the long, winding driveway under the oaks and hickory trees and sycamores, he saw that the paint had flaked from the tall Corinthian columns—which no longer had the effect of propping up the sky—and that the iron balcony behind them drooped like a disillusioned mouth.

And at the rear, where all coloured people were supposed to enter and his feet took him of their own accord, the arms of the tall fig tree couldn't hide the broken shutters at the windows, the gaps in the railing of the upstairs porch, nor the rotting boards of the steps—the air the old place had of dropping minutely into ruin, bit by bit.

The harsh smell of fig leaves in the sun came to him strongly, and he took a sudden sharp breath. It brought back his father more vividly than even the sight of his dead face had done. Tampa Simmons seemed to be standing against the big three-fingered leaves, heavily listed to the left on account of his lame leg, just as he had stood that day when he had brought cream (and Woodie) to the back yard and Miss Jinny had come out to talk with him.

"Miss Jinny, ma'am," he had said, "Ah don't want mah li'l' boy ter grow up ter be lak' Ah is! Miss Jinny—look at me!" He had spread out his work-twisted hands in the mellow sunshine of late afternoon and looked at her earnestly, and Miss Jinny (and Woodie) had looked at him. "Ah don't know nothin'; Ah can't read an' Ah can't write; Ah ain't got nothin' an' Ah ain't never goin' ter have. Ah'm jest er cawnfiel' nigger—er li'l' better'n er mule. Don't yer expec' that mebbe somehow it might be fixed so's mah li'l' boy might be—diff'rent?"

Woodie heard again the grave, self-respecting bass and saw the deeply furrowed, kindly face looking out at him with what had come to be to the boy the wistfulness of their race.

Miss Jinny, too, had seen and heard, and felt, and in the end had found a man in Boston—and Jerusalem seemed no farther from the Piney Woods—to send Woodie away to school and give him such an opportunity as had fallen to the lot of no other coloured child he had ever known. Even his vacations were provided for: that the experiment might have a thorough chance, he had spent them, until this year, with a prosperous Negro family who had a summer place in Maine.

Behind the humble Simmons family always, as protection, somehow, from any hardship too great to be borne, had stood the great rock of Miss Jinny Pickens: impoverished, elderly, and alone, but a Pickens; knit into the fibres of the state; indomitable by nature and affiliations. Woodie felt her there. He stepped up and knocked at her door with confidence.

The door was opened by a woman of his own race whom he did not know. "*She* ain't hyeh!" she said, with inflections that suggested that only the undesirable wouldn't have known it. "She done gone ter Leestown, ter see Miss Sadie Lee."

The Lees were cousins of the Pickenses. He hadn't thought of any of the old names for a long time. He asked when Miss Jinny would return.

"Mebbe ter-morrer an' mebbe not. Is you Tampa Simmons' boy?"

When he said he was she told him what Draper meant to

do at the funeral. She told him with sympathy, but with a strange gusto. There had been a trace of it even in the kindly Charity.

He had come through the woods. As he went back by the road and one Negro after another stopped him to tell him the same thing in the same way, the sick consciousness dawned within him of something which he could not have expressed. The sympathy of these people was real enough, but there was in it an excitation of horror that they craved; a brushing near of occult and of awful things. They awaited his father's funeral in a state of delicious, morbid expectancy.

If Miss Jinny failed him! . . .

He got out the old white mule and started for Leestown.

When he returned the mule to the stable a round white moon was pouring light steadily into the velvet darkness. Sore and stiff, he stumbled into the kitchen, where a pallet had been fixed for him on the floor.

He had ridden the mule to Leestown and back—twenty-four miles. He had had to ride slowly, because the old mule tired easily and had gone a little lame. He would have made the trip by stage, but no stage went in the afternoon. Both towns were off the railroad.

He had gone to Miss Sadie Lee's house, and again Miss Jinny had been away. Miss Sadie had taken her motoring. The best he had been able to accomplish was to leave a note, to be delivered to Miss Jinny immediately upon her return. He hadn't dared wait for her. If she wasn't going to stop Zach Draper, he had to do it himself.

He couldn't sleep. His mind ran all night, as uselessly as the arms of an unconnected windmill. It showed him scores of unrelated pictures: the faces of boys he knew off at school; the little white New England church in the village there; Draper, laughing at him; a bend in the creek where he used to swim; his father's body; the corner of a cornfield behind a snake fence covered with purple morning glories. It repeated scraps of the day's conversations. On and on and on. It reverberated soundlessly with the voodooistic terror that ran through the Negroes of the Piney Woods at the prospect of the morrow's sensation. Fear, like a hot wind, blew across it, searing and drying his thoughts. He felt things older and bigger and more terrible than he had realized threshing around him in the hot, humid Southern air. . . .

Finally he got up and rummaged in a cupboard and slipped his father's old pistol into the pocket of his coat, where it hung over the back of a chair. He had a plan now. It was as simple as Cain's. . . .

Toward morning he slept a little.

Woodie sat on the front pew in the Old Ship of Zion, between his mother and Maria Knox. His mother was heavily swathed in borrowed black. Her plump, innocent features, still swollen from weeping, looked purged and peaceful beneath her veil. She alone was unaware of the air of tense expectancy that bound the rest of the congregation together.

In front of them stood his father's coffin, on two sawhorses banked deep with cape jasmine, which had just begun to bloom; dead-white, half-opened flowers set stiffly in stiff, glistening green leaves. Their heavy odour lay like a blanket over the place in spite of the open windows. A score of spring scents outside strove against it in vain.

Behind him the church filled steadily. He could feel the waiting people: row on close-packed row, all their faces turned one way—tense—expectant—frightened. They were all very still. Somewhere in the distance a man was calling hogs. The long-drawn notes of his voice sounded like a horn. It died away, and the kind of silence that belongs only to funerals fell upon the little church. Into it the clock on the wall plumped nine twangy notes.

Charity spread her thin black fingers over the keys of the melodeon. Draper erected his bulk in the chancel and began lining out the first hymn: "Shall We Gather at the River?"

Woodie's hour was on him, and Miss Jinny hadn't come.

Things swam together and went black. He clutched the butt of the pistol in his coat pocket with a cold, damp hand and stared at Draper. The man seemed of superhuman size. He was like something the little church had been built to hold. Woodie shook with fear.

His mother laid her hand on his arm. "Is yer all right, Son?"

"Yes'm," he muttered thickly, "I'm all right." But he scarcely heard her and was barely aware that he had replied.

The first notes of the hymn came whining out of the old melodeon. He rose with the rest, and the congregation sang. It passed over his mind in a blur of sound.

Draper knelt beside the pulpit and prayed, and the people bowed their heads to the roll of his voice. Woodie listened long enough to be sure the prayer held no menace for the dead man; the rest of it became a confused rumble in his ears.

Draper rose from his knees. Omitting the hymn between the prayer and the sermon, he looked out over his people—gathered them in with his eye. A hush fell upon them. The faint, lazy call of a distant flycatcher pulsed its way clearly through their midst, and he spoke, slowly.

"Brethren an' sisters, de hymn done ax yer, shall we gather at de river, de beautiful river dat flows by de throne uv Gawd? An'*Ah'm* a-axin' yer"—he paused, spread out his arms in a slow gesture of restrained power and let his voice fall upon a note that went through the waiting people as a wind through leaves—"*Ah'm* a-axin' yer, brethren an' sisters, when yer gits ter de river, de beautiful river dat flows by de throne uv Gawd, is yer gwine ter be fitten ter *git on de boat:* de big boat dat's a-waitin' by de bank, wid de steam a-shootin' outer de chimbley an' de paddles a-splashin' in de water—de big boat dat's a-waitin' dar ter take yer on down ter de throne itse'f? *Is yer gwine ter be fitten?*"

A groan went over the people. A scarcely audible sigh of anticipation came out of them. Draper caught it and fanned it. His voice began its steady march toward its goal. Woodie's mouth grew dry. His heart seemed about to burst.

"It ain't gwine do yer no good ter *sneak* on ter de big boat ef yer ain't fitten, caise' yer can't fool de Lawd Jesus! Yer might fool de cap'n er de boat, or de Angel Gabriel, but"—the creak of an automobile brake came through the window—"yer can't"—his outstretched hand sank to his side—"fool——"

His big features stiffened with displeasure. He stood silent, staring toward the door.

Woodie turned with the rest. His heart bounded like a toy balloon and then crowded up into his throat and stuck there.

Miss Jinny Pickens was coming down the aisle.

But not the Miss Jinny Pickens he remembered: a frail, little old woman with bent back and brown time spots on her wrinkled cheeks, who wore shabby clothes and walked slowly, leaning on a cane.

A swift sense came back to him of the Miss Jinny whose foot had tapped the floor as positively as a woodpecker's beak against a tree; whose back had been as straight as a child's; whose movements had been marked with crisp decisiveness; whose clothes had been magnificent.

Or had they only seemed so to the ragged little boy who had never owned a pair of shoes or seen a train? Was it possible that she had been old and frail and shabby then?

He couldn't tell; but then and always she had been *Miss Jinny Pickens*, and a member of the super-supreme court which in the last analysis settled everything of importance in that countryside. No Negro in the state had ever openly crossed one of them and lived out the day. He looked with swift hope at Draper—and saw that things had changed.

Something inhered in Miss Jinny that stood for power, but Draper didn't see it. He waited there in haughty, calculating silence, watching her progress down the aisle, through contemptuous, half-closed eyes, unimpressed and unafraid. The consciousness that the issue lay solely between him and Draper grew tight about Woodie's heart. Miss Jinny faded out for him almost before she had settled herself in the chair that someone brought from the little room behind the melodeon.

And Draper, too, as soon as he began to talk again, forgot her. His voice took on the sound of something started on its way which could not be stopped—not even by the preacher himself. There had been but one rebellion in the Old Ship of Zion since he came: now was the time to stamp out any last lingering embers of it. As he slowly raised his hand and swung back into his march of words, Woodie's vitals seemed to melt and flow downward. Despair boiled in him like vomit.

"De Lawd Jesus'll be a-waitin'! He'll be a-settin' on de edge er de great white throne, a-waitin'—a-waitin' fer dat boat! An' when He see it comin', He'll holler out ter de angels: 'Hi'st up de silver spyglass ter Mah eye!' An' de angels'll h'ist it. Twelve angels it'll take ter h'ist up de silver spyglass ter His eye.

"An' den He'll p'int de silver spyglass, |an' ef dere's anybody on dat boat dat don't belong—*He'll see um! He'll see spang through um!*

"An' He'll say: 'Lean de silver spyglass erginst de throne, an' lif' up de speakin' trumpet dat's made er gol'!' An' de angels'll do it. Twenty angels it'll take ter lif' up de speakin' trumpet dat's made er gol'!

"An' den de Lawd Jesus'll put His mouth ter de speakin' trumpet, an' He'll holler out loud an' cl'are: 'Mistah Cap'n, yer hyeh Me?'" very slowly and solemnly: "'*Yer got er on-believer on dat boat!* Yer'll have ter stop an' go back, Mistah Cap'n, an' lan' um——'"

Woodie's hand closed round the pistol, when his eye chanced to fall on Miss Jinny's face. Her look of quiet certitude startled him. He leaned forward, scarcely breathing.

"'—an' lan' um whar he belongs!'"

Miss Jinny cleared her throat, but Draper didn't notice.

"'Back whar de brimstone's at, an' de fire——'"

Miss Jinny moved her chair, but Draper didn't even look her way.

"'Back whar de smoke's a-curlin' out de groun', an'——'"

The sharp pounding of Miss Jinny's cane fell across his sentence and broke it as brittlely off as if it had been a rod of glass.

Woodie dropped back limply into his seat. He opened his mouth to still the sound of his breathing. He grew weak under the surge of his relief. For a moment all that he could realize was that he hadn't had to shoot—that Miss Jinny had saved him from that.

She sat on the edge of her chair, as delicately separate as a white hepatica, looking straight at Draper, and as the sense of her sank into Woodie it seemed to him that she was a part of the backbone of life itself, and again he looked at the preacher with a flaming up of hope.

But the big Negro was staring at the white woman in blank amazement, without meeting her eyes, much as he might have stared at the roof if it had fallen in; uneasy only because the mood he had induced in his people had been threatened.

For a moment he was silent, while he reassembled his scattered powers. He shifted his weight until the floor creaked. He leaned forward and began to speak again, and Woodie's hope sank slowly and heavily. It was going to take more than the pounding of a cane to stop Zachariah Draper.

With his hand on his father's old pistol, that had never

been pointed at anything bigger than a chicken-hunting
skunk, he leaned forward breathlessly, while Draper, out of a
deep instinct in such matters, and as though rebuking his
antagonist, laid his tongue to stronger words than any of his
own.

"De Good Book say"—with sombre emphasis—"'Take
heed lest dere be in any uv yer an evil heart uv onbelief!
Take heed, fer de sword uv Gawd am quick an' powerful, an'
sharper dan any two-edged sword, piercin' even ter de
dividin' asunder uv de soul an' de sperret, an' uv de j'ints an'
de marrow!'"

"Amen!" a woman said startlingly in a clear soprano; the
others groaned in chorus, "A-amen! A-amen, brudder!" and
the shattered mood of the people came together again.

Draper fanned it as a wind fans a prairie fire: "Brethren
an' sisters, ef yer want ter lan' at de great white throne, yer
got ter git shed uv dat evil heart uv onbelief!"

Tap, tap, went the cane, mild and premonitory, but he pre-
tended not to hear.

"De Good Book say: 'He shall set de sheep on His right
han', but de goats on de lef'. An' He shall say unter dem on de
lef' han', Depart from me, ye cursed, inter everlastin' fire, prepared fer de Devil an' his angels!'"

A gleam came into his eye. He in his pulpit, in the midst of
his people, and the white woman down there alone. . . ! Almost alone too, now, in that part of the state: ten Negroes all
about her now to every poverty-stricken white. . . ! He within
his rights, and she a trespasser. . . ! His voice rolled out over
her like a river:

"Yer got ter pull off from de goats! Yer got ter come inter
de fold!"

He chanted like a warrior leading hosts, with a rhythm as
heavily marked as the beating of a drum.

"Ah been down yander in de canebrake, a-lookin' fer dem
goats—a-studyin' in mah min' an' a-wrastlin' in mah soul!
Ah been down yander in de canebrake, an' what yer think Ah
see?"

A moan of anticipation—pleasure and horror and fear—
ran over his human harp strings. "What yer see, brudder?"
"Glory, hallelujah!" "Praise de name er Jesus!" "What yer
see?"

"Ah done see de Devil, de big, black, shiny Devil, a-scorchin' up de canebrake wid his breath!"

A bass voice began to moan heavily. An alto joined. Others took it up, improvising with a sure sense of harmony an elaborate background for Draper's trampling barytone.

"His tail was long an' shiny lak' er blacksnake! His eyes was lak' de haidlights on de train!"

Woodie shut his eyes and prayed. The long-continued pound of emotion had beaten from him all acquired white folks' methods of speech and feeling. "Gawd gimme strength," he prayed, "ter shoot um through de heart ef Ah have ter!"

The trampling barytone went on: "His feet was p'inted lak' er crowbar an' cloven in de midst, an' his mouth was lak' et watermillon full er seeds!"

Woodie sat there stiff and cold with sweat, in his excitement almost as white as a white boy. He looked childlike and harmless and pitiful, but he was the most dangerous kind of potential murderer: the determined coward, rapt out of himself past the reach of reason; ready to shoot when Draper's words should pull the trigger.

Draper's words crept toward it steadily. "His long white teeth was a-champin' an' a-scrunchin' an' a-gnashin'—*fer dem goats !*"

He got his people rocking and moaning to the drunken rhythm of his feelings and his words. He got them ten thousand miles away from the mind of the white woman, so that her lonely, pale face in their midst seemed strange and unnatural. And suddenly, under cover of the eerie din, he dropped like a waiting eagle straight for his prey:

"An' de Devil say ter me: '*Whar's dat backslider?*"

Tap, tap, tap, insisted the cane, steady and sharp.

Woodie moved farther from his mother, for elbow room.

Tiny beads of sweat broke out on Draper's face, but he didn't swerve. "'*Whar's de man dat laid his 'ligion down?*'"

"Gawd gimme strength!" Woodie prayed.

"'He ain't so dark,' de Devil say, 'an he ain't so light.'"

Woodie cocked the old pistol in his pocket.

"'He's middle-sized,' de Devil say, 'an' he's got er limp ——'"

Woodie leaned forward to shoot, but Miss Jinny was on her feet.

She had risen casually, as if to smooth the folds of the shawl that lay over the back of her chair, but the straight thrust of her keen blue eyes seeking the preacher's made the air between them crackle with life.

Draper drew himself up to the full of his enormous height. He was as superb and as sincere as a great coiled snake. He thrust out his jaw and frowned; his eyes lightened in the way they had, and the essential spirit within him met Miss Jinny's steadily.

The whole church held its breath. There was a moment of intense silence, through which the call of the flycatcher fanned its lazy way, and then an inward and spiritual something behind the frail old countenance broke something behind the big, glistening black face, with its prow of a nose, its curling lips and heavy jowl and restless, predatory eyes—broke it with a snap that might have been audible, so definite it was.

Draper raised his hand and lowered it; opened his mouth and closed it again; drew forth the polka-dotted handkerchief and mopped the perspiration from his face.

And then Miss Jinny sat down, and he found that he could speak.

But whatever it was that had snapped in him had snapped, too, in his people. An uneasy sense of shame lay over them. There wasn't one who didn't know Tampa Simmons as he knew his own hearthstone; not one whom the dead man hadn't helped and comforted when he could; who didn't believe in him as no human being had ever believed in Draper. The tide of feeling flowed away from the preacher; ebbed faster and faster with his every word.

He couldn't tell what was stopping him. He was like a bird trying to fly through the pane of a window. Because he could not see it, he thought there was nothing there, and battered himself to pieces against the realest thing in all that country, going down at last before his congregation, a beaten man, jabbering meaningless sentences out of which one fact only stood up: that the soul of Tampa Simmons went to heaven, where Miss Jinny Pickens wanted it to go.

And in the midst of the debacle a strange thing happened. Softly, spontaneously, without a leader, the people began to sing: "Done got over!" they sang:

> "Done got over!
> Had a hard time;
> Had to work so long;
> But I done got over,
> Done got over,
> Done got over at last!"

The deep, old, patient, humble melody fell upon them like the spirit of Christ, and they bowed their heads and sank to their knees, and most of them wept.

And that night Woodrow Woodson Simmons, the son of Tampa Bay Florida Simmons, who was the son of Wisdom, a chattel without surname belonging to the Pickens estate; who was the son of Zebulon, likewise a slave; who was the son of a naked savage of the Congo jungle, walked alone through his native woods like a murderer reprieved, with a heart too big for his breast; and, throwing the old pistol far out into the swamp, caught the sound of the myriad feet of his people stumbling painfully along the way his father had travelled, out of the land of ignorance and out of the house of fear, and swore that some spark of his father's spirit should march in him at the head of that army until he died.

MONKEY MOTIONS

By ELEANOR MERCEIN KELLY

From *Pictorial Review*

HAVING lately discovered our Aunt Lady after a lapse of years, we made the most of it, and frequently accepted her standing invitation to motor over to the old town for Sunday dinner, saving up our Hooverized appetites for days beforehand, since no mere world war had been able to affect to any appreciable extent Aunt Lady's table.

"A doctor's got to keep his strength up these days," she explained apologetically, "and it isn't as if we didn't raise 'most everything on the place."

On such an occasion—and they were occasions—we noticed for the first time a singularly limber, spindling, knock-kneed youth of a pale saddle colour, who was being taught, with some difficulty, to wait on table. He moved about his duties in a sort of rhythmical, high-stepping manner that made one rather nervous, especially when soup was being served. His eyes had the mournful, wistful anxiety of a young hound's, but his manner affected an easy pomposity, modelled obviously upon the best of butler traditions, which are good in that part of the country.

"Sarvent, Moddom, sarvent!" he murmured as he placed me in my chair at table; and at my husband's ear he breathed solicitously, "I hopes de julep was to Yore Honour's tas'e?"

My husband, who is a mere business man and unaccustomed to such attentions and entitlements, sat down with some suddenness as his chair was thrust vigorously beneath his knees.

"Where," he inquired of the Curtises, "did you get that?"

"It's just the Infant Samuel; Mahaly's child, you know." Aunt Lady spoke in rather a *distraite* manner, her ear turned toward the pantry, whence issued sounds of more or less repressed African mirth. Suddenly there was a crash, and the mirth rose beyond repression.

"Excuse me one moment," murmured Aunt Lady. "I expect Sam'l's dropped the shoat again."

He had. It appeared that when the small roast pig, the *pièce de résistance* of the feast, was laid out prettily upon its platter, fore feet folded on its breast and parsley arranged all round, it so suggested to Sam'l's vivid imagination a baby laid out for burial that he could not make up his mind to bring it in to be carved. The shoat had to be rescued, reinstated upon an unbroken platter, and brought to table by Aunt Lady herself, the rest of the domestic force being entirely demoralized. Only Sam'l remained serious, painfully, shudderingly serious.

"He's very fond of children," observed our host, "and does not come of a cannibal tribe, probably. Besides, he seems to have inherited his mother's nervous temperament. You remember Mahaly, I dare say?"

Certainly I did. She was one of the happiest memories of my childhood, though overlaid, as such memories often are, with events more immediate.

I would no more have missed the weekly visit of Mahaly to our wash house than I would have missed the circus, and for much the same reason. She stimulated the imagination; she brought far things near; in her companionship nothing seemed impossible, neither hippopotami, nor miracles, nor "ha'nts."

She moved in a world of her own, amid events invisible. One frequently heard her conversing, giggling, coquetting with persons who were not there, which might have been disconcerting to older and more rigid minds.

But we loved to hear her tell about them, these invisibles: the King of Yearth, for instance, one of her suitors, who came to court her in the guise of a simple mole, although he lived in underground palaces as gorgeous as Aladdin's cave. (From which of the classic fables could this have derived, and how?)

And there was the Queen of Sheba, African, like herself, but of a "brighter" shade, who was not really dead, but sometimes chose to manifest in the body of some descendant— "ef she kep' herse'f *to* herse'f," added Mahaly significantly. That was the reason she lived quite alone in a ramshackle

cabin on the far side of the graveyard, where "nigger folks
wouldn't come pesterin'."

The Negroes were only too content to leave her alone,
less out of fear, apparently, than out of scorn. They regarded
her as "foolish in the head." They jeered and laughed at
her whenever she appeared, to poor Mahaly's wincing surprise; the penalty an artist pays for living in a conservative
community.

For Mahaly was unmistakably an artist in the broader
sense of the word. How the queer creature could sing! I am
haunted yet by the dramatic pathos she used to put into her
favourite washtub ditty:

> Hark, fum de tomb come do'fum soun'
> (Jay-bird jump an' jar de groun').
> I once was los' but now I'se foun'
> (Wash dem dishes an' set 'em erroun').

Why this rather inconsequent song should contain so
much of pathos I could not have told then, nor can I now;
perhaps one sensed the contrast between her supernatural
yearnings, the Jeanne d'Arc voices which guided her, and
the humble round of Mahaly's daily life: "Washin' dem
dishes" (other people's dishes) "an' settin' 'em erroun'."

On occasion she was moved to dance for us; not the ordinary, frivolous clap-and-patter, buck-and-wing steps, for
Mahaly had got religion and was very much saved indeed
—so much so that she gave nearly all her earnings to the
church—but a stately ceremonial prance, with odd jerks of
the body and long, rhythmic pauses, to the tune of a muttered
chant. Her eyes were half closed as in an ecstasy. So might
some ancient jungle priestess have danced before the great
god Mumbo-jumbo.

And she had the true artist's passion for colour, for beautiful fabrics, which was doubtless the reason our mothers
found her such an invaluable laundress. With what loving
tenderness she would "rub out" some silken treasure en-
trusted to her care, or flute a delicate ruffle, or clear-starch a
sheer organdy! And her cabin walls fluttered queerly with
rags and tags of brilliant colour, discarded finery, bright garments which had ceased to function; meaningless, savage,
more than a little mad, of course, yet cheerful to the eye as a

patchwork quilt. Mahaly was, indeed, an advance agent of the decorative doctrines of Bakst.

Yet I recalled her most clearly—such is the sadism of child-hood—not as the wistful seeker after beauty, the patient and adoring friend (for the most pestiferous of children never seemed to pester Mahaly), but as the guy she always looked when she started off for camp meeting. This great event of her church, known as "Conference," took place annually at a camp ground in the next county, and during the week or so it lasted our kitchens were deserted, also our stables and gardens. An enforced holiday was declared for all but the leisure classes.

Mahaly used to prepare for "Conf'rence" weeks before-hand; and on the day of departure we youngsters would collect in groups to watch her pass, hurrying by short cuts to fresh points of vantage, sniggering, nudging one another, jeering at her, I am afraid, as cruelly as any of the Negroes. But Mahaly never seemed to realize it; we were only "the chillen," whom she trusted and loved.

Moreover, she was uplifted beyond reach of our mocking, rapt in high inner contemplation; and moved along the road with her queer, rhythmic, jerking step to music that we could not hear, trailing clouds of glory—literally. Sheba herself, on her way to the court of Solomon, could have been no more magnificent. She wore, although the sun is hot in "Conf'rence" time, a pink velvet opera cloak trimmed with swan's-down, which had belonged to Miss Mabilla Cornish in her days of bellehood; beneath it glittered and swept a voluminous span-gled yellow evening gown from the same prolific source.

Her feet were encased in a pair of Dr. Tom Curtis's rubber-sided *Romeo* slippers, with the toes removed for greater ease; and she wore my mother's Paris bonnet of many seasons past, an erection of jet which sprouted purple ostrich tips at intervals. There were other details, such as square gold-rimmed spectacles without glass, a *Janice Meredith* curl (blond) draped coquettishly over one shoulder, an ancient carpetbag which bulged with sacrifices destined presumably for the altar: a fat roasting pullet, a jar of brandied peaches, a bottle of elder-berry wine, other delicacies which she could not afford.

But Mahaly never got farther than to the railroad station. Whether the other Negroes would not let her go with them,

whether their jeers caused her to lose confidence in the suita-
bility of her appearance before the Lord, or whether at the
last she dared not put to the risk of possible disillusionment
her secret dreams, her hidden ecstasies, we never knew. But
the train for camp ground invariably went off without Mahaly. She would reappear that evening, shorn of her glory and
much subdued, to a welcome she was sure of, in some grateful
kitchen. Never within my knowledge did Mahaly get to
"Conf'rence."

Except once. Aunt Lady told us about it, all these years
afterward. It chanced that Dr. Tom, driving past the station
just after the annual exodus to camp ground, was struck with
the forlornness of the solitary figure which remained; and,
being Aunt Lady's husband and that sort of man, he had offered to drive Mahaly over in state behind his fast span of
trotters, having a patient to see in that part of the country.

Mahaly had stared incredulously. Then, with a wild shout
of "Glory to Gawd! Here I come!" she had clambered into the
buggy, and said not another word until, after many miles, he
deposited her at the gates of the Promised Land. Then she
came down to earth sufficiently to smile her gratitude speech-
lessly, radiantly. "I declare, the old wench looked almost
handsome!" murmured Dr. Tom, remembering it.

And that was the last of Mahaly for many a long day. Nobody knew what had become of her.

It was a year later that they saw her coming home along
the pike, still wearing the pink opera cloak, bedraggled, weak,
exhausted, but bearing in her arms a puny yellow baby.

"Not her own?" I gasped, incredulous.

Aunt Lady nodded. "For all the world like an old cow
that's gone off into the woods to calve, and don't know
whether to be proud or sorry for herself," she said with
the rich tang of the soil that is her heritage.

Mahaly never told where she had been, nor with whom.
I thought of the King of Yearth, in his Aladdin cave; I
thought also of the sacrifices and libations she had prepared
for the altar, and of priests who might well have appreciated
them. But nobody ever knew. Once, pressed too closely, she
had made some cryptic allusion to "a merracle"; and a miracle
indeed it seemed to those who had known her half their lives
as a man-hating spinster of uncertain age.

But people pay heavily for miracles. Mahaly never recovered from hers. She had the child christened "Infant Samuel" after an admired picture in Aunt Lady's parlour; and then she died, vaguer and more queer than ever, babbling of mystic things. She left the Infant Samuel, of course, to Aunt Lady, who seemed to find the legacy quite natural. It was not her first.

"And, besides, I can't help feeling that Tom was sort of responsible," she admitted, ignoring her husband's startled disclaimer.

Sam'l's infancy was no problem; he just grew up, she said, "like any of the puppies," in and out of the kitchen, the barn, the wash house—who minded an extra piccaninny or two around? But the school age brought difficulties. Not that Sam'l was mischievous, or disobedient, or lazy, like ordinary coloured children. His name seemed to have affected his nature, thus proving a theory of George Moore's: the Infant Samuel was, like his pictured prototype, a model child. But the other coloured children failed to appreciate him.

"Dey mocks at me all de time," he said quite patiently, not at all complaining.

No matter how serious Sam'l was, the teacher reported, he seemed to move his schoolmates to ribald mirth.

And for this there may have been some cause. He not only looked peculiar, with his long, pointed head, his anxious solemnity, and his extreme limberness of body, but he did peculiar things. For example, the sums on his slate looked like real sums, quite neatly done, until one examined them more closely, when they were found to be composed of mere pothooks, meaningless hieroglyphics which resembled figures, and which he seemed to think did quite as well.

"Ha, the imagist theory!" murmured my husband, who interests himself in movements.

And once during geography class, when there were visitors, the teacher had invited Sam'l, who drew quite nicely, to do a map of the United States upon the blackboard from memory. The result was a vaguely familiar outline which resembled a map, in that states and lakes and rivers were all neatly marked, the mountains very handsomely shaded indeed. But one of the visitors, examining it in a puzzled manner, had discovered that its outline was the profile, face downward, of George Washington.

Sam'l was sent home in disgrace for poking fun at company. But he protested earnestly that he "hadn't never poked fun at nobody," not he. That was the way he saw his native land, and he had drawn it so.

"Ho! The subjective school," muttered my husband.

Later, under the influence of his name picture, Aunt Lady had thought to make a preacher of the Infant Samuel; but after a brief trial the coloured seminary had returned him with thanks. Their young brother, they reported, was undoubtedly an earnest seeker, even sanctified; he preached with fluency and was powerful in prayer; but though his language and gestures were most superior, neither prayers nor sermons seemed somehow to make sense; they sounded more like poetry. Nor would his fellow theologs take him seriously. Whatever he said or did, they sniggered at; a fatal handicap in the preaching profession.

So Dr. Tom took him in hand and decided to make a stable boy of him. Sam'l became at once every inch a horseman; he had great adaptability. True, whenever he entered a stall he got kicked, horses being intuitive creatures, not easily deceived. But Dr. Tom bore with him until one morning he found Sam'l running his aged, cherished buggy mare, Miss Susy, round and round the back lot, riding her neck like a jockey, plying the outraged favourite with whip and spur— "jes' givin' the ol' gal a breath-out," he explained, "to take the rheumatics out'n her knees." Incidentally, he gave Miss Susy an attack of heaves from which she never recovered.

After that Aunt Lady thought best to take Sam'l into the house under her own eye, where there were less valuable things than horses to learn upon; and that was the period during which we had discovered him, dramatizing himself on the model of Judge Cornish's stately old factotum, Romulus. He had already, in his zeal, polished most of the silver off Aunt Lady's tea set, and he averaged one smash a meal; whereas Romulus had never been known in his long career to break so much as a teacup.

"Sam'l can't seem really to *do* things, somehow," said Aunt Lady, sighing. "He just does *at* 'em. Play-acting, like. 'Monkey motions'; you remember?"

It was a game the little darkies used to play when we were all young together, a left-over from the care-free days of slavery and the plantation "street." A leader, chosen for skill at pantomime, would select something to imitate, and the circle around him must represent the subject as best they could each in his own way, singing as they went:

> "I ack monkey moshuns, too-ra-loo;
> I ack monkey moshuns, so I do.
> I ack 'em good, and dat's a fack;
> I ack jes' like dem monkeys ack."

And so they did—"gemman moshuns," "lady moshuns," "preacher moshuns," and other less polite—absurd little skinny-shanked, mop-headed creatures, with their soft, bright animal eyes and ingratiating ways; the bandar-log indeed. But why should his fellow bandar-log object so consistently to Sam'l's monkey motions? For the grown-up Negroes were as unkind to him as his schoolmates had been. Was it, I suggested, that they thought him a "white-folks' nigger"?

On the contrary. Sam'l had great ambitions for his "race," as he loved to call them; yearned to lead it on to victory (against what enemy was not stated—presumably the Germans); treated his persecutors—for they amounted almost to that—with a magnanimity that was not without pathos.

"It's jus' ign'ance," he would apologize for them kindly. "They ack so mean an' ornery an' outrageous 'cause they got such woolly heads; that's all!"

Sam'l's own hair happened by some odd freak to be quite straight and thick and silky, like coarse floss.

"If he didn't show off so much, I'd be downright sorry for him," said Aunt Lady. "The boy's lonesome for his kind; but—just listen to that!" (as a burst of song reached us from the pantry). "He can't even sing like other people!"

The pantry door having been thoughtfully propped open, we got full benefit in the parlour of a fine falsetto aria done after Caruso's best manner, the impassioned tremolo, the husky little break at the climax, all complete.

"Do you mean to say," murmured my husband respectfully, "that the Infant Samuel is serenading us in Italian?"

"Practically," said the doctor. "As near as he can make it. He's been that way ever since I made the mistake of bringing

Lady home a phónograph from the city. She lends it to Sam'l to take to his room on holidays, and our housework is accomplished to the strains of *I Pagliacci* and *Lucia*."

"Never mind, it won't last long," his wife soothed him. "Sam'l's going off to be a hero soon."

It appeared that, although the draft had twice rejected him, once because of insufficient age and once because of defective vision, Sam'l had managed to overcome all difficulties and was shortly to report at training camp.

I exclaimed with surprise, not able somehow to visualize the temperamental child of Mahaly as a warrior, and such a determined warrior. It did seem in his case peculiarly heroic, he was so inept and helpless-looking; so what the Negroes call "shackly" in the knees.

"Humph!" remarked Aunt Lady to my praise of this patriotism. "Showing off, as usual. 'I ack soldier moshuns, so I do.' If Sam'l ever hears a cannon he'll start for home like a gun-shy setter. A mere ocean won't be able to stop him."

It was a prophecy that came to pass, as many of Aunt Lady's prophecies do. But in the meanwhile Sam'l got as far as France; supplied by me, because of auld lang syne, with the sort of comfort kit that would have pleased Mahaly. It included a Bible, perfumed soap, a box of chocolate, some very fancy notepaper, and a fountain pen; also a letter of sound advice, as I rather dreaded the effect of foreign travel upon so adaptable a temperament.

His reply is one of my cherished possessions. He had been allotted to a labour battalion, diggers, road makers, and the like, of whom he wrote modestly:

We are the Chosen People who must go before, like a Voice in the Wilderness, to puppare the way. Hallelujah, praise the Lord. What we'll do to them en'emies, respeckted Madam, is a plenty. These yere foreign nations is wusser than what you write about them. The way they ack, respeckted Madam, is somethin' scand'lous. Specially the French. White wimmen makin' over a sanctified cullud boy like who but he! But don' you fret, respeckted Madam, for fear I mought fergit my raisin'. Pussonally I wouldn't so demeen myself as to 'sociate with no white wimmen what would demeen theirselves by 'sociatin' with cullud.

It was reassuring to feel that a representative from our old town was keeping so stern an eye upon the morals and manners of our volatile ally.

We learned not long afterward that Sam'l had been invalided safely home, suffering from something like shell-shock. As Aunt Lady put it in her letter, he must have heard a gunshot somewhere.

We forgot about Sam'l for a while after that, until one very early morning I heard our furnace being shaken down with a sort of rhythmic emphasis, and asked the maid who brought in my coffee what all the racket was about.

She tossed her head. "Hit's de new houseman," she reported, "and he 'lows don't nobody but him know how to shake a furnace nohow." She giggled angrily.

Intuition told me what had occurred, even before a voice came floating up the furnace pipes:

> "Hark, fum de tomb come do'fum soun'
> (Jay-bird jump an' jar de groun')."

Nobody but Mahaly's child could have given this song its old, peculiar eeriness. Sam'l had abandoned the coloratura type of vocalization and returned to an earlier manner.

"Yes, M'dame, hit's me," he called up cheerily (since his sojourn in France he no longer pronounced me "Moddom"). "Miss Lady done sent me along to work for you-all a while," and he presently handed me his credentials.

Since his return from the war, Aunt Lady wrote, the other Negroes had treated him so unsympathetically that she thought best for him to convalesce elsewhere, in the care of people like ourselves who could understand his sensitive nature. While Sam'l, she went on to say, was not and could never be a decent house servant, he was certainly better than the city sort, who, she understood, were likely as not to sit down beside you in the street car.

He did not drink or gamble, he was not light-fingered (though of course he sometimes borrowed things, like anybody), and he was willing and anxious to do whatever was expected of him, whether he knew how or not. His shell-shock merely took the form of a sort of nervousness in the feet, resembling St. Vitus's dance.

We did not, as it happened, either need or want a houseman, particularly one afflicted with St. Vitus's dance; but Aunt Lady, having never in her life failed a friend, is naturally not a person whom her friends can fail. Sam'l and I engaged each other.

It proved a relation which, while pleasant, was of short duration. Sam'l was neglecting his operatic interests at the time in favour of interpretative dancing, and his habit of constant practise in kitchen and basement not only bade fair to disrupt our domestic arrangements, but even to endanger the foundations of the house. At all hours of the day and some of the night there was to be felt a certain measured vibration in the atmosphere, accompanied by a slight warning rattle of chandeliers and crockery.

We might have ignored this growing menace in the interests of friendship, but that one day my husband happened to observe our houseman going off for a holiday sporting golf tweeds and stockings whose vivid pattern was unmistakable. Sam'l, as Aunt Lady had forewarned us, was merely borrowing these articles, and had every intention of returning them to my husband's closet at the first favourable opportunity; but husbands have their little crotchets. I parted with Sam'l, to our mutual regret.

He bore no hard feelings, confessing that he was really on his gradual way northward to join some influential acquaintances he had made during his military career. We were, it appeared, merely a stepping stone, albeit an honoured and a valued stepping stone, upon his upward progress.

That should by all rights have been the end of Sam'l so far as we were concerned, for when Negroes go North they are usually lost to us. But some years later a visitor was announced, who had sent up no card.

"Leastways he *tried* to gimme a card," bridled the housemaid, giggling, "but I never took'n it off him."

The drawing room was empty. I asked where she had put the caller.

"In the kitchen, whar he belongs at!" was the emphatic response.

The prodigal had returned, but a metamorphosed, almost an unrecognizable prodigal. He had grown a neat little shoe-brush moustache (in itself quite a feat for a coloured man); he wore an extremely well-tailored cutaway, mouse-coloured trousers and gloves to match, immaculate white spats, and a gardenia in his buttonhole. His manner was even more of a metamorphosis; it had become as simple as his appearance was elaborate; crisp, clear, decisive, very much the manner, in fact, of my husband closing up a business deal. Sam'l invariably profited by his contacts.

"I shall not take up mo' than a moment of yore vallyble time, Madam" (pronounced in plain American now), "but I have come to tender you and His Honour some free tickets for the performance to-morrow night. I also mailed free tickets," he added, "to Doctor and Miss Lady Curtis, and I took'n the libbuty to suggest that they better come and stay with you-all for the event."

"Quite right, Sam'l; I'm glad you did," I murmured, rather dazed, "but what is the event?"

In silence he handed me a card—the one my housemaid had rejected—printed in Old English lettering, "Professor Samuel K. Curtis, Esq." Mahaly's child had evidently paid his "white folks" the compliment of incorporating their names with his own.

"How nice!" I murmured. "But what are you professor of, Sam'l?"

"The art of Terpsichore, Madam. I thought perhaps you'd reckernize the name. But it's natural you wouldn't," he added, "being as how I'm better known to the public as 'Slippyfoot.' Also," he added simply, "as 'the Charleston King.'"

I began to understand. One knew by hearsay—our personal ambitions in that line having ceased with the fox trot—of the new dancing step which was taking America and even Europe by storm; and I remembered reading that our own city was to be the privileged scene of a coloured Charleston contest, with competitors from all quarters of the country.

"So you've come to compete in the Charleston contest?" I asked.

"Hardly to compete," he replied gently, looking rather disappointed in me. "Rather to expound, Madam. To show 'em," he elucidated further, "how the Charleston should be did; its origins, methods, and significations, like I showed 'em," he added very, very modestly, "in London and in Paris."

I rose to the occasion sufficiently to invite the Charleston King to remain for supper; an invitation he accepted on condition that he be allowed to wait on us at table, which he did, white spats, gardenia, and all. Greatness had not gone to his head; he still remembered his "raisin'." Incidentally, he dropped and broke my favourite salad bowl.

None of us had happened to see the Charleston danced before, or so we thought, until the contest begun. Then we recognized it: the same old clap-and-patter, wriggling and prancing, familiar to any Southern childhood, with some elaborations: a constant St. Vitus-like movement of the feet, odd sidewise skating-motions, a slow dipping of the body up and down and up again, with flapping arms, as of some clip-winged bird trying to fly.

"Good gracious!" exclaimed Aunt Lady, beside me. "You don't tell me *ladies* and *gentlemen* are carrying on like this in the ballroom? And what's the crowd making such a to-do about, anyhow? They can see this sort of thing any day if they look out the back window!"

Yet the large auditorium was packed as for a prize fight; white people on the main floor, standing up, mounting their chairs in order to see better; coloured people packing the gallery, in delegations, with appropriate banners; and all shouting together, catcalling, yelling for Slippyfoot Sam.

What a descent from his christened name! I was glad for the moment that Mahaly was not present at this apotheosis of her miracle child. But only for a moment.

He came in the place of honour on the programme, the spotlight full upon him, heralded by a fanfare of snare drums and saxophones. To my surprise, it was not the elegant gentleman I had promised my companions. He had left to lesser luminaries the fine raiment, the spats, and the gardenia. Even the neat moustache had been sacrificed to art. He had deliberately reverted to type. Barefoot, in ragged trousers, and a hat without a crown, it was a Sam'l any one in that audience would recognize, as we did, and love because he was their own. He had shown the intuition of genius; achieved the crowning artistry of imitating himself.

The audience, with one gasp of surprise, went wild. There were shrieks of welcome and approval, congratulatory howls. "Attaboy, Slippyfoot!" they yelled. "You show 'em, King!"

And of course they laughed at him, as people always did

and always would. But it was a new laughter, sympathetic, almost affectionate. Sam'l, I realized, had become to his public a sort of symbol, like the Charleston itself, like the tune "Dixie"; a reminder of a South that was passing now, and would never come again.

He paid no attention to laughter or to cheers; a ludicrous enough figure with his great flat feet and exquisitely awkward body, yet oddly dignified. It was the dignity of conscious power; Sam'l knew what he was about. Those melancholy, anxious hound's eyes roamed over the enormous audience till suddenly they paused and lighted. He had found his white folks. He smiled at us; I think I had never seen Sam'l smile before. It was an experience; sudden, irradiating, infinitely proud and trustful. He was among friends.

He began to move, a strange, slow prance with measured jerks and pauses, which I recognized—Mahaly before the great god Mumbo-jumbo! Suddenly he crouched, shivering, trembling, and began to run desperately—all without leaving one spot; he fought against unseen enemies, shield before him, thrusting his spear, flinging his assegai; he moved away, drooping, heavy, a captive in chains; never losing a single beat of the wild rhythm, a single intricate double pat of the foot.

I began to understand what he was doing. This was no mere exposition of the Charleston "as it should be did, its origins, methods, and significations." Sam'l, the despised and rejected of them, was interpreting his people for our benefit, dramatizing in dance the history of his race, even as Roland Hayes in song, as others in literature.

There was something hypnotic in that ceaseless beating rhythm, those constant, significant movements of the half-naked body. We saw through his imagination; we remembered through his race-memory. Hoeing and sowing; picking cotton under the eye of an overseer with a lash; escaping into the swamp, with bloodhounds following; terror he danced for us, the terror that crouches and prays and kills; ecstasy, the shouting joys of religion, the release of freedom—springing up and up as if he would dance with the stars.

There followed the humble, happy life of the quarters: picking a banjo, crooning as he patted and swung, flashing his teeth at a girl; rocking a child in his arms, tenderly, lovingly;

bending up and down over a wash-tub, testing a flatiron with wetted forefinger; "washin' dem dishes an' settin' 'em er-roun'." (We heard him humming his mother's old working song to the tuneless steady thump of the orchestra, and Aunt Lady smiled at me dimly.)

Now and again the music changed, and for a moment some familiar tune emerged. To the beat of "Greased my heel wid hog-eye lard," we saw him slip stealthily along the hen-roosts, seize his prey and still it with a quick twist of the wrist; later he seemed to be shooting craps, down on his knees, shaking the dice and rolling them out, to delighted cries from the audience:

"He fives! He sevens! Attaboy, King! Roll your own! Babies, come to Papa!"

We rode a race with him, jockeying home to a grand-stand finish. (I thought of poor, astonished Miss Susy.) We saw him off to the war, strutting gloriously, twirling his baton at the head of a brass band, and we saw him slipping ingloriously home again, peering back over his shoulder as if he had seen a ghost; for Sam'l did not spare himself. Next he mounted the pulpit, wrestled with the Lord in prayer, laying off his hands in eloquent gesture, giving us the Word straight from the shoulder, so that a sudden hysterical voice out of the gallery shouted, "Yas, O my Lawdy! *I* hears You callin' me!"

And all the time his feet kept up that steady, monotonous, hypnotic beat and shuffle, shuffle and beat, as if they could never stop; as if they could never stop until the unseen force that manages the puppet show should cease to pull the strings.

When at the end he stumbled away out of the spotlight, dancing still, bent over double like an old rheumatic that leans upon a stick, there was a moment's quiet.

Some two thousand people felt for that moment, perhaps, just what he intended them to feel: the loneliness of children in a world that has grown old, the helplessness of a simple jungle folk, a bandar-log, set down in the life of cities and expected to be men. "They ack so mean an' ornery an' outrageous 'cause they got such woolly heads!"

Then the audience followed him, as it had welcomed him, with shouts and shrieks of laughter.

But Sam'l's white folks would never laugh at him again;

dreamer of dreams that he was, seer of visions. Aunt Lady's dear, wrinkled face was frankly wet with tears.

Her husband put an arm around her.

"Why, old honey, it's only Sam'l at his monkey motions! What are you weeping about?"

"*I* don't know. What are you!" she countered snappishly.

FOUR DREAMS OF GRAM PERKINS

By RUTH SAWYER

From *American Mercury*

GRAM PERKINS was not my grandmother. I had good reason to believe that she had died and received Christian burial a half century before I first set foot in Haddock harbour. Neither were the dreams of my dreaming; so my connection with her was always remote and impersonal. Nevertheless, I came to know through her all the horror and the fascination of a perturbed spirit.

For those who may not know the harbour, let me explain that it bites into the northern stretch of Maine coast. Summer resorters are still in the minority, and peace and beauty serve as perpetual handmaidens to those few exhausted, nerve-racked city folk who have found refuge there. I was there only a few days when the immortal essence of Gram Perkins confronted me. Perkins is a prevailing name at the harbour. A Perkins peddles fish on Tuesdays and Fridays. A Perkins keeps the village store in whose windows are displayed those amazing knickknacks somebody or other creates out of sweet grass, beads, birch bark, and sealing wax. A Perkins is framed daily in the general delivery window of the post office, and his brother drives the one village jitney.

It was Cal Perkins of tender years who indirectly introduced me to the mysterious dreamer of the dreams. Cal took me on my first scaling of the blueberry ledges. Standing like Balboa on the Peak of Darien he swept a hand inland and said: "Somewhars, over thar, lives Zeb Perkins. Hain't never laid eyes on him myself, but Pa says you doan't never want to hear him tell of them four dreams he's had of Grandmother Perkins. Woan't sleep ag'in fur a month ef you do." It was not long before I discovered those dreams were as firm a tradition at the harbour as the "Three Hairs of Grandfather Knowital" are in Eastern Europe—only with a difference. Natives in the Balkans pass on their story for the asking; whereas in Haddock harbour they evade all questions leading to Gram Perkins, while their tongues travel to their cheeks.

One day Cal took me to the cemetery and showed me the Perkins monument. It was a splendid affair in two shades of marble with a wrought-iron fence and gateway, and all about it were the head stones marking the graves of the separate members of the family. I read the inscription on Gram Perkins's stone:

> Sara Amanda Perkins
> Beloved wife of Benjamin Perkins, Sea Captain
> 1791–1863
> May she rest in perfect peace!

"Wall, she didn't!" Cal hurled the words at me as he catapulted through the gate, shaking all over like the aspen back of the lot. I caught a final mumbling: "Never aim to stop nigh *her*. Pa says I might git to dreamin', too."

Here was distinctly unpleasant food for thought. Already she had a firm grip on my waking hours, and there was no relish to the idea of her haunting my sleeping ones. The manner in which she possessed the town was astounding. She lurked wherever one went, popping out with the most casual remark when one was buying a pound of butter or a pint of clams. And yet, for all the daily allusions and innuendoes, one never got at the heart of the matter; one never rightly understood why Gram Perkins was and yet was not five feet below the sod. As for the dreamer of the dreams, one never found him clothed in anything more solid than words.

I questioned Peddling Perkins one Friday when he came to our house with the makings of a chowder. "Tell me," I began, "where does Zeb Perkins live and what relation is he to you?"

He paused in his weighing. The scales hung from a rafter in his cart and worked somewhat mysteriously. He might have been weighing out the exact amount of relationship he cared to claim. "Fur as I can make out he's sort of a third cousin."

"Did he ever tell you about those dreams?"

"No, m'am!" He fixed me with a fore-warning eye. "What's

more, he hain't never goin' to. I seen Scip Perkins—time he told him. Scairt! Never seen a feller so shook up in his life. Didn't take off his clothes and lay good abed fur a week. No, m'am!"

I questioned the post-office Perkins one day: "Do you happen to know what Zeb Perkins dreamed about his grandmother?"

"Dreamed! Gosh, what didn't he dream? Think of anything a sensible woman, dead and buried fifty years, stands liable to do and you wouldn't have the half of it." He finished snapping his teeth together to signify that he had gone as far with those dreams as he intended to go—for the present, anyway.

A few days later I took the matter to the village store. I even bought a chain and earrings of sealing wax to make my going seem less mercenary. "Those dreams," I ventured, "how did they happen and do they belong entirely to Zeb?"

"They do, God be praised!" Whereupon the storekeeper retired behind the necklace for a good two minutes, and then partially emerged to whisper, "No one's layin' any claim at all to those dreams but Zeb. And I've always thought myself if he hadn't had them, no knowing what he mightn't have had."

II

For two recurring summers I stayed fixed at this point. And then came a spring when I slipped off early to the harbour for trout. The Perkins who drives the jitney met me at the wharf as I stepped from the Boston boat. "Hain't a summer resorter nor a bluejay here yit," was his greeting. "Weather's right smart—nips ye considerable." And it did. The water in the brooks was so cold my fingers remained stiff and blue all day. But the fishing was good, and in the end I caught something more than trout.

A morning came with a southeast wind. Up to that I had lost almost no flies, so I started out with little extra tackle. The middle of the morning found me a mile deep in an alder swamp, bog on one side and piled-up brush on the other. It was what you would call dirty fishing, and in half an hour I had lost every fly and leader I had with me. There was nothing to do but put up my rod and go back. In an effort to strike higher ground I came into what was new country to me. A trail led up toward where I judged the blueberry ledges would be, and climbing for a mile or so I suddenly broke through into a clearing and a wagon road. A grayish house stood beside the road. A thin spiral of smoke curled out of the chimney. On a split stake, even with the road, teetered a sign reading:

HAND MADE TROUT FLIES FOR SALE HERE

I attacked the door without mercy. A moment's knocking brought the sound of stirring from within, and the door finally creaked open, displaying the oddest cut of a little man in a wheel chair. He blinked at me like some great nocturnal bird, and soon there was an intelligent wag of the head—more at my clothes than at me.

"Come in. Doan't gin'rally git lady fishermen. Hearn tell they git 'em down to the harbour lookin' jes' as he-ish as the men." He rolled his chair backward from the door, beckoning me to follow. I could hear him repeating the last of his words under his breath as if by way of confirmation: "Yes, sir, looking jes' as he-ish as the men."

He led me into a room that might have been identified even in the uttermost corner of the world as having been conceived and delivered in the State of Maine. An airtight stove centred it, and on its pinnacle stood a nickel-plated moose at bay. There were half a dozen pulled-in rugs: fruit pulled in; red, yellow, and purple roses pulled in; a rooster pulled in; and other things that defied the imagination. The two window sills were gay with geraniums and begonias. Crayon portraits panelled the walls, and between each portrait hung a hair wreath. Fronting the door was a shower of coffin plates, strung together with a fish line. A large coloured print of a clipper hung over the mantel, while all about hung trophies of the South Seas—strings of shells and beads and corals. But the most amazing exhibit was the feathers: peacock, egret, flamingo, pheasant, turkey, and cock tails, yellowhammer and bluejay wings, breasts, crests and what not. The work bench was littered with tiny feathers, partridge and guinea fowl, and spools of bright silk. He brushed all these aside and reached underneath to a drawer, bringing out a handful of trout flies. It took no close scrutiny to tell their exquisite workmanship.

"Pick out what ye want. Swamp back yonder jes' eats 'em up, doan't it?" And he smiled an ingratiating, toothless smile.

I made my selections slowly, studying the little man more than the flies. His head was as bald and pink as a baby's. His lips were tremulous, and his eyes showed that pale blue opacity of the very old or very young. It was his hands that held me confounded. They were twisted like bird claws. How they could have ever taken wisps of feather and fine lengths of silk and wound them into the perfect semblance of tiny aërial creatures was more than I could conceive. He caught at my wondering and with a burst of crowing laughter he held the claws closer for inspection. "Handsome, hain't they? Cal'ate I work 'em steady as most folks work a good pair. Can't stand wet nor cold, no better 'n Gram Perkins could in hern. Good days she was the smartest knitter in the county."

So here was another Perkins. I aimed my habitual question at him, expecting no better results. "Tell me, do you know anything about those four dreams?"

He sat a moment, motionless, in what one might have termed a vainglorious silence. He sucked his lips in and out over those vacant gums as if he found them full of flavour; then he suddenly burst into the triumphant crow of a chanticleer. "Yes m'am! Cal'ate I do know them dreams—seein' I dreamed 'em. I be Zeb Perkins!" He said it with as sweet an unction as if he had announced himself King of the Hejaz. In a flash the room stood revealed anew. It spoke aloud of Sara Amanda Perkins, beloved wife of Benjamin Perkins, sea captain; of his clipper, of the relics of his voyages, of her handiwork in rugs and wreaths. The very begonias might be slip grandchildren of the ones she had planted. Here, indeed, was a stage set for those dreams. Here sat Zeb Perkins, playwright and stage manager, picking excitedly at his pink head, eternally ready to ring up his curtain. He caught my eye on the wreaths.

"Them little tow-headed fergit-me-nots belonged to her first son as died a baby. She set a terrible store by him. The black in them susans come from her sister Ida, my great-aunt Perkins. See them coffin plates. Ye'll see every one of them was copper, nickeled over, every one but Gram's. Hers was solid."

There was a wealth of information conveyed in that last word. I had been standing until now. One of Zeb's claws waved itself away from the coffin plates to a chair: "Set, woan't ye?

Ye'll see them rockers under ye are worn as flat as sledge runners. That was Gram's chair; and we wore them rockers off luggin' her 'round. She was all crippled up, Gram was, same as me; only in them days there warn't no wheel chairs."

The chair was all Zeb claimed. There was no more rock to it than to a dray sledge. From the chair his eyes flew to the crayon portraits. "Look at them! Look at Marm—then look at Gram. Why, there was nary a thing Gram couldn't do, for all her crippled-upness. Bake a pie, fry a batch o' dough-nuts, clean up the butt'ry. But Marm seems like she was born fretty and tired. Made ye tired jest to watch her travel from the sink to the cook stove. She'd handle a batch o' biscuits like she never expected to live to see 'em baked. Jes' lookin' at 'em, can' ye make out a difference?"

I did and I could. In spite of everything the artist had done to obliterate all human expression he had mastered the single point of difference. One face sagged utterly, the other looked out with sharp alert eyes on a world that interested her im-mensely. There was a grim humour about the mouth, and a firmness that spoke a challenge even at the end of a century.

"I tell ye," Zeb's eulogy was gathering momentum. "We boys set a terrible store by Gram. She was cuter and smarter tied to that chair than Marm was on two good legs—hands to match 'em. Golly! How sick boys git bein' whined at. Didn't make no odds what we done—good or bad—Marm al'ays whined, but Gram—she stood by like she'd been a boy herself. She'd beg us off hoein' fer circus and fair days and slip us dimes for this or that. Cal'ate she's slipped us enough nickels and dimes to stretch clean to the upper pasture. Pasture! Golly! When we was up thar, hot days, hayin', she'd al'ays mix us a pitcher o' somethin' cool—cream o' tartar water or lemon and m'lasses. When she had it ready she'd take a stick and tick-tack on the wind'y. She could whistle, too; whistle through them crooked fingers o' hern like a yaller-hammer. She'd whistle whenever she wanted to be fetched anywhars; then one of us boys would come runnin' and heave her to wheresomever she aimed to go—kitchen to butt'ry—butt'ry to settin' room—settin' room to shed."

Zeb stopped here and illustrated. He put two of his crooked fingers to his mouth and shrilled out a thin, wailing note as eery as a banshee's.

"That's the way she done it," he continued. "And Marm would fuss and fret and say she didn't see why the Lord 'lowed a little crippled-up body like Gram's to stay so chuck full o' spunk. Some days she git sort o' vengeful, Marm would, and tell Gram she'd better quiet down decent, or more'n likely she'd never rest quiet in her grave after she died."

III

A hush fell on the room. There was a baleful light shimmering through Zeb's dull eyes, his claws began a nervous intertwining. "Wall . . . " he broke the silence at last, "Gram died. Night afore she died seems like she got scairt. She grabbed us boys one after another and made us all promise we wouldn't bury her twell we were good and sure she was dead. 'Keep me five days—promise me that,' she kept a-sayin'. And we promised. Recollect it didn't seem to me then as how Gram could die—so full of smartness and spunk. Even after old Doc Coombs come and pronounced her, seemed like she'd open her eyes any minute and ask us boys to lug her somewhars. 'Stead o' that she lay so quiet, seemed like I could hear Doomsday strike."

The air about us became suddenly supercharged with something. Was it that ravenous desire for life that must have consumed Gram Perkins? Under their glass domes the hair wreaths seemed to move as if fanned by a breath. The feathers about us swayed. The rooster in the pulled-in rug seemed to pulse with life and a desire to crow. A crowing shook the room, but it came from Zeb.

"Hot! Golly, Gram died in the sizzlingest spell, middle of August, folks can remember. Didn't embalm in them days, so 'twas ice or nothing. We drew lots for shifts—us boys. Ben and Ellery drew day; Sam and me night. Mebbe we didn't work! Lugged in hunks from the ice house to the shed; thar we cracked and lugged in dish pans to the settin' room. Crack —lug—mop—lug—crack. Five days! It's been a powerful sight o' comfort sence to know we kept Gram's promise. Then come the funeral—smart one. Slathers o' flowers and mourners and hacks. Cal'ate you've seen the lot whar we buried her?"

At the mention of burial a sense of enormity made me shudder. I was beginning to realize that the further Zeb pro-

gressed in the matter of the obsequies of Gram Perkins the
more alive she became. At that moment she possessed the
house—every crack and cranny in it. She possessed Zeb, and
she possessed me. I found myself straining my ears for the
rattle of dishes in the butt'ry or the sharp thin note of a whistle.
Zeb's ear was cocked as well as mine.

"Them dreams," he said, pulling himself together. "First
one come fifteen years after Gram died. All was gone from the
harbour by that time but me. Ben took the pneumony and
died quick. Ellery got liver complaint, turned yaller as arnicy
and thinned out to a straw. Sort o' blew away he did. Sam—
he got trampled on by a horse. That left jes' me. Night after I
buried Marm I come back here and had my first dream. I
was young ag'in. Boys back, Marm back, all of us settin'
thar at Gram's funeral. Parson was a-prayin'—had been fur
a considerable time. I could hear Nate French fumblin' fur
his tunin' fork, so's to lead the departin' hymn when plain as
daylight I heard a whistle. Yes, m'am. Then I heard a tick-
tack—like Gram was knockin' on some wind'y. Kept hopin'
she'd quiet down when out shot another whistle—clear above
the parson's prayin'. Nobody but me seemed to notice, so I got
up gingerly and tiptoed over to the coffin and raised the lid.

"Thar she was—fixin' fur to tick-tack ag'in. I grapped her
fingers quick and shoved 'em back whar they belonged. Then
I leaned over and whispered, loud as I durst, 'Lay still,
Gram. Parson's nigh through and we'll be movin' along
shortly. Folks 'll be passin' 'round in a moment to view the
remains. Fur the Lord's sake, close your eyes and act sensible.'
Wall . . . that fixed her. She give me a wink so'd I know she'd
act right, and I tiptoed back to my place. They was all still
a-prayin'—kept right on a-prayin' twell I woke up. Three
years later, come November, I had the second."

Zeb shivered, and so did I. I wanted that second dream
and yet I did not want it. Had I chosen I could no more have
stayed it than one could have held back the second act of a
Greek tragedy.

"We was on our way to the cemetery." Zeb's voice lifted
me free of all choice in the matter. "I was ridin' outside the
first hack, bein' the youngest, and I was thinkin' what a fine
day it was fur that time o' year. Sort o' funny, too, fur Gram
died in August and here it was November and we was jes'

gittin' to bury her. I was lookin' at the hearse when it happened. Hearses was different in them days, black urns at the four top corners with black plumes stickin' out and a pair o' solid wooden doors behind. Above the poundin' of the horses' hoofs I heard a hammerin' on them solid doors. Bang . . . bang . . . plain as daylight. Old Jared Sims was drivin' and I didn't want he should hear so I sung out, 'Cal'ate they're shinglin' the Coomb's barn.' He turned 'round in his seat to look, and jes' that minute thar come a regular whale of a hammerin' and the doors of the hearse bust open. Thar was Gram—top of her own coffin, peekin' down low at me and beckonin' fur me to come and git her.

"Mad! I was as mad as a hornet. I went back to that wink she'd given me in t'other dream and seemed like she'd gone back on her word—something Gram had never done livin'. I was off the seat of that hack in a jiffy, runnin' aside the hearse. When the goin' slowed up I stuck my head inside and hollered, 'Ye git straight back whar ye b'long! And what's more ye stay thar!' Then I begun to whimper like I couldn't stand my feelin's another minute. 'Gram,' says I, 'hain't ye got any heart? Do ye want to disgrace us boys? How'll ye cal'ate we'll feel to have the neighbours thinkin' we're tryin' to bury ye ag'in your will? We give ye them five days like we promised—can't ye lay down decent and proper now?'

"That settled her. She turned, meek as a cow, climbed back into her coffin and closed the lid down. I went back to the hack and climbed up. We was still a-goin' when I woke up."

IV

An interlude followed. I tried to bring back my mind to the reality of life as I knew it to be. I fingered my trout flies and did my best to image the still, deep pool below the swamp where I had been on the point of casting just as my last leader broke. Half an hour more I could be back there, casting again. But the pool and the trout faded into oblivion beside the sterner reality of Gram Perkins. I was on the hack with young Zeb, my eyes fastened in growing perturbation on a pair of solid black doors.

"Jes' started on our January thaw when the next dream took me," broke in Zeb. "We'd reached the cemetery. Grave dug, coffin lowered, folks standin' 'round fur a final prayer.

To all appearances everything was goin' first rate. But the sexton hadn't more than picked up his shovel, easy-like, when out comes a whistle, clear as a fog horn. I opened my eyes quick and looked down. Thar was Gram, poppin' out like a jack-in-the-box, lid swung wide open and both hands reachin' fur the dirt the sexton was shovellin' in. Yes, ma'm! Ye never saw dirt fly in all your born days the way Gram made it fly. At the rate she was goin', I knew we'd be standin' thar twell Doomsday, gittin' her buried.

"Everybody else was prayin' hard along with the parson, and he was 'most to the Resurrection. I knew somethin' had to be done quick, so in I jumped. I slapped the dirt out of her hands hard like you would with a child and says I, 'Land o' goodness, Gram, what ails ye? We've fetched ye along to what the Bible calls your last restin' place. All we boys is askin' of ye now is to keep quiet and rest twell Jedgment Day.'

"The words warn't more'n out afore I knew I'd said the wrong thing. She didn't lay any more store 'bout this eternal restin' than what ye would, settin' thar fingerin' them flies. She give me the most pitiful look ye ever saw on a human face. It said, plain as daylight, 'Zeb, lug me back home and let me git to work ag'in.'

"Wall . . . I took to whimperin' like a two-year-old. 'Ef ye woan't do it fur the Bible,' says I, 'do it fur us boys. Ye've al'ays been terrible proud of us—al'ays wanted we should have jes' what we wanted, and thar's nothin' in the whole o' creation we want so much this minute as to see ye restin' peaceful. Git back in. Close your eyes, fold your hands, git that listen fur the last trumpet look on your face. Hurry, woan't ye? The sexton's shovellin' like sixty.'

"She give me another of them pitiful looks—nigh broke me all up—and she sort o' slid back and slammed the lid down on her fur all the world like one of these cuckoo clocks. I lit out and landed side o' the parson jes' as he said 'Amen.' . . . 'Amen,' says I, thankful-like. 'Amen,' says the sexton. . . . 'Amen,' says the mourners in a roarin' chorus like the sea. And then I swear to ye that way under the dirt I heard Gram sing out Amen! Tell ye I woke in a sweat!"

"Cold sweat?" I asked. It was all I could think of.

"Cold as a clam, dripped with it."

"That makes three."

"Three!" Zeb tolled it out like a passing bell. "All bad enough—the fourth, worst of all. Ye wait."

I waited.

"Three years I lived comfortable in my mind. Seemed like that last Amen had settled things. Then May come along. I'd been slippin' some of them geraniums to take up to the cemetery Memorial Day. I could still walk some—slowly, but git about—and I went to bed mighty real happy at the idea o' fixin' up Gram's grave. Right on top o' that came the fourth dream!

"I was swingin' up the road toward the cemetery, and in one hand I carried a pot with the slips in, and t'other held my stick I walked with. Jes' about reached the lot when up comes a jedge from Boston—nice feller—and I asked him to come along and see the view from our place. 'Most famous in the State,' says I. 'Clear days we can see 'most anything.'

"I fetched him through the iron gates and stood him up close to the monument and begun pointin' places out. 'Thar's Mount Washington,' says I. 'Some days ye can see the whole Presidential Range. . . . Thar's Katahdin . . . thar's . . .' But I stopped thar dead. I'd caught something move in the grass by Gram's headstone. The next minute out come a whistle, loudest I ever heard. I swung the jedge clear 'round and pointed out to sea. 'Thar's Mount Desert,' says I, and 'thar's Isle au Haut. That's the Rockland boat ye hear whistlin'—consarn it!'

"I looked at Gram. She'd got her head and shoulders clear and she was whistlin' ag'in fur dear life. Then she took her fingers out of her mouth and nodded her head toward out back. Seemed like she was askin' me fur the last time to take her home. The jedge seemed lost in the scenery, and I stepped up to Gram and showed her the geranium slips. 'Look at them,' says I. 'Fetched 'em all the way over to decorate your grave, and here ye be, bustin' loose and cuttin' up. Hain't ye ever goin' to give in and rest in peace?'

"Wall, she never said a word, jes' kept working herself further and further out. I was terrible scairt the jedge would turn round any second and ketch her. Stood thar on pins and needles watchin' Gram rise from her grave. 'Have a heart, Gram,' I begun coaxin' ag'in. 'How'd ye like a city feller like that jedge to ketch a Perkins turnin' ghost like?' . . . Never finished what I set out to say. She looked so queer and upset—so like she wanted to tell me something and didn't know how. I stood thar, geraniums in one hand, stick in t'other, tryin' to make out what it was Gram wanted to tell me. Then it come over me, all of a flash. 'Twasn't she that wanted to git out; 'twas that smart, spunky body o' hern. It was drivin' the sperrit same as a strong wind drives a cloud afore it. She was ready to rest if that doggoned crippled-up, pie-bakin', doughnut-fryin' body would have let her be. But it wouldn't. It was draggin' her out of her coffin, out of her grave, turnin' her loose about the county like no decent sperrit could stand.

"'I'll fix it,' says I, droppin' the geraniums and grabbin' the stick with both hands, 'I'll fix it so it'll let ye rest quiet twell Doomsday,' and with that I laid on Gram with that stick. I beat her up twell thar warn't nothin' left but a scat-terin' of dust on the spring sod. Yes, ma'm! I reduced Gram to dust and ashes like the Bible said had to be."

A long sigh swept the stillness of the room. The face of Zeb Perkins underwent a sequence of changes. Triumph had been there, but it dwindled out and sorrow took its place; and then a fear, a tremulous commiseration and, finally, bewilder-ment. He now looked straight at me. His eyes were dull, fearful. "They doan't understand, them Perkins to the har-bour. They doan't think I ever ought to have done that to Gram."

I gathered up my flies and was halfway to the door before Zeb spoke again. His voice had now grown querulous: "Wall —what do ye think?"

I gave my answer as I slipped out of doors, into the wide spaces again. "I think the trout are going to bite," said I.

THE LITTLE GIRL FROM TOWN

By RUTH SUCKOW

From *Harper's*

I WONDER who that is coming here," Mrs. Sieverson said, looking out of the kitchen window.

"Somebody coming?" Mr. Sieverson asked from the sink. "Oh, I guess that's Dave Lindsay, ain't it? He said he'd be out."

"Yes, but he's got someone with him. Oh! I believe it's that little girl from back East somewhere that's visiting them. Leone! Children!"

Mr. Sieverson went outdoors, and then Mrs. Sieverson, and, by the time the car stopped, rounding the drive, all four children were on hand from somewhere. Even Marvin and Clyde, the two boys.

"Anybody home?" Mr. Lindsay called out jovially.

"You bet!"

They were all looking at the little girl in the car beside him. They had heard about this little girl, and how "cute" she was. Her mother was some relative of Mrs. Lindsay. Leone and Vila looked at her eagerly. The boys hung back but they wanted to see her. Mr. Lindsay was proud. He said:

"Well, sir, I've got somebody along with me!"

"I see you have!" Mr. Sieverson answered with shy heavy jocularity and Mrs. Sieverson asked, "Is this the little girl been visiting you?"

"This is the little girl! But I don't know whether she's visiting or not. I've just about made up my mind I'll keep her!"

They all laughed appreciatively. Leone pulled her mother's dress. She wanted her mother to ask if the little girl couldn't get out and play with them. "Now, don't. We'll see," Mrs.

Sieverson whispered. The little girl was so pretty sitting there with her soft golden-brown hair and her cream-white dress that Mr. and Mrs. Sieverson were both shy of saying anything directly to her. Mr. Sieverson cried, still trying conscientiously to joke:

"Well, ain't you going to get out?"

Mr. Lindsay asked, "Well!—shall we, Patricia?"

The little girl looked gravely at the other little girls, and then nodded.

"All right, sir! Patricia's the boss! I've got to do as she says."

She consented to smile at that, and the two boys giggled. Mr. Lindsay lifted her out of the car. She put her arms around his neck, and her little legs and her feet in their shiny black slippers dangled as he swung her to the ground. The children felt shy when he set her down among them. Mr. and Mrs. Sieverson didn't quite know what to say.

"*There* she is! This is the first time this little girl has ever been out to a farm. What do you think of that, Marvin?"

Marvin grinned, and backed off a few steps.

"Yes, sir! But she and Uncle Dave have great times driving round together, don't they?"

The little girl looked up at him and then smiled and nodded her head with a subtle hint of mischief.

"You bet we do! We have great times."

The Sieversons all stood back in a group shyly grinning and admiring. Leone's eyes were as eager as if she were looking at a big doll in a store window. They had never seen any child as pretty as this one, and Mr. Lindsay knew it and was brimming with pride. Her short dress of creamy linen, tied with a red-silk cord at the neck and embroidered with patches of bright Russian colours, melted its fairness into the pure lovely pallor of her skin. The sleeves were so short that almost the whole of her soft, round, tiny arms was bare. Her hair was of fine gold streaked and overlaid with brown—the colour of a straw stack with the darker, richer brown on top—but every hair lay fine and perfect, the thick bangs waved slightly on her forehead, and the long soft bob curved out like a shining flower bell and shook a little when she moved her head. Her skin wasn't one bit sunburned, and so white and delicately grained that there seemed to Vila, in awe, to be a little frost upon it . . . like the silver bloom on wildflower petals, picked in cool places, that smudged when she rubbed it with her fingers.

Mr. Lindsay became businesslike now that he was out of the car. "Well, Henry," he said, "you got it all figured up and ready to show me? I think we've got Appleton where we can make a deal all right."

"Yeah, I guess it's ready."

While the two men talked, the little girl stood beside Mr. Lindsay, her hand still in his, with a grave, trustful, wondering look. Leone, smiling at her, was getting closer. Mr. Lindsay seemed to remember her then and looked down at her.

"Well, Patricia, what about you while I'm looking after my business?" He smiled then at the other children. "Think you can find something to do with all these kids here?"

Leone looked up at him and her blue eyes pleaded brightly in her eagerness. "I guess they's plenty of them to look after her," Mr. Sieverson said shyly but still grinning. "They can entertain her," Mrs. Sieverson put in. She could do the baking without Leone this morning, she thought rapidly, but feeling hurried and anxious.

"You going to play with them for a while, are you?" Mr. Lindsay felt responsible for Patricia. All the same he wanted her off his mind for a while until he had finished his business. "I don't know whether——"

"Oh, Leone'll look after her," Mrs. Sieverson assured him, and Mr. Sieverson repeated, "Sure! She'll be all right with Leone."

Leone came up now, smiling eagerly and with a sweetness that transformed her thin freckled face. She shook back the wisps of uneven, tow-coloured hair. She took the little girl's hand protectingly and confidingly in her hot palm that had a gleam of dusty perspiration along the life line and the heart line. The tiny hand felt like a soft warm bit of silk—or a flower.

"That's right! Uncle Dave won't be gone long. Don't take her out where it's too hot, kids. You know she isn't used to things the way you are."

"No, you be careful," Mrs. Sieverson warned them.

"Will you go with Leone?" The little girl did not say that she would or wouldn't, but she was courteous and did not draw back. "You'll be all right! *You'll* have a good time! Oh, I guess Uncle Dave didn't tell these kids who you were, did he? This is Patricia."

"Can you say that?" Mrs. Sieverson asked—doubting if *she* could.

Vila drew shyly back, with one shoulder higher than the other; but Leone laughed in delight. "I can say it!" She nodded. She squeezed Patricia's hand.

"You can say it, can you? All right, then. Well, now, you kids can show this little girl what good times you can have on the farm. That so? All right then, Henry."

Mrs. Sieverson went into the house to get back to her baking. She had a lot to do to-day. She wasn't at all worried about leaving their little visitor so long as Leone was with her. But she turned to call back to the children, who were still silently grouped about Patricia in the driveway:

"You better stay in the yard with her. Mr. Lindsay won't like it if she gets her dress dirty. Leone! You hear me?"

"I heard. Do you want to come into the yard, Patricia? You do, don't you?" Leone asked coaxingly.

Patricia went soberly with her. Her eyes, gray with threads of violet in the clear iris, were looking all about silently. Her little hand lay quiet but with confidence in Leone's. The other children followed, the boys lagging behind, but coming all the same.

"There, now! Here's just the nicest shady place, and Patricia can sit here, can't she, and just be so nice?" Leone placed Patricia in the round patterned shade of an apple tree, and spread out her linen dress, making it perfectly even all around, and carefully drew out her little legs straight in front of her with the shiny black slippers close together. "There!" she said proudly. "See?"

She sat down on one side of Patricia, and then Vila shyly and with a sidelong confiding smile sat down on the other. The boys hung back together.

"Leone!" Mrs. Sieverson called from the house. "Ain't you got something to entertain her with? Why don't you get your dolls?"

"Do you want to see our dolls, Patricia?"

So far Patricia had been consenting but silent. "You go in and get them, Vila," Leone ordered, and when Vila whined,

"I don't want to!" she said, "Yes, you have to. I can't leave her. I have to take care of her. Don't I, Patricia?" But when Vila came back with the scanty assortment of dolls Patricia looked at them and then reached out her hand for the funny cloth boy doll in the knitted sweater suit. The boys laughed proudly and looked at each other, the way they had done when the swan in the park at Swea City took the piece of sandwich they put on the water for it. "Isn't that doll cute, Patricia?" Leone begged eagerly.

Patricia touched its black-embroidered eyes, and its red-embroidered lips—done in outline stitch—and then looked up at the eager, watching children and smiled with that gleam of mischief.

The boys laughed again. They all came around closer. "That's mine," Vila said softly. She reached over and touched the big stuffed cloth doll, with the hair coloured yellow and the cheeks bright red, that was smooth along the top and bottom sides like a fish but crisp along the edges from the seams. Patricia took it and looked at it. She looked at every one of their dolls—there were five, one of them was a six-inch bisque doll from the ten-cent store—and then smiled again.

"I'll bet you have nice dolls at home, haven't you, Patricia?" Leone said in generous worship. "I'll bet you've got lots nicer dolls than we have."

Patricia spoke for the first time. The children listened, with bright eager eyes wide open, to each soft little word.

"I have fifteen dolls."

Marvin said, "Gee!"

"Have you got them named?" Vila leaned over the grass toward Patricia, and then quickly hitched herself back, frightened at the sound of her own voice asking the question.

"Oh, yes, I always name my dolls," Patricia assured them. "My dolls have beautiful names. They're all the names of the great actresses and singers." And she began gravely to repeat them. "Geraldine Farrar, and Maria Jeritza, and Eva LeGallienne, and Amelita Galli-Curci . . ."

While she was saying them, the boys looked at each other over her head, their eyes glinting, their mouths stretched into grins of smothered amusement, until Clyde broke into giggles.

Leone was indignant. "Those are *lovely* names! I think Patricia was just wonderful to think of them!"

Vila stretched across the grass again. She touched the cloth doll and drew back her fingers as quickly as if it were hot. "Her name's Dor'thy," she whispered.

After Patricia's gracious acceptance of the dolls, the children wanted to show her all the treasures they had—even those they had never told anyone else about. Everything, they felt, would receive a kind of glory from her approval. They liked to repeat her name now. "Patricia." "She wants to see the little pigs. Don't you, Patricia?" "Aw, she does not! Do you, Patricia? She wants to see what I've got to make a radio." Patricia looked from one to the other with her violet-gray eyes and let the others answer for her. But after a while she said with a cool, gentle, royal decision:

"No. I don't want to go anywhere. I want to stay right here in this round shade."

The children were highly delighted. They began to bring their treasures to her. Vila had run off to the edge of the garden and dug up two glass precious stones she had buried there, but when she came back to Patricia she was too shy to show them and kept them hidden in her hot little hand that got sticky and black from the earth clinging to them. The boys were getting quite bold. Marvin said:

"I bet you never saw a mouse nest, Patricia."

"Patricia doesn't care anything about that," Leone said impatiently. "I wish you boys would go off somewhere anyway and let *us* look after Patricia."

"I can show it to you, Patricia."

"*She* doesn't want to see that!"

"Yes, I do," Patricia assured them with an innocent courtesy that made Clyde giggle again.

The boys ran off to the woodshed to get it. It was all made of wound-about string and little bits of paper and a soft kind of woolly down. Patricia examined it with her large grave eyes. She reached out one finger toward it delicately, and drew the finger back. She looked up at the boys.

"What is it?" she breathed.

"A mouse nest," Marvin said nonchalantly.

He held it carefully in his brown sturdy hands, partly to keep it together, but more because he liked to have Patricia's soft little fingers come near his. They were as smooth as silk, and rosy at the tips as the pointed petals of the dog-tooth

violets he had found near the little creek in the woods, when
he was out there one day last April all alone. A happy shiver
went over him at the thought of their touching him, silvery
and cool.

"Do the mouses—*mices*—live in it?"

"Sure! They did before we took it away."

"Oh, but can't they live in it any more? What will the
mices do?"

"Gee! What can they do?" Marvin swaggered. Clyde
giggled.

Her pink mouth opened into a distressed O. She looked from
one to the other for help, and the violet in her eyes deepened.
"But they won't have anywhere to live! You must put it
back." She was very serious.

"Shoot! Why, they've run off somewheres else by this
time!"

What did it matter about mice anyhow? Gee, they were
something to get rid of! Why did she suppose Pop kept all
those cats and fed 'em, if it wasn't to get rid of the mice?
But she looked so distressed that Leone, with an angry
glance at the boys, assured her hastily leaning over and hug-
ging her:

"No, they haven't, Patricia! Boys just like to say things
like that."

"Aw, gee——!"

"But what will the mices *do?*"

"The boys'll put the nest back, and then the mice'll come
there," Leone warmly promised her. She didn't care if it wasn't
true.

The boys had never heard anything so funny in their lives.
Gee whiz! They despised her for such ignorance, and could
hardly keep from laughing, and yet they felt uneasily ashamed
of themselves for they didn't quite know what. They had
just wanted to bring her the mouse nest to make her interested
and then to show her, too, that they weren't afraid of things
most people didn't want to touch. But they seemed to be out
of favour. They hung around while the girls talked a lot of
silly talk, and laid all the dolls out in the grass in front of
them.

"I'll bet you've got awful pretty clothes for your dolls,
haven't you, Patricia?"

Patricia didn't like to say, or to talk about her dolls because she didn't really think that these dolls' dresses were one bit pretty. Leone went on questioning her, with naïve admiration, and Vila listened with her eyes glistening.

"I'll bet you've been into lots of big stores, Patricia. Did this dress you've got on come from a big store?"

They both bent and examined the creamy shining linen with its coarse silky weave and the large roughened threads that Vila scarcely dared to touch with her fingers all dirty from the precious stones. Patricia graciously let them touch and see until, gently but with a final dignity, she drew the cloth out of their fingers.

"Now you mustn't touch me any more."

The boys giggled again at this, admiring but feeling abashed.

A striped kitten came suddenly into sight at a little distance—became motionless, saw them—and flattened and slid under the cover of the plants in the garden. Patricia gave a little cry. Her face bloomed into brightness.

"Oh! Do you have a kitty?"

"A cat! Gee!" They all laughed. "*One* cat! I bet we got seventeen."

"Really seventeen kitties? Did your father buy them all for you?"

"Buy them!" The boys shouted with laughter. "Gee, you don't buy cats!"

"Oh, you do," Patricia told them, shocked. "They cost twenty-five dollars, the kitties that sit in the window in the shop."

"Twenty-five dollars! Pay twenty-five dollars for a *cat!*" Cats, when you had to drown half of 'em and couldn't hardly give the others away! The boys were hilarious with laughter over such ignorance.

Leone couldn't help knowing that Patricia was ignorant, too. But she gave the boys a hurt, indignant, silencing look— it was mean of them to laugh at Patricia when she didn't know! Anyway, she was so little. Leone put her arm around Patricia, in warm protection.

"But they do!" Patricia's eyes were large and tearful and her soft little lips were quivering. It was dreadful to have these children not believe her, and she couldn't understand it. "Some of them cost a hundred dollars!"

"Oh, gee!" the boys began.

"Maybe some of them *do*," Leone said quickly. "You don't know everything in the world, Marvin Sieverson." She knew, of course, that cats couldn't—but then, she wasn't going to have the boys make fun of Patricia. "Come on now, Patricia," she pleaded. "We'll go and see our kitties. Shall we?"

The boys watched anxiously. They didn't want Patricia to be mad at them. They wanted to take her out to the barn and have her look at everything.

She considered. Her eyes were still large and mournful and a very dark violet. At last she nodded her head, held out her hands trustingly to Leone to be helped from the grass, smoothed down her skirts—and the whole tribe went running off together.

Patricia had to climb up the steep stairs into the haymow one step at a time. She felt along the rough sides carefully with her little hands. The boys would have liked to help her and were too bashful, but all the time Leone was just behind her, telling her, "Don't you be afraid. Leone's right here, Patricia. Leone won't let you fall." When they got up into the haymow Patricia was almost frightened at first; it was so big, and there were such shadows. A long beam of sunlight fell dimly and dustily golden from the high window in the peak, across the great beams and the piled hay, and widened over the great stretch of wooden floor.

"Haven't you ever been up in a haymow before?" Clyde demanded.

"Of course she hasn't," Leone answered indignantly.

Patricia looked around at them, and her face was pale with awed excitement. "It's like the church!" she breathed.

"Gee, a *hay*-mow!"

Still, it really was. Even their voices and the way they walked sounded different up here. The boys were tickled and a little embarrassed that Patricia had thought of that.

"Is this where the kitties live?"

"The little ones do. Where are the little bitty ones, Marvin?"

"*I* know!" both the boys shouted. They leaped up into the sliding mounds of hay, calling back, "Come on if you want to see, Patricia!"

"I'll help you, Patricia," Leone encouraged her.

She boosted and got Patricia up on to the hay pile and helped her flounder along with her feet plunging into uncertain holes, and the long spears of hay scratching at her bare legs above the half socks, and the dust making her eyes smart. Then Patricia began to laugh. She liked it!

"Here they are!" the boys shouted.

A bevy of half-grown cats suddenly fled down the hay like shadows. "No, no!" Patricia screamed when the boys tried valiantly to catch a little black cat by its tail. Leone was assuring her, "Never mind, they won't hurt the kitties, Patricia."

"Look here! Come here!" the boys were calling.

Patricia was almost afraid to go. The boys had found the nest of little kittens. They had got hold of the soft, mousy, wriggling things and were holding them up for her to see. Fascinated, she went nearer. The little kittens had pink skin fluffed over with the finest fur, big round heads, and little snubby ears, and blue eyes barely open.

"Oh!..." She looked up at Leone with her pink lips pursed. She loved the little kittens but she was afraid of them. "Oh, but they aren't kitties! They don't look like kitties."

The boys were highly amused. "What do they look like?" Marvin demanded. "What do you think they are? Cows? Horses?"

She said tremulously, "No, I *know* cows are big. But their heads look the way little baby cow heads do in the pictures. They do."

"I think they do, too," Leone asserted stoutly. She coaxed, "Touch them, Patricia. They won't hurt you."

The boys grinned at the way Patricia put out her fingers and drew them back. How could these little bits of kittens hurt her? Didn't she know they couldn't bite yet? Their little teeny teeth couldn't do anything but nibble. It was fun to feel them. Marvin caught up the white one and held it out to her, and they all kept urging her. He hoped her fingers would touch his. She cringed back, her mouth pursed in wonder.

"Oh, but they have such funny tails!"

"No, they ain't. They got tails like all cats got."

"Oh, no, Marvin. In the show the kitties have tails so big, and they waved them—just like the big plumes on men's hat's riding on horses."

The boys doubled up with laughter. "Who'd put cats in a show?"

"Oh, but they are!" Patricia looked at them in distress.

"Why shouldn't they be?" Leone demanded.

Of course she knew why, as well as the boys did. Nobody would pay to see a cat! Patricia had meant the tigers. She was so little she didn't know the difference. The boys were not to tease her though! Clyde was giggling. Gee, if she didn't have the funniest notions!

At last they got her to touch the kitten. She did it first with just the pink tip of one finger—then it felt so soft, so little and fluffy, with tiny whiskers like fine silk threads, that she reached out her hands. Marvin felt the brush of her fingers, as if a cobweb had blown across his hand, and a shiver of joy and pain went down his backbone. Patricia laughed in delight, and looked from one to the other of the children with her large shining eyes, to share her wonder.

"Take it!" Marvin urged.

"Oh, no, I wouldn't!"

"Why not? Go on and take it!"

She shook her head.

"She doesn't have to if she doesn't want to," Leone said warmly.

"Yes, she does!" Marvin thrust the kitten into her hands. She gave a little shriek and squeezed it by its soft belly, while the weak pinkish legs wavered and clawed out of her grasp.

"I'm going to drop it!"

"No, you won't!"

Its fluffiness filled her with ecstasy. "Oh, see its claws! They look like little bits of shavings from mother's pearl beads!" The boys grinned in amusement and delight at each other. Vila laughed happily. "Oh, and inside its little ears! Just the way shells look inside—only these are *silk* shells!" The boys grinned broadly. She caught the kitten to her cheek and held it wildly wriggling. "Oh, kitty, I love you! I want to have you to take home!"

"You can—you can have it," the children all urged her eagerly. Marvin said, "Gee, we got all kinds of cats, and that old gray one——" Clyde pinched him. "Shut up!" He grinned and blushed. Patricia laid the kitten gravely and reluctantly back in the rounded nest. She shook her head until the fluffy bell of shining hair trembled. She said solemnly, and as if she had forgotten that the others were there:

"No. I won't. Because all its other little sisters and brothers would be lonesome for it. And its mother would."

The boys stood grinning but they said nothing.

What were the kittens' names? Patricia asked. She was horrified that they had none. "Gee, we call 'em kitty," Marvin said; but Leone hastened to add, "Well, we call that one we have Old Gray."

Patricia said: "Oh, but they must have names! That's wicked. Nobody goes up to heaven to our Lord Jesus without a name!"

The boys just barely glanced at each other. They kept their red faces straight with agony. Then Marvin went pawing and rolling through the hay over to the other side of the pile, where he buried his flushed face and snorted.

"I'm going to give every one a name," Patricia asserted solemnly.

"What are you going to name 'em, Patricia?" Leone and Vila were impressed.

"I'm going to give them jewel names. Because the cats make me think about things like jewels. This is what I'm going to call them. I'm going to name this one Pearl because it's white, and this bluey one Sapphire, and the other bluey one Turquoise, and this little pinky one Coral, and this one . . . Jade!"

"Aren't you going to name one Di'mond, Patricia?" Leone asked eagerly. Vila thought that, too.

"No." Patricia was very decided. "Cats don't look like diamonds. They look like coloured jewels."

The boys giggled. Besides that one she had named *Pearl*—gee, they had already looked at these kittens and they knew very well that one was a he-cat! If she wasn't funny!

Vila was looking at Patricia so intently that she trembled. Now she said, "Patricia's eyes are jewel eyes, too. They're—they're——" She didn't know how to say it, and yet she felt what she meant and wanted to say—felt it so that it hurt! The whites of Patricia's eyes gleamed, and a little blue spread out into them from the circles of the coloured parts, and in these there were all sorts of threads of colour woven together, the way they were inside the glass of marbles—bluish and violet-coloured and gray, and a sort of golden! All just as clear . . . Vila reached out and took Patricia's wrist quickly and with shy ardour, but then she only smiled and couldn't think of anything to say . . . she would have been afraid to say it, anyway.

"Now she must see all our places!"

They went through the big barn. "Look here, Patricia!" "Patricia can't. She's looking at this." She looked at everything, but when they urged her, "Touch it! Go ahead!" she wouldn't quite do that. When they went out of the barn they all took hands and ran pounding down the long slope of heavy boards and out into the farmyard. Patricia was afraid at first and then shrieked with laughter and wanted to do it over again.

"Now we mustn't do it any more," Leone said after the third time. "Her little face is all red. Let go her hand, Marvin! Now, darling, stand still, and Leone'll wipe off her little face."

They thought it was funny the way she ran when the chickens came near her. "Oh, gee, if we had time we'd go down to the pond and show her the geese. Wouldn't she run if that old goose got after her!" Leone said, "Marvin Sieverson! We shan't go there."

But the very best place was the orchard. Even the boys were not so wild and noisy there. Their feet made only soft swishing sounds when they went through the long grass. The boughs were loaded, some broken and sweeping the ground, and the sky was patterned with leaves.

"Patricia!" Marvin hinted, tempting her, holding out a little green apple.

Leone snatched it from his hand. "Why, Marvin Sieverson, shame on you! Do you want to make little Patricia sick?"

"Aw, gee!" He had just wanted to see if she would take it. He and Clyde had both been hunting through the grass for some apples that Patricia could really eat.

Only the yellow transparents were ripe. The large apples had a clear pale colour against the leaves that were only slightly darker—mellow and clear at the same time, a light pure yellow-green through which the August sunshine seemed to pass. Patricia took the big yellow apple that Marvin picked for her and carried it all around with her. "*Eat* it, Patricia, why don't you?" But she wanted to hold it. "Oh, thank you!" she said very earnestly for every single thing the children gave her—the red dahlia, and the tiny bunch of sweet peas, the bluebird's feather. Whenever she saw a bird she stopped. She put her little silky hand on Leone's wrist. "Look!" "It's just a bird." She stood and watched with fascinated eyes until the bird was lost in the sky and she had to turn away dazzled with blue and gold.

"Do you wish you could stay here and belong to us, Patricia?" Leone asked her wistfully. "We'd play you were my little girl, wouldn't we?"

Patricia wished that she could stay. There were streaks of dust down the shining linen dress and on the soft little arms, a damp parting in the lovely wave of the bangs, and around her mouth there was a faint stain of red from the juicy plums the boys had brought her to suck. Oh, yes, the country, she said, was *nice!* She looked about with shining innocent eyes of wonder. She loved the animals. In the city, she told them, animals weren't happy. There were the beautiful green birds in the shop—just the colour, almost, of these apple-tree leaves!—but her father wouldn't buy them for her because he didn't believe in keeping things in cages, and he wouldn't get her the big gray dog because it wasn't right to take dogs out on chains.

"Oh, if I lived in the country," she cried, "do you know what I'd do? I'd just run around and run around——"

"You'd play with *me*, wouldn't you, Patricia?" Marvin cut in jealously.

"I'd play——"

"Children!"

The grown people were calling them. Disaster showed on the children's faces. "Oh, we don't want Patricia to go home!" There were so many things still that they hadn't shown her. But Mr. Lindsay came into the orchard calling out jovially:

"Well! Here she is! Ready to go home now with Uncle Dave?" He took it for granted that she was. He took her reluctant little hand, and the other children trailed after them. When they reached the farmyard, he said, "See what's going with us!"

Patricia looked in awe and wonderment. "What is it?" she breathed.

"Don't you know what that is?"

Mr. and Mrs. Sieverson, standing back, both laughed. The children too were grinning.

Patricia ventured, " A baby cow!"

Then they all laughed to think that she had known.

"That's what it is, all right. But don't you know what baby cows are called? Calf! That's a calf! Well, sir, do you want this little calf to go with us?"

Patricia didn't know whether or not Uncle Dave meant that for a joke. But the little calf was so sweet—she loved it so terribly the instant she saw it—that she couldn't help risking that and begging, "Oh, yes!" Its head really was shaped like the tiny kittens'. But its eyes were very large and coloured a soft deep brown under a surface of rounded brightness, so gentle and so sad too, that it seemed to her as if the colour showed in each eye under a big tear. The calf turned its head toward her. Its frail legs bent inward, to prop it up. Its coat looked like cream spilled over with shining tar. There were curls, like the curly knots showing in freshly planed wood; and the shining ends of the hair looked as if they had curled because the whole coat had just been licked by the mother.

"Oh, yes, Uncle Dave! Is it going *with* us?"

"It's going to be our back-seat passenger. If the boss permits?"

It made Mr. Sieverson laugh—feel tickled—to see how the thought of riding to town with that calf pleased the little girl. But he said dutifully to Mr. Lindsay:

"Now, if that calf's going to be any nuisance to you——"

"No, no. As long as I've got the old car, put it in. Tie it up."

Patricia saw the rope then in Mr. Sieverson's hand. She cried, "Oh, not *tie* the little calf!"

"Sure," Mr. Sieverson said, grinning kindly at her. "You don't want it to jump out, do you?"

She looked at Uncle Dave for confirmation of that. He said:

"Sure! Calves won't go riding any other way."

The two boys laughed.

Patricia stood back close to Leone but not saying anything more. She looked frightened. Mr. Sieverson said, with some feeling of reassuring her still more:

"You don't want to let this calf get loose or you won't get any of it!"

She didn't understand that.

"Get any of it to eat. This calf's going to make veal."

"Eat it?" she cried in horror; and she earnestly put him right. "Oh, no, I wouldn't *eat* it." Mr. Sieverson was joking.

"Why, sure!" he said. "Don't you eat good veal? You're going to take this calf to the butcher."

"Oh, no!" He meant that! Patricia was suddenly wild with crying. They all stood back, shocked, never expecting such a storm as this. "Oh, no! The little calf isn't going to be killed! I won't! I won't! No!" She put out her hands blindly and turned from one to the other for help. Mr. Sieverson didn't know what to do. She turned to him and beat the air with her little fists, shrieking, "Oh, you're *wicked!*"

He couldn't stand that. His face got red. Even if she was just a child, he demanded, "Don't you eat veal?"

"No! No!" Patricia shrieked.

"What, then?" he demanded.

She had to look at him. Her little pink mouth was open and her bright eyes drowned. She quavered, "Other kinds of meat . . . I'll eat chicken," and turned piteously to Uncle Dave.

Mr. Sieverson didn't like to be called "wicked" by anyone. The injustice, when he had just been trying to be nice to this little girl, too, hurt him. His wife murmured, "Well, now, Henry——" But he insisted, "Don't chicken have to be killed before you can eat it?"

But even Mr. Sieverson, although he was in the right of it, felt ashamed when he saw the little thing cry. Mrs. Sieverson gave him a look, stroked Patricia's hair, and said, "They won't take the calf." Mr. Lindsay hastened to promise, "No, no. Of course we won't take the calf." They were all trying now to reassure her. Vila was crying, too. The boys were pleading, "Patricia!" although they didn't know just what they would say to her in comfort if they got her to look at them. "No, no, it isn't going. It won't have to be tied up. See, he's put away the rope." The two men settled the thing with a look above her head. Patricia looked up at last, with piteous drowned eyes, as dark as wet violets. She broke away from all of them and, running to the calf—fearful of touching things as she was—she threw her arms in protection around its neck and stared fiercely at the shamefaced people.

"Oh, no, we couldn't take it!" Mr. Lindsay muttered. He cleared his throat.

The children surrounded Patricia again. They were begging her not to cry. Her cheek was laid against the little calf's silky ear, and she was telling it, in her own mind, "Don't you care, don't you mind, precious little calf, I've saved you." She let herself be drawn away but said "No!" when Mrs. Sieverson wanted to wipe the tears from her cheeks, and held up the little wet face trustingly for Leone to do it. That pleased all the Sieversons greatly.

"So now we can go! Hm?" Mr. Lindsay asked her.

She seemed to have forgiven them. She didn't want to look at Mr. Sieverson, but when she said good-bye to Mrs. Sieverson she touched her little skirts and made a curtsey. Clyde pinched Marvin to tell him to look. The children watched her with as great delight as they had watched the tightrope walker in the "show." Mr. Lindsay lifted her into the car. She smiled faintly at the children, but there were stains of tears on her pearly cheeks, and her eyes were still as dark as violets.

"You children go get her something—apples or something," Mrs. Sieverson whispered.

"We have, Mamma! We've got a whole lot of things for her."

They began piling presents into her lap. "Don't forget your little feather, Patricia!" Marvin ran off to find something else. The wilting flowers, the apple, the six rosy plums, the bluebird's feather she carefully took again. Marvin came panting back with his new game of "Round the World by Aëroplane." But Mr. Lindsay wouldn't let him give her that.

"No, no, my boy! You keep your game. She's got more things at home now than she can ever play with."

Now she seemed happy and appeased. The children crowded close to the side of the car and pleaded, "Come out again, won't you, Patricia?" Vila whispered in her shy voice, "I'll take care of Pearl and Samphire and those others, Patricia." Marvin said fiercely, "If any tomcat comes round, I'll——" and ground and gnashed his teeth and made fiercely appropriate motions. Leone gave him a look for making her think about the tomcat! But Patricia was still smiling and happy and hadn't understood. Now, in her relief and in the flurry of going, she was more eager and talkative than she had been all afternoon. She promised everything they asked.

"I will. I will, Leone. I will, Marvin. Thank you for all the beautiful things."

In the midst of it Mr. Lindsay leaned over to say in a low tone to Mr. Sieverson, a little ashamed, "Well, somebody else'll take that in for you, Henry, if you can't go."

"Sure. That's all right, Mr. Lindsay."

"Well, now, my little girl, tell them all good-bye."

"Good-bye." "Good-bye, Patricia!" They called and waved madly to her, all standing back together. She answered them. At the very last minute, just as the car was going out into the driveway, she leaned out with her shining hair mussed and blowing in the breeze, and cried:

"Good-bye, calf! I forgot to say good-bye to you."

Marvin laughed in delight, and then Clyde echoed him.

Mr. Sieverson stood looking after the car. That "wicked" still rankled. He said, as if very much put out, "Well, now, I'll have to find another way of getting this calf in or else take it myself before night." Then he said, as if ashamed, "Gosh! I don't know. I almost hate to take it. That little thing put up such a fuss." He couldn't help adding, "She was a pretty little kid, wasn't she?"

Mrs. Sieverson did not answer at once. Then she said in an expressionless tone, "Well . . . maybe you better take the other one, then."

He looked at her and seemed to want to assent. Then he cried, "Oh, no! We can't do that. This is the one we'd picked on." He looked angry, and yet in his light-blue eyes under the shock of lightish hair there was a hurt, puzzled look. "Oh, well," he muttered. "Folks can't be foolish!" If ever folks were to start thinking of *such* things . . .

He went forward resolutely, saying "Hi! Stand still, there!" as he took hold of the calf. His wife stood back watching him and saying nothing. The calf turned, bolted a little way, and then let him take hold of it again. It did not seem to know whether to be afraid of him or not. Its eyes looked up into his. In the large eyes of dark mute brown and the smaller eyes of light blue there was much the same reluctant bewilderment in some far depths. But the man knew what he was after, and the calf did not know what was to come.

"Come on here!" Mr. Sieverson said sharply.

He put the rope around the calf's neck.

SHADES OF GEORGE SAND!

By ELLEN du POIS TAYLOR

From *Harper's*

IT WAS one of those April mornings when the sun lacquers yesterday's rain puddles with gold, and the meadow larks melodiously promise a month of blue weather with violets to match it. But all this fruitful fuss did not warm one apathetic drop of Matilda Gessler's young blood nor soften one scornful angle of her averted face.

Matilda was weighing sugar in her father's dingy little grocery in Crittenden, South Dakota, when she should have been dozing under ancestral lace in a château somewhere in France. If Mathilde Lantier, her paternal grandmother, hadn't lived with such unwise intensity that one moonlit hour in a certain French garden, and if old Franz Gessler hadn't been so conveniently eager to shoulder the consequences, and if . . . but then Matilda knew nothing of all this. But she knew enough. She knew what her mother's Methodist God had done to her. He had created her under a morally tight roof in Crittenden for the good of her soul when every Latin molecule of her belonged in one of those sophisticated centres of the earth where it's dinner in low-cut brocade at eight and philosophy before kissing.

And so Matilda, weighing sugar, sniffed at the plucky April trying to make a bright island on the muddy floor. What was the use of looking like a bayadere when it meant breaking her lithe back over flour bags, the contents of which were destined to nourish the grace of girls less graceful than she? She was doomed to make beans into bundles that others might be strengthened for flight. Only last week Hazel Amberton, the thick-ankled daughter of the jeweller, packed her gauzy traps and went forth to conquer Minneapolis.

Matilda shrugged her shoulders. It was a gesture inherited

from Mathilde Lantier and worthy of Ninon de Lenclos herself, but there was no one to appreciate it except three tobacco-sodden farmers who tramped out, leaving her to resume her futile musing.

If ancestors would only stay where they belonged and live their lives in straight lines and leave the tangents to those who deserved them! Well, no good rebelling against anything as irrevocable as your grandmother's mistakes, your father's failures, or your mother's God. That left one thing to rebel against . . . the store.

The store was a place of odorous chiaroscuro. Smells fairly nudged one another and often knocked one another down. There was the fetidness of stale codfish, the acrid pungency of freshly ground coffee, the penetrating foulness of rancid butter, and the sickening tropical odour of decaying bananas. It wasn't worth looking at either . . . rows of tins whose faded labels betrayed the probable age of the victuals within; jars of moribund prunes and molasses-coloured horehound drops, counters piled with coarse denim garments leaking threads, bolts of grotesquely sprigged calico. Even the dusty jumble of decorated china on the top shelf didn't look destined for anything but cooling pork fat. And, if all this wasn't enough, they have to live over it. Four of them lived up there in the huddled stuffiness of a half-dozen rooms . . . horrible, uneasy rooms tenanted by lumpy pieces of golden-oak furniture whose sharp corners and glittering hostile surfaces constantly threatened one with eviction.

But there was one member of the family before whom the whole domineering conglomeration was powerless. That was Minnie Gessler, Matilda's fat, unimaginative mother. Every rocker dreaded her relentless dimensions. There was but one place where she looked properly engulfed and that was under the steepled bulk of the red-brick church around the corner. She waddled there regularly. Matilda often puzzled over her mother's voluptuous devotion to something that couldn't be poked or eaten or wasn't her son Fred.

Matilda sighed resentfully when she thought of her brother. The dispatch with which he made his dreams come true was nothing short of indecent. He rarely came near the store except to eat and sleep over it. He made quick, successful love to the dimpled daughters of the Crittenden gentry and bragged about it afterward in Lemke's Pool Room. He never kissed the mother who adored him, but he wheedled a Ford car out of her and went tearing up and down the long yellow road between Crittenden and a half-dozen towns, seeking other lips to conquer and getting them. Now Matilda dutifully kissed her mother every night but it had got her nothing. Minnie Gessler hadn't even allowed her daughter to have a French name in peace. It was 'Tilda she grumbled at and not Mathilde.

Matilda's father was shy and the only German thing about him was his name. There was a foreign gleam in his hazel eyes and the hair that fimbriated his bald head was black. He had not inherited Mathilde Lantier's fire—that fire which had made the submitting required of her a thing almost as prismatic as the unrealizable dreams of other people. But he hated the store. Matilda was the only one who suspected this and she knew it from the gingerly manner in which he handled grubby potatoes and the delicate way he turned up his nose over a slab of ancient cheese. Once Matilda caught him trying to carve the head of a Greek goddess out of a bar of American Family Soap, and after that she had a dim kind of respect for the thin man who shuffled uncomplainingly about the murky store at all hours.

This, then, was Matilda's family. It was no worse than the usual run of families, but Matilda thought she was uniquely cursed. The trouble was that Matilda's frustrations blinded her to everything but her own point of view. If only her French blood were given an opportunity to riot uncensored! But no opportunity had materialized . . . that is none which iridescently mattered. To be sure, she had taken a degree from the little sectarian college on the edge of Crittenden, but that experience had only enabled her to rebel against fate in terms of bad poetry.

Matilda deserted her sugar and went over and stood in the doorway. She glanced up and down the clapboarded vista of Main Street. Dora Todd, the blue-and-gold daughter of the banker, clicked by on her new red heels. Envious tears smarted Matilda's eyelids. She did not envy Dora because the wind tossed her curls flaxenly, nor did she covet eyes made of azure china, but those heels were another matter. They typified Dora's power to dress herself up. Matilda adored her own dark obliqueness and she would have liked to keep it in the style to which it deserved to be accustomed. Those heels now —they might have been those of her ancestress, young Mathilde Lantier, setting Paris boulevards to music! Matilda shook herself impatiently. Why couldn't her grandmother stay out of it? She even appropriated the heels of that silly cream-coloured girl who didn't know Balzac from buttons! And that wasn't the worst of it. Pretty soon that other woman would take command of her resentment—that irritatingly brilliant woman who had flooded the world with printed proofs that she had lived the fullest life of her generation and who had given Mathilde Lantier such vivid advice one afternoon in her drawing room at Nohant. Sometimes Matilda wished that her grandmother had kept that memory to herself, for the bright taint of it simmered through her blood like some high and mighty poison.

This was what had happened.

It was the summer Matilda was twelve. Mathilde Lantier Gessler had come to Crittenden from Baltimore to see her son once more before she died. Grandmother Gessler was tall and every inch of her was swarthy. Her eyes were as black as bottomless water and as imperishable as diamonds. There was a tuft of hair on her jutting chin, and it was proudly apparent that her lips had curved once. She came and stayed three days. Before she left she took Matilda aside.

"*Ma petite*," she whispered harshly, "I am content that it is the *père* you resemble and not that fat *other*."

"Why?" asked Matilda, perversely delighted at this allusion to her mother's size.

"Because, *ma cherie*, it is the dark and slender ones of the earth that know how to suffer, and yet keep their joy."

"Oh, Grandma," exclaimed the child, "you are happy then!"

"Of course," the old woman assured her gallantly, "and a great number of tears I might have shed and did not. I laughed sixteen hours out of the twenty-four and smiled in my sleep the other eight. The dreams I had under the crimson canopy of that ancient bed across the sea! But that was before it was decided that I marry Franz Gessler, the merchant, and make an end in Baltimore."

"Merchant?" queried Matilda. "Is that why Papa keeps a store?"

Mathilde shrugged her aristocratic old shoulders.

"God punished us. I was young and dark and it made trouble. Franz Gessler was fat and yellow and he dropped dead of it."

"Is that why we are so poor and the store smells so awful?"

And then it had seemed to Matilda that her grandmother peered down at her for the first time. "Ah, yes," she sighed, stroking the braided silk of her granddaughter's hair. "Ah, yes!"

"Tell me more," begged Matilda. "Tell me everything."

But the old woman had suddenly grown stubborn or weary. She sat there and kept quiet about the walled gardens in which she had strolled; the suitors she had tormented over sundials; the mistake she made that night the moon shone with such Hellenic tenderness; the tearful morning they packed her into the eager arms of the old German merchant and hurried them both off to Baltimore. But she did rouse from her romantic napping long enough to say:

"*Ma petite fille*, there was a thing or two I had from a woman who knew how to love beyond bounds and suffer with triumph. One summer afternoon I saw her at Nohant. There were books on the floor, an unfinished letter to Flaubert on the writing table, and Dumas sitting in a corner. She deserted everything to talk to me. Her eyes were wisdom, her hands were comforting, and her smile contagious. I left, but before that she gave me these," and the old woman drew up a yellowed package from the capacious pocket of her gown.

"They are for you." And she smiled a wise and curious smile.

The package contained a picture and a book, and very old they both looked.

"The original," explained the grandmother, holding up the picture, "was painted by Delacroix."

"It's a man," observed the child ruefully, taking in the long aquiline face framed by short thick hair above a tightly buttoned waistcoat.

Mathilde Lantier snorted. "You have only to observe how the mouth is of a sympathy and the bosom of a tenderness to know!"

"Oh," said Matilda, "excuse me!"

"And this," continued the woman, "is just one of the so many books she wrote. Ah, *ce roman dépeint une existence malheureuse d'artiste!*"

"C-o-n-s-u-e-l-o," spelled Matilda, bending over the tattered cover.

"*C'est ça, ma cherie.*"

"You talk funny, Grandma."

The grandmother pointed to a line of faded script on the fly-leaf. A long bony finger caressed each word as the foreign staccato of it sharpened the air like thin music: "*Quand on a aimé un homme, il est bien difficile d'aimer Dieu . . . c'est si différent!*"

There was a silence in which the stately reveries and tingling regrets of an old coquette mingled with the timid wonder of a child.

"She said truly," sighed the withered woman at last, "too truly for peace."

"Peace?" asked the little girl, "and what is that, Grandma?"

"A thing a woman longs for but does not want, *ma petite fille.*"

Mathilde Gessler returned to Baltimore. A week later a telegram came announcing her very sudden death. But she hadn't quite died. A goodly fraction of her alternately dreamed and despaired under the olive-tinted skin of her granddaughter, and her granddaughter thought at times she would die of it. And that wasn't all. There was that unholy booty from Nohant. Matilda longed to achieve the expression which illumined the experienced features of the woman Delacroix painted, and the unintelligible copy of *Consuelo* with the scribbled sentence on the fly-leaf finally drove her to the little college just outside of Crittenden. It had been rumoured that French was taught there.

Doctor Pusey, professor of Romance languages, was a retired Presbyterian. He threw up his hands at mention of the lady's name. His attitude, combined with her dead grandmother's enthusiasm, put Matilda into a palpitation that drove her to the little college library ransacking for information. One short paragraph in the encyclopedia rewarded her:

Sand, George (1804–1876), the pseudonym of Madame Amandine Lucile Aurore Dudevant, *née* Dupin, the most prolific authoress in the history of literature and unapproached among women novelists of France. Her life was as strange and adventurous as any of her novels, which for the most part are idealized versions of the multifarious incidents of her life.

Matilda fumed at the inadequacy of it. It gave no clue as to why the college curriculum had been cleansed of her. Of course there was that reference to an adventurous life, but that might mean anything from tea parties with kings to lions in Africa. And Delacroix had made her look like a clever Madonna masquerading as a nobleman up to nothing more damnable than courageous benevolences.

There came a day, thanks to old Pusey's French exercises, when she could spell her way through *Consuelo* and make what was scrawled on the fly-leaf her own. That sentence tormented Matilda like music which must be experienced to be appreciated: "*Quand on a aimé un homme, il est bien difficile d'aimer Dieu . . . c'est si différent !*"

No wonder old Mathilde had looked a bit wan over that sentiment! But before a woman could look wan like that she would have lived some intoxicating moments in ballroom corners and rose arbours. Love . . . it would be slow and silken and happen in a far place. How fiercely and, at times, almost resentfully Matilda envied this George Sand who could be so flip about the love of God! She had more or less ceased envying Mathilde Lantier. After all, that lady had in some subtle fashion wound up in Crittenden.

Crittenden . . . every harsh tight syllable of it made Matilda feel manacled. Her history had run a quarter of a century and here she still was loitering in the doorway of her father's store while another girl's red heels made the minutes flash and click on Main Street. Of course, before the sun shortened April another hour a thing would have happened to her, too, but Matilda was not aware of this. She just stood there in the doorway shifting her unhappy weight from one miserable foot to the other and thought bitterly of all the drawing rooms she could make historic if God would only stop being a Methodist.

Matilda snatched up a hat faded by last summer's sun and

walked down a street paved with clay, past houses whose eaves were dripping with sunlight to where a wet yellow road cut uncertainly through the pastures. She walked until a rickety wooden bridge spanned Sandy Creek. Matilda liked Sandy Creek. The willows that bent to it reminded her of churchyards filled with people who had died loving one another. A cottonwood or two dropped white fluff and it floated on the sluggish water like tufts of foam. But the water wasn't so sluggish this morning. Last night's rain made it behave like the brooks one read about. Matilda leaned over the rachitic railing and looked at it.

If one had the nerve one could start being adventurous from this very spot. All one would have to do would be to follow Sandy Creek as it flowed through three great rivers and sprayed into a gulf on the brink of which was a French town where dark men lurked passionately under iron balconies.

Just then Matilda noticed something which disfigured the sandy smoothness of the creek bank. Her fingers tightened resentfully on the railing. It was so like any one of those people back there in Crittenden to sacrifice beauty to the easiest way by dumping worn-out shoes, broken bottles, and old papers off the only bridge within ten miles! And there was something almost shamelessly revelatory about such rubbish. Matilda leaned over and peered down at it. Well, of all things! Somebody had tossed away his library, for edging the heap were a half-dozen books, their backs broken and their tattered leaves flapping hysterically in the wind. Matilda scrambled down and turned over the mass with a stick. Her lip curled. They were well thrown away—nothing but a lurid copy or two of the adventures of Nick Carter and the pale experiences of Elsie Dinsmore. Just as she was about to abandon the pile a name caught her eye. She snatched up the volume and rubbed the black lettering with an unconvinced finger. It wasn't merely a coincidence. It was probably Providence warning her, or the shade of the mad mistress of Nohant mockingly reminding her that the road to a salon is paved with something more definite than intentions.

A man named Francis Gribble had been so intrigued by those daring feet which had blazed the way to a high banned place that he had written a volume about George Sand and Her Lovers and somebody in this town had bought it—a woman, perhaps, who had glimpsed it in a window in a city and to whom it had appealed as a Baedeker to romance intoxicatingly beyond the stilted prelude to a husband and a family of children. And she had tossed it away. . . .

Matilda hurried home. And it was only the excessive brightness of the sun that prevented her seeing a waistcoated shade striding gallantly along beside her.

Once home, she locked the door of her room so she could have her mythical headache in peace. She threw herself flat on the bed and was oblivious to everything but a certain world compressed between those two brown covers. One paragraph of the preface gave everything away.

> Living in an extravagant age, George Sand gloried in her own contributions to its extravagance. She not only lived her own life but boldly asserted her right to do so. Her feeling was that when she loved she was making history.

A pretty brazen creed for the timorous daughter of a sad little grocer in a prairie town, but we must not forget that Matilda had inherited a way of dreaming. That was why these words burned slogan-wise in her brain after every other page was devoured and why at six o'clock the following evening she was able to seize her opportunity by something more than the tenuous tail of it as it whisked over her dazzled head.

The whole point about George Sand was that she would have got nowhere if she had been content to be a home girl. The fact that she was a descendant of kings and that a grisette gave birth to her in an alcove adjoining a ballroom wouldn't have availed her much had she not answered when Paris called. She could have stayed down in the country, being a dutiful wife to Casimir Dudevant until kingdom come and that would have been all there was to it—no Latin Quarter to be free in, no salons to dominate, no editors to cajole, no poet to be adored by—and what woman doesn't dream of being adored by one of the shallow ethereal creatures? Then, too, George Sand had a sense of values. It would be more interesting to coddle Chopin on an island than to keep Maurice and Solange tidy at Nohant; so she up and had the courage of her romantic convictions.

Just as the dawn was turning the blurred square of her window to rose Matilda decided what she would do. She would go to a city, Chicago, perhaps; change her name to Mathilde Lantier, and open a salon. She might even write when she had lived long enough to have a viewpoint about her lovers. In the meantime she would make a collection of bon mots. To hear her one would think that opening a salon in Chicago was as simple as setting up a millinery shop on Main Street at home.

The next day Matilda went about the detested store in a daze of intrepid graciousness, and so hypnotized was she by her borrowed boldness that she verily believed she was bringing something to pass.

When the school children trooped in at noon she tossed lemon drops across the counter as if they were largesse. She sold farmhand overalls with the charming condescension of a princess. A notoriously stingy old fellow who "batched it" in a tumbledown cottage across the tracks came in and bought china recklessly because Matilda's way among the chipped dusty cups was that of a hostess tendering a senator tea.

At six o'clock that evening it was her father who swung open the door she dreamed of.

The four of them were at supper. The fat, hairy mother headed the board like a pink general whose idea of relaxation is being as plump as possible in a flowered wrapper. Her handsome son Fred sat there glorying sullenly in a prowess which enabled him to juggle night into day and make sibyls, sheriffs, virgins, and hoboes stand in awe of him or succumb, as the case might be. There was Matilda herself, hollow-eyed, brooding, with a heritage in her breast clamouring to be aired and a book upstairs which was making her poignantly sure that at last she had found a way up the hill. At the foot of everything sat Franz, the grocer, who clung to the tangled faded ends of dreams with the same kind of shamefaced pride that he clung to the last faint fringe of his hair. He was gumptionless and meant too well for his own good, but it was he who spoke.

"I'm thinkin' of puttin' in a line of fancy glassware and some electrical stuff. We gotta be more modern."

"A fool notion," grunted Minnie Gessler.

"Go to it, Dad," said Fred. "When you get the place fixed up maybe I'll clerk for you."

"Where you plannin' to get the truck?" asked Minnie,

Fred's interest making her visibly weaken in favour of the proposition.

"Chicago," confessed poor Franz, hanging his head.

"Well, you're not goin' traipsin' off there and leave the store. Runnin' up and down those stairs would jest kill me ... my corns. ..."

"Fred'll go," decided her husband, growing sallower and stringier than ever under her accusation and his own disappointment.

"And I'm going with him," announced Matilda, clutching the tablecloth between her knees with hands that tingled and trembled.

"For the land's sakes, what for?"

"To buy hats," said Franz, going white with inspiration. "I'm thinkin' o' puttin' in a line o' women's hats."

"Hats," snorted Minnie, "in a grocery store!"

"It's a general store," he reminded her courageously, and his eyes sought help from his daughter. But Matilda was silent. Gratitude and pity choked her.

"I won't have 'Tilda tagging me to Chicago," objected Fred sourly.

Minnie Gessler became as alert as her bulk would permit. Suspicion twitched at her features. It was one thing to give this beloved son the trip he wanted but jeopardizing his purity might be another. Chicago was sheer Babylon.

"Go 'long with him, 'Tildy," she said, "and keep your eye on him."

The train shuttled noisily through the windy dust of two states and finally deposited them on the station platform in Chicago. A terrifying kaleidoscope this platform. Was it possible for a city to be big enough to supply destinations for all those people? Matilda clung to the arm of her brother and was in despair about theirs. Fred hailed a taxi and gave the chauffeur a number out on North Dearborn Street.

"What's that?" asked Matilda timorously.

"Boarding house run by Old Lady Campbell. Clyde Eggers, the drummer, told me about it. Said just to give his name and she'd treat us white."

"How nice!" agreed Matilda meekly. Where had this uncouth brother of hers kept all this unsuspected savoir faire?

He didn't know George Sand from Adam, and yet he was the one who was brave and unabashed. Matilda leaned back in the taxi, which was very swift and very yellow. Time enough to check up on her own courage after the cinders were washed off and she knew where she was.

They were dropped in front of a high narrow brownstone house. Flora Campbell met them. She was a large imposing woman with coarse black curly hair which she wore in a high chignon. A tight black-satin gown accentuated the amplitude of her bust and the grotesque narrowness of her hips. There was something innately gaudy about her which her clothes barely hinted at. Notwithstanding her advanced ideas about adventure, Matilda would have been shocked had she even so much as suspected what her prospective landlady had been through. Carl Eggers, the drummer, knew by what perilous, unconventional steps Flora Campbell had finally arrived at this boarding house—the genteel goal of her dreams. And, in spite of the flagrant past of its mistress, it had turned out to be the most respectable of boarding houses. The only off-colour thing about the establishment was the violent toilettes of the owner herself, but she was complacently confident that she dressed as all dignified matrons must eventually dress.

She eyed Matilda and Fred proprietarily.

"So you're friends o' Clyde's from Crittenden! Glad to take care o' you. I have only the nicest people. People like Mr. Goodwillie who is at Field's, Mrs. Kelsey whose daughter paints, and Mr. Eugene Walter who writes."

"Writes?" asked Matilda, hypnotized by Mrs. Campbell's tone.

"Yes," answered Flora importantly, "books in his room."

Matilda turned to Fred. "We'll stay, won't we?" she asked timidly.

"'Spose so," grunted Fred. He didn't much care where he slept.

They stayed a week. Matilda helped Fred with his buying and spent the rest of her time poking purposelessly in and out of the stores on State Street and gazing despairingly at the flashing modishness of the boulevard. She could fairly feel herself shrinking under the expensively turned out gaiety of the city, so impersonally musical and so inexorably full of motion!

The boarding house hadn't been a success either. Mr Goodwillie turned out to be an amiable old bore with a manner which was a courtly hang-over from his floorwalking days. Mrs. Kelsey was a plump gray woman whose only claim to distinction was a lorgnette on a silver chain studded with amethysts, and a daughter who studied at the Art Institute. Enid Kelsey was a yellow-haired, green-eyed, freckled little creature with a large shapely mouth full of white teeth. She and the young man who wrote books in his room seemed to have a great deal in common.

Eugene Walter was tall, lank, and mouse-haired. He had an Adam's apple and blue eyes that twinkled behind horn-rimmed glasses. He seemed to have unlimited leisure. Matilda wondered when he wrote his books, but the mere fact that it had been said that he wrote them was glamorous enough. Mr. Walter was anything but an Apollo; but even the irresistible George Sand had had to make a choice between beauty and genius. There had been that lover of hers, Michel de Bourges. He must have been queer enough with his shrunken body and his unwieldy head several sizes too large for him. And yet in spite of Matilda's willingness to overlook his lack of pulchritude, Mr. Walter continued to ignore her. The only person in the house who noticed Matilda was a Miss Slattery who taught English somewhere and she was acidly superior to everything but hot water and the Elizabethans. The week wore on. Fred was out every night. Matilda smelled whisky on his breath and once she surprised him amorously counting a roll of dirty greenbacks. Had he gambled and won? He apparently had. Matilda sighed. Fred, as usual, was making his dreams come true.

It was Monday evening. Matilda and Fred were due to start back to Crittenden in the morning. They were sitting in the parlour. Enid was playing the piano, and Eugene Walter was hanging loosely over her. Matilda watched them narrowly and bitterly. That giggling little blonde was monopolizing the only male in the room worth talking to, while she, Matilda Gessler, the granddaughter of a certain not inconsiderable French coquette, was forced to sit moping beside a brother whose mind was busy with exploits which he meant to turn into cash or kisses.

Why hadn't Eugene Walter noticed her? God knows, it

only needed one warm word or a bent look to make all her stifled vividness leap into flower. She could be ten times more arresting than that stupid flaxen-topped creature who used her gleaming teeth to make up for her lack of brains. What was the matter?

And then a strip of iridescent silk slipping from a white shoulder made her divine the truth with devastating thoroughness. It was the clothes. She leaned forward, studying her rival from a purely sartorial angle. She *was* effective in spite of her freckled skin and turned-up nose. The green gown emphasized the emerald lights in her eyes. Gold banded her hips, and a large cornelian made a splash of flame against her breast. Matilda looked down and fingered her own brown serge disgustedly. Why had she been so blind? She gritted her teeth. Then her hot rage cooled into a resolve. She wouldn't let her French blood go to waste. She would warm it yet or know the reason why. There was a woman once who charmed a romantic doctor out of Venice by the velvet eccentricity of her attire.

"I'm not going back to Crittenden," announced Matilda with soft suddenness.

"Gee!" he whistled. "What's the big idea?"

"I'm going to stay here and be an authoress."

"Like fun you are."

"Yes," said Matilda, and wondered why more people didn't lie for the sheer intoxication of it. It could miraculously commit one to anything. "Yes," continued Matilda, "Dad will miss me. Mother won't like it, but you must lend me two hundred dollars." She held out her hand.

Fred shifted his gum from one cheek to the other. He chewed peppermint gum so that his sister would not detect the odour of liquor on his breath.

"I ain't got any money," he said sullenly.

"Yes, you have. I saw you pull a roll of it out of your pocket. You must lend it to me. If you don't I'll write the folks what you've been up to. Mother'd be furious if she knew you drank and gambled. She'd take the car away from you."

Poor Fred looked shaken. Life in Crittenden without that Ford would be awful. They had sent Matilda to Chicago to spy on him and this was the result.

"Two hundred," insisted Matilda ominously.

He squirmed miserably as he counted the money into her palm.

The next afternoon Matilda's locks made a dark swirling island on the floor of a State Street barber shop. Then a department store claimed her. She could imitate George Sand's haircut but the waistcoat was another matter. Something intuitive counselled her that if she didn't dare be mannish she must be as feminine as possible. So she bought a dinner gown of flame-coloured crêpe de chine. To this she added a long swathing kind of cape and a pair of black-satin pumps buckled in gold.

She spent a whole hour before dinner nerving herself to the point of slipping that sheath of ignescent silk over her cropped head. She finally surveyed herself in the mirror and was panic stricken at what she saw. She was too lithe, almost colubrine, and every inch of her from shoulder to knee cap looked on fire. She cooled herself at a window and then returned to the mirror practising nonchalance. How broad and white her back was! But would George Sand have hesitated knowing that she was probably beautiful? Matilda shuddered and snatched up a long black motor veil from a hook. It would do duty as a scarf. She would let her shoulders slide out by inches.

Matilda slipped into her seat at table and nervously attacked her soup. She did not raise her head. She felt that the least motion on her part would ignite a neighbour. Mr. Goodwillie coughed, and Miss Slattery sniffed. It was over the last spoonful of bread pudding that she caught Eugene Walter's eyes fixed upon her. Flora Campbell gave the signal to rise. Mr. Goodwillie ceremoniously escorted her into the parlour.

"Very tasty . . . that frock. Going to the theatre?"

"No," she answered, "I just got tired wearing that stuffy serge."

"One does," agreed Mr. Goodwillie stiltedly, seating her on the sofa.

Enid floated to her place at the piano, where she postured and shook her flaxen halo in vain. Mr. Walter was not disposed to lean over her to-night. He sat gazing at a herd of fluffy sheep framed in hard gold which was suspended over Matilda's head. Miss Slattery glared at her over the flapping pages of a woman's magazine. Mrs. Kelsey inspected her through her lorgnette. They both left the room. After strumming fruitlessly on the piano for awhile, Enid whirled and murmured something about being bored and drifted out, leaving a faint odour of lilies of the valley.

Matilda sank into a silence so absolute that even the brook-like garrulity of the loquacious Goodwillie could not weather it, and so he, too, rose and left.

It was nine-thirty.

She and Eugene Walter avoided looking at each other. It was as if they wordlessly conspired to rid themselves of the others and now that they were alone it was meet and proper they should sit there in a moment's decent silence and not gloat. He advanced finally and stood in front of her, his eyes still on the white animals huddled under a white storm.

"I wonder," and he did not succeed in making his voice casual, "why artists paint sheep? Inane things."

"Isn't that the trouble with everything?" asked Matilda heavily.

"That gown isn't inane. It's gorgeous." And he gave her a direct look.

"I was so sick of that old serge," she said weakly, drawing the veil about her shoulders a shade more tightly.

He sat down beside her and gave the veil a little pull which exposed one shoulder. It glistened in the light like marble and made her feel like a Diana submitting to the brazen teasing of a satyr. "You've no right . . ." she murmured.

"You've no right to cover up such eburnean loveliness," he whispered.

Eburnean? What was that? Her whole being wondered what it meant and it thrilled her because she did not know.

"Take that funereal rag off," he said pettishly twitching the veil.

"I feel funereal," she said, despondent once more at his touch.

"Why?" he asked, his hand barely touching her knee.

"Because I've been in Chicago a whole week and nothing has happened."

"Doesn't eating dinner in the presence of a novelist thrill you?"

"It did at first," she admitted ruefully.

"Well, you thrill me in that gown. You're epical."

Matilda gasped. He talked like a book. She became suddenly oblivious to Eugene Walter's Adam's apple, his pasty pallor, and the clamminess of his fingers as they caressed her elbow. She glowed under his elaborate infatuation and told him everything. More than everything.

She told him about her French grandmother who had jilted a title to follow an adventurous lover to Baltimore; how she herself lived in a copy of a French château surrounded by a vast western garden; about her father who sat all day in his tapestried library, reading Balzac. She told him about her majestic mother who sceptred it over everybody and dispensed formidable charity to a grateful countryside. But she did not dare refer to the one thing that would have impressed Eugene Walter more than all her guilty exaggerations. She did not dare refer to her grandmother's momentous interview with the famous chatelaine of Nohant; for to have brought Madame Sand into it would have in some subtle fashion given her own secret away. Therefore, there was nothing for it but to gild everything else.

At midnight Eugene Walter stooped and gallantly kissed her hand.

"Good-night, Egeria," he whispered, and his eyes were two promises lighting her up the darkened stairs.

Matilda tottered happily to her room. She had been flattered for over two hours in words five syllables long, and her adroit fictions had enabled her to measure up to the flame of her gown. And he had called her Egeria. That sounded involved and classical. Just who was this divinity? Some goddess, perhaps, who had turned Mount Olympus upside down by appearing on it attired in a crimson tunic.

Matilda hung her own bright gown caressingly away in the closet and tumbled into bed too stirred for sleep. This was it. This was the beginning. George Sand herself had probably hung around Paris a week or two before Sandeau noticed her. And hadn't Eugene promised to introduce her to his crowd and dedicate his novel to *Mathilde* Gessler? And out there among those powerful literary friends of his perhaps there was a poet whose hands were not moist and who looked like Byron.

Matilda Gessler and Eugene Walter stole out every night after dinner. She descended Flora Campbell's stairs in scarlet silk with the long dark cape wrapped romantically about her. They wandered along the shore of the Lake, and while the spray misted the sidewalk with pearl, he concealed the thinness of his soul under trappings borrowed from Oscar Wilde. Occasionally he stepped back and allowed Swinburne to make love to Matilda. And Matilda was satisfied.

Once when a scimitar-shaped moon cut the wet purple clouds with silver, Eugene wound his long arms about Matilda and kissed her on the mouth. His lips were thin and cold and savoured in some ridiculous fashion of bitter tea. She very nearly cried out against she knew not what, but ten minutes later the old complacency came surging back when he murmured in her ear, "*Ma Mathilde . . . Ma belle . . . Ma princesse adorée.*"

French! How many generations of dark heads in France had dropped to catch the flattering music of those very words! Just so De Musset must have apostrophized George Sand. . . .

Every night it was the same. Once she hinted that it was time to invade that literary circle of his, but he passionately flouted the idea. He must keep her to himself awhile, for all too soon the clamouring world would claim her. This made Matilda prey to conflicting emotions. She wanted above everything to feel the world under her feet, but the only way of getting it there seemed to be via somebody's arms—somebody whose head was above the horizon. Ah, yes, she would marry Eugene when he asked her and then slip from one pair of arms to another until . . .

And so it was that they strolled every night by poetic water, and when she wearied of the interminable contacts that got nowhere he would lure her back by a quotation.

It was two o'clock in the morning, Eugene had preceded her up the damp stairs. Matilda had taken off her shoes so that she could steal up in noiseless security. Just as she was turning to tiptoe down to her room, she felt a soft plump hand on her shoulder. She turned sharply, suppressing a scream. It was Flora Campbell in a sky-blue kimono latticed with yellow roses. "Come into my room," she hissed, the gold in her teeth gleaming.

Matilda mutely allowed herself to be propelled into a tiny alcove garishly ruffled in pink cretonne and stuffed with bird's-eye maple.

"Sit down, miss," ordered Flora, shoving a low stool toward her.

Mathilda took it heavily, although she had no intention of doing so. Flora remained standing, her two hands ruthlessly crushing the blossoms on her hips.

"I ran a decent house until you came, miss," she accused shrilly. "I've had complaints."

"Complaints," hazarded poor Mathilda, "what are those?"

"Do you mean to sit down there and tell me that you can dress yourself up in flashy low-necks and sit in my parlour and make eyes at my best-paying boarder and philander on park benches with him until two in the morning and then pretend you don't know what I mean when I say I've had complaints?"

"I don't," answered Matilda, her lips trembling childishly. Oh, it was dreadful being pushed into this horrible pink place minus the dignity of shoes and to be hissed at by this awful harpy in a terrible wrapper!

"You can't put over any of that big-eyed innocent stuff on me. I ain't lived fifty-seven years for nothing. I'll give you until to-morrow to pack and find a new place."

"Who—who complained about me?" quavered Matilda.

"Everybody," replied Flora cryptically. "There's that sweet little Enid Kelsey. What kind of an example are you for her, I'd like to know? And Miss Slattery can't bear the sight of that red dress and she's been with me five years."

"But," objected Matilda faintly, "there's Mr. Walter. He was out, too."

"He's a man. I never interfere with what they do. Besides, he was friendly with that Kelsey kid and going to bed at ten until you came along. Why should I turn him out?"

Why, indeed? Matilda rose. "Good-night," she said succinctly and opened the door.

"If I was you," warned Flora, "I'd reform. Men don't marry light women."

Matilda did not reply to this excellent advice. It was doubtful if she heard it. Her head hummed and something in her throat whirred. Once in her room, she threw herself full length across the bed and sobbed. She didn't weep because she felt guilty. She wept because the vulgar words of that coarse woman had pounded her brilliant conception of herself into the dust. It was like seeing a beloved rose go worm-eaten—to have her dream go like that. She wasn't in love with Eugene. It was more tragic than that. She was still in her Crittenden cage. A bar would have to be broken, and she had counted on Eugene's ardour. He represented her only way out. Once out, there would be countless hands to help her up. And now she was about to be driven into the street like the scarlet-lettered women one read about. How had George Sand managed things? How would she have managed an irate landlady? Well, she was done for . . . done for . . . Then a ray of hope filtered through the gloom. She had one more night.

She would put Eugene to the test. He adored her. He had said so over and over until her ears ached with it.Confronted with the possibility of losing her, he would make something happen—something that would make it radiantly unnecessary to return to Crittenden.

Matilda slept finally—slept across her bed in wrinkled crêpe de chine while a noisy gas jet drew the hot yellow walls together. . . .

When she awoke it was past noon. Her temples throbbed and her gown was a wreck, but that didn't matter. Eugene would be glad to take her, headache and all, in her old serge; for deep down inside Matilda Gessler there was an inherited technic which up until now she had not been stirred enough to use. She would use it now. She would return Eugene's kisses. Perhaps she would find herself in love with Eugene if she returned one of his kisses, and then she, too, would be entitled to feel that, "*Quand on a aimé un homme, il est bien difficile d'aimer Dieu . . . c'est si différent!*"

Matilda hummed under her breath as she crammed her dingy wardrobe into a wicker suitcase.

At six o'clock Matilda stole out and ate a hasty sandwich in the little white-tiled lunch room around the corner. She would have died rather than face the polite hostility in Flora Campbell's dining room. At six-thirty she slipped back into the front hall. Uncertainty assailed her and made her cheeks tingle with something not unlike shame. If only Eugene would appear and they could unobtrusively slip out together! She smiled as she visualized his probable uneasiness about her non-appearance at dinner. He might even omit pudding and rush out.

She wavered there at the foot of the stairs, her breath shortening and thickening in her throat.

Then the portières between the parlour and the hall parted. Enid appeared muffled to the chin in a green-velvet cape edged with soft gray fur. Over the top of her spiralling mop of hair towered Eugene Walter. Matilda gasped and her despair sharpened. It was wretchedly evident that in the glow of Enid's pride in being reappropriated by him and under the unbearable intensity of her own need of him, Eugene Walter had taken on some of the remote perfection of an Adonis and the poetic dignity of a Galahad. He paused in front of the rack and took down his hat—the very hat that had lain crushed between them last night on that bench by the Lake when he had all but promised her the Mediterranean. Matilda made a brown blot against the wall and somehow managed to ascend three steps.

"If there isn't Miss Gessler!" lilted Enid, nudging Eugene. Matilda turned and looked unseeingly down into their faces. She felt curiously like a person who had died and after a fitting funeral had had the bad taste to come back to life.

"We thought you'd gone," said Enid, balancing her fairy proportions against her escort.

"I'm going," apologized Matilda dully, "in the morning."

"How distressing!" exclaimed Eugene nervously, twirling his hat.

"How funny!" chanted Enid, laying her white fingers on his sleeve.

"Is there anything I can do?" he said with that cool, impersonal courtesy which is not meant to be taken advantage of.

"No, thank you," answered Matilda mechanically, heavily, mounting another step.

"Good-bye then, *Mathilde* . . . and good luck!" he called up to her, feigning a casualness he clearly did not feel. He made a forward motion as if to take her hand, but Enid with birdlike deftness fluttered in front of him and sank gracefully down on the bottom step.

"My slipper's unfastened," she murmured.

He knelt and took the slender golden foot in his hand.

Matilda gained the upper hall. Just as she turned to enter her room she glimpsed Flora's coloured bulk in close communion with Mrs. Kelsey's gray dumpiness. Matilda clenched her fists. How fast they must have tossed her name about at dinner and with what eager celerity they must have sprayed it with venom! And there was Eugene. How easily he was filling the gap between dessert and bedtime with the fluffy green and gold that was Enid! And yet if those two hens had held their tongues she might have . . .

Matilda sank down in the darkness beside her window and leaned her forehead against the sooty glass. Paint peeling from clapboards, pork fat congealing on thick china, dust sifting through the vulgar meshes of coarse lace curtains, smells crowding one another through the damp tumult of the store, bolts of cross-barred gingham stuffily waiting to become high-necked dresses, two books and a picture under a pile of cotton chemises reminding one of freedoms taken in silk . . .this was what she was doomed to return to. Matilda writhed there beside the window on the other side of which a city went adventuring without her. She even cried out to her mother's Methodist God.

Then something seemed to materialize close beside her— something that laid a cool shadowy hand upon her shoulder and brushed its dark velvet waistcoat against her cheek. For one ghostly moment she believed that she was her grandmother being comforted at Nohant. Then she looked up. It was as if she were aware of eyes . . . mocking at first and then softly united with hers.

They sat there for hours grimly enjoying an old disillusionment together.

THE END